THE ULTIMATE
WITCH

THE ULTIMATE
WITCH

BYRON PREISS
& JOHN BETANCOURT
EDITORS
▼▼▼

ILLUSTRATED BY
LARS HOKANSON

BOOK DESIGN
BY FEARN CUTLER

A BYRON PREISS BOOK
A DELL TRADE PAPERBACK

A Dell Trade Paperback

Published by Dell Publishing, a division of Bantam Doubleday Dell Publishing Group, Inc., 1540 Broadway, New York, NY 10036

Special thanks to Leigh Grossman, Jeanne Cavelos, and Leslie Schnur

Design: Fearn Cutler

This book is a work of fiction. It does not endorse or imply any endorsement of witchcraft or any of the content herein.

CONTENTS

INTRODUCTION
▼▼▼

PHILIP JOSÉ FARMER

THEY flourished in the Old Stone Age, and they are still with us.

But, whereas they were the only game in town in the Paleolithic, they are, today, up against stiff competition. Their rivals, believers in different religions, far outnumber them. Moreover, these do not play fair. They loathe and detest witches as evil heretics and would like to kill them.

"Thou shalt not suffer a witch to live," the Old Testament declares. Ever obedient to Biblical precept, the ancient and medieval Jews stoned them to death. The medieval Christians hanged or burned them. Until the early nineteenth century, a witch could be executed after due process of law in many countries. Only because many enlightened people ceased to believe in magic as a reality did the legal persecution of witches cease.

However, despite the myth that we are a civilized and nonsuperstitious nation, many in the United States (and elsewhere in the world) believe that magic does exist and that its "laws" are as valid as those of physics. They also believe that magic can be used only for evil purposes. There is no such thing as a good witch, the Christian literalists declare. (This would be news to Glinda the Good.) Though fear of punishment by the law restrains the Christian fundamentalists (of the fanatic branches) from murdering witches (or those they think are witches), they do persecute them to the extent that law allows. Sometimes, they go beyond the law.

By coincidence, the day after I was asked to write an introduction to this anthology, the *Chicago Tribune* published a full-page article on early and modern witches in its Women News section. One of those cited is a self-declared witch who has lived in Salem, Massachusetts for eight years. Some of its citizens still cross the street to prevent closeness to her and, thus, contamination by evil. Some also call her names such as "Child of Hell" and "Satan's daughter." Another witch, who lives in Medford, a Boston suburb, was ousted from her apartment along with her family when her landlord found out that she was a witch.

The Salem witch mentioned above is a graphic artist and a Girl Scout troop leader. Her aerospace engineer husband, who is no witch, has been asked by fellow workers to get his wife to cast spells for them. She refuses to do this because she never uses her magic on others without getting their permission. When she does so, she only uses her magic for good.

This witch and many others claim that they are neopagans and that their religion must not be confused with Satanism or any form of devil worship. She states that she and her "sisters" base their religion on spirituality and environmentalism. Earth is sacred; Earth must not be polluted. Men and women should be allies and symbiotes of our planet, not exploiters and ravagers. Also, these witches' spells are more like prayers than curses, like benedictions, not harmful works of evil.

Witches, genuine witches, would like to overthrow the patriarchal system for one based on the true equality of men and women.

It is no coincidence that Salem is a magnet for witches and that many live in its area. Salem became famous, or, rather, infamous, because of the witch trials of 1692. Twenty citizens, mostly women, were hanged, and over one hundred were put in prison. Then good sense triumphed, shame replaced the hatred, and the hysteria died out. But the laws against witchcraft stayed on the books long after the unfortunate victims of Salem had died.

I have stated above that the fear of witches ceased when the majority of people lost its belief in magic. I'll have to modify that. Here we are, the twenty-first century on the horizon, supposedly a rational people, surrounded by an ever-burgeoning technology which is itself a magic of the mind. Superstition should be an evil which flourished only in the barbaric past. It should have been cast into the dustheap of the long-ago. But this has not happened. Far from it.

Many people still believe that magic is viable. They also believe that certain men and women can use its principles and powers as scientists use science. Witches can cast spells, don't have to use airplanes to fly, can summon up storms, can kill or cure you at a distance with a spell, can make people fall in love with you, can give you good fortune or ill fortune, and can bring up demons from Hell. They can ensure good crops or blight them, and they can make women fertile or cause stillbirths.

In olden times, they could make your cow's milk turn sour in the udder. Nowadays, I suppose, they can put a spell on your new car so that it doesn't run.

Those who believe in the witchly powers include both witches and nonwitches. Many among the latter are certain, as I've said, that magic can only be wielded for evil. But the nonwitches are ignorant of the very long history of and lore about witches. They don't know that many legends and folktales in many areas of the world are about good witches. That is, white witches. And, in certain areas, such as in Dartmoor, Devonshire, England, gray or "double-ways" witches figure in many folktales. These use their magic for good or for bad, depending upon whether or not they like the person who is the target of their powers. This belief was not confined to Devon by any means. Among many tribes in North America, the shaman could cure you or put an evil spell upon you.

Then there's the Devil, Satan, Auld Hornie, Old Nick, The

Black Man, the ancient fallen angel Lucifer. Many envision this supreme evil spirit as having the form of a man with horns, hooves, and a tail. They also affirm that he commands a horde of lesser demons. They name his worshipers "Satanists," and are one hundred percent certain that all witches are servants of the Devil. This belief is, however, chiefly held by Christian literalists, that is, those who insist that the letter of the Bible is to be taken as expressed. No part of it, except for the obviously poetic, is symbolic or allegorical. Thus, God really did take one of Adam's ribs and transform it into the first woman, Eve. There really was a worldwide flood brought about by God because of the general wickedness of mankind then. Only Noah, his family, and specimens of every animal in the world survived by riding out the deluge in a huge boat, the Ark. Also true according to the literalists is the Old Testament story that King Saul got the Witch of Endor to evoke the ghost of Samuel, a prophet.

Thus, the literalists, also called fundamentalists, believe that magic is an evil science. It was created by the Devil, and witches, devotees of the Devil, have been taught by him to wield their evil upon the worshippers of God. Since magic is a creation of the Devil, all witches have to be evil. No such thing as a white witch exists.

This belief has driven the literalists to some strange conclusions and even stranger behavior. They object to the Oz books because they depict witches. It's not just that one of the characters is a good witch. They don't want their children—or any adults, for that matter—to read books depicting witches, good or bad. They object to TV or movie shows about witches. They have made efforts in several cities to ban the Oz books in public libraries.

Just why they have this attitude about witches in books and movies is incomprehensible. It may be that they fear that the supposed evil of the witches will rub off onto the reader. But, if the literalists were logical, their efforts to repress all such books would lead them to ban the Bible. After all, witches and demons are described in it.

Pathetic. But dangerous. The most absurd case of this of which I know is a book written by Jane Yolen, one of the contributors to the book at hand. It's titled *The Devil's Arithmetic*. But it's not about the Devil or devils, unless you consider the Nazis to be fiends incarnate, as the cliché phrase goes. It's a time-travel story in which a modern Jewish girl, one who doesn't take much interest in her religion or traditions, is carried back in time to the Holocaust. Not through magic but, seemingly, by a slip in time. Her experiences make her realize the horror and inhumanity of the Holocaust.

Only the title has anything to do with the Devil. Yet, a fundamentalist in a city protested publicly against the book. She had not read the book and assumed that it was about witches and Satanists. So vehement were her protests and so strong was the adverse publicity she generated, she succeeded in making the publisher withdraw Yolen's book from the stores.

Absurdity plus. Ad nauseam.

Jane Yolen has been living in Scotland off and on for some time. Scotland used to be overrun with witches, which means that some are still around. If I were Jane, I'd hire a Celtic witch in the Fife area to make the house of the woman who's given Jane so much trouble burn down. Or cause the woman to bear sextuplets, all horned and hooved.

Hiring the witch would at least be a test to determine if witches do indeed have such powers. And I'm sure Jane could use the hire-money as an exemption on her income tax.

I cite Jane Yolen's situation to show the moronicity of anti-Satanists and the power they have. Also, to demonstrate that there are people, well-organized though, I hope, not numerous, who firmly believe in witches and the Devil. Yet, the woman who is so fanatical and irrational that she objected to the "Devil" in the title obviously knows very little about his genesis, history, and evolution. But she does embody the beliefs of many people, whether they are Christians or not.

Where do Satan's horns, hooves, and tail come from?

He has these because he derives directly from sorcerers of the tribes of the Old Stone Age. The earliest known image of him is found in the Caverne des Trois Frères in Ariege, southern France. It's dated as being in the late Paleolithic (Old Stone Age). Thus, sometime between 40,000 B. C. and 10,000 B. C., the image of the half-man, half-animal was painted deep within the cave. Other paintings of animals appear with it. But the Horned Man is a misnomer for this magic-evoking figure painted on a wall deep within a cave. The sorcerer bore stag antlers.

The wordage limit in this foreword forbids an extensive survey of the evolution of the truly ancient, cave-dwelling, man-stag witch into the horned Devil of a later era. Suffice it here that later witches formed groups of thirteen, a coven, and that the male leaders of these groups were known as the Horned Man. The witches' religion of western Europe derived from those of the Old Stone Age and maintained an unbroken (though not undistorted) continuity in time.

When Christianity became the state-supported religion of Europe, a fierce warfare against the pagans began. It continued up to approximately the middle of the seventeenth century. Since the Christian priests have written the records about this warfare, they give the impression that complete conversion to Christianity occurred. But this is not true. Much of the rural populations continued to cling to the Old Religion, though many pretended to be Christians.

There is evidence to show that even the nobility and the monarchs were secret Old Religionists up through the medieval and Reformation times. *The God of the Witches* by Margaret Murray, for instance, states that such kings and well-known people as Rufus, son of the William the Conqueror, Gilles de Rais, Marshal of France, Joan of Arc, the maiden savior of France, and Thomas à Becket were voluntary ritual sacrifices of the Old Religion.

In any event, much larger numbers of pagans continued to believe in their faith than the Church historians would like you to believe. The Old Faith was never stamped out, and it flourishes in this somewhat tolerant late twentieth century in Europe and the Americas.

But the old gods become the demons of the new religion. Thus, the Church identified the Horned Man as Satan, the Devil. His worshipers were said to do evil through their magic, and the Church sought to eliminate them entirely by burning and hanging. Many genuine witches, that is, Old Faith believers, and many innocents were killed. During this period, Satan acquired in the popular mind the horns (once antlers), hooves, and tail (though deer don't have much of a tail) of the ancient sorcerer. However, the more enlightened Christians did not believe in this image of Satan. The Bible does not describe Satan as such any more than it portrays angels as winged.

Despite the Horned Man as the leader of the coven, the Old Faith also had female goddesses, higher in the deity level than men, the most important being the fertility goddesses. Much of this lingers in present-day witchly belief. In fact, many witches have stated that their supreme deity is Mother Earth and that the Horned Man (under various names) is secondary to Her. Some don't even acknowledge his existence in their religion.

Now, having dealt with Old Faith from the rational viewpoint, I'll write briefly of it from the irrational viewpoint. By irrational, I don't "insane" or "crazy." I mean the Irrational, those supernatural things and beings which science rejects as impossible or highly unlikely. I am human, therefore both rational and irrational. There is in me as in all humans, a feeling, often subconscious, that the Irrational: God, spirits, demons, and ghosts may exist. The Old Stone Age savage lives in all of us, no matter how vehemently we deny it. Perhaps, just perhaps, I think, there may be genuine witches here and there. Magic does exist; its practitioners exist. I like to think of myself as open-minded. Thus, I don't finally and forever reject the possibility. After all, I've twice seen ghosts and twice had mystical experiences. The latter convinced me, however briefly, that the universe does have meaning and that all is well in God's world despite its never-ending horrors.

These intimations of the Irrational (or were they emotional hallucinations?) and those of other people I know demonstrate that there are two worlds within our seeming physical limits. They occasionally touch each other at points where humans happen to be. Perhaps, just perhaps . . .

Whatever the truth, I've loved stories and movies about witches since my childhood. Not all of them are Grimm; many are fun. But the more threatening stories always strum a fear-filled chord deep within me. The Old Stone Age caveman still lives.

Whether or not you believe in the magic of witchcraft, you do believe in the magic of the written word. Read the stories at hand, and shiver a little or enjoy. Or both.

GINGERBREAD

▼▼▼

S.P. SOMTOW

WHEN we went to live in Hollywood, we saw many wonderful things. We saw many cruel things. Some people touched our hearts and some people touched our bodies. We grew up much too fast, and when we were all grown we found we'd been trapped in our childhood forever.

This is me, Greta Blackburn, writing all this down so my brother Johnny will one day remember if he chooses to. I can write real good now because there are a lot of books here and they let me take as many as I want into my room and I can keep them there without signing for them or anything.

On Sundays, a screenwriter comes to the institution and tells us stories. His name is Bob, and he is unemployed. But I've never seen him panhandling for money, and he wears expensive clothes. He is nice, kind of, and he never lays a hand on us. He is a volunteer. The Writers Guild has this program where they send writers to talk to people like us. It's supposed to keep us anchored to the real world.

Bob encourages me to write and he makes me keep a diary. Every week he reads what I've written and corrects most of the grammar. He doesn't correct all of it because sometimes he thinks it's charming the way it is.

I know I am too old to listen to stories, but I go because of my brother. He doesn't talk much anymore, but I think he is taking it all in. The time Bob told us the story of Hansel and Gretel, I could see that Johnny was paying attention, because he fixed on Bob with those clear blue eyes. That made me listen too. That's how I finally figured out what Titania Midnight was. I hadn't been able to put my finger on it, not until I heard Bob read us that fairy tale, but the moment I realized it, it was obvious.

Titania Midnight was a witch.

▼▼▼

We didn't meet her until the second time. The first time our parents tried to dump us, they didn't succeed. That's because Johnny had snuck down to the kitchen for a Snickers bar, and he overheard them in their prayer meeting. He woke me up by banging on the ladder that goes up to the top bunk. "Greta," he said, "they're gonna take us away and . . . and they're gonna *ditch* us."

I was groggy and I thought he'd wet the bed again, but he just kept shaking me, and finally I crept out of bed, just so he'd calm down, and I went downstairs with him.

They were in the living room. There was a drape we used to hide behind whenever we listened to them arguing. It was a nice living room with big vinyl sofas, a mahogany piano and a painting of Jesus over the fireplace, with big kind eyes. I couldn't see Daddy but I knew he was standing right in front of that painting and drawing his authority from the Lord. "It's all settled, Martha," he was saying, "no ifs, ands or buts about it. I've prayed on it, and I've begged the Lord to take this cup from us, but he said, 'I've made up my mind, Jed, and there ain't nothing more to say about it.' And you'd best obey me, because you're my wife, and the apostle Paul says—"

"Maybe it wasn't the Lord talking to you. I mean, to abandon your own kids . . . maybe it was . . . someone else . . . you know . . . *mimicking* the Lord."

"You calling me a Satanist, Martha?"

"Told you," Johnny whispered, and he gulped down his second candy bar.

"But how can we know they'll be all right?" Mom said.

"We have to trust in the Lord. They'll be provided for, long as they don't stray from the paths of righteousness."

I hugged my brother and said, "We have to make a plan."

Later, when we were settled in again, Daddy came into our bedroom. He checked to make sure Johnny was snoring. Then he sat down on the bottom bunk next to me and slowly peeled down the sheet. I half opened my eyes. In the blue glow of the Smurfs nightlight my father's face looked like the face of a demon. As usual, I pretended to be fast asleep, and I waited for it to end. But this time he didn't start right away. Instead, he began to talk, in a sweet voice full of hurting, a voice I'd never heard him use before.

Daddy said, "Forgive me, I'm not a bad man, there's just something that comes over me and I can't help myself . . ." and then, "if only you knew how much I love you baby but I can't talk about those things I'm just a sinner and your mother don't understand . . ." and then he called me tender nicknames he would never use when I was awake. But after a while his voice grew harsh, and he said, "God damn them to hell, them ayrabs and them chinks that take away a decent Christian's job, and them usury-practicing kikes that caused this damn recession and take bread out of our mouths . . . the krauts should've never let them crawl out of them ovens, damn them, damn damn damn," and he called me *bitch* and *whore* and I just squeezed my eyes tight shut and made myself very small and very far away until he was all done with me.

The next morning, after breakfast, they made sure we brushed our teeth, then we got into the station wagon and set off. Daddy had to go to a job interview first, and we waited in the car. He came out looking dour.

"God damn all them Goldbergs and Goldsteins and Goldfarbs and Gold-shitass-Satan-worshiping baby-sacrificing jewboys," he said. "A decent Christian can't get enough to feed his family, and they own half the damn country."

"Jed, please don't curse," said our mother, "not in front of the children."

They left us at some shopping mall, told us they'd pick us up in an hour, and went away. But we were prepared for that, and we had memorized every turn and every street name, and by sunset we managed to walk all the way home.

Daddy prayed on it all night. He didn't even come into our bedroom. Johnny peed the bed, but I overslept and didn't strip the sheets. They didn't notice, just fed us breakfast and told us to wait in the garage.

The second time, they locked us in the trunk and they drove and drove, and Johnny was carsick and we could hardly breathe. Johnny cried all the way. Partly it was the sugar that made him hard to deal with. I guess that's why they wanted to ditch us. Still, I was the one who took care of him most of the time. I'm a good girl.

▼▼▼

When we woke up, we were in a blind alley, and it was night. There was a dumpster leaning against the wall, so I knew that we wouldn't go hungry. But it was cold and I didn't know how late it was or how long we had been there. Johnny was whimpering because he hadn't had a candy bar in a long time. From beyond the wall we could hear a buzzy kind of music and there were neon lights flashing in rhythm to it. There were people chattering, too, and the sound of spiked heels on concrete, and, now and then, a police siren. But inside the alley it was all quiet and dark.

"It hurts all over," Johnny said.

"Maybe we should go back to sleep for a while," I said, because I knew that when you're asleep there is no pain. We curled up together but the pavement was damp and cold, and finally we climbed up on the dumpster and found comfy places among the trash, which was not bad; back home, Daddy sometimes made us sleep in the garbage to teach us a lesson. He'd say, "You're poor, and you're white, so you might as well be trash too." I got a better deal because Johnny had a lot of fat on him and his butt made a pretty good cushion after I wedged it tight against the metal casing with a beer bottle.

The next time I woke up, it was still night, and I was looking into Titania Midnight's eyes. She was shining a flashlight in my face, and she was all in shadow, except for her eyes. They were sunken into a mess of wrinkles, but they were young eyes, and kind, like the painting of Jesus in our living room. "By Isis and Hecate," she said, "I've struck gold tonight."

That was when Johnny woke up and he started carrying on like he always does. "Double gold," said Titania Midnight, "even though the second nugget is a little . . . dare I say it . . . *larded*."

"That ain't nice," I said. "Johnny can't help being, um, *ample*. It's his glands."

"Oh, I daresay, I daresay. But within the chrysalis, something beautiful, no? You'll come with me, of course; you'll want food."

"I had pizza earlier. It was still warm even, two slices, pepperoni. But Johnny has to have his sugar fix or he'll get crazy."

"I've just the thing." She rummaged in a tote bag and gave something to Johnny. "Baked it meself. Gingerbread is best. I think it blends a lot better than brownie mix."

"Blends with what?" I said.

"Oh, oh, you innocent, wide-eyed creature. Fundamentalist parents, I'll bet. Raped you too, I wouldn't wonder. Maybe not the boy, he's so *gelatinous*. No wonder you bolted."

I didn't understand what she was talking about, but she seemed kind, like in the parable of the good Samaritan. Johnny gobbled the gingerbread cookie greedily and asked for another one.

"Oh, nonsense," she said, "you'll be stoned out of your everloving mind."

She asked us our names and she told us hers. I thought it was a fishy-sounding name, but I didn't want to be impolite. I'm a good girl.

"Well," she said. "Come along now. You'll be wanting to freshen up. Get a decent night's sleep and all that. No time to stand around chit-chatting. Hollywood's like the Forest of Arden. Anything can happen. Sorcery. Gender confusion. Love potions that make you see a donkey as a sex object. Whew! But it's a magic place. You'll see. Wonder piled on wonder."

I helped Johnny out of the trash and dusted him off a little bit. We followed Titania out of the alley and that's when the lights and the music hit us full blast. God, it was wild. Posters tall as buildings with painted ladies on them and musclemen in just their underwear, and a big Chinese dragon that lit up and wall-to-wall cars and hip-hop making the pavement quake and skateboarders with long hair on one side and bald on the other and people snapping pictures everywhere and stars on the sidewalks and a dinosaur climbing up the side of one building . . . oh, it was Disneyland. I held Johnny's hand tight because he gets frightened easily. But actually he didn't seem to mind even though he had never been among so many people in his life. His eyes just seemed to go all glassy. The gingerbread must have been real good.

Everyone seemed to know who Titania was. People would come up to her and she would smile at them or wave. The colors of the lights kept changing and sometimes she seemed young and sometimes she seemed old. She had a nose like a parrot's beak and her lips were red as cherries and her eyelids were all covered with gold paint. A man in a white suit came up to her and pointed at us, but she said, "Don't you touch any of my babies, you hear? They're too good for the likes of you."

And I whispered in Johnny's ear. "She's nice. She'll protect us. Maybe she's our guardian angel."

"Yeah," Johnny said, and then he giggled for no reason at all.

We turned down a side street and then another one. This was a narrow street and all dark, except for one neon sign, blinking, and it read

PSYCHIC READER AND ADVISOR
DONUTS

and I knew that there had never been any place like *that* where we came from. From the street it seemed like just a regular doughnut place and there were a couple of customers inside, including a policeman. Next to the entrance was a narrow un-paved alley with high walls and there was a side door. Titania used three keys to let us in, and then she punched in a code on the security pad inside the doorway.

Inside there was a dingy living room. A black girl was lying on the rug watching *Murphy Brown*. The clock on the wall said three A.M., so it must have been a videotape. She looked up at us. "Hey," she said, "I thought you said no more kids."

"No jealous fits, now, Laverne," said Titania, "you really must learn to share."

"Where they gone sleep?" Laverne said. "And what about *lardass* there? You could strip him and sell him for parts, maybe, but in one piece, he wouldn't even make it round the block." She frowned and flicked the remote to MTV. I knew it was MTV, even though we didn't have cable back home, because it showed Satanic stuff.

"Oh, you cruel heartless beast," Titania said, but there was no malice in the way she said it. "Put on the light; let's have a look at this one. Ai, ai, ai . . . what are we to do with him?"

Laverne got up and switched on a naked light bulb that swung from the ceiling. All of a sudden everything was harshly lit. One side of the room was all drapes; they were a tad open and I could see through to a big kitchen, maybe where they made the doughnuts. The walls were covered with signed photographs of famous actors. The shag carpeting was spotty . . . one or two places looked like puke stains. Titania and the black girl were leading Johnny by the hand until he was right under the light, and they were studying him, like dissecting a frog in school.

"You know," Titania said, "Laverne, you are too ready to flush people down the toilet bowl of existence. This one has possibilities. Notice the eyes, how big they are. They are the eyes of an angel. And the flesh, well, the flesh . . . even though we are not Michelangelo, can we not see David in this block of marble? Can we not whittle? Hone? Hollow the pudginess so the cheekbones stand proud, even arrogant? And look at his sullenness. The lips can be worked into a willful pout. Strip him for parts indeed!" They were all poking him and looking at his teeth and looking down his shorts and Johnny started to cry. And Titania let go of him and made Laverne step back, and she said, "That's it. The finishing touch. Listen to that weeping. It's like the cry of the sea gulls over some solitary isle in the bitter cold North Sea."

"I think I know what you're getting at," Laverne said slowly.

"What *is* she getting at?" I said, and I could feel my stomach curl up.

"He will be our fortune!" Titania cried, and kissed Johnny wetly on the lips, which caused him to make one of his goofy faces. They laughed. "He'll have the beautification room," Titania said. "As for . . . Greta, was it? . . ."

"I ain't sharing my room with no honky greenhorn," Laverne said.

"Oh, you were always selfish."

"You can tell she's not right for us!" Laverne said. "She gots a strong firm body like a ho', but she don't have a ho's eyes. She be needing one of your magic potions every time she goes to work."

Suddenly, for the first time, I panicked. "You can't split us up!" I said. "We've never been apart, not for one minute! And I'm the only one who can tell when his sugar's off."

That set both of them to laughing, and Johnny to carrying on still more, and I could feel a few tears brimming up in my eyes too, until it dawned on me that there would be no visit from Daddy tonight. I realized I had died and gone to heaven.

▼▼▼

The beautification room was about the size of a large closet but it had a TV and a VCR. It could only be locked from the outside. The door had a little glass pane where you could look in. There was no toilet but Titania gave him a potty that she made me empty once a day. She fed him on nothing but water and little blue pills. I told her he needed sugar but she said, "It's okay, hon, this is just for a little while; the dexies will get him thinned down, bring out those dimpled cheekbones."

Titania was the only one who had the key, but you could talk to Johnny by sticking your ear right on the pane to listen, and putting your lips up to the glass and talking soft enough so the sound wouldn't carry beyond the corridor. But I couldn't touch Johnny and I knew that upset him. Still, I didn't want to complain too much to my host. I was a good girl, and I had been through a lot worse times than this.

It wasn't much fun sleeping with Laverne at first, though. She used to hog the thing you folded out to sleep on (she called it a "foo-ton") and she would talk about me as though I wasn't there, and even when she talked directly *to* me, she made it sound like I was stupid. But a lot of the time she was gone all night, and I could sleep by myself, which was great because it was a tiny room, the size of a large bathroom maybe, with no windows.

When Laverne got home—it didn't matter how late it was— she kicked me out of the futon so I was at least halfway on the floor. She would turn on the television and smoke cigarettes.

She was addicted to the Jeffrey Dahmer case, which was on the late, late news every day. "I *love* Jeff," she would say. "I think he's beautiful. He eats people alive. He's the grim reaper."

I didn't know if that was a satanic thing to say or not. I shut up about it mostly. But no matter how late she came in, she would always go flick, flick, flick with the cable controller until she found some piece of news about him. It was scary how obsessed she was. The third night, even though I was afraid she'd bully me and tell me to shut up, I just came out and asked her why she didn't watch something more pleasant. She only said, "Sometimes I wish he'd carve *me* up."

"But why would you say that?" I said. "Aren't you happy here?"

"Sure," she said, "sure, Laverne happy."

In the dark room all I could see were her eyes, large and

round and full of disappointment. I thought she was just contrary. Things were good for us girls. We had a lot to eat. And even though Titania didn't let Johnny eat anything at all, it was true that Johnny was shedding his rolls of fat. By the third day, looking at him through the pane in the door, I could see what Titania meant. Johnny was beautiful, and I cussed myself out because I, his own sister, hadn't seen fit to notice a plain fact like that, right under my very own nose. His eyes were getting more and more like the eyes of the Jesus that hung in our living room over the fireplace.

"Titania," I said over dinner, "you must know magic or something."

"I do," she said. "Finish your corn muffins and take Johnny his pills. And empty his chamberpot and weigh him and get dolled up, because we're going into Beverly Hills."

I used to watch *Beverly Hills 90210* every week, of course, so naturally this was the most exciting moment for me since we arrived in Hollywood. Titania made me borrow some of Laverne's clothes. They were tight and skimpy but Titania kept telling me I looked beautiful. Then she made me put on makeup so I looked like a painted whore of Babylon. I guess I did anyway, because though I had never been to Babylon I'd heard Daddy talking about them often enough, and I knew they weren't good girls like me. But I was afraid not to do what Titania said because she had been so good to me. And then again I thought of Johnny, locked up in the beautification room, with the ugliness melting away from him with the pills and the starvation, and I knew that what Titania was doing was a dark mystery . . . like the changing of water into wine. If Titania could really work miracles, she had to be connected to the Holy Spirit somehow, because Daddy told me that Satan can't *really* do miracles, he can only deal in illusion.

And when I looked in the little hand mirror Titania gave me, I really was beautiful. It wasn't an illusion. I looked like, I don't know, Julia Roberts. It sure made me happy to know I could be beautiful even though I had never been in a movie.

Titania came out of her room and she was wearing a long black gown, studded with rhinestones. She wore so much makeup she seemed to have no wrinkles at all. In the harsh light of the living room her face seemed to be made of porcelain. Laverne came in for a moment and when she saw me dressed that way she turned her nose up at me.

"Bitch," she said.

"Now don't you carry on," Titania said. "You can be *so* immature sometimes, Laverne."

But I was sorry because I figured Laverne was a little envious because she wasn't coming with us, and I said, "Why can't we bring her along?"

Laverne said, "She taking you 'cause you white."

"Now you know very well that that simply isn't true," said Titania. "Each of us has his appointed place in the cosmos. You have yours, and Greta will have hers . . . and a splendid place it will be," she added, handing me a gingerbread cookie out of her clutch. I nibbled it as she went on, "Come on, now, Greta. It's time you learned the ropes. And really, dear, we must do a little better than *Greta*. So *plain*, so, I don't know, *teutonic!* What about Anastasia? Or Renée? Carina? Perhaps some advice, Laverne? You people always have such unusual names."

"I hate you," Laverne said. "Gimme one of them cookies."

"In time," said Titania, and it seemed that her porcelain face grew taut and brittle, "but now, get your black ass back out on the street and don't come back until you've made your quota for the night." She didn't sound like the same woman at all; she had a scary voice, like those women who sometimes get possessed and have to have the devil cast out of them in church. Then Titania turned on the charm again and said to me, "Honey, we're off."

▼▼▼

A limo picked us up and we went onto the freeway. Actually we went way past Beverly Hills—I got a chance to look at all the posh houses—and then down a winding road that hugged the ocean. I watched television and Titania fussed with my hair. I flick-flick-flicked until I saw the image of Jeffrey Dahmer on the television. He was being tried and his face filled the whole screen. I didn't think he was beautiful at all, and I sure didn't want to get cut into pieces and eaten. I wondered what it could be that made Laverne think that way. After all, life is a precious gift.

The limo drove past solitary beach houses. There was a house shaped like a monster's face, peering from the side of a cliff. There was a house that seemed to be made of vines, and another all glass, and another all chrome. It was gloomy and you could hear the ocean sighing even through the closed windows of the limo. Titania was putting on more makeup. For the first time since I'd known her, she seemed nervous, tapping the armrest with her tapered fingernails, smudging and redoing her lipstick over and over. When she thought she was all done, she said to me, "Now, Anastasia, I'm going to introduce you to a *very important* person. He can really change your life if you're good to him. I want you to do what he says, even it if seems a tad peculiar to you . . . do you understand?"

I nodded as I watched on television that they weren't going to send Dahmer to the electric chair after all, since they don't do that kind of thing in Milwaukee. That was strange to me, that you could kill all those people and not be killed yourself. It went against the Bible. But I had been thinking less and less about the Bible the last few days.

Where the party was there was a long wooden deck that ran on stilts beside the sea. The house was wooden and all white. There were maids in black uniforms and all the guests wore black even though it wasn't a funeral. Inside the house there were big splotchy paintings and sculptures made of wire and the guests sat in small groups, drinking and sniffing some kind of Nutrasweet into their noses. I was scared and stood in a shadowed corner, but Titania just plowed right into the crowd, screaming out endearments like "darling" and "honey" to people even though I could tell she didn't care about them at all.

"Titania Midnight!" said a woman who was wearing enough jewelry to sink a ship. "You have just *got* to do a reading for me."

"Well," said Titania, "the moon is full and the night is bright." She blinked her gold-lidded eyes and her lashes *rippled*. I don't know how to describe it except once, in school, before my parents took us out because they'd been teaching about evolution, I saw a paramecium-thingy in a microscope, and it had those little legs, *cilia* they call them, and they were just like Titania's eyelashes. "Come, Anastasia," she said, and it took me a minute to remember it was me, and we went out to the deck, to a private place that was surrounded by potted plants.

Titania sat on the redwood planks, in front of one of those electric waterfalls where the water comes down all beads, and she pulled a deck of cards out of her clutch, and she handed them to me. The woman squatted across from us and I realized I had seen her before, in *All My Children* maybe. Titania shuffled and the television star woman shuffled and then they handed me the deck and whenever Titania held out her hand I was to give her one of the cards, face down. And Titania would turn it up and lay it down on the deck in a cross kind of pattern, which reminded me of the Lord's crucifixion. Then she closed her eyes and mumbled to herself . . . I guess she was praying in tongues . . . and she said things like, "Oh no, oh no. You won't want to hear this, honey, but . . . the other one . . . he is darker, isn't he? I think, a swarthy man, hairy also, and . . . wearing a gold chain—thick."

"Oh, my God," said the movie person, "I can't wait until I totally tell all my friends . . . this is, oh God, *uncanny*. Well, it's a platinum chain actually. Herbie's, you know, *allergic* to gold and all. Can you relate?" she added, turning to me, but I don't think I was supposed to answer.

Then I looked up and saw the blond beautiful man with long hair. He was wearing a black suit and he had an earring in the shape of a scythe dangling all the way down to his shoulder. He wore mirror shades. Maybe Laverne was in love with Jeff Dahmer, but she'd probably think again if she saw *this* man. He had a little stubble, like Jeff did in the courtroom.

"You old witch," he said to Titania. "What have you conjured up today?"

Titania saw that I was staring at him with my mouth wide open. She said to me, "Anastasia," and she nudged the base of my skull so I'd look more demure, with downcast eyes, "this is your host and mine, Dana Harrington. I think you had better call him Mr. Harrington."

"But what about the dark hairy man with the platinum chain?" said the movie star woman. "Do we get to, you know, like, *do* it?"

"Hold your horses, hon," said Titania, taking the next card and flipping it through the air, "you have the death card. I think you should wait until after the divorce. Or else . . ." She made a throat-slitting gesture.

"*Shit,*" said the movie person, "the fucking trust fund. The palimony. I'd better lay in a supply of Seconals."

"Go with Mr. Harrington," Titania said to me.

I followed Mr. Harrington through the party crowd, which parted for him like the sea. We reached a bedroom that was all white and didn't even have a television in it. There were toys on the white carpet . . . boy's toys, but the kind that are a few years out of date, I mean, Transformers, TMNT action figures, and stuff. Above the bed there was a huge painting in a gold frame, and it was a picture of a boy. He was a thin boy with big eyes, but in a strange kind of way he reminded me of Johnny. I couldn't help thinking of Johnny at that moment, wondering what he was doing and whether he had wet himself yet. There was a tray of chocolates next to the bed and the man offered them to me. I had one. There was a weird liquid in the middle, which tasted the way Daddy's breath used to smell some nights. It made me feel a bit woozy, but part of that was from the gingerbread I'd had earlier. I had a few more chocolates.

"How old are you, Anastasia?" said the blond beautiful man.

"Fourteen. And my name's really Greta."

I said I was older than I really was. Later I found out you can get more money if you say you're younger.

"Do you like the chocolate liqueurs? Have some more." He

smiled. He was nice. I wondered if he would start calling me names, like Daddy. But he just made me sit next to him on the bed and he toyed with my hair. I was scared my hair would get messed up and Titania would be mad at me so I just sat there, all stiff, eating the chocolates.

"I want you to know that I'm not a bad man," said Mr. Harrington. "I do have . . . *weaknesses* . . . but I'm in therapy now. You really needn't worry about me hurting you or anything like that. I'm the last person in the world who would do that."

"I know you're a good man, Mr. Harrington," I said.

"I'm an important man," said Mr. Harrington. "Maybe I could do something for you one day."

"I got everything I need," I said. "You don't have to worry about me, Mr. Harrington." But he had already slipped a hundred dollar bill into my hand. "You sure got a lot of art here."

"I'm a collector. I only have the most beautiful things in the world here. Like you. I have an insatiable appetite for beauty. I eat it up. I consume it and afterward I'm still hungry. You know, the Chinese food syndrome."

I wasn't sure what was so great about some of those splotchy paintings, but I was too good a girl to point that out to him. Mr. Harrington took off his shades. He had the clearest eyes; I couldn't decide if they were more like Jeff Dahmer's or more like Jesus's.

"Who's that?" I said. I pointed to the portrait that reminded me so much of Johnny . . . not fat little Johnny but the Johnny that Titania was squeezing out of Johnny's flesh . . . the ideal Johnny, Johnny Angel.

"It's my son," he said.

"He looks nice."

"He's dead."

"I wish I'd of known him."

"You would have liked him. Everyone did. He was everybody's favorite Hollywood kid. He was precocious but not obnoxious. He was bright enough to be witty but not enough to be an egghead." Mr. Harrington looked away from me, remembering.

"How did he . . . I mean . . ." I knew I shouldn't have said that. Because Mr. Harrington turned to me and he was so full of rage I was afraid he was going to slap my face.

"Don't!" I said, and I shrank back, and that left him kind of dazed, staring at his hand.

"Violently," he said at last. "He died violently." I saw a tear in the corner of one eye form slowly, like a drop of condensation on a glass of soda, and slide down his cheek. I wondered whether, right now, Daddy was crying over me. Probably not, I thought. Mr. Harrington was a very special kind of man, blond, beautiful, and caring. He wiped his eye on a sleeve, and he smiled a little, and put his mirror shades back on again so I couldn't see his eyes anymore.

Then he fucked me.

▼▼▼

Titania Midnight allowed me to keep ten dollars out of the hundred, and things got better for me after that night. I did parties and dates every night except Sunday, when I helped out in the doughnut shop, stirring the big vat of batter and putting the croissants into the monster oven in batches, a hundred at a time. Sometimes I made as much as a hundred dollars a week. I became good at makeup. I became more beautiful. And so did Johnny. But when I went into his little room to take him his pills and empty his potty, I tried not to look at him too much. He would mumble things I didn't understand. I think it was because of all the videotapes he watched. He didn't have anything to do but look at television. It was lucky there were a lot of tapes: musical comedies, slasher movies, pornos, and even some that weren't in English.

Johnny's skin had a shine to it now, like a polished vase. It glowed as though there were a candle burning inside him, and I could see what Titania meant about his cheekbones. But I'd clear out of the room as quickly as I could every morning. I felt guilty, I suppose. I knew that somehow I had betrayed him. Once in a while I'd slip him a piece of gingerbread.

Titania had taught me how to make it, from sautéing the dried marijuana in butter beforehand to kill the taste, to rolling the dough and fashioning it into flat little men with raisin eyes, noses, and mouths. "Creating life in the laboratory," Titania called it, sipping her coffee and wolfing down three or four powdered doughnuts, her favorite. It sure seemed to give Johnny life because he'd just wolf that thing down. He was always sad and that was part of what made him beautiful.

Titania even showed me the larder where she kept all the fixings for her special treats. There was a jar full of white powder, a mortar and pestle, and dried toadstools, and a big brown envelope full of marijuana. There was a corrugated brown box marked *Valium*. And a whole lot of other stuff that you could use in baking to get unusual results.

The best times of all were when it was real late at night, and Titania would let me sit in on her readings. They were in a big room way in back, and it was hung with black velvet drapes and there would always be music playing there, the kind of music where you can't quite catch the melodies even though they are almost the same thing, over and over, twisting around one or two notes. I would sit in shadow and hand her the cards. Sometimes she told them I was a mute, or retarded, because they were afraid I would betray their secrets. They would look at me and say, "Poor thing," and stuff, and I had to pretend I couldn't understand.

After the last customer left, Titania would show me how it all worked. Every card, she said, is a window into another world. There's what you see and there's what you don't see. Look at this one: what are the wolves howling at that's just beyond the edge of the picture, the thing that we can't see? Is that a lobster or is it a scorpion in the water? When you open yourself up, she told me, you can hear what the wolves are saying. And more. You can hear the voices that speak from all over that hidden world. You can hear the weeping of the moon. Listen. Listen. Turn over another card.

Tonight the card was Death.

The first time I'd flipped up Death had been at Mr. Harrington's party. Death was a bent old skeleton-man with a scythe, grinning. Mr. Harrington had a scythe hanging from his left ear. The ground beneath Death was strewn with severed heads. Jeffrey Dahmer had heads in his refrigerator, apartment 213, the same number as our area code in Hollywood. Looking at the card this time made me all shivery and I wanted to cover it with another card.

Laverne poked her head in the doorway. "Eww," she said, "someone gone die tonight."

Titania took both my hands in hers and said, "Dear, dear, dear! The first lesson for the good clairvoyant is this: *Thou shalt not kill the goose that layeth the golden eggs!* Imagine, honey, the horror of telling some Hollywood fashion plate, 'Eww, someone gone die!' You'd never survive a fortnight in the biz."

"But what if I get the feeling that someone *is* going to die?" I said. "I have to tell the truth, don't I? Ain't that what the gift of prophecy is all about?"

"Laverne, go check on the chocolate dips, there's a dear." Laverne threw a roll of twenties on the floor, slammed the door, stalked off down the hall. The money crossed the death card and all you could see was the tip of the scythe. Titania flicked the money out of the way and whispered, "Now, my dear dear dear disciple, now we come to the greatest mystery of them all. Death is not death. Death is transformation."

"Oh, I get it. Like the death and resurrection of the Lord."

"Bingo! Aren't you the clever one."

"So if I draw the Death card, I have to tell the questioner that . . ."

"There will be a transformation. No, no, there is no death. Chrysalis and butterfly, corpse and maggot, life rolls over into life, death is a tango through eternal night. Look at your little brother . . . how he has shed his fleshy self . . . how he is translated into the ethereal! Ai, ai, ai, Johnny Angel indeed!"

I stared and stared at that card, but I couldn't figure it out.

▼▼▼

In the morning, Johnny moaned and carried on, and he was mumbling and muttering and he had a fever. His skin was all translucent, and you could see the veins. I mopped up his sweat with a dish towel. He tossed and turned in my arms, but I couldn't understand anything he was saying, until, looking straight past me, he said, "The man with the big curvy sword."

The room became all cold. I thought I felt someone breathing on my neck. Johnny seemed to see someone, standing behind me, swallowing both of us in his shadow. Maybe it was the fever, or maybe he really could see something; he's gifted that way. In church, he always used to know when someone was possessed.

After the blast of icy breath died away, I couldn't feel anything anymore. But Johnny could still see whatever it was he saw. I knew it was terrifying him because he started to piss himself, which he normally only does in his sleep.

I fed him gingerbread men until he dozed off. Then Titania came in with a Polaroid camera, and she made me lay him down, very carefully, like a dead body on a bier, and she took three or four snapshots of him all lying there, asleep with his eyes wide open.

▼▼▼

I have a lot of men inside me now. I've sucked little pieces of them into myself. One day the little pieces will dissolve and I'll be able to piss them away and become all clean again inside.

They liked it when I called them Daddy. Maybe they didn't have daughters of their own. Sometimes when she sent me out to work, Titania brewed me what Laverne used to call her magic potion. The potion made me crazy. I learned how to buck and heave and make those little panting noises. But oftentimes they liked it better when I played dead, closed my eyes, pretended to be asleep. That was the easiest to do, because I learned it from home. It was different from home though. Because sometimes they told me jokes, bought me little gifts, tried to treat me like a real person. They didn't call me names. And they gave me money, so that I wasn't worthless anymore.

I hardly ever watch television or go to the movies these days. You never know when one of them's going to appear. And then I'll feel all queasy inside and I have to excuse myself to go to the bathroom.

After a while, maybe because she wasn't Titania's favorite anymore, Laverne kind of drifted away from us, and sometimes she'd stay out all night. One day they were yelling at each other and Titania screamed, "Go away, get what you want, I dare you," and sent Laverne sulking into the neon night, and Laverne never came back.

I saw one evening on *A Current Affair* how Jeff Dahmer had his own groupies who used to hang around the courtroom waiting for a glimpse of him. You'd think they would all be a bunch of fat wannabes but no, some of them were good-looking, not the kind of people who needed to get a life. I had this idea that Laverne had maybe taken the bus out to Milwaukee to become one of the groupies. Since the verdict, Jeff had not come on television as often anymore, so that was probably why I had not seen Laverne on TV. Maybe in a year or two, if they ever had one of those "What ever happened to—?" type shows, I could see Laverne, hovering outside the walls of a bleak gray prison, and she'd still be calling out to him. "Come and get me too, because I love you."

I did see Laverne on television, but it wasn't how I imagined it. They were pulling her body out of a dumpster. I think it was the same one Johnny and I had slept in, that first night in Hollywood.

Later Titania and I went down to the morgue to identify the body, because we were all the kin Laverne had. She was in pieces, but it was her all right. Her hands had been cut off and strung around her neck with a length of her own intestine, and one of her feet was poking up out of her, you know, down there. Her skin was just like Johnny's, translucent. She had never been that

black but now she was almost yellow. Her eyes stared past me
the way Johnny's stared that time, seeing someone I could not
see. It still seemed to me that she was sneering at me, even now
that she had been shuffled and redealt.

In the pocket of her jeans, they had found a Jeffrey Dahmer
trading card. I knew then that this death had been the death she'd
prayed for. It was hard to believe that a man in a prison far away
could have reached out, heard her wishes, and granted them,
maybe by sending down some divine ambassador to wield the
scythe that had sliced her into thirteen pieces. After all, Daddy
had always told me that only God can do things like that. But
he also said God can be anyone, anywhere, anytime.

Maybe even inside a serial killer.

It made me sick, and later I asked Titania how she could still
say to me, "There is no death."

But all she would say was, "You have to look past those
things." And she took a sip of the hospital cafeteria coffee.

Sure, she'd said, *sure, Laverne happy.*

Now I couldn't get any of them out of my head: the bone
man swinging the scythe and Dahmer and the head in the refrigerator and Mr. Harrington and the dead boy who'd died violently,
violently, and my brother transforming into an angel inside that
beautification room. "God, why'd you have to bring me here?" I
screamed at her. "Did you make this happen when you told her
she would get what she'd always wanted? Is this another one of
your magic spells?"

"Temper, temper," she said. "I have to open all the doors in
the dark castle, dear; you have to gaze at the searing face of the
deity; yes! Oh, Anastasia, oh, Renée, you have looked the demon
in the eye and know him to be yourself!"

It was then that I knew Titania Midnight was crazy. Only
Johnny could know if she was sick in the head or whether some
devil had taken possession of her body. I was half crazy myself,
because I loved the old woman, because she was what I had to
cling to in the madness that whirled around me. The city of night
had given me a thousand fathers, but only one mother. I cried

then, and I hugged her and told her it would all come out all right in the end.

After all, she still had me, and I could do double the work to keep us all afloat. And I did.

▼▼▼

There was another party at the Harrington place. It was another Harrington place, actually, not the one in Malibu, but the one actually *in* Beverly Hills. The house was different but the room was the same. It was uncanny. The room was a kind of shrine I guess. There was probably one like it in every house the beautiful blond man owned.

The bed, the portrait of Mr. Harrington's son, even the out-dated toys that were scattered on the rug were in exactly the same places. Mr. Harrington gave me two hundred dollars this time because by now he had found out my real age, plus now I was real good at behaving just the way he wanted. Right after it was over, I fell into a deep sleep because it was the best way to stop feeling the pain.

When I woke up, Titania Midnight was in the room, and so was Mr. Harrington, fully dressed now in his tuxedo, ready to go to some premiere. They were sitting on the edge of the bed.

"Can we talk? She won't wake up, will she?" said Mr. Harrington.

"Not if she drained that Valium cocktail to the last drop."

Mr. Harrington said, "You've been very good to me, Titania. In accommodating . . . well, my tastes. But there was something else you were going to look for . . . I don't know how much progress you've made."

"A lot. I want you to see some Polaroids," Titania said. I kept my eyes closed because I didn't want them to know I could hear them. I could hear Titania rummaging in her purse, could hear papers rustling, and then I heard Mr. Harrington sigh. "The eyes. The sadness. The crisp hard curl of a lower lip that can't quite twist into a smile. He's so beautiful you could eat him up," Titania said.

"No poetry, Titania," said Mr. Harrington. And he sighed again.

"No poetry? But how can you say that when you see these pictures? But it gets better. No papers. No dental records. No milk cartons. No television appeals. He does not exist. Not until you spring him, fully formed, into the world. Come for him tomorrow midnight."

"I'll have the cash."

They didn't talk for a long time. It took time for the weight of what they were saying to settle in. I pretended to sleep until they left the room. Then I got up and prowled around. I didn't go back down to the party because then they might know I'd overheard them. I tiptoed across the toy-strewn rug. Titania had left her purse on the dresser. I was sure she'd been showing Mr. Harrington the Polaroids of Johnny, and I was right. That's what they were. I held one of them up to the lava lamp, then I glanced up at the portrait of Mr. Harrington's son. Titania had caught the look exactly. Somehow, she had turned Johnny into this dead boy. It was like Johnny's body was an empty glass and you could pour in any soul you wanted. Maybe the pills did more than melt away his fat. And Mr. Harrington was a collector, he'd told me. Was he planning to collect Johnny? I became real frightened, and I guess my hand was trembling because I knocked the purse onto the floor.

A lot of stuff fell out: a key ring, a packet of Dunhills, a driver's license. I knelt down and tried to put everything back in. I looked at the license too. It showed Titania's picture, but the name on it was Amelia Goldberg. Hadn't Daddy said something about Goldsteins and Goldfarbs . . . sacrificing babies and taking away his job? It didn't seem possible that Titania Midnight could be one of those people. She didn't even know who my father was, so how could she take his job? And it wasn't *her* who had killed Laverne.

Or was it?

I didn't want to think such terrible things about the woman who had taken me in, given me a job with decent wages, and tried to share so much of her wisdom with me. But it sure made me think. There was more to all this than I had ever dreamed. It really scared me.

Especially when I finally put my clothes back on and I went back down to the party, and I saw Mr. Harrington gliding through the thick of the crowd, smiling a little, in a world of his own, and the scythe in his ear catching the light from the crystal chandelier. He moved among the chatter, and the clinking of cocktail glasses, but he himself seemed to be inside his own private silence.

▼▼▼

That night I dreamed about the beautiful blond man, and the scythe swinging and people screaming and their heads flying through the air like bloody soccer balls. When I woke up I wished Laverne would be lying on the futon next to me, even if she would kick me half onto the floor. It was real late and I knew that even Titania would be asleep by now, either in her bedroom or in the reading room, slumped over a deck of tarot cards, or in the easy chair in the big kitchen among the unbaked doughnuts.

I had a feeling I had to see Johnny. It was Johnny who had spied on Daddy's prayer meeting and who had had the presence of mind to come and warn me. It was only fair I should tell him about things I overheard. So I pulled on a long *Beverly Hills 90210* T-shirt, and I crept down the corridor to the beautification room.

I looked in at my brother. He was leaning against the wall, staring at the television. He didn't seem to see me. I put my lips to the pane and whispered his name a couple of times, but he didn't look up. Then I tried the door. It was unlatched. I wondered how many times it had been unlatched in the past, how many times we could have escaped. Except where would we have escaped to? Titania had fed us . . . me, anyway . . . loved us, for all I could tell. I slipped into the room and I was almost touching him before he seemed to notice me. "Johnny," I said,

"Johnny, I think they want to do something to you, I don't know what."

Johnny said, "I don't like the pornos that much. I seen all that stuff before, at home. Westerns are cool. The horror movies are the best. I love Freddy Krueger's fingernails."

"Johnny, can't you hear me?"

"When I close my eyes, the movie still goes on. The man with the curvy sword is dancing in the street. Under the neon lights. The flashing sign makes a dragon on his face because his face is like a mirror."

God, I thought, thinking of Mr. Harrington's shades as he moved up and down, up and down, seeing my face get big and small, big and small. "Johnny," I said, "are there mirrors over his eyes? Is the curvy sword dangling from his ear? Is he a beautiful blond man dressed in black?"

Johnny giggled. But that was because of something on the television. "You have to tell me," I said, "it's real important."

But Johnny began to babble in tongues. He was always a lot closer to the Lord than I could ever be. He carried on for a while, waving his arms and making his eyes roll up in their sockets, but without the gift of interpretation I couldn't understand what he meant. But finally he switched back to English and he said, "The skull." And pointed straight at the television screen. But all I could see was a Madonna video.

"Come on, Johnny. Let's run away. I don't think this place is safe anymore. I think they're gonna do something really bad to you. Look, I got a couple hundred bucks saved up, tips and stuff. I know we don't remember how we got here, but maybe we can find a better daddy and mommy. I met a hundred new daddies here, and most of them were pretty nice to me. You could have all the candy bars you wanted. You wouldn't have to be this way."

Johnny turned to me at last. The room was dark except for the pool of gray light in front of the television. He sat up. He was wearing only a pair of yellowing BVDs and his whole body was shiny, like the TV screen, and his eyes were haunted and deep. His hair was as pale as the hair of the blond beautiful man, and his fingers tapped at the empty air. "We can't go," he said softly. "You can't run away from the man with the curvy sword."

I hugged Johnny and said, "I got a plan, Johnny. We'll be okay." I didn't know what the plan would be yet, but my mind was racing. We'd use my money to buy a bus ticket to Disneyland. We'd find a mommy and a daddy and a tract house in a green green suburb. We'd overdose on gingerbread and fly into the sky.

I tugged at Johnny. He started to budge, then I heard the key turn in the latch of the prison door. I looked up sharply and saw Titania's face in the television's ghostly light. She must have just come back from a Beverly Hills reading, because her face was powdered to a chalky whiteness, and her lips painted the crimson of fresh blood, and there were charcoal circles around her eyes. She sniffed like a hungry she-wolf, and her lips twisted into a sharp-toothed smile. Then she faded into shadow.

Titania Midnight was more than mad. She was evil.

I held Johnny in my arms the whole night long, and didn't sleep until dawn.

▼▼▼

The blond beautiful man with long hair was coming at midnight. I knew that from overhearing that conversation. I didn't have that long to do what I had to do. I went to Titania's secret larder and pulled out about forty Valium; I ground them up with the mortar and pestle, and I folded and sifted them with a half cup of powdered sugar. I poured the mixture into an envelope, tucked it in my jeans, and went out to work.

Work was not too bad that day. All my dates were regulars, and I already knew how they all liked it. So I didn't really have to concentrate very hard. I just let myself drift, and I swallowed just enough gingerbread to loosen up my soul, and not enough to cut the kite string that held me to the real world. Everyone was pleased with me and I got a lot of extra money, which was good because maybe me and Johnny would need it later.

I stayed out as late as I dared. When I came home it was only an hour before midnight. I found Titania in the kitchen of the doughnut shop. She had turned off the neon and pulled down all the shades and hung up a sign on the door that read **ON VACATION—CLOSED**. She had a whole pot of coffee out and, even though she wasn't going out anywhere, was dressed to the teeth. She had on a long black robe embroidered with suns and moons and stars. Her eyelids were painted in rainbow glitter, and her lips were midnight blue. When she saw me, she became all agitated and she started to cackle.

"Tonight's the night, my baby Anastasia," she said. "No more slaving over a hot kitchen for you! No more blowjobs in BMW's. You're going to be a princess now, and Titania's going to be queen of the wood. Be a dear and do me up some powdered doughnuts. Mama Titania'll be back in a few minutes."

I fetched the doughnuts and dipped them in the Valium powder. She was gone for a long time, and I became more and more nervous. I took the croissants out of the oven and stacked them up. I wondered why she was still baking if we were supposed to be on vacation . . . and rich besides.

When Titania came back, she had Johnny with her. He was wearing a brand new blue suit with crisp, sharply creased short pants. Titania had moussed his hair and brushed it. It was hard for Johnny to stand in the light. He kept blinking and he seemed not to know where he was.

Titania said. "Things will be different now, Johnny. You'll be able to eat anything you want. Would you like some candy? Would you care for a doughnut?" She snatched one from the plate I had so carefully arranged and handed it to him. Then she stuffed one into her own mouth. While she was busy chewing, I pried the doughnut loose from Johnny's fist and gave him something else, a chocolate éclair. He sucked on it, savoring the cream.

"My two little darlings," said Titania Midnight, "tonight Mr. Harrington is going to come for you. Well, the deal is only for Johnny, but I think we can manage to get Anastasia thrown into the package . . . oh, my angels, how I slaved to make you ready for this moment! But tomorrow it's curtains for Titania Midnight, reader, advisor, pimp, and doughnut manufacturer extraordinaire . . . and now . . . for my next transformation . . . enter Amelia Goldberg . . . rich bitch from Encino . . . estate broker . . . millionairess . . . queen of the gliterati . . . oh, it'll be splendid, splendid, splendid, my honey babies!"

I said, "There's a picture on Mr. Harrington's wall. He says it's his son. He says his son died violently."

"I know," said Titania. "So sad, isn't it? Torn to pieces by a mad slasher. Time, indeed, for a new son."

"You're lying!" I said. "You made Johnny into an angel so Mr. Harrington could kill him! He's the man with the big curvy sword, the grim reaper, the Jeffrey Dahmer man!" How could I have been so stupid before? Daddy always told me that people like her liked to sacrifice babies. He said they shouldn't have let them crawl out of the ovens. Titania had sent Laverne out to die with a single sentence. She had said that death and transformation were the same thing, and now she was telling us to get ready for transformation. *Right.* For death.

He's so beautiful you could eat him up.

Wasn't that why the oven was still on?

"We ain't going where you tell us anymore," I said. "We ain't going to die for you. It's too much to ask."

Her face started to transform then. There really was a demon inside. I could tell by the way her eyes burned and her fingernails raked the air.

"Whore!" she screamed. "I take you in . . . you *nothings* . . . I make something of you, I see the chance to pull all of us out of the gutter . . . and you dare defy me . . ." She lunged at me, but that was when the Valium kicked in and she sort of folded up, and then I pushed her with all my might. Right into the oven. She slid in easy. I slammed the door but that didn't keep out the stench. And then fumes began pouring into the kitchen. There was a smell like burning plastic, maybe from her clothes, and another smell, like barbecuing lamb, that made my mouth water in spite of what I knew it was.

I started coughing. The smoke detector went off and the alarm screeched and I could hear clanging and buzzing and a siren in the distance. I stood there for a long time, too numbed to move, until I realized that the fire was going to eat all of us up unless I took Johnny by the hand and steered him out of the doughnut shop.

There was smoke all over the street. The whole place was burning up. There was a Rolls Royce parked in the alley and the blond beautiful man was standing there, all dressed in black, with the scythe dangling from his ear.

"Get away from him," I said to Johnny. "He'll cut you in pieces."

But Johnny just stared at him, and he kind of smiled. And he began walking toward him. I ran after him, trying to pull him back, crying out, "No, Johnny, no!" but he wouldn't listen.

Mr. Harrington took off his mirror shades. He was just staring at Johnny as though he were looking at a man from Mars. Then he started to weep.

"He does look just like him," he said softly. "Titania was right." He started to reach forward to touch Johnny, and that was when I lost control.

"I killed Titania! Now you can get out of our lives too!" I screamed. And I pummeled his black silk jacket with my fists. But he was hard and strong and hollow.

"She's dead?"

"I shoved her in the oven," I said. "God damned baby-sacrificing kike."

"Oh, my God," said Mr. Harrington. "Where did you learn to say such hateful things?"

"From Daddy," I said.

"You killed her." He started to back away from us. "She wasn't an evil woman. In her way she did try to help you. It's true that she trafficked in young flesh . . . but . . . no one is so evil they deserve to be . . ." The odor of burning meat wafted across the alley. "Poor Titania."

"Poor Titania? She was gonna give Johnny to you . . . so

you'd kill him and cut him in pieces and eat him . . . like Jeffrey Dahmer."

"She didn't tell you? I was going to adopt him. Both of you, probably. You could have lived in Beverly Hills with me and had everything you ever wanted. For years I've wanted a new son . . . and Titania knew the dark country where you live, the forgotten, the abandoned children. I promised to pay her well to find me a kid who looked so much like . . . like. . . ."

"Don't give me that bullshit. You fucked me."

He winced. "I wish you wouldn't use that language."

The smoke blended right into the smog of night. I just glared at Mr. Harrington. I think he saw my anger for the first time. Maybe I shouldn't have lain there, leaving my body behind while my mind drifted far away. Maybe I should have looked him straight in the eye and shown him all my rage, all my frustration at being so weak and powerless. Then maybe he wouldn't have done it to me. But it was too late now. I could see now that the powerful emotion that had shaken him when he first saw us might have been the beginning of love. But it was fading now.

"I'm not a bad man," he said. "I'm . . . a weak man. I would have been good to you."

Johnny said softly, "I'm gonna pee my pants."

"But of course I can't adopt either of you now. My reputation . . . the scandal . . . you know how it is. I'd better go." Now I could see that he thought of us as slimy things . . . cockroaches . . . vermin. "I'll call 911 from the car."

He kissed Johnny on the forehead and touched my hair. Then he got back in his Rolls Royce and drove away, and we stood in front of the burning doughnut shop, waiting for the fire department.

▼▼▼

Sometimes I see the blond beautiful man on television. But I change the channel. In a few months the court will send us to a foster home, if they can find one. But it might be hard since I'm a murderer.

After Bob read the last entry in my diary, the one where I talked about the fire at the doughnut shop, he told me that it made him cry. I don't know why. *I* never cry. I don't have time because I have to look after Johnny.

After he read *Hansel and Gretel* to us, I told Bob my witch theory, and he shook his head slowly and said, "Greta, there's only one kind of magic in the world. You made magic when you wrote the words that made me cry. Words can be black magic and they can be white magic, but they are the only things that can transform us. Even a movie starts with just words on a page, a screenplay."

That's why I go on writing it all down. If I write enough words down, maybe we can still have the things we long for . . . the tract house, the mommy and daddy, the green green suburb far away. But so far nothing has come true.

I guess I'm not that good at witchcraft.

THE WITCH OF THE MOON
▼▼▼

TANITH LEE

IN the garden behind the hut, Flawna's grandmother had been gathering herbs. Above, in the lavender sky, a pale blushed moon stood over the hills. And Flawna's grandmother told her then that a witch lived on the moon.

"But how can a witch live there?" asked Flawna, who that day was ten years old. "Does she live alone?"

"All alone, but for her livestock and her hares," said the grandmother.

"Is she not lonely?" said Flawna.

"Perhaps," said the grandmother, "but she is powerful too."

"More powerful than my father?"

"Much more."

"More powerful than a king?"

"A king is like a child to her."

Flawna thought about this as she tied the herbs in bundles and put them in the basket. Finally she asked: "What will she do?"

"If ever you should need her help," said the grandmother, "there is a way to call to her. And I will show you. Then she will help you. That is what she will do."

Behind them in the hut the warm light had risen on the clay

lamps, and at the hearth Flawna's mother and sisters were cooking in their bronze caldron. Out of the land the men had not yet come from their hunting and farming.

Flawna's grandmother held up her old bone hands to the moon, and then she said, "You must do this, and then you must shut your eyes, and inside your eyes you must see only the moon. And then you must take a cup of water, and let the moon shine in the water. And then you should drink the water. Mind, the moon must be full, as now it is, and nothing standing between you and it. You will feel the water cold in your throat and belly. And then you must say *this*," and she told Flawna the secret words, and made Flawna repeat them. When the old woman was satisfied, she nodded and went on plucking the herbs, singing as she always did under her breath.

At last Flawna said, "Why have you told me this?"

"Because you may need to know."

▼▼▼

Some years passed, and the grandmother died, and Flawna was thirteen. Her hair was long and dark as smoke, and her eyes gray-green. She had breasts, and every month she bled. Being a woman, she had now learned the woman's crafts of cooking and weaving and singing, and she would soon enough be married, for there were young men who came to look at her, and one had given her a copper band for her wrist.

But then on a still evening, a thunder rushed down the hills. It was made of warriors in chariots, and they burned the huts and the fields and killed the men. Flawna's father and three brothers they killed; she saw it. In the dark of dawn, as the red smoor of the huts smoldered on behind them, they took the women away, tied by ropes like the cattle.

Three days and three nights the journey was, and on the way Flawna's mother stabbed herself, sticking a brooch-pin into her throat. Flawna's sisters lived and wept, but once they reached the King's Town, Flawna did not see them again.

There was a market, a great square of beaten earth under the King's House. And here the women and the cattle were sold.

Flawna had not wept. Now she sat on the ground, her hands tied to a wheel, with her dark hair round her. The King's House was like no place she had seen before. Thick pillars, the color of her father's blood, held up its roof that was thatched with straw and sun, like gold. Eventually a woman came out of the King's House. She wore a blue gown and had gold wire in her plaits. She looked over the remaining captives on the square, and a silence fell. Then the woman pointed to Flawna.

"Make her stand up."

So they told Flawna to get up and loosened the rope so that she could. Flawna stood, and looked at the woman from the House.

"Yes. She will do. She need only sweep and clean. But we must have only the pretty ones in the High House."

So Flawna became the King's slave.

▼▼▼

The High House was full of riches and strengths. Spears and pelts and enemy skulls set with jewels were on the walls, and there were in the wide Hall lamps made of alabaster, and the King's seat was plated in gold.

Fifty warriors served the King, but he had only one son. The King's son, who had been a warrior, now lay sick. The House was under this shadow, and it was cruel.

The lower slaves, in whose order Flawna was, wore rags and slept amid the kennels of the dogs. Their food was the scraps the other servants left unwanted. Though no one in the House might be taken in if ugly, yet these slaves became so after a time from ill use.

Flawna swept the floors of the kitchens, scoured the pots, ground the flour on the unkind stone, washed fairer garments than her own in the river that ran below the King's orchards. Always she was slapped and cuffed, and once, when she stole a ripening apple among the gnarled and silent trees, another slave

noticed her and told what she had done. Then came the master
of the kitchen, who oversaw the lowest slaves. He thrashed Flawna
with a switch of twigs until she bled, and then before them all
he made her rinse out her mouth with dog's urine. The people
of the kitchen laughed and mocked Flawna. But this awfulness
she endured, because all her life was now so terrible she expected
nothing of it but horror. At night she lay to sleep in the filthy
straw, as far from the angry dogs as she could get, and nearby
she heard the other slaves at their sexual sport, and knew that in
time she too would be the prey of it, although so far, finding her
unwilling and others less so, she had been left alone.

Months passed and a winter came. Deep rains and then a
wing of snow covered the Town and the House. In the whiteness,
with rags bound about her feet, Flawna went to the frozen well
and broke the ice and brought back the pots. And there one day
a priest stood, in the kitchen's center, and everyone cowered about
him. His hair was bound with bones, and his clothes were the
skins of wolves and lynxes, set with eyes of amber and green
quartz. On his ringed hands were the smokes of tattooes, and his
forehead had on it a crimson eye.

"Girl," he said to Flawna, "is it true you have never lain
under a man?"

Flawna put down the brimming pots and at the core of her
body her virgin's seal seemed to twist and tighten. He was a priest,
so she must speak, before them all, all these who had cuffed and
scorned her and given her the piss of a dog to drink.

"I have never known a man."

"Lie down on that table," said the priest, "and spread your legs."

Flawna, at this, backed away from him. It was only a leap of
her soul; she knew there was no escape.

Two of the men slaves who had tried for her were glad enough
now to catch and throw her down. She was forced open, and
into her second heart the priest peered squinting.

"It is true, she is a maiden. Get up, slut," said the priest.
"Go to the river and wash yourself clean. Dress yourself in this
gown. Then I have a deed for you."

Flawna ran to the river, through the snow. She broke the ice and entered the black cold like a swan. She washed herself with water and with tears. They were the first woman's tears she had shed, and they came from her like blood, the blood of her father and mother, the dead fire of her burning home.

When she was finished, she put on the gown the priest had given her, at which before she had not looked. It was white as the bones in his hair, a gown of linen. So she returned, cold as death through the snow again, and went in, and the priest said to her, "Fill this cup with the water you brought from the well. Then follow me."

In the kitchen was a great quiet. They did not look now, only bowed to their tasks. But now and then one darted a glance. When Flawna had filled the cup, which was of gold, the priest beckoned her away.

They went up through the House, and no one was there, as if the path had been cleared before them. Through the wide Hall they went, which she had only glimpsed. Two dogs lay by the hearth, but they did not stir. The golden seat was empty. No warriors sat dicing or sharpening their spears.

Above was a narrow chamber, under the roof.

"You are a maiden. They have had word that only a maiden, and a stranger not of his blood, may cure him with water. Go in and give it him. Do not speak. If you speak, I will have you killed."

So Flawna took the golden cup of water to a couch of fine rugs that was over in the corner under the painted wall. Someone lay there, and she kneeled down to do as she had been told she must. As she did so, she remembered all at once her grandmother, and how she had spoken of the cup of water that had held the moon. Then she knew that the one who lay here was the King's only son, and she ceased to think of her grandmother.

He was young, and as the day is to the night, the night to the day, so he was to the world. His hair was black as young ravens, and when her shadow touched his face, he opened two eyes blue as blue never was. He looked at her without a word, and then he raised himself a little, and took the cup from her hand, and drained it.

"How cold the water is," he said.

She would have spoken. She would have said, "There was ice in the well." She would have said, "It is not cold from the moon." But the priest had promised she would die if she spoke to the King's son, and so she did not speak.

And he, he lay back and closed his eyes again.

So she got up and left him, and at the door she gave back the cup to the priest, who took it and said, "Very well. Go away now."

And she went down again through the quiet suspension of the High House, and in the kitchen they shrank from her, and she stood in her linen gown, cold as the moon.

▼▼▼

Birth is pain, and in the river Flawna was reborn. She hurt now, unhealed and unsolaced. The death that must come before the birth, that too lay heavy on her. And memory. And strange terrible sweetness.

For never had she known so many things of anguish, and one new thing. For though she had never loved, now she recognized that she did so. Diermod was his name, she had heard it often and it had had no form, but now it had a form. The King's son.

She had been the slave of the High House almost a year, but that one day was a year in itself. And when the sunset came, and still they left her alone, the crew in the kitchen of her misery, Flawna took up a rough clay cup, and she went out into the gleaming shadows of the snow-dusk.

Down to the river she went in her linen gown, and there she filled the cup, and turned to face the east between the slender naked trees. And up through the web of them the moon was rising, round as the head of a child.

Far off, the torches lit in the King's House, russet red. And in the King's Town the dogs barked and the cattle moaned in their stalls, and there was the narrow murmur of human life. But across the orchard came the stillness of eternity, the moon speaking to the earth.

Flawna raised her arms to the moon. And then she shut her eyes and saw only the moon. She knelt and drank the water that the moon reflected in. And it was cold. Then, she said the magic words her grandmother had told her. And perhaps after such a time and such events, she did not say them quite right, but even so, their nature was unchanged.

Kneeling on the snowy ground under the bare trees of the orchard, Flawna waited.

"There is a witch lives on the moon," had said her grandmother. "She will help you. That is what she will do."

The sky was mauve, like a mallow, and only the moon was in it. And then, there issued out of the moon a faint thin glowing white line, and it spread away, separated, and grew softer, as if the sky had melted it. But also it fell down and down, nearer and nearer, and Flawna saw it was a great white cloud, long like a boat. It sank in upon the trees, and came through their branches, unbroken, and drifted to the edge of the river, where Flawna knelt on the snow.

The cloud lay, attending on Flawna.

She knew, and her heart filled with tears, but not her eyes. She rose, and went into the cloud, and there was the slightest quiver, like the motion of a soft sleeve. She was borne upward then, she knew, for through the depth of the cloud she saw the ghosts of the trees, and then the red glare of the House, but these drew away below, and then the purple sky opened above, full of dawning stars.

But soon after the cloud covered Flawna over, and she fell asleep at once, like a tired child.

So she did not see how they came there, to the opal island of the moon.

▼▼▼

When she woke, Flawna had arrived, and the cloud had left her.

She saw that she was in a vast valley that was white, like the snow, yet it was warm there, and a soft breeze blew. The grass was white as clover. In the distance rose the white hills, dark white as bone, and behind these the white mountains, but they were tinged with mauve from the dark purple sky. The stars stood bright and large.

All across the valley, flocks and herds of white beasts grazed on the grass, sheep with long fleeces and cows with crystal horns. And there were pale trees where pale fruit hung like drops of silver.

A river ran across the valley, but it was full of clouds, not water, though here the cattle came to drink.

On the brink of the river was a hut with silver thatch, and there a woman was before the doorplace, as if she waited. Her hair was black, and hung to the ground.

Flawna had begun to walk across the white grass, toward the hut and the woman, and it was strange, for though the distance was great, she moved with peculiar swiftness, and in less than a minute she had come to the stones in the river, and so to the far bank and the hut.

The woman wore a white gown, and in her left hand there was a golden distaff, but her right hand was empty.

She had a face that was too perfect for any feature, and even her eyes were only as if two stars shone through her head. At her feet played seven white hares, running miles off in a second, coming back to her in another.

"Lady," said Flawna.

"Enter my house," said the woman.

Flawna walked through a garden of tall golden flowers, and they went in. No fire burned in the hut; only a light bloomed on the floor, and over it hung a silver caldron from which pink steam like a feather gently rose.

"What will you have?" asked the Witch.

"Do you know where I have been?" asked Flawna.

"Yes," said the Witch of the Moon, "I know it all. That you are a slave, that you have given water to the King's son."

"If I ask for justice," said Flawna, "what will I have?"

"Everything you desire," said the Witch, "and I can give it you. But in return, I will take also one thing."

Flawna did not feel afraid. There was no fear there. "What is that one thing?" Outside, the hares ate the golden flowers, but the flowers grew again at once.

"You will know, when the time comes."

"I have nothing," said Flawna. "Nothing to give."

The Witch of the Moon put her empty right hand directly into the steaming caldron. She drew out a powder like salt, and offered it to Flawna.

Flawna took the powder, but somehow the Witch did not touch her at all.

"You must not," said the Witch, "let a grain of it fall, until you are ready. Then, throw it in the well, before you draw the water."

"What can it be?" said Flawna. She had always asked questions, and now the knack had come back to her.

"It can be," said the Witch, "what it is."

Then she motioned Flawna to sit down, and Flawna, with her left hand closed tight upon the powder, as the hand of the Witch stayed closed on the distaff, sat on the rugs of the Witch's house. And the Witch brought her clouds to drink in a cup of white polished wood, and the clouds tasted of apple beer. And then the Witch dropped a tiny fruit into Flawna's mouth, and for the first time in almost a year, Flawna was not hungry.

Then the Witch sang, and Flawna sang. They sang together as the women did on the Earth. And although she could not see it in the perfect featureless face, Flawna knew that the Witch smiled at her.

After this they stood in the doorway, and looked in the opposite direction, up the valley of the moon. And there in the purple sky was the other island, the Earth, huge, blue and gray-green as eyes, garlanded by stars.

"Must I go now?" asked Flawna.

"Only if you wish to."

And Flawna thought that the Witch of the Moon was lonely, as she had supposed.

"I will go," said Flawna, "for I want what you have given me."

"Farewell, then," said the Witch.

And out of the river rose a cloud, perhaps even the first cloud, and folded Flawna round. And she slept again, and only once it seemed she saw a snowy cow that jumped across the sky, and then she awoke lying on the Earth under the orchard trees of winter and the King.

But her left hand was fast closed, the moon had set, and in the east the dawn was beginning.

▼▼▼

Flawna went to the well of the King's House, and cast in the powder from the moon, all of it. And then she drew the pots of water and brought them to the kitchen.

Water, like blood, ran everywhere about the body of the House.

Flawna sat still in her corner, where now they let her be. She rested her head upon her knees.

Presently she heard cries, then the crash of metal things, then screams. And at last a greater scream, close by.

And looking up, she saw the master of the kitchen, he that beat her and gave her the water of dogs; he had changed. He was down on the floor, grunting and snorting. He was black and tusked, a barrel on foolish little legs. He had become a pig.

All through the High House, those that had abused Flawna had become swine. The servant girls who had slapped her and torn her hair, the boys that had tried to force her, the ones who had cursed her and spat at her. And the woman in the blue gown who had bought Flawna, she too, a bluish grunting pig with swinging dugs.

And then from the house they were chased out with brooms and spears, and they ran away, these ensorcelled ones. Stones were flung at them and blood patterned their skins as, naked and speechless, on their trotters, they fled toward the forest. For pigs see the wind, how terrible anything worse.

But up above, Diermod the King's son rose from his couch, strong and sound, like a young wolf, a stallion. And standing in his beauty, he shouted that he must see the girl again, the virgin girl, who had cured him.

Then they came to Flawna and told her, and meek as before, she went up the ways of the High House, where now the people clustered, staring. She went into the Hall, where he stood, a tree of light, clad in bronze and gold, gold in his raven hair, and looked long at her from his eyes that were the blue that had never ever been till he had been.

"This is the maiden," he said. And to Flawna, "What is your name?"

She told him, for no one had said, this time, she must not speak.

"Flawna, you are my spirit. You are more lovely than sunrise. Your hair is night and your eyes are the great lake that meets the sea."

The King moved his body as if to stay his son, but Diermod looked at the King and said, "Would you rather, then, have had me dead?"

So the King said nothing more.

And Diermod went down and put his hand quietly upon her breast, over her heart, and kissed her mouth.

"Am I yours?" she asked.

"Till the sun goes out."

And she felt again that twisting within her, but now it was joy.

She forgot her father's death and her mother's death, and her home burning, and her grandmother. She forgot the Witch of the Moon. She put her hand into his.

▼▼▼

So she came to be Queen in the High House, for the old King did not live long after that, and Diermod was the King. For half a year they were lovers. They did all together. They woke as one in the King's bed, and came to each other like fire. And then they ate and dressed and went hunting in the forest, and there he would draw her down under the greening trees of spring, and later under the green roofs of summer. And in the westering light they would ride home and in the end of day they would feast in the Hall, and she had a seat of silver he had had made for her, set by his seat of gold. And at last, under the dark, when the fallen torch of the sun had lit the world to bed, they coupled again with sighs and cries, and slept as one.

And sometimes the moon put down a white ray into the chamber, and waking for a moment, Flawna saw it. But she thought nothing of it. For if cruelties may be endured, so may kindness.

Then one morning she woke and her body was no longer hers, and she put her hand out not to embrace but to stay her husband.

"I am with child of you," she said.

And at her words, she wondered, for it was as if she no longer belonged to herself at all, as if she hung far off and only looked on. But Diermod was glad and told her that she would bear him a son.

Then they were no more lovers, and Flawna was no more Flawna, but a woman heavy with her burden. She waxed large and how slowly she moved. She lingered alone with only the young women round her, while Diermod hunted the forest. And when she sat in her silver chair she seemed to see the world at a mile of distance. Food tasted strange to her. Sleep deserted her. And so by night she beheld the passing of the white finger of the moon, writing on the floor of the chamber, but what it wrote she did not know.

One blood-red dawn, in agony, she gave birth to Diermod's son. He was flawless, a wondrous child. Flawna was now another person. Not lover, wife and queen, but mother. She nursed the child at her body and out of her he seemed to draw his life. Like a golden plant he grew against the milk-white tower of her breast.

Diermod played with his son, throwing him up and catching him, having made for him small bronze spears and bands of gold. Diermod hung his son with amulets of blue stone and green beryl. He called the boy Culen, which had been the old King's name. Culen curled quietly from Flawna, and twined instead into the men's side. He strode about the house, a tiny image of his father, with black hair down his back.

But Diermod and Flawna were lovers once again, and she said to him, "Do you prefer me to all others?" For she knew he had had other girls of the House when she lay heavy with the child.

"You are my spirit," said Diermod, "and my son is a spark of you."

Yet now their love was lust, it was hunger, and it was dicing, too, and soon the dice fell upon the special place, and again Flawna was possessed of another child.

"What troubles you, Flawna?' asked her husband. "Why do you sit at the window looking up? The moon will burn your eyes."

"Once, long ago, I traveled to the moon," said Flawna, great with life, round as the moon her belly, but the light hidden inside.

"Did you so?" he asked. "And what did you find there?"

"The grass is white, and from the trees hang silver fruits. The cattle there have horns of crystal."

"And were there no people there?" he asked, smiling at her. And she saw, for the moonlight showed it, that he did not believe her, and that perhaps he loved her less, for now he was all mild consolation, where love had made him fierce as fire.

"No. There are no people on the moon," said Flawna. "And perhaps I only dreamed it."

▼▼▼

Birth is pain, and with agony once more, now in the violet dusk, Flawna let forth her second child. White as snow, it was a girl.

Diermod named the child for his mother. But Flawna did not

call the baby by a name. Flawna held her daughter to her breast, and the white child turned her head aside.

When she was strong enough, Flawna went out alone in the sunfall, down through the trees of the King's orchard. It was summer now, and every tree was massed with leaves like copper in the sun's end, and on them the young fruits stood in beads of life, all the children of the orchard. But the river was brown and over its stones the frogs sat, waiting for the night.

Night came. The stars were cool, and presently the moon rose, dim and yellow.

Flawna stayed, with her girl child in the curve of her arm.

And suddenly from the moon there stole a faint yellow vapor that stretched and separated and fell slowly down and down, down through the leaves, unbroken, and lay attending on the Earth.

Flawna did not weep. Her heart was full of tears.

She put her daughter into the cloud, and the cloud wrapped up the child, then lifted away, away, and Flawna stood alone on the bank of the river.

"I will take also one thing," she had said, the Witch of the Moon.

And Flawna had said, "I have nothing."

And now, "I have nothing," she said.

▼▼▼

Diermod sat frowning in the Hall, upon his golden seat, and Flawna sat still at his side on the silver one.

Diermod's people, his counselors and warriors, murmured together, then spoke to him again.

They said his wife was a witch. It had always been known. How else had she cured him of his sickness? How else had she turned her foes into pigs? And now, this business of her child. What had she done with the King's daughter?

Diermod said, "That is between her and me. It is not yours to ask or to be answered. And that she cured me, did not the priest see to it?"

Then the priest stepped forward in his skins, and in his hand he had a staff with a fox's head with blue eyes.

"She is the Queen. She is the King's wife," said the priest. "If the King does not speak against her, who am I? Then too," he said, "she has borne him a son. And she will bear him others."

Flawna looked at them all and saw them as far away as when she had carried her babies. But now her womb was full of silence. She felt no fear, for she had been stunned, as if by a fall. Her eyes were so green, and clear as the eyes of the magical fox. When the mutterers and murmurers looked into them, they thought that she was curious, not of this Earth maybe, and perhaps they should think of the pigs and keep quiet.

As for Diermod, he would not hear a word against her. He kept her at his side in the Hall, and in his bed by night. They thought she had bewitched him, and they had better think of that too.

They did not know how the King and his wife had spoken together. When she had said to him, "Your daughter has gone away."

"Gone to where?" he asked, thinking her playful.

"I will not tell you," said Flawna. "To tell you would be as useless as not to tell. Therefore I will not."

"But is it true?"

"True as I stand here before you."

"Then what have you done?" he cried, in sudden deep alarm.

"Nothing. She is not harmed. But," said Flawna, "perhaps you will kill me for it."

"How can I kill you? You gave me back my life."

"And I gave life to the child, but she is taken from me."

"Who took her?"

"I will not say."

Then he struck her. She lay at his feet and the touch of her smoking hair upon his ankle went as harshly into him as a spear. He lifted her up and held her on his breast, but she was like a stone. Both knew in that instant they were no longer lovers, nor even husband and wife, save in name only. Then he said, "Whatever you have done, I will keep you safe."

She thanked him.

She thought how she had seen him lying on his bed, and had given him the plain cold water, and then how some other, that she did not even know, had taken to him the other water, in which had been the Witch's sorcerous salt. *She* had not cured him. She had not deserved him, or to be Queen. If his father's warriors had not gone raiding, she would have lived among the huts of the valley. She would not have been a High Woman with gold wire in her hair and bands of silver on her wrists. She would not have given one of her children to the moon.

So, although the priest had said she would have more sons by Diermod, Flawna gave him only one, Culen. For they did not lie together any more, only back to back, sleeping, and often not even this. Since in the moonlit nights, while Diermod sank dreaming, Flawna would stand at the window. She would gaze up at the moon's face, and image her daughter there, playing in the white meadows under the white hills and the shadowed mountains tinted mallow from the sky. She saw her daughter growing into a maiden, and that the sheep followed her, and the white cows let her ride upon their backs. She bathed in clouds, and she sang with the Witch in her hut with the silver thatch.

But Culen grew up and was a man of bronze, and in Diermod's dark hair came chains of iron. But they said of Flawna, "See, she stays the same." And it was true, she did not age very much, for the moment of loss had been her death, as the moment of the freezing river was her birth. In the amber of unhappiness she poised, a young girl with a few thin lines upon her face, the bones of her body showing a little more, and one gray lock in her dark hair, by her badger husband.

▼▼▼

One day in spring, a girl was brought into the High House. She was a slave, but so beautiful, they thought her fit to serve only the King. And beautiful she was.

Her name was Riad, and from her head poured hair redder

than the morning sun. Her skin was cream, her eyes a blue that only once before had been.

When he saw her, Diermod became as motionless as a rock, hard all over, his flesh, his brain, his sex.

Soon enough, he lay with Riad, in a secret chamber kept for his pleasure. But when he had had her, he was not sated. He held her pure face between his strong, hard hands, and said, "You are my spirit, Riad."

And Riad smiled and wept and said, "Never till now was I happy."

The spring swelled into summer, and the womb of Riad burgeoned too. Diermod went to his thin and green-eyed witch-wife.

"I must say my heart," said Diermod. "Forgive me, but I am sick of you. When I look at you my soul cringes. I know that you put some spell on me. My people fear you. Our son will not come near you. I have slept in a bed with you all these years and my dreams have been evil. You worked some terrible thing upon your own child. I will not put you aside. Forgive me. I will say what you are, and you will die."

Flawna lifted her eyes. She glanced at him. Who was he? Her death? No, she had died long before.

She said, "I have always obeyed you."

"No, you have obeyed some wickedness in your own heart."

Diermod denounced his wife.

All of them spoke up then.

They said, they had seen her gather herbs and strange plants. That she communed with animals in weird languages. That she could become invisible and visit upon them illness. She had made women barren. She had dried up the river.

The priest talked to her all one day. She watched his tattooed hands, and the eye on his brow, and did not know what he said.

In the evening, they led her out, out into the marketplace of baked earth, where, at the very first, she had been tied to a wheel.

Now they pushed her up into a chariot without horses, and tied her to a stout oaken pole, and round her were heaped bundles of sticks and dried sere grass.

The King's Town was there, looking up at her, one soundless stare, and from a high wall of the House, Diermod looked, and Culen by him, and elsewhere red-haired Riad would be watching with her sun-round belly pressed to the stone, and perhaps Diermod's new son watched too, through the chink of Riad's navel.

But then the moon came up above the High House, rosy white.

Flawna called down to the men who pushed the sticks against the chariot, "Give me some water."

"That will never put out the flames, Lady," said the men.

"I am the Queen. Give me some water," repeated Flawna.

But the men said, "You are a witch. Soon you will be nothing."

Another said, "She will. She will be ashes."

So Flawna raised her head and looked at the moon. She had no water. She could not lift her arms, for they were tied to the pole. She shut her lids, and saw the moon within her head.

She said in her heart: "I cannot make the sorcery. I cannot say the words, for I do not now remember them. Nevertheless help me."

But then she opened her eyes and over the moon a bird was flying; it had come between them. There was no hope.

The priest put a torch to the bundles of grass and wood, and the fire leaped through like fierce red love, to have the chariot, and to have the woman.

Flawna put back her head again, and she saw a faint thin vapor in the sky beside the moon. The vapor fell and fell, downward. It fell through the King's Town, and into the fire, unbroken. It was a cloud, and it covered her. She slept at once, like a child.

▼▼▼

When she woke, Flawna was on the moon.

Sheep grazed nearby; cattle fanned her with warm sweet breath.

The white grass of the valley was starred by golden flowers, and in the meadow a young girl was running toward her, with her black hair flying.

"Are you my mother?" cried this girl, reaching Flawna in a second. "How long you have been in coming. Yet, it was only an hour."

Above the sky where white birds flew was pink as strawberries, and it tinted the mountains. Silver moths danced on the flowers.

Before the doorplace of the hut on the riverbank, stood the woman with long ebony hair that fell to her feet. But beside her were some others that, across the great distance, Flawna could see well. And her mother and sisters and her grandmother too were there, all laughing at Flawna, because she had been so long in coming, because she had arrived at last.

THE APRIL WITCH
▼▼▼

RAY BRADBURY

INTO the air, over the valleys, under the stars, above a river, a pond, a road, flew Cecy. Invisible as new spring winds, fresh as the breath of clover rising from twilight fields, she flew. She soared in doves as soft as white ermine, stopped in trees and lived in blossoms, showering away in petals when the breeze blew. She perched in a lime-green frog, cool as mint by a shining pool. She trotted in a brambly dog and barked to hear echoes from the sides of distant barns. She lived in new April grasses, in sweet, clear liquids rising from the musky earth.

It's spring, thought Cecy. I'll be in every living thing in the world tonight.

Now she inhabited neat crickets on the tar-pool roads, now prickled in dew on an iron gate. Hers was an adaptably quick mind flowing unseen upon Illinois winds on this one evening of her life when she was just seventeen.

"I want to be in love," she said.

She had said it at supper. And her parents had widened their eyes and stiffened back in their chairs. "Patience," had been their advice. "Remember, you're remarkable. Our whole family is odd and remarkable. We can't mix or marry with ordinary folk. We'd lose our magical powers if we did. You wouldn't want to lose your ability to 'travel' by magic, would you? Then be careful. Be careful!"

But in her high bedroom, Cecy had touched perfume to her throat and stretched out, trembling and apprehensive, on her four-poster, as a moon the color of milk rose over Illinois country, turning rivers to cream and roads to platinum.

"Yes," she sighed. "I'm one of an odd family. We sleep days and fly nights like black kites on the wind. If we want, we can sleep in moles through the winter, in the warm earth. I can live in anything at all—a pebble, a crocus, or a praying mantis. I can leave my plain, bony body behind and send my mind far out for adventure. Now!"

The wind whipped her away over fields and meadows.

She saw the warm spring lights of cottages and farms glowing with twilight colors.

If I can't be in love myself because I'm plain and odd, then I'll be in love through someone else, she thought.

Outside a farmhouse in the spring night a dark-haired girl, no more than nineteen, drew up water from a deep stone well. She was singing.

Cecy fell—a green leaf—into the well. She lay in the tender moss of the well, gazing up through dark coolness. Now she quickened in a fluttering, invisible amoeba. Now in a water drop-let! At last, within a cold cup, she felt herself lifted to the girl's warm lips. There was a soft night sound of drinking.

Cecy looked out from the girl's eyes.

She entered into the dark head and gazed from the shining eyes at the hands pulling the rough rope. She listened through the shell ears to this girl's world. She smelled a particular universe through these delicate nostrils, felt this special heart beating, beating. Felt this strange tongue move with singing.

Does she know I'm here? thought Cecy.

The girl gasped. She stared into the night meadows.

"Who's there?"

No answer.

"Only the wind," whispered Cecy.

"Only the wind." The girl laughed at herself, but shivered.

It was a good body, this girl's body. It held bones of finest slender ivory hidden and roundly fleshed. This brain was like a pink tea rose, hung in darkness, and there was cider-wine in this mouth. The lips lay firm on the white, white teeth and the brows arched neatly at the world, and the hair blew soft and fine on her milky neck. The pores knit small and close. The nose tilted at the moon and the cheeks glowed like small fires. The body drifted with feather-balances from one motion to another and seemed always singing to itself. Being in this body, this head, was like basking in a hearth fire, living in the purr of a sleeping cat, stirring in warm creek waters that flowed by night to the sea.

I'll like it here, thought Cecy.

"What?" asked the girl, as if she'd heard a voice.

"What's your name?" asked Cecy carefully.

"Ann Leary." The girl twitched. "Now why should I say *that* out loud?"

"Ann, Ann," whispered Cecy. "Ann, you're going to be in love."

As if to answer this, a great roar sprang from the road, a clatter and a ring of wheels on gravel. A tall man drove up in a rig, holding the reins high with his monstrous arms, his smile glowing across the yard.

"Ann!"

"Is that you, Tom?"

"Who else?" Leaping from the rig, he tied the reins to the fence.

"I'm not speaking to you!" Ann whirled, the bucket in her hands slopping.

"No!" cried Cecy.

Ann froze. She looked at the hills and the first spring stars. She stared at the man named Tom. Cecy made her drop the bucket.

"Look what you've done!"

Tom ran up.

"Look what you *made* me do!"

He wiped her shoes with a kerchief, laughing.

"Get away!" She kicked at his hands, but he laughed again, and gazing down on him from miles away, Cecy saw the turn of his head, the size of his skull, the flare of his nose, the shine of his eye, the girth of his shoulder, and the hard strength of his hands doing this delicate thing with the handkerchief. Peering down from the secret attic of this lovely head, Cecy yanked a hidden copper ventriloquist's wire and the pretty mouth popped wide: "Thank you!"

"Oh, so you *have* manners?" The smell of leather on his hands, the smell of the horse rose from his clothes into the tender nostrils, and Cecy, far, far away over night meadows and flowered fields, stirred as with some dream in her bed.

"Not for you, no!" said Ann.

"Hush, speak gently," said Cecy. She moved Ann's fingers out toward Tom's head. Ann snatched them back.

"I've gone mad!"

"You have." He nodded, smiling but bewildered. "Were you going to touch me then?"

"I don't know. Oh, go away!" Her cheeks glowed with pink charcoals.

"Why don't you run? I'm not stopping you." Tom got up. "Have you changed your mind? Will you go to the dance with me tonight? It's special. Tell you why later."

"No," said Anna.

"Yes!" cried Cecy. "I've never danced. I want to dance. I've never worn a long gown, all rustly. I want that. I want to dance all night. I've never known what it's like to be in a woman, dancing; Father and Mother would never permit it. Dogs, cats, locusts, leaves, everything else in the world at one time or another I've known, but never a woman in the spring, never on a night like this. Oh, please—we *must* go to that dance!"

She spread her thought like the fingers of a hand within a new glove.

"Yes," said Ann Leary, "I'll go. I don't know why, but I'll go to the dance with you tonight, Tom."

"Now inside, quick!" cried Cecy. "You must wash, tell your folks, get your gown ready, out with the iron, into your room!"

"Mother," said Ann, "I've changed my mind!"

▼▼▼

The rig was galloping off down the pike, the rooms of the farmhouse jumped to life, water was boiling for a bath, the coal stove was heating an iron to press the gown, the mother was rushing about with a fringe of hairpins in her mouth. "What's come over you, Ann? You don't like Tom!"

"That's true." Ann stopped amidst the great fever.

But it's spring! thought Cecy.

"It's spring," said Ann.

And it's a fine night for dancing, thought Cecy.

". . . for dancing," murmured Ann Leary.

Then she was in the tub and the soap creaming on her white seal shoulders, small nests of soap beneath her arms, and the flesh of her warm breasts moving in her hands and Cecy moving the mouth, making the smile, keeping the actions going. There must be no pause, no hesitation, or the entire pantomime might fall in ruins! Ann Leary must be kept moving, doing, acting, wash here, soap there, now out! Rub with a towel! Now perfume and powder!

"You!" Ann caught herself in the mirror, all whiteness and pinkness like lilies and carnations. "Who are you tonight?"

"I'm a girl seventeen." Cecy gazed from her violet eyes. "You can't see me. Do you know I'm here?"

Ann Leary shook her head. "I've rented my body to an April witch, for sure."

"*Close*, very close!" laughed Cecy. "Now, on with your dressing.

The luxury of feeling good clothes move over an ample body! And then the halloo outside.

"Ann, Tom's back!"

"Tell him to wait," Ann sat down suddenly. "Tell him I'm not going to that dance."

"What?" said her mother, in the door.

Cecy snapped back into attention. It had been a fatal relaxing, a fatal moment of leaving Ann's body for only an instant. She had heard the distant sound of horses' hoofs and the rig rambling through moonlit spring country. For a second she thought, I'll go find Tom and sit in his head and see what it's like to be in a man of twenty-two on a night like this. And so she had started quickly across a heather field, but now, like a bird to a cage, flew back and rustled and beat about in Ann Leary's head.

"Ann!"

"Tell him to go away!"

"Ann!" Cecy settled down and spread her thoughts.

But Ann had the bit in her mouth now, "No, no, I hate him!"

I shouldn't have left—even for a moment. Cecy poured her mind into the hands of the young girl, into the heart, into the head, softly, softly. *Stand up*, she thought.

Ann stood.

Put on your coat!

Ann put on her coat.

Now, march!

No! thought Ann Leary.

March!

"Ann," said her mother, "don't keep Tom waiting another minute. You get on out there now and no nonsense. What's come over you?"

"Nothing, Mother. Good night. We'll be home late."

Ann and Cecy ran together into the spring evening.

▼▼▼

A room full of softly dancing pigeons ruffling their quiet, trailing feathers, a room full of peacocks, a room full of rainbow eyes and lights. And in the center of it, around, around, around, danced Ann Leary.

"Oh, it *is* a fine evening," said Cecy.

"Oh, it's a fine evening," said Ann.

"You're odd," said Tom.

The music whirled them in dimness, in rivers of song; they floated, they bobbed, they sank down, they arose for air, they gasped, they clutched each other like drowning people and whirled on again, in fan motions, in whispers and sighs, to "Beautiful Ohio."

Cecy hummed. Ann's lips parted and the music came out.

"Yes, I'm odd," said Cecy.

"You're not the same," said Tom.

"No, not tonight."

"You're not the Ann Leary I knew."

"No, not at all, at all," whispered Cecy, miles and miles away. "No, not at all," said the moved lips.

"I've the funniest feeling," said Tom.

"About what?"

"About you." He held her back and danced her and looked into her glowing face, watching for something. "Your eyes," he said, "I can't figure it."

"Do you see *me*?" asked Cecy.

"Part of you's here, Ann, and part of you's not." Tom turned her carefully, his face uneasy.

"Yes."

"Why did you come with me?"

"I didn't want to come," said Ann.

"Why then?"

"Something made me."

"What?"

"I don't know." Ann's voice was faintly hysterical.

"Now, now, hush, hush," whispered Cecy. "Hush, that's it. Around, around."

They whispered and rustled and rose and fell away in the dark room, with the music moving and turning them.

"But you *did* come to the dance," said Tom.

"I did," said Cecy.

"Here." And he danced her lightly out an open door and walked her quietly away from the hall and the music and the people.

They climbed up and sat together in the rig.

"Ann," he said, taking her hands, trembling. "Ann." But the way he said the name it was as if it wasn't her name. He kept glancing into her pale face, and now her eyes were open again. "I used to love you, you know that," he said.

"I know."

"But you've always been fickle and I didn't want to be hurt."

"It's just as well, we're very young," said Ann.

"No, I mean to say, I'm sorry," said Cecy.

"What *do* you mean?" Tom dropped her hands and stiffened.

The night was warm and the smell of the earth shimmered up all about them where they sat, and the fresh trees breathed one leaf against another in a shaking and rustling.

"I don't know," said Ann.

"Oh, but *I* know," said Cecy. "You're tall and you're the finest-looking man in all the world. This is a good evening; this is an evening I'll always remember, being with you." She put out the alien cold hand to find his reluctant hand again and bring it back, and warm it and hold it very tight.

"But," said Tom, blinking, "tonight you're here, you're there. One minute one way, the next minute another. I wanted to take you to the dance tonight for old times' sake. I meant nothing by it when I first asked you. And then, when we were standing at the well, I knew something had changed, really changed, about you. You were different. There was something new and soft, something . . ." He groped for a word. "I don't know, I can't say. The way you looked. Something about your voice. And I know I'm in love with you again."

"No," said Cecy. "With me, with *me*."

"And I'm afraid of being in love with you," he said. "You'll hurt me again."

"I might," said Ann.

No, no, I'd love you with all my heart! thought Cecy. Ann,

say it to him, say it for me. Say you'd love him with all your heart.

Ann said nothing.

Tom move quietly closer and put his hand up to hold her chin. "I'm going away. I've got a job a hundred miles from here. Will you miss me?"

"Yes," said Ann and Cecy.

"May I kiss you good-bye, then?"

"Yes," said Cecy before anyone else could speak.

He placed his lips to the strange mouth. He kissed the strange mouth and he was trembling.

Ann sat like a white statue.

"Ann!" said Cecy. "Move your arms, *hold* him!"

She sat like a carved wooden doll in the moonlight.

Again he kissed her lips.

"I do love you," whispered Cecy. "I'm here, it's me you saw in her eyes, it's me, and I love you if she never will."

He moved away and seemed like a man who had run a long distance. He sat beside her. "I don't know what's happening. For a moment there . . ."

"Yes?" asked Cecy.

"For a moment I thought—" He put his hands to his eyes. "Never mind. Shall I take you home now?"

"Please," said Ann Leary.

He clucked to the horse, snapped the reins tiredly, and drove the rig away. They rode in the rustle and slap and motion of the moonlit rig in the still early, only eleven o'clock spring night, with the shining meadows and sweet fields of clover gliding by.

And Cecy, looking at the fields and meadows, thought, It would be worth it, it would be worth everything to be with him from this night on. And she heard her parents' voices again, faintly, "Be careful! You wouldn't want to lose your magical powers, would you—married to a mere mortal? Be careful. You wouldn't want that."

Yes, yes, thought Cecy, even that I'd give up, here and now, if he would have me. I wouldn't need to roam the spring nights then, I wouldn't need to live in birds and dogs and cats and foxes, I'd need only to be with him. Only him. Only him.

The road passed under, whispering.

"Tom," said Ann at last.

"What?" He stared coldly at the road, the horse, the trees, the sky, the stars.

"If you're ever, in years to come, at any time, in Green Town, Illinois, a few miles from here, will you do me a favor?"

"Perhaps."

"Will you do me the favor of stopping and seeing a friend of mine?" Ann Leary said this haltingly, awkwardly.

"Why?"

"She's a good friend. I've told her of you. I'll give you her address. Just a moment." When the rig stopped at her farm she drew forth a pencil and paper from her small purse and wrote in the moonlight, pressing the paper to her knee. "There it is. Can you read it?"

He glanced at the paper and nodded bewilderedly.

"Cecy Elliott, 12 Willow Street, Green Town, Illinois," he said.

"Will you visit her someday?" asked Ann.

"Someday," he said.

"Promise?"

"What has this to do with us?" he cried savagely. "What do I want with names and papers?" He crumpled the paper into a tight ball and shoved it in his coat.

"Oh, please promise!" begged Cecy.

". . . promise . . ." said Ann.

"All right, all right, now let me be!" he shouted.

I'm tired, thought Cecy. I can't stay. I have to go home. I'm weakening. I've only the power to stay a few hours out like this in the night, traveling, traveling. But before I go . . .

". . . before I go," said Ann.

She kissed Tom on the lips.

"This is *me* kissing you," said Cecy.

Tom held her off and looked at Ann Leary and looked deep,

deep inside. He said nothing, but his face began to relax slowly, very slowly, and the lines vanished away, and his mouth softened from its hardness, and he looked deep again into the moonlit face held here before him.

Then he put her off the rig and without so much as a good night was driving swiftly down the road.

Cecy let go.

Ann Leary, crying out, released from prison, it seemed, raced up the moonlit path to her house and slammed the door.

Cecy lingered for only a little while. In the eyes of a cricket she saw the spring night world. In the eyes of a frog she sat for a lonely moment by a pool. In the eyes of a night bird she looked down from a tall, moon-haunted elm and saw the light go out in two farmhouses, one here, one a mile away. She thought of herself and her family, and her strange power, and the fact that no one in the family could ever marry any one of the people in this vast world out here beyond the hills.

"Tom?" Her weakening mind flew in a night bird under the trees and over deep fields of wild mustard. "Have you still got the paper, Tom? Will you come by someday, some year, sometime, to see me? Will you know me then? Will you look in my face and remember then where it was you saw me last and know that you love me as I love you, with all my heart for all time?"

She paused in the cool night air, a million miles from towns and people, above farms and continents and rivers and hills. "Tom?" Softly.

Tom was asleep. It was deep night; his clothes were hung on chairs or folded neatly over the end of the bed. And in one silent, carefully upflung hand upon the white pillow, by his head, was a small piece of paper with writing on it. Slowly, slowly, a fraction of an inch at a time, his fingers closed down upon and held it tightly. And he did not even stir or notice when a blackbird, faintly, wondrously, beat softly for a moment against the clear moon crystals of the windowpane, then, fluttering quietly, stopped and flew away toward the east, over the sleeping earth.

ARORA'S CURE
▼▼▼

T. DIANE SLATTON

SYPHILIS banished in scarcely a fortnight was the latest American miracle I wrote to my disbelieving father in Kerala. That his elder son's teenaged bride suffered benefit of such medical magic was a secret best whispered to dust in an empty temple.

"Tell her she isn't sterile," grumbled the tortoise-faced health department woman.

I braved a smile and spoke enthusiastically in Arora's native Oriya tongue. "You and Dev can still have many fine children!"

My sister-in-law dissolved into miserable sobbing no sooner than her husband's accursed name dropped from my mouth. The health department crone leaped up and dashed around her desk to comfort Arora while fixing me with pebble-eyed blame for my brother's poisoned seed.

"Hey, Vijay!" Dev always laughed when bringing me sickening requests; for he saw only sport in his disastrous existence, and high comedy in his mortifying uselessness: "Hey, Vijay! Bar girl cleaned me out last night. Loan me a few dollars, eh?—and get Father to line up a marriage broker back home. I could use a wife." "Hey, Vijay! Be my alibi, eh?—stupid Narc Squad's after me and you *know* I'd never . . ." "Hey, Vijay! I think maybe I gave Arora a wedding present she's not gonna like.

Drive her over to the free clinic for me, eh?—and don't mention this to Father."

However had poor Dev survived the decade-plus-half before I
came to study in his beloved America?

"Mister Rajivishnu!" snapped the sour woman past Arora's
heaving shoulder. "Your brother has missed *both* appointments
we've set up. Please impress upon him the danger of reinfecting
his wife."

I half-bowed, touching fingertips to forehead in a false show
of goodwill that hid my shame and resentment. The woman
sniffed, then reluctantly delivered my sister-in-law back into my
care.

"She spoke something more of Dev?" Arora asked when we
stepped out into late afternoon haze.

In response, I bought her an ice cream and gave silent thanks
that she'd not learned much English. Watching her beside me in
my car nibbling her treat with the concentration of a child, I fed
upon rage at Dev's easy lies. He'd spoken to me of needle and
pill without having endured any venereal curatives at all—even
disease was mere drug-addled sport to him.

"Dev will need his supper," she said in Oriya.

I jerked a nod, answered in English, "May I suggest rat
poison?"

After tilting her face up to study my tense profile for a minute,
Arora apparently declared my words an unbreakable code and
returned to the important ice cream. I dared my traitorous new
habit, considering ways to deliver the girl back to her family in
India without stigma of marital failure, but such thoughts were
useless as long as her passport and important papers were held
hostage by her husband.

"Dev will need his supper!"

I slowed the car at seeing I had passed my brother's place,
but Arora leaped out even before I came fully to a stop. Turning
my body on the seat, I watched through the tinted rear glass as
she dashed toward a cage-windowed high-rise that boasted several
bullet holes in its graffiti-marred metal entrance door. My gaze

lingered upon the girl bright as Kerala sunrise in her yellow/gold sari, its long silk *dupatta* scarf billowing surrender flag from her shoulder.

If only for that night, I thought with a sigh, I would indulge in wine and books to disentangle from the blind servitude Father insists I owe Dev in the name of fraternal Karma. But approaching my residence in the pristine graduate students' apartment complex, memories of my brother's cold, flat stare as he pulled his bride around the wedding fire filled me with new disgust and guilt for tossing little Arora back to her wolf.

"Helluva guy, that brother of yours," slurred the building maintenance drunkard when I reached the elevator.

"Sorry, yes," I answered automatically.

"Looking good now. Gave me five dollars to get my head straight. Helluva guy!"

I glanced at his drifting, rum-dulled eyes and impatiently jabbed the "up" button.

"Know what, Mr. Raji—? If my brother ever took *my* TV to get it fixed, he'd rip me off, cousin. But you foreigners—"

My heart pounded as I bolted past him and into the stairwell and up, taking three steps at a leap. I refused sudden knowledge that Dev would liquidate one of my paltry assets to feed his ravenous veins. Nor would I accept possibility that my only sibling would ask me to attend his wife's most intimate health merely to rid me from my home for a time.

But assuredly my television was gone. My thoughts hurtled to the week past and crystallized upon the vision of myself searching dresser drawers, muttering curses, unable to find the engraved sterling watch Father had presented me upon graduation from Delhi University. I had worn it to a dinner-dance only the week before that, on an evening just prior to delivering Arora to her first clinic appointment . . .

Laughter barked hoarse and painful from my chest as I wondered how many times Dev would have to disease his wife before leaving me with nothing more than my smile. And even that he would steal, for laughter froze at seeing affixed to the gaping new hole in my entertainment unit, a note scribbled in crude Malayalam.

"What is injury without insult?" I asked, shaking my head at his attempt to write my language. I translate approximately:

Vijay Heiyo!

You are a bitch about needing all your money for school stuff that's why I stopped asking for a loan anymore. I know you will understand I've got bad guys looking for me so I'm laying low cool for a few days you understand? Look at Arora for me thanks.

Dev

I dropped the note and stood very still, allowing the descent of darkness to wrap me in its comfortless shroud. For a moment the sun shone harsh as a spotlight upon a childhood noon when I raced out onto a rickety porch:

"Dev! Heiyo! Dev!" I called, waving miniature arms good-bye as my aunt left, taking only my adored elder brother to market— to the airport—to Baltimore USA—TO HELL.

"You left me!" I screamed at the hole where my TV had been.

Rage broke within, releasing and cleansing with tears long denied. How ashamed Father would have been at my fists alternately swinging full force at thin air, and rubbing at relentlessly overflowing eyes. But could he even fathom the weight of protecting him from knowledge of Dev's failure; protecting Dev from police; protecting myself from the allure of casual lawlessness; protecting Dev from self-destruction; protecting Arora from crushing truth; protecting Dev . . .

Protecting Arora.

My sympathy came to rest on the girl who likely fretted over lentils and rice burnt or grown cold. Within a quarter-hour I stood at the graffiti'd entrance door of the cage-windowed highrise, seeking fine-laced lies for a bride whose husband was now ". . . laying low cool for a few days you understand?"

"Good evening-hi-hi!" was my clumsy attempt at Dev's American blitheness when Arora's sweet voice floated from the intercom. I was no more clever standing at her open apartment door, but this was due to unabashed amazement.

For a second in shadows, I presumed Arora was wearing the *salwar kamiz* pantsuit seen on many ladies of India, but oh!—her costume was not that modest coverup at all. Just below capped sleeves of a short, too-well-fitted top were silver arm bands that matched the ones tinkling loosely at her wrists, and more silver at ankles above dainty feet painted festive crimson. Her dark liquid eyes were shadowed blue sky and lined coal black. Silver again was the band encircling her smooth brow beneath parted silken hair.

My attention darted from half-blouse to opaque harem-cut trousers to gauzy gold scarf dissecting her torso from one shoulder to a heavy three-tiered chain belt that trapped it below her navel. The thin scarf concealed nothing; indeed it made her bare midriff appear even *more* naked to my burning eyes. I blinked once, again, forced my stare past her with deep embarrassment at having glimpsed my brother's wife as an adult woman.

"I dance the Odissi," she said.

"What is it?" I asked in her language, keeping my eyes averted. "Do you celebrate something this night?"

Arora's answering laugh sounded slightly wild as she "Chinged" delicate finger cymbals and spun from me into the apartment. "Come, Vijay!" she sang unseen beyond the foyer.

I stepped in and closed the door, weighing the likelihood that my sister-in-law, in her loneliness, had taken to drinking. If so, this was minor corruption in the face of Dev's limitless debaucheries.

"I will have a beer too," I said. As I fetched one, the corner of my eye filled with the thrilling new sight of her in the tiny living room. Without benefit of flute or drum, Arora leaped high and seemed to pause midair before touching the floor again.

This Odissi she danced appeared to traverse strange ground between the spiritual and the sensual. To stop myself from mistaking her intentions, I sat calmly upon a sofa in a room lit only by candles and said, "Tell me, little flower, am I interrupting your prayer?"

She only laughed again and bent backward until she faced me with arms outstretched as if summoning a lover. A bolt of desire—shocking and unwelcome—raced through my body.

"Don't dance for me, girl," I said in a voice thick and strange to my own ears.

"But I dance for Dev," Arora answered sweetly. She raised from her back bend and turned to face me, drawing my gaze to her gleaming, lipsticked mouth. "I dance only for my husband. Even now, dear Vijay, to cure his grave wretchedness. Your presence is the window exposing him to me."

My eyes, searching for someplace—*anyplace*—to rest away from her wondrous body, squinted into the sparkling clean kitchen, noticed that no food had been prepared. Wasn't that why she'd leaped from my moving car that afternoon—to cook dinner?

Taking a single sip from the beer bottle, I asked, "Did Dev telephone you? Did you know he wouldn't return home this night?"

"Ching!" answered finger cymbals, and at once incense filled my nostrils. The room expanded, and the breath trembled from my lungs. It occurred to me that sweet Arora might have poisoned the beer. The bottle thudded to the wood floor and I followed, tumbling freely into an illusion of myself crouched as a sleek panther prowling ancient Khajuraho temples. Torch flames there pulsed forgotten rhythms that moved me toward softly rounded flesh . . .

"No, no—VIJAY!"

My eyes sprang wide to see Arora without makeup or jewelry, dressed in a conservative blue sari. I raised my head from her floor, glanced at the spilled beer bottle near my hand, stared around at electric lamplight where fire had been.

Through my searing headache, I reasoned that her seductive costume and dance had been a dream, that Dev's thievery within my own apartment had brought me there to his in less than sober condition.

"No Eng-lish, sir. No—VIJAY!" Arora brought the receiver to her breast and frantically waved me to come.

I stood and staggered toward the kitchen where a horrendous mess of boiled-over pots and burnt rice revealed my sister-in-law's usual heroic culinary efforts. Arora pushed the phone into my hand and turned away to scour her scorched range top.

"Vijay," I announced to the caller as if to assure myself of my identity.

A gruff voice amid much noise answered, "Hello! Somebody there again? Good. Are you related to, um, Baldev Roger—"

"Rajivishnu, yes. Sorry. He is my brother."

"Right. Detective Cleary, third precinct homicide and I'm afraid . . ."

"Ching!" chimed finger cymbals when Arora swept past me and, as I floated once more beneath the pungent odor of incense, my confused heart filled near bursting with horror that was true reality. I ripped the phone from the kitchen wall, keeping the receiver at my ear to pick up disjointed bits of hallucination fed me in a fake detective's voice: "A shooting . . . drug-related . . . DOA . . . identify the body . . ."

I dropped the dead phone clattering to the floor and stared at dirty pots and pans until they disappeared; at living room lamps until they became candles and candles flared into temple torch-flames; at Arora's sari until the illusion of it dissolved to reveal the dancer in makeup and silver and gauze at her naked waist. She spun madly, dark eyes gleaming a vicious blend of childish spite and the god Siva's gift of destruction.

"Siren!" I accused. My hands clenched to fists, awaiting her move to full battle. "Is your dance the *celebration*, or the *cause* of my brother's death?" The words rushed forth in my language, which I did not realize until Arora stopped her spinning and answered fluently while posed with crimson-painted left foot resting against right knee.

"He is cured!" she sang in my Malayalam.

"My husband, cured!" in her own Oriya.

"Cured, yes!" in bitter Sanskrit.

"Evermore cured!" in snarling Brit-English.

My usefulness to her apparently depleted, the apartment door suddenly burst open and I was ejected violently by forces unseen. I roared terror as my face slammed to a hallway floor; but within this urban asylum so accustomed to sounds of combat, my cries went unheeded. Arora's triumphant laughter raked flesh from my back as I stood, trudged heavily to fire stairs, clutched walls for sanity and dearest life . . .

Six months after Dev fell to sleep forever with his demons, Father writes from Kerala that he himself is miraculously cured of plaguing night-terrors in which his elder son still lay bloodying an alley like a massacred dog. So unburdened is his conscience, in fact, that the old jackal is now betrothed to his widowed daughter-in-law.

I considered several warnings in response to this news before only wiring congratulations with mildest admonition to treat his bride well. But alone with private thoughts, I pray sweet Arora will have had her fill of Rajivishnu men by the time her second one is passed from this existence.

If not, I shall get a gun.

WOODEN DRUTHERS
▼▼▼

E R STEWART

HE always had the knife. It was one of those penknives, they called them. The blades fold into the handle for safe pocketing. His was so old the main blade was getting skinny from all the stroppings, all the accumulated minutes spent spiraling on the grindstone. The small blade he used for detail work, but the bigger blade could work even hard woods, so both must have been razor sharp and of the hardest stainless steel.

Not that it was an expensive knife; he couldn't even afford shoes, that boy. At age eight, he wandered town barefoot even when there was frost or snow. Many locals had discussed the power of those little feet. They must have some pretty big power to withstand the slush he walked them through, the ice he skated them over, and the drifts he kicked when the real snow came. A tough little kid, all the folk thereabouts agreed.

Where he got the knife is not known. He entered town one cold day, carrying it and whittling on a piece of pine. Town wasn't much back then, both sides of it only a house deep at the time, and the road not even paved with MacAdam then; all the improvements and expansions came much later. Todd Meacham, his lower lip sucked in from sight as he concentrated on peeling off flakes of wood with his knife, probably didn't even notice that town's lack of things, or even its wealth of poverty and neglect.

No, Tee Em cared little for the things of that town. He noticed the people in it, though.

"Todd," I called. "Tee Em, how about some tag?"

"Looka this." He held up the knife. It had a white pearl handle, with shiny rivets. There were little tiny words down at the base of the main blade, like magic runes to the likes of us, who read only the looks of fury on adult faces, mostly. "Got it this morning."

I reached to take the knife from him, so I could examine it good and proper, but he snatched it back from me before my fingers even got the hint of a touch. Shrugging, I said, "So you want to play some tag?"

"Sure." He dropped the stick he'd been whittling, folded the blade away, and stuck the knife deep into his trouser pocket.

We ran, and I beat Tee Em most times, but he was evasive at close quarters. My feet found most of the rocks and roots to trip over, while his avoided all but the divots, which tended to stiff-leg him to the ground.

Jumping on him after one of these tumbles, I wrestled him, laughing as he struggled to get away from me. We beat each other a few times, pinning and being pinned as if sharing some expensive toy, very careful of each getting his right turn in the proper amount.

I was about to try bending his arm around behind his back when he started yelling, "Wait."

Piling off, I stood and said, "What?" I looked around, figuring some adult was heading our way with a war-face on or something.

"My knife," he said. He was on his hands and knees swooshing through the leaves, and I got down to help him find the knife.

That's how I got to be the only other one we know of to touch the thing. My left hand skidded sideways over the hard-packed dirt, under a layer of leaves, and came up against the knife almost right away. Had it wanted me to find it?

The knife was warm, for one thing. And it felt good. I mean

it gave pleasure to my hand, like some kind of magnetism that throbbed up my arm and made me smile. It felt too heavy for its size, and there was just the slightest vibration to it, like inside it something was humming a tune from long back, far off.

I brought the knife to me, then dug my right thumbnail into the groove on top of the big blade, to pull it open. That's when Tee Em hit me, all forty-odd pounds of him. He knocked me clean over, and my head was ringing when I came back at him, to hit him, to hurt him back a little, as was only fair. By the time I'd punched his stomach a few times, he had the knife. How he got it I don't know, unless I dropped it.

Maybe the thing flew to him when I let go of it. I just don't know.

"Bob, run," he told me, the look on his face like a crooked mask of fright, with the rest hilarity and high good humor. He dashed off, sprinting out from under the old oak's shade and crossing the village green way ahead of his own shadow, as we used to say about fast-running boys.

I started scrambling to my feet, but before I could push against the ground, a hand clamped on the scruff of my neck and hauled me skyward. I could tell by the feel of the calluses that it was my stepdad, Art. He stank of drinking and sourer things, and I smelled him good and strong then because he shoved his face near mine and yelled, "What do you mean by fighting that retard right here in the middle of town for everybody to see? You shaming me, boy? Is that what? We'll see about shaming."

This for him was a grandiloquent speech, and all the while he was holding me aloft by the neck. You've got to give folks the credit they're due, and his credit was strength. In both smell and muscle, that man was strong.

He proved it further by drop-kicking me just like a football. It wasn't the first time, so I knew how to fall, but there was a lot of forward thrust to it and I kind of rolled too much, and he was on me again before I could scurry to the side. His boots had steel toes. Miner's boots, although he got kicked out of the mines for stealing another man's things, they say. Those boots felt like miner's boots, though, because they felt like they could split the earth itself, if they wanted.

All they did to me was send me flying again. I got to thinking once that I ought to be applying for my junior pilot's license, what with the regular flights I'd been taking since Dad died and Art moved in. Mama'd probably let me, too, for real, but where'd we get the money?

That was always the thing, money. Money made you poor by avoiding you, and it made you mean by letting you down, and it made you hurt by getting adults riled and spit-mad angry. Earning money was one thing we all dwelled on, and I did my share, picking coal by the tracks, selling scuttles of it cheaper than the companies. Between that and running errands for adults too lazy to walk, I got by.

I got by, but Art got my money. And then it was never enough and I would shame him and he'd start to kicking me.

That day, the day I touched the knife, Art kicked me right through town. I guess me shaming him by fighting Tee Em, as he called our roughhousing, wasn't the same as him kicking me with those steel-toed boots of his from one end of town to the other. By the time I got kicked home, I was wearing every kind of mud and dirt there is on that stretch of road, and many samples of shale and red dog, too.

And it was a good thing, or else Mama might have seen the bruises before I got a chance to cool them down at the pump out back. That cold water takes swelling down mighty fast, so it must have Indian magic like the older folk say. All I know is, through it all, the feel of that knife in my hand stayed with me.

Late that night Art finished off another bottle of Wild Turkey and commenced whopping and wailing on Mama, so I got out through my window, the one with cardboard instead of glass. Running through the night helped loosen my stiff muscles.

As always, I ran to Tee Em's. The adults, some of them anyway, call him a retard, but he's not even slow. He's faster in the brains than any adult I know; he's just a different kind of being, like he's blessed or something. I remember Mama, when

Dad was around, telling tales of angels sometimes coming down from those icy, glittering stars to bless the lucky few, the ones with grace. Tee Em was like that. He fit into the world like inlaid silver, especially when adults weren't around to spoil his calm.

"You get a beating?" he asked me.

"Nah, just kicked home." I rolled my shoulders and grinned to show him I was fine. "Whatcha got?"

"Just carvin'." He said it like it was nothing, but what he held in his slender, facile fingers looked like a store-bought toy, so real and detailed was it. I looked closer, and he held it up to a moonbeam, and I saw my own face.

"Tee Em, that's me you're carving. Real good, too."

He just nodded and kept working at it.

"Where'd you learn that from?" I couldn't get over how much like me it looked, like a photograph in wood, kind of, except not flat, but all of me, rounded, three-dimensional. And in it, I wasn't hurting, I could even see that. In his carving, I was okay.

And then he said it the first time, the phrase that still makes me shiver some nights, hell, some days when I think of it. He said, real serious, and not even looking up from his carving, he said, "If I had my druthers every one, I'd have my wooden druthers, too." It sounded like an incantation, or the first couple lines of a poem maybe. It seemed, in the dark and under the moon, like lyrics from a very old song, translated too many times into too many tongues to be traced to ground.

Now, I'd heard that one part—"if I had my druthers"—many times before. It's a common folk saying, nothing special. Sometimes the old ladies of the town said it when they talked about what things would be like if they had a choice of worlds, as they sat quilting or canning currants. "If I had my druthers, no one would be poor," they'd say, or things like that. So I knew it really meant having your "I'd rathers," your preferences. But wooden druthers? That'd be your "wouldn't rathers," I figured.

Who ever heard about having what you wouldn't rather? Or did it maybe mean having your choice of the bad things? Maybe that was it. If you really had your druthers, you'd have your wooden druthers, too.

All this I puzzled out over the years since that night. All I know is what I've come up with on my own, so don't take it to the bank, as they say. In fact, you take anything to a bank, you're a fool. Why give what you earn to other people? Ain't no one going to watch your own things as well or as truly as you yourself. Life's worth more than money, too, keep that in mind. No interest paid is enough to earn back the principle.

Anyway, I watched while he carved me. And a funny thing is, he didn't even look up at me, the way an artist might keep glancing at his subject or model, to get the details right. No, it was more like the details came up out of the wood on their own, with the fast, gentle help of that knife, which shined in the moonglow like a sliver of mountain stream. And the image of me was me, in every detail, but me old, me as an old man. It was eerie, and my skin prickled when I saw the face. The wrinkles were happy ones, earned by smiling more often than crying. My face old looked better to me than my face young, because it seemed like good times knew that face better. The details added up to being happy and living right as the big blade shaped and the little blade detailed.

Those blades made precious few shavings, too, by the way. It was like there was no, or very little, waste. I kind of liked that; it made me feel proud somehow that my image could come out of a common chunk of pine and leave only a small pile of cuttings.

"Done," Tee Em said pretty soon. He folded the knife and slipped it slowly, carefully into his pocket. He looked up at the sky. His face was sad. Looking back down, he started digging a hole with his fingers. He sat with his legs apart, digging a little hole, ignoring me, with that image of me laying there like so much kindling.

"What are you doing?" I asked, having a pretty good idea. And sure enough, he didn't answer me, but buried the little statue of me, and scraped in the shavings, too.

We were sitting in his backyard. The stump for cutting firewood was at his back, the axe embedded with its handle jutting more up than down. I leaned against a stack of logs waiting to be split into cordwood. The ground around that whole area was bare of grass and such, being so often walked on and worked on. That's what made it easy for me to see all the little mounds.

It looked like a miniature graveyard. Tee Em must have had the knife a long time before that day, and he must have been busy most nights, carving and burying.

He looked up, having tamped the new-turned dirt down flat with the heels of both hands. "You're okay now," he told me, again real serious in tone and expression. "I claimed you a time with my wooden druther of ya."

I just nodded. What else could I do?

We went frogging, but didn't catch anything that night. Oh, I caught one frog, but the instant I touched it the darned thing went stiff and died, so we threw it away, figuring it for polluted. It was quiet, so that one frog's splash sounded big enough to drown creation. All the frogs were silent, waiting for summer's end, probably, when they'd bury themselves in cool muck and mud to die for the winter so they could rise again next spring. That was the way of frogs. We knew that much.

I went home nearer dawn than now, approaching the house first with my ears. Everything seemed quiet. I slipped in. Mama was crying, and I peeked around the corner, past my curtain, which is really just an old dress of Mama's hung on cotton rope to screen my bed off from the rest of the room. My gaze found Mama lying on the kitchen floor. On tiptoes I crept to her. Kneeling, I said, "It's okay now, Mama." I touched her hair.

She looked up. "He's gone. Art's gone. He left me."

"Left you bruised and battered," I answered, braver in Art's absence, at least with my mouth.

She only cried, and I thought of Tee Em's carvings. Had his wooden druther of me somehow taken away my biggest hurt?

The very next night I asked if he'd carve one of my mother, and he did. I helped dig the hole, and we buried it together.

"Now just wait," Tee Em told me, face watching the ground expectant.

We sat staring, until I started to nod. Tee Em's elbow roused me from sleep a couple times, and the moon got higher, brighter it seemed, and then I saw the wooden druthers rise up and dance, and there were hundreds of them. They weren't just buried in Tee Em's yard, either, but came dancing up the road, clattering together like rhythm sticks surprised to be alive. Each one pushed up from their holes like moles, slowly at first, then quicker, until some fair shot out of the ground. Some flew up around our heads, and one smacked my ear enough to swell it a little.

Tee Em and I laughed and chased them like fireflies, like moths, like clothespins in a twister. We played with them, and had fun, too, until one by one they went back to their proper holes. Then we climbed trees and stole some apples from Mac-Cready's Orchard. They were too sour to eat, but Mama made nice pies from them, and even sold one to Bethy Ann Mac-Cready, her own fine-clothed, greedy self.

We moved out of that place not too long after that, down out of the hills and into the city, where money's braver about getting within arm's length, but Mama and I felt a lot better right from the time I learned about the wooden druthers. I don't rightly know if it was magic or what. I don't know if they mean anything or not, or if it's all in my mind, or if I'll die when I look exactly like that carving of me, but however it works out, I guess it's a fair swap not to know, because I'd rather live my life for a good long while than chase after pain and death every second like a scared animal.

And these days, when chores or debts or burdens come along that I'd rather not face, I tell myself, "Self, I wooden druther do this, but it's better than many another thing that might take its place," and that gets me through, keeps me going. It's also what keeps me checking the used pocketknives in the secondhand shops. You never know.

And one of these days I might just hike back up into those hills, and see if I can't dig myself up some extra comfort. Then again, I might just leave well enough alone, too.

REUNION
▼▼▼

KATHRYN PTACEK

I was enjoying the warmth of the sun upon my head, the sound
of waves crashing upon the beach, the gritty feel of the sand
beneath my bare toes. The sea gulls wheeled overhead, occasionally swooping down for a tasty tidbit; somewhere a radio played
softly in the background. The white sails of boats dotted the blue
ocean.

I was growing drowsy and thinking of napping when a loud
voice interrupted my sun-induced reverie. I cocked open an eye
and saw the source: the woman who had just married into the
family a year or so ago.

My husband had talked me into attending his family's late
spring reunion at the Jersey shore. I had wanted to stay home
and tend my garden. While I'd already planted most everything,
there is the matter of maintenance; you see, a garden is crucial
to a witch. But my husband convinced me it would be good for
me to get out of the house—he's rarely there, since he commutes
long hours to New York City; often he travels on company business. He thinks nothing of flying thousands of miles, while I
hardly stray from the house.

The loud voice broke into my thoughts again.

The newcomer was holding forth to whomever would listen,

and her voice was much too loud for such a relaxing day. I couldn't hear everything she said, although once in a while individual words floated my way. She wasn't angry; she just had her opinions, and she was determined that everyone would know them, whether they'd asked or not. She approached her husband Michael and his brothers now and pointed at the barbecue, which they were in charge of. Obviously she was unhappy about something she saw there, or perhaps she thought she knew a better way of doing it, and her husband's face was growing redder by the moment as he listened to her. My husband laughed, but Michael shook his head and his lips were pressed tightly together.

Another brother made a dismissive gesture, and realizing she wasn't wanted there at that moment, Sherry—for so she had called herself when we were first introduced; I had not gone to their wedding last year—cornered the teenagers next. From the beginning, the teens had clumped together, bemoaning loudly their fate at having been dragged away from the mall for a weekend. Now they looked bored and uncomfortable as Sherry obviously corrected them on some matter, then began lecturing a dark-haired girl in a skimpy bikini on proper attire, and finally, out of desperation, the teens left to help their fathers. Next she pounced upon the small children—and there were many, for my in-laws have always been prodigious breeders—who up to that minute had been happily engaged in games of tag and Frisbee. Sherry wanted to organize them into regular games, but no one could agree on what kind or who'd be the leader because they all wanted to be it. Minutes later a fistfight broke out between the blonde twins, who were the best natured of children, and one of the children went screaming to his mother.

My husband's sisters had made themselves scarce, and I wondered where they could have disappeared to so quickly and efficiently. Next, Sherry lectured the rest of her new family, including my mother-in-law, who as she lounged on her beach blanket was pretending to be hard of hearing, which she most certainly is not.

It was going to be a long three days. Since she'd driven in

with her husband Michael this morning, Sherry hadn't shut up once.

Yes, a very long weekend.

As I watched a miniature crab scuttle across the sand by my toes, I wished then that I had brought some books with me. I had several paperbacks to read, but the books I'd left behind were the ones with spells in them. There are many tomes to study. I have learned much in my life, but there is still much to master. It's not widely known what I do, because there are in our society certain archaic attitudes still in existence. But I did not need to advertise; word of mouth played a goodly part. Sometimes the neighbor women come to me when they don't feel well, or when they want to attract the attention of a man at work, and when they no longer wish the attention of their husbands, and I prepare certain recipes for them.

I do like to be supportive. And it is crucial that I learn new spells and practice them on a regular basis.

Next week, I thought with a yawn. This is my vacation. I'm here to sit in the sun and stare off into the distance and do nothing harder than lift a glass of iced tea to my lips.

Suddenly Sherry spotted me, sprinted over as if she feared I would leap to my feet and flee, and dropped down onto the sand alongside me. In doing so, she knocked over my glass and splashed sand onto my open book. I managed to retrieve the book before the tea drenched it. I wondered if the tiny crab had moved out of her way in time, then I saw one tiny pincher jutting out of the sand at a broken angle.

"Oh, sorry, did I do that? Geez, I'm such a klutz." She tried to grab the overturned tumbler. I was faster.

I murmured something polite.

"What's that you're reading?" she asked and seized my book before I could do anything. "Geez, you read this kind of stuff, honey?" She shook her head at my apparent lack of taste. "I don't read much, y'know, but when I do, I like the gritty stuff, if you know what I mean. You know, realistic. I don't like fantasy much, or that horror stuff."

"I like to read all sorts of things," I admitted.

"Time's too short to read everything, I say. You know that? I mean we only got so many hours in the day, and if you work all day, you don't have much time at home for dumb stuff, you know? And brother, you better believe I work hard. You know, I've got this important job—I just got promoted—" She paused.

I murmured my congratulations. She had been waiting for that. She went on.

"So, I got this promotion, and my boss says to me we really expect big things out of you, Sher—he calls me that, you know— and I says to him that I won't let him down, and you better believe that I won't. I am in charge of operations for a coupla hunnert salesguys, you know, and you had better believe that that's a damned important thing. I mean, if I weren't there the company would come apart at the seams, you know?" She squinted at me. "So, you're like what, a housewife?"

I smiled.

"Geez, I didn't know there were any of those around anymore. I mean, how can you stand to be cooped up in the house all the time day after day and not doing something really important? I mean, I'm not one of those women libbers or whatever, but you gotta get out of the house and do something for yourself, gotta work to keep the cobwebs out of the mind, if you know what I mean. I mean, working keeps you young. You gotta put some meaning in your life, you know? Plus it's nice to get the extra dough. You got kids yet?"

"Not yet."

"Geez, you guys have been married a long time, like seven or eight years or something, right?"

"Or something."

"Geez, I hope nothing's wrong." She paused.

My smile stretched.

"You know, Tommy and his wife over here have been to the fertility clinic I don't know how many times in the past couple of years. It's gonna cost them a fortune to just have the kid, you know. That is, if they can have one. I kept tellin' them they oughta adopt, and Tina just kept bawlin' like some lost calf or something. Tommy just left in a huff; I don't know why. You know, Michael and me are gonna start our family in about a year or two. I'll be thirty then, and we'll be pretty set with our finances and all by then, and then Michael says he'll stay home with the kid. Pretty good, huh? Geez, I couldn't have asked for a better husband. He sure has done a lot better than his brothers—except for your husband, of course. I mean, the others are, well, you couldn't very well call them successful, could you? Bruce is on his, what, fifth or sixth wife now?"

"Second," I corrected.

"Oh. And then there's Will; I heard him and his wife had to declare bankruptcy. What kind of high living were they doing or what?"

"I believe her mother was dying of cancer and had no hospitalization, and that the medical bills just keep mounting up. You know, hospitals and doctors don't like to wait for their money."

"Oh yeah? I thought it was because they got too many new cars or something. Actually, I thought they had this gamblin' problem cause they live so close to Atlantic City and all. They probably went there hoping they'd win a potful so they could pay those bills." Sherry paused to shake her head. She ran a hand through her hair, which was honey-blonde and quite luxurious; her eyes were blue-green and wide-set, and she had that sort of ingenuous face and shapely figure that would motivate men to leap forward and open doors for her and light her cigarette or otherwise fetch for her. Until she opened her mouth, that was. "And Evan, he's a real souse. I never saw anyone enjoy his beer as much as he does, if you know what I mean. You know, honey, I don't go in for alcohol and that sort of thing; I just don't think it's right."

"Evan's had a hard time. His wife left him, taking their two daughters, and a few days later they were killed in a car crash."

"Geez? Really? That's too bad. I dunno. I guess I can understand then. But the others . . . what's their excuses, I mean? The sisters—our sisters-in-law—they're not that much better, you know? I mean Cindy has had two liposuctions already, and the way she keeps gettin' into the cupcakes and potato chips, she's gonna need a third. And Beth's got a real weight problem. Her kids are kinda chunky too. She'd better set a better example for them; you know, kids imitate adults." She nodded again. "Yeah, I got the real pick of the litter—except for your husband, of course."

Blessedly for a moment she fell silent, then she half-turned in my direction.

"The guys are all cute, though, don't you think?"

She meant the brothers, I realized. "Yes, they're all very good-looking. I understand they look much like their father did when he was young. Of course, I didn't know him long before he died."

"Oh yeah, I heard he had some sort of . . . disease, you know." She looked at me knowingly.

"Disease? I thought it was a heart attack that killed him."

"Oh no, I heard he picked up this . . . disease . . . you know . . . from someone not his family."

My fingers, resting in the sand, clenched.

"Geez, I hope none of the brothers take after him, you know, honey? I mean I'd just kill Michael if he did something like that. But I don't know, him and your husband, they're quite the lookers, huh? I just bet you get women crawling all over your husband all the time."

"Not really."

"I'm amazed. Of course, I'll let you know what the women say about your husband and all."

"What?" I asked, a little startled.

"Oh yeah, didn't I tell you, honey? I work at Fosterfields & Sons. You know, he got me my job at the company. When he was out at the wedding last year, I happened to mention that I was looking for work, and he said he knew a position at his company, and the next thing you know I was interviewing for it, and then I got hired. I'm in the office right next to your husband."

My smile froze.

She winked. "So I'll keep a good eye on him for you, honey." She took a deep breath and swiveled her head, scanning for other family members she could move in on. "Geez, here I've been talkin' about everybody in the family and going on and on, and I hope you don't think I'm a, well, you know," she leaned toward me confidentially, "the 'b' word. I don't wanna use it, because it's not the kind of word you use in polite company, if you know what I mean, it not being a very nice word, if you take my meaning."

"Not at all," I said at my diplomatic best. Indeed, I did take her meaning. "Oh, look, Sherry, I think Michael is looking for you."

"Oh yeah? I guess I ought to go. He's just so jealous, you know; hates to have me talking to other guys. I bet he'd just *kill* me if he saw all the times me and your husband get together to talk at the office. Hey, it was real nice chattin' with you. We'll have to do this again, you know." She sprang up and trotted off toward Michael.

"Not on your life," I said aloud after she had gone. I had never met a more obnoxious woman, and what was worse is they didn't live all that far away from us, which meant I would be seeing her again.

In fact, my husband had mentioned something about getting together with Michael and Sherry after the reunion.

And he had helped her get the job at the company. He had never said a word to me.

I stared at the ocean for a moment, then glanced at Sherry. Then with my left hand I smoothed the sand in front of the towel, and with great concentration began making tracings. I was relying on my memory because I didn't have my special books with me. If anyone saw me, they would simply think I was doodling in the sand.

I glanced back up at Sherry. Nothing seemed to have happened. She was still talking away, and now I thought my husband looked fairly entranced by her. But perhaps I was mistaken.

I swept away the old patterns, began knew ones. Minutes went by, and still nothing happened. One sister had left in a huff after Sherry had converged upon their group.

I realized with some frustration that I just couldn't recall the proper spell. If only I had my books. . . . I closed my eyes and tried to visualize the lines upon the pages.

Nothing.

Angrily I kicked my useless paperback away.

A shadow loomed over my patterns, and I looked up, halfway expecting it to be Sherry.

"Actually, I prefer shells," Chloe, Bruce's wife, said as she dropped to her knees and unloaded the delicate shells she had collected in the front of her sweatshirt. "Does the trick just as well, I think."

"I beg your pardon?"

"Shells. I like to use them when I'm engaged in my . . . work. . . ." She began laying the shells out in intricate patterns.

I watched as the patterns grew, and I recognized them. I was speechless. I had found a kindred spirit, and here in my husband's family!

"How long have you known?" I finally managed to ask.

"Well, I suspected it for a while, but when I saw your expression when Motormouth was here, and then saw what you were doing in the sand, I knew."

" 'Motormouth.' That's not very kind."

Chloe glanced over at Sherry, who seemed now to be bawling her husband out for some reason. His head hung down slightly, as if he had heard all of this before. "She's a gossip, a nag, a bore—and I'm sure we could find a few more choice words for her."

"The 'b' word."

" 'I don't wanna use it' . . ." Chloe quoted.

" 'It's not the kind of word you use in polite company . . .' "

". . . 'It not being a very nice word. . . .' "

" 'If you take my meaning,' " we finished together and then laughed.

"She is indeed that," Chloe said. "I don't know how Michael got involved with her."

"A moment of weakness," I suggested, and we laughed again.

Sherry had moved on to the group of brothers, and it was apparent even from where we sat that she was informing them they were incorrectly barbecuing. Tommy looked thoroughly disgusted, and Evan had opened another beer, and Sherry's husband was standing there with his back to everyone. Two of the sisters were arguing with each other, and a ten-year-old had knocked another down and was kicking sand in his face.

"She's ruining everyone's mood, and this is just the beginning of the reunion. The way things are going we'll all be pissed at each other inside of an hour and heading home by the end of the day. What are we going to do?"

"Well, Chloe, I don't know about you, but I really am having a good time. I admit I didn't want to come, but I'm glad I did. And now that I'm here, I don't want anything to spoil it. Not anything."

We smiled at each other.

"It's a shame I don't have my books here with me," I said. "I've been having a hard time remembering the proper spell."

"Well, I don't have mine with me, either. We could improvise, though," Chloe said, and laid a line of pink shells at a right angle to half of an oyster shell. "I'm sure what we can come up with together would be stronger than one of us alone."

"I'm sure you're right." My fingers moved through the sand. "We can't do anything too terrible. I mean, if she dies, it really will put a damper on the party."

"That's true. Hmm. What about stomach cramps?"

"I thought about that, but . . . no. The others might think it's because of the food, and we wouldn't want that."

"Hmm. You're right. A headache?"

"She'd get sympathy then."

"Can't have that." Chloe tapped her knee with her fingertips. "You know, when we get home, we'll have to swap some recipes. I've got one for a love potion that's the quickest, safest thing I've ever seen."

"I'd like to hear about it. I don't know if you've ever used a poppet before, but I once had occasion to employ a paper one, and it worked beautifully."

The wind had shifted, and now we could hear Sherry's voice more clearly than before. Her tone was becoming increasingly strident, and Michael had just turned and was stomping back to the hotel where we all had rooms for the long weekend. More little kids were wailing, and now some of the teenaged boy cousins had become involved in a shouting match. I noticed that Sherry had a bottle of beer in her hand; it would seem she didn't operate well with alcohol, either.

I looked at Chloe. "I know."

She cocked an eyebrow. "Yeah?"

"Muteness."

We both smiled.

It didn't take long, and before even half an hour had gone by, Sherry's voice began to fail her. She sputtered and choked, although she was never in any danger. She waved a hand in front of her mouth, as if she believed that would make her voice come back, and she tried to talk, but only a squeak came out. She called for Michael, but by then her voice was gone—it would be for the next three days—and when she tried to wave at someone to make them understand she'd gotten an abrupt case of laryngitis, she found they simply stared at her; no one cared that she couldn't talk any longer. Finally, she went off toward the hotel. A few minutes later Michael came out to join the family.

"Time for dinner, ladies," my husband called to us, waving the spatula over his head as if it were a sword triumphant.

"Shall we go?" Chloe said.

"Delighted," I said as I stood and walked back toward the others with my newfound friend. I must, I decided at that moment, have Chloe and Bruce over to dinner when Michael and Sherry came to visit. Chloe would bring her books, and I would have mine at hand and . . . well, imagine what we could do then. . . .

I smiled, fully enjoying the reunion now.

CRAWLING FROM THE WRECKAGE
▼▼▼

ANDREW LANE

THERE are cormorants nesting in the wreckage now. Even after all this time the islanders will still not come near it, and yet the cormorants quite happily hop in and out of the rents in its skin, mate there, lay their eggs and raise their young.

It was less than a year ago that it carried me from the skies, burning and breaking apart around me, crashing onto the shore and letting the waves and the rain put out its fire. The storm was bad that night. The waves carved the shoreline and the dunes into new shapes and threw me far up the beach toward the cliffs, to the point where the sea grasses thin out and the dunes begin.

I can remember only isolated fragments of that night now— the sea rushing up to hit me; sand flowing around my half-buried body as the waves retreated, gathering their strength for another assault on the beach; the crumpled struts of the wreckage emerging like the legs of an upturned crab beside me; the still form of an old woman staring down at me in the sanctuary of a cave. The last thing I saw was her weathered and immobile face; the last thing I heard was the pounding of the waves on the beach.

The sea can never reach the wreckage now; it lies rusted and inviolate above the line of seaweed that marks the tide. Sometimes it seems to me that the seaweed is a fence between the sea and the wreck, but whether it prevents the waves getting to the wreck or the wreck getting to the waves I do not know. But then, sometimes it seems that I can hear the cormorants calling to me with the voices of long ago friends, and then I know that I have been sitting for too long staring at the sea, and the wreck, and the sun.

I think the cormorants know me. I know that their voices are my creation rather than theirs, but I still believe that they have come to recognize me, accept me, and know that I am no threat. They certainly see enough of me. I have my favorite spot, nestled between two steep-banked sand dunes close to the cliffs and protected from the wind and the wind-borne sea spray. From it I can see the wide sweep of the bay and the white caps to the waves that might be the foam as they curl and break, or the cormorants riding them and diving for food. The cormorants are my friends: large birds with gray-brown feathers tipped in black, their beaks curved and cruel. They watch me as they sit on the remains of my craft and survey their isolated kingdom. They glance over, glitter-eyed and suspicious if I shift my position to ease the cramp in my joints. My leg still aches badly at high tide and during storms. The scars on my body have healed, but some injuries take longer. Once in a while I wake sweating, thinking I can hear tortured metal screaming. It is only the cormorants. Only ever the cormorants.

At least the islanders tolerate me now, although the wreckage is outside their experience. They are unfamiliar with the principles of metalworking, although I have seen metal implements on the island, and the burnt, angular struts and crisped skin of the wreck must look to them like the bones of some huge dragon. Or perhaps I overestimate them. The islanders share many characteristics but imagination is not one of them. In a way they are as much outside my experience as the wreck is outside theirs. I am forced to accept what they do, how they think, without knowing why. They shun the wreck, but they do not avoid me. Not anymore.

It was in this spot where I now sit, in the notch between two dunes on the southern beach of the island, that Jethro claims he found me. Perhaps the old woman had dragged me back down the beach toward the wreck. Perhaps I imagined both her and the cave. Jethro later told me I had been unconscious and raving for a week while he bathed the wounds, so any memories I have before I woke up are suspect. My life, my new life, started at that moment.

Glancing up, I saw looming cliffs and heard the sound of waves, but the cliffs were Jethro's weatherworn features and the waves were far away.

"You're safe," he said curtly. Faded blue eyes watched me for some sign of understanding. Behind him there was worn wood, and to my right a window. I could smell the sea. Cormorants were crying somewhere outside.

"How long . . ." I started to say, but my voice was dry and tasted of bile. Jethro eased me up from the mattress I was lying on and handed me an earthenware mug. I sipped the water gratefully.

"Six days," he muttered. "We found you on the beach up near the naming cave. You were injured, so Ruth and I brought you here. I'm Jethro."

"My name is Thomas," I whispered, raising my head weakly. "Thomas Jerome."

Jethro slid his hand beneath my neck to support me as I looked around. The furniture in the hut was handmade from driftwood and branches. There was no evidence of nails, only crude mortise and tenon joints holding it all together. The material from which the curtains and sheets had been made was a rough, homespun wool, patchily hand-dyed.

"Strange sort of wreckage," he said. "Never seen a boat like it."

"It wasn't a boat," I whispered, "it was an aeroplane."

His face creased along existing lines.

"A what?"

"An aeroplane." He still looked blank, and I started to wonder exactly how far I had flown. The storm had been brewing as I took off from my first refueling stop at Dover, so this still had to be England, or, at the very least, an island off the coast. Aeroplanes had been around for enough years for them not to be a novelty, and since the Great War everybody who read a newspaper knew what one looked like.

"An aero . . . plane?" He tried the word hesitantly.

"A machine for flying in," I explained. My voice was firming up with use, but my throat still felt as if I had been gargling sand.

"Witchcraft," he muttered with a strange sort of wariness in his voice. "They talk about flying machines on the mainland. Never put much truck in mainland tales myself, considering what *they* say about *us*."

I suddenly realized how bad the throbbing in my head was, and with that realization the rest of my body clamored for attention. My right leg ached and, looking down, I saw dried blood on my thigh. My chest and legs were covered in cuts and scratches, some rough and deep, some like doodled pencil lines, all of them clean and healing. I could understand the rough-edged scrapes—the spars and supporting members broken in the crash would have clawed at my body as I thrashed my way from the wreck—but the thin scrolling cuts confused me for a moment. I thought back to the last few moments of my old life, and remembered wires under tension suddenly snapping and lashing back into the cockpit, slicing through clothes and flesh alike, as the aircraft crumpled in the fist of the wind. It was not the end. There were bound to be boats, and from what Jethro had said the English coast was not that far away.

Jethro offered me the water again. I sipped in silence, watching the motes of dust that floated calmly on the surface. A shadow moved past the window, then the door opened and then Ruth walked in.

"How do you feel?" she asked, putting down the bundle of rags she carried and coming across to me. I pulled the sheet up to cover my chest, acutely conscious of my nakedness. I tried to tell her how grateful I was for their care, but the words caught in my throat and I ended up gagging violently with both of them holding onto me. As the heaving subsided and they laid me gently back onto the bed, I found myself staring at Ruth. She was not beautiful—her face was too rounded, her eyes too foreign for that—but there was something natural and joyful about the way she moved that absorbed my attention. She was like no woman I had seen before.

"Do you feel strong enough to eat?" she asked. I nodded, suddenly aware that I was ravenous. "Fine. There's stew if you can manage it, and bread as well."

The stew was thick and hot, made from vegetables and occasional chunks of fish, and we washed it down with sweet, dark beer that had been brewed in the village. There was a reserve in their manner at first. Jethro, in his rough island way, questioned me about where I had come from but relaxed when he realized that I was from further away than the immediate mainland. Somehow I gained the impression that there was bad blood there, a feud of some sort. Ruth sat on the end of my bed, holding Jethro's hand. He had pulled up a rough-hewn wooden chair in order to sit beside me.

They were both interested in my aeroplane. Ruth was inclined to dismiss it, first as a fanciful tale and then, when she realized that I was serious, as a trivial boy's toy of no practical value. Jethro asked me technical questions without knowing what words to use, and I found to my shame that my dependence on my mechanics had been more profound than I had realized. When he asked me what kept it up in the air, I found myself waffling about the cormorants and the curve of their wings. Jethro thought I was trying to make a fool out of him, and left in a temper. I was too busy to care, wondering what I had been thinking of, setting off with a decrepit De Havilland DH16 on the long flight to Barcelona and the Spanish Civil War with a storm brewing and without the faintest idea of what to do if something went wrong. As, of course, it had.

Idealism can make fools of us all.

I slept for most of the next few days. When I woke either Jethro or Ruth was there with me, offering me food, or water, or a hand to hold. If it was night then it was Jethro. If the sun slanted in through the broken glass and the cormorants cried outside then it was Ruth. She was still living with her family at the time, but she and Jethro were betrothed, and she seemed to spend most of her time unchaperoned at his hut. I developed a slight fever again, not as bad as before but enough to blur another few days together in my mind. I can remember waking sometimes to find myself screaming in the middle of a nightmare as I relived the crash and the struggle to shore. Occasionally in my thrashing I reopened old wounds, and awoke to find the sheets smeared with blood.

Eventually I woke one morning soaked in sweat, but my mind was whole and mine once more and my body was weak but responsive. Jethro was there with me. I wolfed down breakfast— crusty black bread and water—and I could have eaten lunch right after. I felt complete, in control again. I felt like the man I had been before I crashed, and my thoughts turned to how I could leave. Jethro and I talked of generalities again: how I felt, what the weather was like, the prospects for a good harvest that year. Jethro always avoided asking me anything personal. He always left it up to me to talk, and I never did.

Instead I asked Jethro what he did, how he survived and earned the money to buy food and clothes for himself and Ruth. He went and stood by the window. I thought for a moment that he would not answer. His manner toward me was usually little better than wary, and sometimes downright suspicious.

"I weave nets for the fishermen," he said finally. "The storms are always pulling them onto the rocks and ripping them, so they come to me for repairs. Patched nets are never as good the second time around, so I usually end up making new ones." He looked out at the cormorants. "My father taught me how to make them, and his father taught him. Trouble is, I don't know everything he knew, and he didn't know everything his father knew. Things change, and never for the better."

I could see cormorants wheeling aimlessly in the sky past his head.

"And what about Ruth?" I asked.

"She looks after the old 'un," he said, then stopped, as if he had said too much.

"The old 'un?"

"The old 'un used to live in the village, long time ago now," he muttered eventually. "Decided she preferred it down on the beach, near where we found you. Only likes to be bothered for namings and . . ." he looked at me strangely, "marriages. Ruth looks after her needs."

"I think I remember her. She pulled me to safety, I think . . . There was a cave . . ."

"Yes," Jethro said, "a cave."

The sun made a buttress against the shadows, bracing the windowed wall against the floor. Dust motes sparkled briefly as they danced lazily through the beam. Outside, the cormorants called to each other in a private tongue.

"I would like to express my gratitude," I said. "Could we . . ."

"She won't see you."

"Even so . . ."

He sighed, and looked out of the window.

"Ruth's been on at me to get you up and about. She reckons the exercise will do you good."

He dug out some old, faded clothes to replace my ripped flying kit, and supported me as I stumbled down the rocky path to the beach to look over the wreckage. It was difficult to associate the broken struts and burnt, salt-caked skin with the graceful creature that had carried me through the sky. I felt nothing for her. Both of us had changed too much.

I looked around for the cave I remembered seeking sanctuary in, but the cliff face behind us was riddled with holes and fissures, none of which looked familiar. I made to move toward them, but Jethro took my arm. His face was crinkled with concern and . . . could it be? . . . fear.

"Best not," he said. "She doesn't take kindly to newcomers."

"But she saved my life!"

He frowned, and looked out at the calm gray sea.

"I'm sure she had her reasons," he said quietly.

I wanted to ask more, but Jethro turned and started back toward the path up to the hut. It was clear that he was going back, with me or without me. I looked back toward the cliff face. I thought I could see Ruth leaving one of the caves, but then Jethro called me, and I had to hurry to catch up with him.

We walked back in silence. My joints ached, but the sea air filled my lungs and invigorated me. My thoughts turned again to leaving. I would ask Ruth about the fishing fleet, and the mainland.

Back at the hut Jethro and I sat in uncomfortable silence for a while. After time I could only measure by the movement of the sun across the floor, Ruth arrived with food. The atmosphere in the hut shifted in some subtle way as we ate lunch, and twice my eyes caught Ruth's across the space between us. Or perhaps my mind was still clouded with sleep and I misinterpreted the expression in her eyes. I still felt light-headed, and my joints ached, so when Ruth suggested we take a slow walk into the village and back I took little persuading. Jethro looked regretful, but said that he had some mending to do. The storm that interrupted my flight had also ripped many of the nets against the stone reefs that surrounded the fishing grounds. We walked out into the afternoon sunshine and took a path that wound through the grassy dunes and up the face of the small cliff. Jethro sat cross-legged in front of the hut, a diminishing figure as we climbed together. Within five minutes he had faded into the heat haze.

The path to the village led up along the cliff top above the beach, and I could feel my muscles gratefully stretching, easing and unknotting as we walked. I breathed in the clear, sharp air and I was happy. Ruth smiled up at me. I grinned back. No words. We did not need them.

After a while I realized that we were walking along hand in hand, although I could not remember our hands linking. Cormorants were sailing above our heads, catching the breeze in their wings and drifting wherever the gusts took them, calling mournfully. In the distance I could make out the shapes of fishing boats heading out for the day. I supposed that somebody in the village should be in a position to offer me a berth to the mainland, but something in me unexpectedly rebelled at the idea. England and the Spanish Civil War seemed like a dream to me now. The sun on my cheeks, the breeze on my neck, the heat of her hand in mine. This was the only reality.

"I don't know how I can properly repay you," I said after a while, and my words were just the vocalized part of a whole string of messages between us, passed in the pressure of our hands and the warmth of our expressions.

"No need," Ruth replied, smiling gently. "Friendship isn't a debt."

We both stopped walking at the same moment and turned to face one another. We were in a bare area some thirty feet across on the cliff edge. A carved pole had been stuck into the ground in the center of the clearing, its pointed cap thrusting proudly into the sky. With the crunch of sand under our feet silenced, the soft whisper of the waves flowed in to fill the space. We stood quietly, still with our fingers entwined. The pupils of her eyes were large and deep. I could see myself reflected in them, and behind me the sky and the cormorants wheeling and swooping.

"We don't know where you came from," she said, the smile fading into seriousness, "and we know you don't want to talk about it. That's all right. You've been hurt and you're still not healed, but as long as you want to stay you're perfectly welcome to, with no need to repay us for anything. There's some in the village who say we shouldn't have anything to do with strangers, but Jethro and I don't agree. You were hurt, and it's our obligation to heal you. We don't know what your plans are, or whether you want to stay on the island or not, but for as long as you want to be with us, our home is yours." Her lips began to curl as she tried to suppress a grin and failed. "So long as you do the cooking and the washing up, clean the hut every day, fetch the food and the water and . . ."

My hands caught her just underneath her ribs and squeezed. Ruth squealed, wide eyed in surprise, and writhed as I tickled her. Laughter tingled in the air. Her surprise and her giggles were so natural that I could not help joining in, even as she attempted to escape. Somehow she ended up pressing closer to me. Her body was warm and soft. She smelled of summer. Our laughter grew quieter, grew quiet. I remembered Jethro.

"I think we'd better get going," I said.

Ruth nodded, silent. Our eyes held, then we moved apart and started walking again.

We were both more subdued on the way to the village, but as the first few stone houses appeared along the edges of the path, Ruth began to unbend.

"It's market day today," she confided. "The whole village'll be there, and the ones like Jethro who live further away—nigh on two hundred people. There'll be stuff that's been made, and stuff that's been grown, and stuff that's come from the mainland. We still trade with the mainland folk. Some of them, anyway. There's things like cloth, and rigging for the boats, that we just can't make ourselves, and there's always mainlanders who wouldn't let bad words spoil a bargain."

"Bad words?" I asked. I had already realized that contact between the islanders and the mainlanders was slight, but this was the first time that either Ruth or Jethro had referred to it directly. I supposed that it might make returning to England more difficult, but I was not sure whether to be annoyed or pleased.

"They say we're heathens," she said, turning her face away. "They say we're going to go to Hell."

Houses appeared in huddled twos and threes. We passed a church, dilapidated and empty, and I asked Ruth if there was a priest or a pastor on the island. She glanced oddly at me and shook her head. People with closed, suspicious faces stared at me as we walked past. If I smiled back at them they looked away. There seemed to be a marked similarity between many of the people, as if they were all part of the same extended family. After a while I could pick out characteristics—flat stares, heavy eyebrows, wide faces—that seemed to be common. Many of them seemed to resemble Jethro, or perhaps Jethro resembled them.

One or two looked like Ruth. A large woman in mismatched clothes who had fine, downy hair covering her face and hands watched us pass. She had two children with her who gazed up at me with unreadable expressions on their furred faces.

We walked on like this for ten minutes or so, with the number of houses and people around us increasing, until we were in the center of a bustling crowd in the market square. Brightly colored stalls were scattered haphazardly around the cobbled area, selling food, clothes, household items, animals and roughly made pieces of furniture. The smell of cooking and tanning drifted over everything. I followed Ruth from stall to stall as she bartered and dickered and promised, all with a smile on her face. I smiled too, but the faces of the islanders turned sour as they glanced at me out of the corners of their eyes.

As I walked I became aware of a small figure flitting through the crowd. Whichever way I turned, it seemed to turn with me. I was being followed. I tried to get a closer look, but the crowd seemed to thicken wherever it moved. I tried to attract Ruth's attention, but she was busy bargaining over a loaf of bread. Leaving her side, I attempted to edge toward the figure, but my progress was suddenly impeded by villagers suddenly too slow or too clumsy to get out of my way. By the time I got to the spot where I had seen it, leaving a flurry of elbows and muttered apologies in my wake, it had gone.

I turned to make my way back to Ruth but, as I did so, a sudden eddy in the throng opened up a space across which I caught sight of my pursuer. I was only afforded a momentary glimpse before the crowd moved again, closing the gap, but in that long moment my eyes met hers. She had the body of a child, and yet, as she looked over her shoulder at me, her face was baggy and wizened, and her eyes were vacant.

The sights, the sounds, and the smells of the market swirled around me as I tried to understand what I had seen. Eventually, when nothing more happened, I turned back to the stalls. Ruth was arguing happily over a box of root vegetables, but as I moved to join her, I caught sight of a stall selling pieces of driftwood carved into animals, faces, and abstract forms. It was the first time that I had seen anything resembling art on the island, and I took a closer look. One particular sculpture caught my eye. It must have weighed a couple of pounds, and took the shape of a curved, slightly fluted, column with a conical cap—a mushroom, perhaps, or something more symbolic. It was a crude piece of work, but it had an undeniable power. It reminded me of the pole in the clearing that Ruth and I had stopped by, up on the cliff.

"How much?" I asked the man on the other side of the stall. He stared at me for a long moment.

"Not for sale," he said eventually, reaching over and taking it roughly from me. His face was weatherworn and old, the skin cracked and grained like one of his carvings. I guessed him at about fifty.

"I'm a friend of Ruth and Jethro," I said, more to fill the silence than for any other reason.

"Aye, you'll be the one they salvaged from the sea." He spat on the ground.

His casual manner offended me.

"They've been very kind."

"Aye, well they've got good cause."

"What do you mean?"

He smiled. His teeth were tobacco-mottled and rotting.

"You'll find out."

A woman with a deeply lined, wary face came over and stood beside him. I smiled at her, but there was no response.

"He's the stranger," she said to the man.

"Excuse me," I said, "but is there somebody with a boat I could talk to?"

"He'll not get off the island," she muttered. "She'll not let him go."

"Who won't?" I made as if to move around the stall and confront her, but the man put his arm around her shoulders protectively.

"You'd best catch up with your lass," he said. "There's nothing for you here."

I wanted to continue asking him about boats, and who exactly it was that wouldn't let me off the island, but I had noticed that something was wrong with his hand. Trying not to be obvious, I shifted to get a better look, and recoiled, shocked, as I realized that the index finger of his right hand branched into two smaller fingers at the first knuckle.

Ruth was suddenly at my side, with a brittle smile on her face. She took my arm and moved me away.

"They don't like me," I said.

"You're a stranger," she said. "Tobias and Rachel don't like strangers."

"Do any of them?" I asked, looking around at the sea of suspicious faces.

"Some of them are reasonable," Ruth responded with a quirk of her lips. "Rachel's husband, Elisha, has no bad feelings for anybody. But then, he's a stranger, like you."

"I thought Rachel was married to Tobias," I said, determined to avoid any future misunderstandings by getting everybody's name and relationship down pat.

Ruth looked confused. "She is."

Now it was my turn to look confused.

"But you just said she was married to Elisha."

"She is."

We were both frowning now, unsure of our ground.

"So . . . hang on a second. Rachel is married to both Tobias *and* Elisha?"

"Yes . . . What's wrong?" Ruth looked genuinely puzzled.

"I . . ."

There was a voice behind me, calling. Ruth smiled over my shoulder and began to wave.

"Sarah!" she yelled. "Sarah!" Her eyes flickered onto me semi-apologetically. "Sarah's my half-sister." Then she was pushing past me and slipping like a fish through the crowd shouting, "You're looking so well, Sarah. How much longer?"

"A few months yet, the old 'un told me," said Sarah. She was young, about the same age as Ruth, but broader and blond.

What I had taken to be puppy fat was, on closer inspection, a pregnant bulge. I tried to move toward them but Ruth was smaller and more used to the crowds than I, and I was swept sideways by a good few feet before I could recover and fight my way through. People stepped aside for me, but not out of kindness. I fielded their hostility with smiles and murmurs of thanks. By the time I got to Ruth and Sarah they were saying good-bye. There was a quick introduction, a flashed smile, and a silent look exchanged between the two of them. Then Sarah was gone, escorted by two young men and an older woman who had been standing silently beside her.

"No doubt she's married to all of them," I said quietly, watching them go. I do not know if I was being facetious or not. Sarah was holding hands with the two men as they walked. The woman trailed behind.

"Of course not," said Ruth. She sounded . . . not shocked, but some lesser level closer to surprise. "She hasn't had the baby yet."

That halted the conversation for some time.

We walked around the market for a while longer, then I asked Ruth if we could make a move for home. I was tiring, and my leg was beginning to throb.

It seemed to be a shorter walk back. We said little. As we drew nearer to Jethro and the hut, Ruth gestured down at the beach.

"The tides are funny around here," she said suddenly. "Somehow the pebbles get sorted in the water. The sand gets washed up by the hut, and the larger pebbles end up down by the village. The fishermen say that wherever they beach their boats they can tell where they are, just by the size of the pebbles."

"Ruth, how can Rachel be married to two men at once?"

"That's the way it happens," she said.

"Not in other places."

"We're a long way from the mainland."

"Why does that matter?"

"It matters."

Silence for a while. The trees lining the path cowered backward from the sea in positions of frozen horror. Years of storms had fixed them into the best shape for survival. Down below us, by the seashore, the hut came into sight. It looked so small. I could not see Jethro anywhere. Beyond it lay the wreck—graceless, like a beached whale.

"And Sarah? My God, Ruth, the girl's not even married yet and she's having a baby."

"What's so wrong about that?"

"She should marry the father."

"She will. Both of them."

My face must have reflected my shock. Ruth stopped and grabbed my arms, trying to make me understand.

"Sarah will get married, just as soon as she's had the baby. As soon as it's been named. What's wrong with that?"

"Married to who?"

"To all of them."

"And what about that woman who was with them?"

"Betty? She's already married to them. She's had four children named already."

"What's so special about naming a baby?"

She frowned, unsure of how serious I was. "You can't have a baby named unless it's whole."

"Whole?"

She was angry now. "Two arms. Two legs. A face. Not deaf or blind. Not dead."

"Don't be an idiot!" I was angry too. She had no right to be furious at my ignorance. "How often does that actually happen?"

Silence. A small voice. "One in every three." Suddenly her face crumpled and she began to cry. I moved forward and took her in my arms. Warm tears dampened my shirt. Jethro's shirt. I took her face in my hands and raised it until Ruth was looking at me with bleary, beautiful, almond-shaped eyes. I leaned forward and kissed the tears away one by one. They tasted of salt.

"Oh God, I think I'm pregnant too," she whispered into my ear. I moved my head back to look at her. Silent tears still trickled from screwed-up eyes. I kissed her properly this time, long and slow. Her body pressed into mine. Time and identity melted together and it seemed only seconds later that we were naked, although I cannot remember removing her clothes or mine. We fitted together like two perfectly machined engine parts, moving in a regular rhythm. Her face was screwed up tight. The breeze was cool on my back, the sand warm beneath my hands and knees. My body tingled. As she gasped and I cried out I felt her hand tighten on my shoulder, but then her arms slid around my waist as she gazed up into the cloudless blue sky, and I looked up, and Jethro stared down at me. He was smiling, and one of his hands held my shoulder while the other caressed Ruth's face with gentle, loving strokes. He was so pleased for us. God help me, he was so pleased.

I still remember his expression, although it was months ago now. Sarah—Ruth's half-sister—gave birth last week. She married the two men who might have been the father as soon as the baby had been pronounced whole, and named. I was not allowed to attend. Ruth had been tearful, Jethro resolute. The old 'un would not have permitted it, I was told. I had not yet been accepted by the islanders.

I asked who the old 'un was, to dictate their marriages, their lives, their loves? I said that I did not understand how they could let their lives be blighted by one person's word. Ruth started to explain, but Jethro cut her short.

"We should go," he said, and took her arm. She glanced back at me as he opened the door.

"I'm coming," I said, and got up.

"Thomas . . . no!" The fear in her eyes stopped me cold. "Thomas, I . . ."

The door closed before she could finish.

I watched from the window as they made their way along the foot of the cliff. Part of me wanted just to lie down and rest, but I knew that I had to follow. Something was sour at the heart of this island, and I cared enough for Ruth—yes, and for Jethro too—that I needed to know what it was.

I left the hut and sprinted along the beach, staying close to the sea, hidden from Ruth and Jethro by the low rolling dunes. By the time I caught up with them, they had joined a procession from the village that had Sarah, her baby, and her suitors at its head. Although I only caught glimpses of them as I ran, it seemed to me that there were more people in the procession than I had believed were on the island. Somehow it did not surprise me that they were heading for one of the many caves along the base of the cliff. Under cover of the dunes I managed to run ahead, so that by the time Sarah led the way in to the shadowed opening I was crouched, watching, behind a large clump of sea grass. For the first time I could see the villagers clearly, and the sight made me almost sick.

I saw abominations in that procession the like of which I have never seen before, and pray to God I never see again: twins joined at the shoulder, people with enlarged or shrunken heads, a man whose lips were mere ragged fringes surrounding his teeth and who chewed at his fingers as he walked. One by one they entered the cave.

"They still make my stomach turn," said a reedy voice behind me. I looked over my shoulder. A thin man in an overly large sweater was crouching some yards behind me. His gray hair hung in greasy ringlets about his ears but thinned out to the point of baldness above his brow.

"Elisha," he said. "You'll be the other stranger."

"Other?"

"My fishing boat foundered on the rocks twenty years ago now. They still call me stranger."

"You're Rachel's husband," I said, remembering the market and the start of my argument with Ruth.

"Rachel's *other* husband," he reminded me gently, and glanced over at the cave mouth, from which the sounds of distant chanting echoed.

"They only come out for special occasions," he said. "The feeble ones. The crippled ones. The ones who aren't quite right in the head. Only come out for namings and marriages. They're kept apart the rest of the time. The islanders don't like to be reminded."

"Reminded of what?"

He looked at me strangely. "God's judgment," he said quietly.

"What did they do wrong?"

"They married each other. No limit on this island. Marry who you like."

The sound of massed voices raised in song drifted across the sand.

"How did it all start?" I asked. "They can't always have been like this, surely?"

Elisha smiled sadly, and rubbed his nose.

"They claim a wise woman came to live amongst them, long time ago now. She'd been persecuted on the mainland, and came here for refuge. They say she could do the most incredible things: tell the future, make potions for lovers, fly through the air. Must have been a forceful personality, by all accounts; after all, her mark is still on the island. She took lots of lovers, and encouraged the islanders to do the same. There were ceremonies in which they would all dance around a pole set in the ground, stark naked, and then take each other like so many animals rutting." He laughed suddenly. "Like I say, she must have been a forceful personality, because they're still doing it. Or perhaps the hexes she cast are still working on the islanders."

"What about . . ."

"The Church?" He snorted, and spat onto the sand. "The local pastor was driven out according to one story I was told, driven mad according to another. Can't say I'm surprised."

He fell silent, listening to the singing.

"What happened to this wise woman?" I asked.

"She's still here," Elisha said, and nodded toward the cave mouth. "They call her the old 'un."

"Have you seen her?"

Elisha smiled, and looked out to sea.

"Oh yes," he said, "I've seen her."

Odd facts and throwaway lines started to meet up in my mind like a child's join-the-dots puzzle.

"That's why the mainlanders won't have any contact with the islanders!"

"They say the islanders are Godless," Elisha confirmed. "One or two whose greed overcomes their piety will trade, but that's on the sly."

"But that means . . ." My thoughts were racing ahead of my mind now, but I didn't dare articulate my thoughts. Elisha did it for me.

"Oh, they're all related," he said, nodding toward the cave. "There's been no fresh blood for generations now. The island's all one big happy family. Didn't you know? Jethro is Ruth's brother."

I felt as if I had become detached from the world I thought I understood. The feel of the sand beneath my feet faded away; the sound of the surf retreated into a faint hissing. I heard a voice ask a question, and it was only when Elisha answered that I realized it had been me who said: "So that was God's punishment? Deformities?"

"That or barrenness. Couples aren't allowed to marry here until they prove they can bear a normal child. If they can't, then they aren't allowed to have any more children. That way the islanders try not to spread the deformities through the population."

He smiled proudly at me. "I'm not saying it's to do with marrying within the family, but all ten of my children are healthy." The smile faded from his face. "Not that it's done any good. It seems like every year there are more freaks and misfits on the Island. That's why the old 'un wants you to stay. You're an injection of health into a decaying population."

Elisha's quiet, normal tone had pulled me back from wherever I had floated off to. "They don't kill the children?" I asked.

"No. But they don't like having them around. If it makes my stomach turn, what does it do for them?"

There was silence from the cave, and suddenly the islanders

started to emerge, blinking, into the daylight, like parishioners leaving church. Sarah and Ruth were last, gossiping and laughing. Jethro held back from the crowd and reached out a hand to Ruth. She took it coyly. I looked within myself for any hatred toward him, but could find none. If Ruth loved him, how could I not?

"She's a beautiful woman. You're very lucky."

"Am I?" I whispered.

"They'll be heading up to the marriage pole now," he said wistfully. "Sarah'll get married to the two lads, and then they'll all follow the old tradition. They still don't let me join in, being a relative newcomer and all, but I like to watch." He put his hand on my shoulder. "Do you want to come?"

I turned away. After a few moments, he muttered, "Suit yourself," and left.

After I was sure that all of the villagers had left, I walked across to the cave. The sun was dipping toward the sea, turning the waves to crimson and silhouetting the soaring cormorants. The closer I got, the more familiar it looked.

A few feet past its entrance the cave widened out into a chamber the size of an aeroplane hangar. The last rays of the sun shone through potholes and fissures high in the cliff face and cast thin beams of light across the empty space. Stalactites like folded sheets of dirty lace hung from the high ceiling. As I stepped forward into the main body of the cave I looked down. The floor appeared to drop away before my feet, plunging into shadowed depths where grotesquely twisted stalagmites reached up blindly toward their cousins. I could see no path, no space where the islanders could have congregated. Then, as the stalagmites rippled slowly in my vision, I realized that they were too perfect, too close a representation of the stalactites above. I bent and reached forward. For a second my fingers were cold and the cave shook before my eyes, and then my fingers met rock. I let out a breath I did not even realize I had been holding. A thin layer of water covered the floor of the cave, and it was the reflection of the stalactites above that had fooled me.

I stepped forward, my feet splashing the water and causing

ripples to spread out, making the illusory stalagmites shimmer like a dream. Ahead of me a large chunk of stone obstinately refused to change. As I got closer I realized how large it was—a chunk of limestone slightly smaller and almost as broad as I was. It was the only stalagmite that rose from the floor of the cave. The centuries-old dripping of water from the roof of the cave had weathered it into complex patterns, and constant trickles had etched deep folds into its body. In the half-light of sunset it could almost be taken for a cowled figure with folded arms. The stone on a level with my eyes had even been weathered into features— rounded approximations to the human face, like the gargoyles poised around old churches, waiting for the souls of the dead.

Like an old woman with cruel, lined features.

If there ever had been a wise woman living in the village then she was long dead, her memory kept alive by the islanders and by the accidental similarity of a chunk of stone. I turned to go.

"Thomassss . . ."

I spun round. Water splashed around my feet. Nothing moved.

"Thomassss . . ."

"Who's there?" I shouted. "Jethro? Ruth?"

"Join ussss . . ."

The wind whistling through fissures in the rock? The half-heard trickle of far-off water? The noise echoed in the shadows, fainter and fainter, until it was gone. Nothing moved and nothing spoke as I stalked out of the cave.

▼▼▼

I spend a lot of time on the beach now. I have my favorite spot, nestled between two steep-banked sand dunes and protected from the wind and the wind-borne sea spray. From it I can see the wide sweep of the bay and the white caps to the waves that might be the foam as they curl and break, or the cormorants riding them and diving for food. I often come here to sit, remembering the life I used to have, watching the fishing boats heading out for the day and wishing I had the courage to be on one of them.

The wreck of the old De Havilland DH16 is overgrown now. Grasses and weeds have sprouted unchecked through and around it, tough sea grasses that can adapt to any conditions and survive anywhere. The cormorants seem quite happy. I got angry with them last week and chased down the shingle toward them, arms flapping hysterically, driving them away if only for a moment. Flushed with my success I sat on one of the charred struts. The structure creaked under me. As I adjusted my position, my foot brushed an object half buried in the shingle. I bent to pick it up. It was a book, old and faded now, pages made brittle by the sea. The leather cover cracked as I opened it up. A tiny puff of dust bled onto my palm. The ink had faded of course, but I still remembered the words I had written on the flyleaf all those years ago.

Thomas Paul Jerome. Flight logbook, August 1933.

With a strong overarm cast I managed to hurl it a few hundred yards closer to the English coast. A cormorant was ducking for food near to where it sank. The bird looked up at me disdainfully, then returned to its feeding. I watched it for a while. Food, and the sea, and the wreck—these were its world. The island was mine. The cormorants could fly away to the mainland, or further if they wished, but habit bound them here. I was tied by love, and I could not, would not, leave.

INSCRIPTION
▼▼▼

JANE YOLEN

Father, they have burned your body,
Set your ashes in the cairn.
Still I need your advice.
Magnus sues for me in marriage,
Likewise McLeod of the three farms.
Yet would I wait for Iain the traveler,
Counting each step of his journey
Till the sun burns down behind Galan
Three and three hundred times;
Till he has walked to Steornabhagh
And back the long, hard track,
Singing my praises at every shieling
Where the lonely women talk to the east wind
And admire the ring he is bringing
To place on my small white hand.
—Inscription on Callanish Stones, Isle of Lewis

IT is a lie, you know, that inscription. From first to last. I did not want my father's advice. I had never taken it when he was alive, no matter how often he offered it. Still I need to confess what's been done.

If I do not die of this thing, I shall tell my son himself when he is old enough to understand. But if I cannot tell him, there will still be this paper to explain it: who his mother was, what she did for want of him, who and what his father was, and how the witch cursed us all.

Magnus Magnusson did ask for me in marriage, but he did not really want me. He did not want me though I was young and slim and fair. His eye was to the young men, but he wanted my father's farm and my father was a dying man, preferring a dram to a bannock.

And McLeod had the richest three farms along the machair, growing more than peat and sand. Still he was ugly and old, older even than my father, and as pickled, though his was of the brine where my father's was the whiskey.

Even Iain the traveler was no great catch, for he had no money at all. But ach—he was a lovely man, with hair the purple brown of heather in the spring or like a bruise beneath the skin. He was worth the loving but not worth the waiting for. Still I did not know it at the time.

I was nursed not by my mother, who died giving birth to me, but by brown-haired Mairi, daughter of Lachlan, who was my father's shepherd. And if she had married my father and given him sons, these troubles would not have come upon me. But perhaps that, too, is a lie. Even as a child I went to trouble as a herring to the water, so Mairi always said. Besides, my father was of that rare breed of man who fancied only the one wife; his love once given was never to be changed or renewed, even to the grave.

So I grew without a brother or sister to play with, a trouble to my dear nurse and a plague to my father, though neither ever complained of it. Indeed, when I stumbled in the bog as the household dug the peat, and was near lost, they dragged me free. When I fell down a hole in the cliff when we went for birds' eggs, they paid a man from St. Kilda's to rescue me with ropes. And when the sea herself pulled me from the sands the day I went romping with the selchies, they got in the big boat that takes four men and a bowman in normal times, and pulled me back from the clutching tide. Oh I was a trouble and a plague.

But never was I so much as when I came of age to wed. That summer, after my blood flowed the first time and Mairi showed me how to keep myself clean—and no easy job of it—handsome Iain came through on his wanderings. He took note of me I am sure, and not just because he told me the summer after. A girl knows when a man has an eye for her: she knows it by the burn of her skin; she knows it by the ache in her bones. He said he saw the promise in me and was waiting a year to collect on it. He had many such collections in mind, but I wasn't to know.

His eyes were as purple brown as his hair, like wild plums. And his skin was dark from wandering. There is not much sun on Leodhas, summer to winter, but if you are constantly out in it, the wind can scour you. Iain the traveler had that color; while others were red as rowan from the wind, he was brown as the roe. It made his teeth the whiter. It made the other men looked boiled or flayed and laughable.

No one laughed at Iain. No woman laughed, that is.

So of course I loved him. How could I not? I who had been denied nothing by my father, nothing by my nurse. I loved Iain and wanted him, so I was certain to have him. How was I to know the count of days would be so short.

▼▼▼

When he came through the next summer to collect on that promise, I was willing to pay. We met first on the long sea loch where I had gone to gather periwinkles and watch the boys come in from the sea, pulling on the oars of the boat which made their new young muscles ripple.

Iain spoke to all of the women, few of the men, but for me he took out his whistle and played one of the old courting tunes. We had a laugh at that, all of us, though I felt a burn beneath my breastbone, by the heart, and could scarcely breathe.

I pretended he played the tune because I was watching out for the boys. He pretended he was playing it for Jennie Morrison, who was marrying Jamie Matheson before the baby in her belly swelled too big. But I already knew, really, he was playing just for me.

The pipes told me to meet him by the standing stones and so I did. He acted surprised to see me, but I knew he was not. He smoothed my hair and took me in his arms, and called me such sweet names as he kissed me I was sure I would die of it.

"Come tomorrow," he whispered, "when the dark finally winks," by which he meant well past midnight. And though I thought love should shout its name in the daylight as well as whisper at night, I did as he asked.

▼▼▼

Sneaking from our house was not easy. Like most island houses, it was small and with only a few rooms, and the door was shared with the byre. But father and nurse and cows were all asleep, and I slipped out, barely stirring the peat smoke as I departed.

Iain was waiting for me by the stones, and he led me down to a place where soft grasses made a mat for my back. And there he taught me the pain of loving as well as the sweetness of it. I did not cry out, though it was not from wanting. But bred on the island means being strong, and I had only lately given over playing shinty with the boys. Still there was blood on my legs and I cleaned myself with grass and hurried back as the sun— what there was of it—was rising, leaving Iain asleep and guarded by the stones.

▼▼▼

If Mairi noticed anything, she said nothing. At least not that day. And as I helped her at the quern preparing meal, and gave a hand with the baking as well, all the while supressing the yawns that threatened to expose me, perhaps she did not know.

When I went back to the stones that night, Iain was waiting for me and this time there was neither blood nor pain, though I still preferred the kisses to what came after.

But I was so tired that I slept beside him all that night, or what was left of it. At dawn we heard the fishermen calling to one another as they passed by our little nest on the way to their boats. They did not see us: Iain knew how to choose his places well. Still I did not rise, for no fisherman dares meet a woman as he goes toward the sea for fear of losing his way in the waves. So I was forced to huddle there in the shelter of Iain's arms till the fishermen—some of them the boys I had lately played shinty with—were gone safely on their way.

This time when I got home Mairi was already up at the quern, her face as black as if it had been rinsed in peat. She did not say a word to me, which was even worse, but by her silence I knew she had said nothing to my father, who slept away in the other room.

▼▼▼

That was the last but one I saw of Iain that summer, though I went night after night to look for him at the stones. My eyes were red from weeping silently as I lay in the straw by Mairi's side, and she snoring so loudly, I knew she was not really asleep.

I would have said nothing, but the time came around and my blood did not flow. Mairi knew the count of it since I was so new to womanhood. Perhaps she guessed even before I did, for I saw her looking at me queer. When I felt queasy and was sick behind the house, there was no disguising it.

"Who is it?" she asked. Mairi was never one for talking too much.

"Iain the traveler," I said. "I am dying for love of him."

"You are not dying," she said, "lest your father kill you for this. We will go to Auld Annie who lives down the coast. She practices the black airt and can rid you of the child."

"I do not want to be rid of it," I said. "I want Iain."

"He is walking out with Margaret MacKenzie in her shieling. Or if not her, another."

"Never! He loves me," I said. "He swore it."

"He loves," Mairi said, purposefully coarse to shock me, "the cherry in its blossom but not the tree. And his swearing is done to accomplish what he desires."

She took me by the hand, then, before I could recover my tongue, and we walked half the morning down the strand to Auld Annie's croft, it being ten miles or so by. There was only a soft, fair wind and the walking was not hard, though we had to stop every now and again for me to be quietly sick in the sand.

Auld Annie's cottage was much the smallest and meanest I had seen, still it had a fine garden both in front and again in back in the long rig. Plants grew there in profusion, in lazybeds, and I had no name for many of them.

"She can call fish in by melted lead and water," Mairi said. "She can calm the seas with seven white stones."

I did not look impressed, but it was my stomach once more turning inside me.

"She foretold your own dear mother's death."

I looked askance. "Why didn't I know of this?"

"Your father forbade me ever speak of it."

"And now?"

"Needs does as needs must." She knocked on the door.

The door seemed to open of itself because when we got inside, Auld Annie was sitting far from it, in a rocker, a coarse black shawl around her shoulders and a mutch tied under her chin like any proper wife. The croft was lower and darker than ours, but there was a broad mantel over the fire and on it sat two piles of white stones with a human skull, bleached and horrible, staring at the wall between them. On the floor by a long table were three jugs filled with bright red poppies, the only color in the room. From the rafters hung bunches of dried herbs, but they were none of them familiar to me.

Under her breath, Mairi muttered a charm:

> I trample upon the eye
> As tramples the duck upon the lake,
> In the name of the secret Three,
> And Brigid the Bride. . . .

and made a quick sign against the *Droch Shùil*, the evil eye.

"I knew it, I knew ye were coming, Molly," Auld Annie said.

How she knew that—or my name—I could not guess.

"I knew it as I knew when yer mam was going to die." Her voice was low, like a man's.

"We haven't come for prophecy," I said.

"Ye have come about a babe."

My jaw must have gone agape at that for I had told no one but Mairi—and that only hours before. Surely Auld Annie *was* a witch, though if she threw no shadow one could not tell in the dark of her house. Nevertheless I shook my head. "I will keep the babe. All I want is the father to come to me."

"Coming is easy," Auld Annie said in her deep voice. "Staying is hard."

"If you get him to come to me," I answered, suddenly full of myself, "I will get him to stay."

From Mairi there was only a sharp intake of breath in disapproval, but Auld Annie chuckled at my remark, dangerous and low.

"Come then, girl," she said, "and set yer hand to my churn. We have butter to take and spells to make and a man to call to yer breast."

I did not understand entirely, but I followed her to the churn, where she instructed me in what I had to do.

"As ye churn, girl, say this: *Come, butter, come. Come, butter, come.*"

"I know this charm," I said witheringly. "I have since a child."

"Ah—but instead 'a saying 'butter,' ye must say yer man's name. Only—" she raised her hand in warning, "not aloud. And ye must not hesitate even a moment's worth between the words Not once. Ye must say it over and over till the butter be done. It is not easy, for all it sounds that way."

I wondered—briefly—if all she was needing was a strong young girl to do her chores, but resolved to follow her instructions. It is a dangerous thing to get a witch angry with you. And if she could call Iain to me, so much the better.

So I put my hands upon the churn and did as she bid, over and over and over without a hesitation till my arms ached and my mind was numb and all I could hear was Iain's name in my head, the very sound of it turning my stomach and making me ill. Still I did not stop till the butter had come.

Auld Annie put her hands upon mine, and they were rough and crabbed with time. "Enough!" she said, "or it will come sour as yer belly, and we will have done all for nought."

I bit back the response that it was not *we* but *I* who had done the work and silently put my aching arms down at my sides. Only then did I see that Annie herself had not been idle. On her table lay a weaving of colored threads.

"A framing spell," Mairi whispered by my side. "A *deilbh buidseachd*."

I resisted crossing myself and spoiling the spell and went where Annie led me, to the rocking chair.

"Sit ye by the fire," she said.

No sooner had I sat down, rubbing my aching arms and trying not to jump up and run outside to be sick, when a piece of the peat broke off in the hearth and tumbled out at my feet.

"Good, good," Auld Annie crooned. "Fire bodes marriage. We will have success."

I did not smile. Gritting my teeth, I whispered, "Get on with it."

"Hush," cautioned Mairi, but her arms did not ache as mine did.

Auld Annie hastened back to the churn and, dipping her hand into it, carved out a pat of butter the size of a shinty ball with her nails. Slapping it down on the table by the threads, she said: "Name three colors, girl, and their properties."

"Blue like the sea by Galan's Head," I said.

"Good, good, two more."

"Plum—like his eyes."

"And a third."

I hesitated, thinking. "White," I said at last. "White—like . . . like God's own hair."

Auld Annie made a loud *tch* sound in the back of her throat and Mairi, giving a loud explosive exhalation, threw her apron up over her head.

"Not a proper choice, girl," Auld Annie muttered. "But what's said cannot be unsaid. Done is done."

"Is it spoiled?" I whispered.

"Not spoiled. Changed." She drew the named colors of thread from the frame and laid them, side by side, across the ball of butter. "Come here."

I stood up and went over to her, my arms all a-tingle.

"Set the two threads at a cross for the name of God ye so carelessly invoked, and one beneath for yer true love's name."

I did as she bid, suddenly afraid. What had I called up or called down, so carelessly in this dark house?

Auld Annie wrapped the butter in a piece of yellowed linen, tying the whole up with a black thread, before handing it to me.

"Take this to the place where ye wish to meet him and bury it three feet down, first drawing out the black thread. Cover it over with earth and while doing so recite three times the very words ye said over the churn. He will come that very evening. He will come—but whether he will stay is up to ye, my girl."

I took the sachet in my right hand and dropped it carefully into the pocket of my apron.

"Come now, girl, give me a kiss to seal it."

When I hesitated, Mairi pushed me hard in the small of the back and I stumbled into the old woman's arms. She smelled of peat and whiskey and age, not unlike my father, but there was something more I could put no name to. Her mouth on mine was nothing like Iain's, but was bristly with an old woman's hard whiskers and her lips were cracked. Her sour breath entered mine and I reeled back from her, thankful to be done. As I turned, I glanced at the mantel. To my horror I saw that between the white stones, the skull was now facing me, its empty sockets black as doom.

Mairi opened the cottage door and we stumbled out into the light, blinking like hedgehogs. I started down the path, head down. When I gave a quick look over my shoulder, Mairi was setting something down by Auld Annie's door. It was a payment, I knew, but for what and how much I did not ask, then or ever.

▼▼▼

We walked back more slowly than we had come, and I chattered much of the way, as if the charming had been on my tongue to loosen it. I told Mairi about Iain's hair and his eyes and every word he had spoken to me, doling them out a bit at a time because, truth to tell, he had said little. I recounted the kisses and how they made me feel and even—I blush to think of it now—how I preferred them to what came after. Mairi said not a word in return until we came to the place where the path led away to the standing stones.

When I made to turn, she put her hand on my arm. "No, not there," she said. "I told you he has gone up amongst the shielings. If you want him to come to you, I will have your father send you up to the high pasture today."

"He will come wherever I call him," I said smugly, patting the pocket where the butter lay.

"Do not be more brainless than you have been already," Mairi said. "Go where you have the best chance of making him stay."

I saw at last what she meant. At the stones we would have to creep and hide and lie still lest the fishermen spy us. We would have to whisper our love. But up in the high pasture, along the cliffside, in a small croft of our own, I could bind him to me by night and by day, marrying him in the old way. And no one— especially my father—could say no to such a wedding.

So Mairi worked her own magic that day, much more homey than Auld Annie's, with a good hot soup and a hearty dram and a word in the ear of my old father. By the next morning she had me packed off to the shieling, with enough bannocks and barley and flasks of water in my basket to last me a fortnight, driving five of our cows before.

▼▼▼

The cows knew the way as well as I, and they took to the climb like weanlings, for the grass in the shieling was sweet and fresh and greener than the overgrazed land below. In another week Mairi and I would have gone up together. But Mairi had my father convinced that I was grown enough to make the trip for the first time alone. Grown enough—if he had but known!

Perhaps it was the sea breeze blowing on my face, or the fact that I knew Iain would be in my arms by dark. Or perhaps it was just that the time for such sickening was past, but I was not ill at all on that long walk, my step as jaunty as the cows'.

It was just coming on late supper when we turned off the path to go up and over the hill to the headland where our little summer croft sits. The cows followed their old paths through the matted bog with a quiet satisfaction, but I leaped carelessly from tussock to tuft behind them.

I walked—or rather danced—to the cliff's edge where the hummocks and bog and gray-splattered stone gave way to the sheer of cliff. Above me the gannets flew high and low, every now and again veering off to plummet into the sea after fish. A solitary seal floated below, near some rocks, looking left, then right, then left again but never once up at me.

With the little hoe I had brought along for the purpose, I dug a hole, fully three feet down, and reverently laid in the butter pat. Pulling the black thread from the sachet, I let the clods of dirt rain back down on it, all the while whispering, "Come, Iain, come. Come, Iain, come." Then loudly I sang out, "Come, Iain, come!" without a hesitation in between. Then I packed the earth down and stood, rubbing the small of my back where Mairi had pushed me into the sealing kiss.

I stared out over the sea, waiting.

▼▼▼

He did not come until past dark, which in summer is well into the mid of the night. By then I had cooked myself a thin barley gruel, and made the bed up, stuffing it with soft grasses and airing out the croft.

I heard his whistle first, playing a raucous courting tune, not the one he had played on the beach when first I had noticed him, but "The Cuckoo's Nest," with words that say the one thing, but mean another.

In the dim light it took him a minute to see me standing by the door. Then he smiled that slow, sure smile of his. "Well . . . Molly," he said.

I wondered that he hesitated over my name, almost as if he could not recall it, though it had been but a few short weeks before that he had whispered it over and over into my tumbled hair.

"Well, Iain," I said. "You have come to me."

"I have been called to you," he said airily. "I could not stay away."

And then suddenly I understood that he did not know there was magic about; that these were just words he spoke, part of his lovemaking, that meant as little to him as the kisses themselves, just prelude to his passion.

Well, I had already paid for his pleasure and now he would have to stay for mine. I opened my arms and he walked into them as if he had never been away, his kisses the sweeter now that I knew what he was and how to play his game.

▼▼▼

In the morning I woke him with the smell of barley bread. I thought if I could get him to stay a second night, and a third, the charm would have a chance of really working. So I was sweet and pliant and full of an ardor that his kisses certainly aroused, though that which followed seemed to unaccountably dampen it. Still, I could dissemble when I had to, and each time we made love I cried out as if fulfilled. Then while he slept I tiptoed out to the place where I had buried the butter sachet.

"Stay, Iain, stay. Stay, Iain, stay," I recited over the little grave where my hopes lay buried.

For a day and another night it seemed to work. He did stay— and quite happily—often sitting half-dressed in the cot watching me cook or lying naked on the sandy beach, playing his whistle to call the seals to him. They rose up out of the water, gazing long at him, as if they were bewitched.

We made love three and four and five times, day and night, till my thighs ached the way my arms had at the churn, and I felt scrubbed raw from trying to hold on to him.

But on the third day, when he woke, he refused both the barley and my kisses.

"*Enough*, sweet Moll," he said. "I am a traveler, and I must travel." He got dressed slowly, as if almost reluctant to leave but satisfying the form of it. I said nothing till he put his boots on, then could not stop myself.

"On to another shieling, then?"

"Perhaps."

"And what of the babe—here." It was the first time I had mentioned it. From the look on his face, I knew it made no matter to him, and without waiting for an answer, I stalked out of the croft. I went to the headland and stood athwart the place where the butter lay buried.

"Stay, Iain," I whispered. "Stay . . ." but there was neither power nor magic nor desire in my calling.

He came up behind me and put his arms around me, crossing his hands over my belly where the child-to-be lay quiet.

"Marry another," he whispered, nuzzling my ear, "but call him after me."

I turned in his arms and pulled him around to kiss me, my mouth wide open as if to take him in entire. And when the kiss was done, I pulled away and pushed him over the cliff into the sea.

Like most men of Leodhais, he could not swim, but little it would have availed him, for he hit the rocks and then the water, sinking at once. He did not come up again till three seals pushed him ashore onto the beach, where they huddled by his body for a moment as if expecting a tune, then plunged back into the sea when there was none.

I hurried down and cradled his poor broken body in my arms, weeping not for him but for myself and what I had lost, what I had buried up on that cliff, along with the butter, in a boggy little grave. Stripping the ring from his hand, I put it on my own, marrying us in the eyes of the sea. Then I put him on my back and carried him up the cliffside to bury him deep beneath the heather that would soon be the color of his hair, of his eyes.

Two weeks later, when Mairi came, I showed her the ring.

"We were married in God's sight," I said, "with two selchies as bridesmaids and a gannet to cry out the prayers."

"And where is the bridegroom now?" she asked.

"Gone to Steornabhagh," I lied, "to whistle us up money for our very own croft." She was not convinced. She did not say so, but I could read her face.

▼▼▼

Of course he never returned and—with Mairi standing up for me—I married old McLeod after burying my father, who had stumbled into a hole one night after too much whiskey, breaking both his leg and his neck.

McLeod was too old for more than a kiss and a cuddle—as Mairi had guessed—and too pigheaded to claim the child wasn't his own. When the babe was born hale and whole, I named him Iain, a common-enough name in these parts, with only his nurse Mairi the wiser. At McLeod's death a year later, I gave our old farm over to her. It was a payment, she knew, but exactly for what she never asked, not then or ever.

Now I lie abed with the pox, weakening each day, and would repent—of the magic and the rest—though not of the loving which gave me my child. Still I would have my Iain know who his mother was and what she did for want of him, who and what his father was, and how the witch cursed us all. I would not have my son unmindful of his inheritance. If ever the wind calls him to travel, if ever a witch should tempt him to magic, or if ever a cold, quiet rage makes him choose murder, he will understand and, I trust, set all those desires behind.

Written this year of our Lord 1539, Tir a' Gheallaidh, Isle of Lewis

EASY TOM AND THE SEVEN HIGHWAYS TO CONSTANTINOPLE AND ALL POINTS SOUTH

▼▼▼

JONATHAN BOND & THOMAS J. LINDELL

EIGHT ways into the damn mansion, all locked and all with alarms. Seeing those bars gave me a warm, safe feeling. Oh well, Momma always said I had a stupid streak in me.

After my last round of checking the perimeter, I fell asleep in the bat-cave-sized living room with my ten-millimeter pistol in my lap and a brown Mexican throw-blanket over my shoulders.

Woke up just after midnight with the chilly feeling that Easy Tom was in the house despite the locked doors and all of Old Lady Brisbane's guru, black-magic, earth-mother-goddess bullshit.

As I eased the heavy blanket back, I caught the tangy scent of goat's blood mixed with ginseng and slippery elm bark. Brisbane had slaughtered Stuckey—the family's pet goat and all-around garbage disposal—then used the blood to whip up a batch of her witch's brew. She then proceeded to slop the foul stuff everywhere. By the time twilight hit, there were off-kilter pentagrams covering most of the floors and walls.

When I met Old Lady Brisbane about five years before, I'd heard the rumors. Everybody in town knew she and Tom were into some weird shit. I mean, they showed up out of nowhere with tons of cash and started pushing some of the bigger mob bosses around like tinker toys. Didn't take long for the word to spread that the Brisbanes did things best left unmentioned by the light of day.

That kind of shit didn't hold water with me back then, and the Brisbanes were paying the highest price going for contacts and muscle. So what's a poor ex-con to do?

I'd signed on as an independent information broker, which is a nice way of saying "snitch," and wound up making friends with Tommy Brisbane. People didn't call him Easy Tom for his laid-back attitude. No, they called him that because he could break kneecaps easier than most men break breadsticks. People said that had to do with black magic as well. I'd just laughed at the time.

Now, I wasn't so sure. The scent of death and bad herbal tea filled the room like L.A. smog in the middle of July. And if the stench wasn't bad enough, there was a breeze coming from the foyer to the south.

Even I knew a breeze in a locked, sealed house was bad news.

I slipped from the tan leather couch and made sure the pistol's safety was in the off position, just like Billy Chin showed me.

Didn't hold much with guns because they add years to a jail sentence, but I didn't hold much with dying either. See, while I was checking the greenhouse for possible entry points, Brisbane wheeled up to me in her motorized chair and told me in her hissing, wasted voice that I would probably need some protection of sorts.

Eager to please, not to mention stay alive, I drove the Chrysler over to Billy Chin's Demolition Emporium and picked up the biggest piece of hardware I could find.

Billy told me to just point the Heckler and Koch ten-millimeter (with the extended clip) in the general direction of whatever

I wanted dead, and keep pulling the trigger. If something didn't fall down before I went through sixteen shells, then I deserved to bite it.

But when I showed up with the pistol earlier this evening and flashed it to the old lady, she just croaked out that froglike laugh of hers. "What the hell are you going to do with *that?*"

"Protection," I said, trying my best to sound like the ruthless wise guy my business cards proclaimed me to be. "You told me I needed protection."

She laughed and turned up the driveway. "You might as well have brought a condom."

"I wasn't planning on killing Tom, you know, I just want to have something to slow him down a little," I said, as I followed her into the foyer of the large mansion.

Brisbane just dismissed me with a wave of her hand, backed her wheelchair up to the staircase, and hooked it onto the elevator.

"So, just what type of protection did you have in mind?" I said.

"Rabbit's foot, boy. Piece of jade carved into the shape of Tyche. Shit, even a St. Christopher's medal would do more good than that *heater.*"

She actually said that: heater.

I watched the elevator carry her backward up the stairs, and for a minute she looked just like the Wicked Witch-lady riding her bicycle in the tornado scene from *The Wizard of Oz*. "Why'd you call me here," I called out after her, "if my protection is worth less than a goddamn rabbit's foot?"

"You got special talents, Danny Fairfield," she said as she detached her wheelchair and vanished into the upstairs of the house. "Talents I'm going to need when the Seven Roads open." Then there was that froglike laugh that sent a nasty chill down my spine.

Seven roads, my ass. I tested the weight of the H&K and examined the flat-black surface of the gun. I thought about sticking it back in the Chrysler.

I kept the pistol, mostly because the weight in the palm of my hand was more comforting than nothing at all, and partly because I would have laid even odds a bullet from that pistol had a better chance of stopping Easy Tom than waving a magic wand or using Stuckey the Goat as Mop 'n Glo.

So now, eight hours later, there I was clinging to the gun like it was a fuckin' teddy bear.

It took a second for me to get my bearings in the giant living room. I stalked across the thick pile carpeting and around the love seat, guided by the moonlight filtering in the massive window that looked onto Shilshole Bay. The smell of Stuckey's blood and ginseng got stronger.

Damn you, Brisbane. Told you all that mystic voodoo wouldn't do any good.

As I stepped from the living room into the foyer, I could hear the sounds of Brisbane doing her chanting clap-trap upstairs. I breathed a sigh of relief.

Maybe Easy Tom hadn't gotten in after all.

High-adrenaline stomach butterflies and the gaping front door told me that was wishful thinking. I stopped at the foot of the curved oak staircase and started counting my options. I got as far as two, then I was stumped.

I put my foot on the first stair. I almost yelled for Brisbane, hollered out that things weren't quite as under control as I'd promised her they would be. Then, I saw myself standing in the dark, shouting to an old woman in a wheelchair. I passed. I still wasn't sure what Easy Tom was planning to do, but I figured that letting him know I was in the house by yelling wouldn't be my smartest move.

Turns out it wouldn't have mattered either way. Must have walked right past Tom and never noticed him in the shadowy entryway. God knows, I never said my mother was *wrong* about my smarts, and tonight my luck was running true to form: shitty.

"Howdy, Fairfield," Tom said in a voice that made me think of cold, dark river bottoms.

The kidney punch caught me just as I was stepping back off

the stairs. The flash of pain made everything go hazy for a second, and my knees buckled as I tried to turn around.

That half-turn ended up saving my life, for what it's worth. If Easy Tom had hit me dead on, I would have sunk to my knees, straight on the stair, and lost my head a moment later. As it was, I was out of alignment. One knee missed the stair and I toppled as the blue steel arc of Tom's machete swung out of the dark and sank three inches into the oak stairwell with a sound like an ax hitting marble.

Missed taking off the top of my head by a fraction of an inch, and I got an even closer haircut than I did the day Big Billy Thompson and Dead Eye Joe held me down on the floor of my prison cell and shaved the word "punk" down the center of my scalp.

As I toppled off the stairs, I tucked into a ball and continued to roll backward. Easy Tom's cursing turned into a quick shout as I barreled into him at thigh level.

He lost his grip on the handle of the machete, and we both sailed out of the foyer and ended up in a heap in the living room. I wound up on top, which was probably the second luckiest thing that happened to me all night.

Easy Tom slipped his arms around me, and I knew that if the big sonovabitch got me in a bear hug I'd get thin and pulpy in a hurry. I kicked off him and slid under the ugly, bronze coffee table with the tacky lion's claw feet.

Moving like a snake across the living room floor, I tried to find a patch of darkness big enough to hold me. I managed to keep ahold of the Heckler and Koch, and I firmly intended to plug sixteen lead balls into Easy Tom as soon as I could get enough distance on him. Sixteen bullets may sound a little much, but the last person to put just *one* bullet into Tom Brisbane was a dirty, little killer named Victor Spetz. Vic wasn't normally stupid, but when he came up against Easy Tom, he must have had a brain fart.

Asshole plugged Tom once with a Browning .44 magnum and then just stood there waiting for the big guy to drop. Without so much as a flinch, Easy shambled over and shoved Vic's nose cartilage into his brain. Made us stop for a drink on the way to the hospital afterward, too.

As I scrambled, I reasoned that one bullet wasn't going to be enough for Easy Tom. I just didn't have any idea how many it would take to do the trick.

From the entranceway, Tom chuckled. Count on Easy Tom to find the funny side. Tonight, though, his chuckle sounded dead and cold. "I gotta hand it to you, Fairfield." He stood up slowly and looked around the room. "You ain't smart, you ain't strong, and you ain't mean, but shit-o-dear you do move pretty fast."

"I was gonna add that to my business cards," I said as I slid into the pool of darkness at the foot of the leather couch. Easy Tom was silhouetted like some childhood nightmare against the large bay windows that faced Puget Sound.

"Watch the birdie," I said, and, holding the pistol in my right hand just like the studs in the movies, I waited for Tom to turn toward me.

Playing John Wayne nearly got me killed. Everything was going smoothly until I actually fired the H&K. I was planning on emptying half the clip into Tom's head and chest, but I only got two shots off.

The first one hit Easy Tom. Even a blind man could have hit him at that distance, but the second one went right into the ceiling as the gun sailed out of my hands.

Hey, so who knew they had such kick? I promised myself that I was going to live at least long enough to smack the shit out of Billy Chin for not telling me to hang on with both hands. I dropped to the floor and started doing my snake imitation again, scrambling around trying to find the damn gun.

Easy Tom grunted, then laughed. "Don'cha know, Fairfield? Shooting me might have worked a day or so ago; now it just pisses me off." Tom shuffled toward me, and in the shadows he looked like Frankenstein's monster.

I started to whine. I couldn't help it. "Jeezus, Tom, it isn't like I *wanted* to kill you or anything. You tried to scalp me with the machete!"

Tom didn't say shit, which meant that he was ready to kill me. I found the gun in the dark and rolled over onto my back. Easy Tom was standing over me, his arms outstretched to fold, spindle and mutilate.

Ever heard of hitting the broadside of a barn? That was how big Tom looked. I held on with both hands and squeezed the trigger four times. It was point-blank. I know I couldn't have missed unless the bullets swerved to go around him.

Tom took two shuffling steps back and grunted. "If I weren't already dead, Fairfield, you'da really hacked me off." Tom paused for a moment, as if he were expecting to keel over.

The longer he stood there, the faster my hopes fell.

Finally, he shook his head. "But since I can't feel dick anymore, I'll kill you quick 'cause we used to be pals."

Okay, sure, Billy Chin had told me they found Easy Tom swinging from the rafters down at Woodside's warehouse. My own fault for not listening. I got a warning and laughed it off. Hell, I was feeling kind of proud of myself for not swallowing the whole zombie thing, even after I saw Tom take four bullets that should have cut him in half. I mean at that point I still hadn't ruled out Kevlar.

I'd figured that if Tom were dead it would make the security job for Old Lady Brisbane that much easier. How was I supposed to know a chicken-foot and a braid of garlic would have been more useful than a gun.

It had occurred to me when Old Lady Brisbane handed me six grand in cash, that if she was worried about Tom coming back it was because she'd pissed the boy off, not because he was dead. Though, I guess when you think about it, killing a person has got to be one of the best ways to piss them off.

Mainly because I'd run out of options, I decided to pump some more lead into Easy Tom, thinking that it might knock him backward enough for me to squirm around him. And failing that, I figured on doing it just to be ornery.

Before I could squeeze the trigger, lights came on all over the house and I heard Old Lady Brisbane croaking from the top of the stairs, "Stop your roughhousing!" in the loudest hiss I'd ever heard.

Easy Tom turned toward the foyer, his voice gentle. "Momma?"

"So, you made it, eh Tom?"

Tom turned his back on me and stumbled to the foot of the stairs. "Why'd you have to go and kill me, Momma?"

"I can't holler down the stairs at you, Tom." Her voice sounded more like a bucket of bugs and broken glass being flattened by a steamroller than anything human. "You come up here, and bring that Danny Fairfield with you. Don't hurt him, Tommy. I need his help too. The Seven Highways have opened. It's time to go home."

Easy Tom came back for me, and though I tried to evade him, he managed to grab a handful of my shirt. I flew into the air like I didn't weigh a thing. When Tom held me up, I could see the tight, narrow bruises and rope burns on his neck. Hung.

I also saw five bullet holes in his chest that weren't bleeding, they were just oozing a little bit of stuff that looked like Vaseline.

"Jeezus, Easy," I said softly. "You really *are* dead, aren't you?"

Tom frowned and looked a little sad. "Yup. Dead." Then he laughed that scary laugh of his. "Kind of a kick, ain't it."

"Kinda kick I'd rather avoid for a while, Tom," I said.

He nodded. "Guess I ain't gonna kill you just yet, Danny. Probably won't kill you at all."

"Thanks, Easy Tom." I did my best to sound sincere, 'course I kept hold of the ten-millimeter too.

He carried me gently into the foyer where his machete was sticking out of the stairwell like a bad joke. He pried it out and up we went.

The floor was swaying under me as Easy Tom's shoulder dug into my stomach. The coppery scent of Stuckey's blood mixed with the overwhelming odor of ginseng had me nauseous and dizzy by the time we reached the top of the stairs.

"I'm in the study," Old Lady Brisbane said.

Tom set me down in front of a doorway that had been painted with a large, black crucifix that looked strange until I realized it was upside down.

Easy Tom opened the door by pushing my face into the center of the crucifix.

Lucky for me, the door wasn't locked. I stumbled into the study and looked around. The room was filled with pots of incense and candles made out of some kind of black wax. The smell of sickness and death caught me with a close-fisted punch in the throat. I retched and tried to stagger backward into the hall, but Easy Tom pushed me all the way into the room.

Old Lady Brisbane sat in her wheelchair in the dead center of the room, surrounded by a pentagram of blood. The walls and windows were covered with tapestries that smelled musty and old. They deadened the sounds and closed in the space until I started to feel the twitches of claustrophobia. As I stared at the tapestries, I could tell that they were ancient. They looked kind of like the stick figure drawings you see in pictures of Egyptian tombs, only they had a different feel to them. More ancient, somehow. The scenes on the wall hangings showed a group of people in robes dancing around an altar and killing animals. As I followed the story from tapestry to tapestry around the room, I realized that the rituals became more and more obscene until I had to jerk my head away and focus on something else.

The other thing that took up the rest of the space in the study was an ebony table with bronze trim and lion's clawfeet like the table downstairs. Stuckey the goat had been split open along the stomach, and his intestines were spread across the table. I had been wondering what Old Lady Brisbane had done with Stuckey, but I wasn't prepared for the sight of goat guts tacked to ebony-stained wood with large, bronze needles. Stuckey's head was facing me, his tongue sticking out to give me a raspberry.

I looked down at my shoes and started swallowing furiously to keep from throwing up.

Easy Tom ambled toward Brisbane and stopped at the edge of the pentagram.

"Can't come any farther, can you boy?" She cackled. Sounded like she was gargling glass shards.

"Why'd you have to go and have me killed, Momma?" Tom said again.

Brisbane narrowed her eyes and looked across the gulf at her son. "If there had been another way, boy, I surely would have done differently. I needed a hand'o'glory, Tommy, and the only murderer I knew was you."

Tom stood silently and let that sink in.

"Hannah Glory?" I asked. "You mean the porn star?" I figured if I was going to be in on this, I'd better find out just what the hell was going on.

Brisbane glowered across the pentagram. "Hand . . . of . . . Glory, you imbecile," she spoke slowly, with an angry little grunt after each pause. "The left hand of a freshly hung murderer is an artifact of incredible power in this reality. I had to have one." Brisbane cackled again. "I researched it carefully," she said, "and as far as I could tell there were no restrictions on turning the dead man into a zombie as well, so I did both."

"Okay," I said. "I have had enough of this. I don't believe in voodoo zombies walking the streets of Seattle. I don't believe in magic circles. I don't believe in any of this hokey pocus. What, exactly, in the fuck is going on here?"

"Don't believe your own eyes, boy?" she asked softly, gesturing in Easy Tom's direction.

She had me there, so rather than face facts, I changed the subject. "So, just supposing for an instant that I actually buy all this shit, and Tom here isn't just wearing a Kevlar body suit, then what is all this Hand-of-Glory-seven-roads-zombie stuff, and why is it coming down on my head now?"

"I read Stuckey," Old Lady Brisbane said.

Trying not to look at the gutted animal, I said, "You read a goat? Gimme a break! I don't read much, but I'm pretty sure I didn't see any goats hanging on the book rack the last time I went shopping."

Her face pinched with anger again. "You wanted an explanation, shut up and listen to it. We aren't from around here, Danny."

Like I couldn't have figured *that* out for myself.

"We come from a filthy and decadent reality where magic is the dominant force. Tom's father was a wicked man, and a very powerful one. You know how girls just go crazy for the dangerous type." She gave me a sly, sick smile that showed all the gaps between her remaining teeth. "Or maybe you don't. . . ."

I didn't know what to make of that comment, so I kept my mouth shut and stared at her.

"After a while, the terror and excitement wore thin. I started to get older while Tom's father stayed the same age. Eventually, I found his last four wives, stuffed and mounted in his *sanctum sanctorum*. I decided to head for the hills, so to speak, but there was nowhere on our world to hide from a wizard like Magda. I took the only option possible. We took the North Road and found ourselves here, my boy and I."

"So, just where is this place you're from? Sounds a lot like Tacoma to me."

"Don't get smart, boy. Our history is similar, but different. Where we come from, there isn't any science as such. All the fairy tales you've ever heard, all the ancient rituals—all of them are true if you know how to make them work. I have tapped forces in your world that have remained untouched for almost two thousand years.

"I consulted the entrails of a goat just as legend dictates, and I saw that Magda has weakened, and the seven roads have cleared. The way home is open, and we must return to Constantinople— the city you call Istanbul. Where we come from, the Turks were kicked all the way back into the Mediterranean." She turned to Easy Tom who had been standing silent during this whole conversation. "Tom, I want you to take that machete and chop off your left hand. I need it, and I need it soon."

I knew Tom was easy, but I didn't think he'd do it.

Wrong.

Tom knelt on the floor. He braced his left wrist on the ground and raised the blade.

"Waitaminnit, Tom!" I shouted.

Easy Tom stopped the downward arc of the blade with a look of relief on his dead face.

I looked at Brisbane and she looked at Easy Tom's left hand. "Tom!" she croaked, "Cut off your hand now!"

"Don't," I said. I know that I'm not the smartest person in the world—been told that since I was in the fourth grade—but every once in a while, someone opens the refrigerator door in my head and the light comes on.

Tom was doing everything he was told, as long as someone told him to do it and made it sound serious. "Throw the knife away, Tom. Don't cut off your hand if you don't want to."

Brisbane sighed. "I am afraid I just don't have time for this. The portal must open now."

The old crone pulled a wand out of her lap that looked like it was made of bones. She waved it at Tom, and I saw him stiffen. "Poor Tom ain't got much left," she said. "He has traces of his personality 'cause he's so fresh. When he rots a little more, he'll just wander around and kill things. I need his services before that."

She turned and waved the wand at me. "I need you too, Danny."

I felt a chill crawl through my bones and freeze me where I stood.

"You're making me waste my power, boy. I hate that." Old Lady Brisbane let her hand sink back into her lap. "Well, I would have had to ensorcell you sooner or later. I couldn't have afforded to have my virgin sacrifice fighting back at a crucial moment."

Brisbane turned to Easy Tom, who was still kneeling on the floor. "You know what you need to do, now, don't you boy?"

Tom nodded and raised the machete.

I tried to scream. Realizing I still held the H&K, I tried to raise the gun and shoot Tom just to distract him. I tried to run for my life. I couldn't do any of it. Brisbane had me pinned, and it actually began to sink in what she meant by virgin sacrifice.

I found out I could still sweat.

Tom brought the machete down and lopped off his left hand cleanly at the wrist. I expected a spray of . . . something, but Tom just leaked some goo on the floor. He didn't scream, or cry, or anything. He just put down the machete and picked up his left hand. He held it out to his mother, but she couldn't reach it through the pentagram. She was trapped in the wheelchair. "Okay, Tom, go ahead and throw it to me."

Easy Tom looked down at this left hand and back at his mother. "Momma . . ." he said.

"Do it boy. Don't make me show you that you can remember pain."

"I'm sorry, Momma, I can't."

Brisbane turned toward me and raised the wand again. "Danny, take the hand from Tom and pass it through the pentagram to me."

My body started to move without me telling it to. Fighting it with everything I had, which wasn't a lot, I walked over to Tom and took the hand from him.

The Hand of Glory was cold, and it felt like wax.

Shuddering, I walked through the pentagram to hand the hand to Old Lady Brisbane.

She pulled out a Zippo lighter and ignited the tips of Easy Tom's fingers. They lit with a green flame that sucked the heat out of the room. I stood beside her wheelchair and watched her make incantations over the Hand of Glory. Tom stood on the other side of the ring looking like a little boy who'd just had his ice cream cone taken away.

I thought there was more of Tom left inside his brain than Old Lady Brisbane did, but I wasn't in much of a position to do anything about it.

The old woman cackled and croaked her way through a terrible song with words that I could almost understand, and then she pulled out a long knife with a bent blade—like an old gurka fighting knife—and more of those tacky lion's claws on the hilt.

She told me to bend over.

"Momma," Easy Tom said. "Aren't you going to take me with you, even?"

Brisbane stopped for a moment and looked across the room at her son. She shook her head sadly and looked as though she wanted to say something but didn't want to interrupt her train of thought. Bent over her as I was, I could see one tear crawl across her pitted and shriveled cheek.

For the second time that night, someone opened the refrigerator door. When the light came on, I knew how come I could get through the pentagram and Tom couldn't. Tom believed the circle of Stuckey's blood would keep him at bay. I didn't believe it for a second.

Brisbane told me earlier that science was a kind of anti-magic. Well, I grabbed ahold of all the bad attitude and disbelief I could and concentrated on the two pieces of technology within sight.

The Heckler and Koch, and Brisbane's Zippo lighter.

With a strain that drenched my entire body in sweat, I said, "This is a whole load of shit."

Lack of belief and a Zippo turned out to be worth a whole lot more than a bunny foot from the local Pay-N-Save.

It worked.

I stood up and stepped back from Brisbane.

"My virgin!" she shrieked.

I took another step back and turned to Tom. "I gotta tell you, Tom. I'm pretty pissed for this whole virgin thing."

Tom shrugged.

Old Lady Brisbane jerked her head around and tried to stab me with the curved knife, but the wheelchair prevented her from making the turn.

As Brisbane struggled with the brake on her wheelchair, I lifted the ten-millimeter and looked her in the face. For the first time, I actually saw Old Lady Brisbane's eyes clearly. They glittered like a jackal's eyes, and there was fear behind them as well as power. Her hand scrabbled in her lap for the black wand. "I'll take you, Danny boy!"

Slowly, I pulled back the slide and chambered a round. With just as much deliberation, I pointed it at her head. "Drop the wand, or I'll read the future in the splatter marks your brain makes on the far wall."

"Momma," Easy Tom bellowed and charged the pentacle. When he hit the outer circle, his body lit up with sparks, and the smell of burning flesh filled the room. I wanted to tell him to stop, but I knew I couldn't afford to take my eyes off Old Lady Brisbane.

She pointed the wand at me. This close, I could see it really was the arm bone and hand of a human child. I shuddered, and then I felt the cold start to flow from the base of my skull.

"You can't shoot me, boy. You don't have the brass to do a woman."

"I ain't convinced you're a woman, you old bat." I fired off two quick shots and sprayed Old Lady Brisbane's skull all over Stuckey the Goat.

The windows blew open and there was a huge flash of light, and then there was a sensation like an elevator floor dropping out from under you.

And then there we were. Wherever the hell *that* was, exactly.

It was a clear night, with a full moon shining down on us standing in the middle of what looked like a pseudo Stonehenge, except that the formations all looked like upside-down crucifixes. Off in the distance, I could see the glow of a city with great rounded rooftops coning up into deadly-looking spikes.

The fabled city of Constantinople.

Well, one of them, anyway.

Tom says it's like the one from his childhood, but not quite perfect. The spell worked, just not all the way. I guess Old Lady Brisbane must not have been a virgin.

Well, that was going on a year ago. First thing I did was convince Tom not to turn me into cold cuts for offing his Mom, then we headed into town to get Tom patched up and preserved. We even managed to have his left hand reattached. The fingers were a little singed, but they seem to work fine.

Turns out on this side, being a zombie isn't really the end of the world. We just have to keep him cool until we can afford the resurrection.

And since resurrections cost some serious shekels, I decided to take a page from Old Lady Brisbane and use technology against a society that didn't have any. I found an artisan who could recreate bullets for the H&K, and with a dead guy for a bodyguard, we introduced Constantinople to the concept of organized crime.

Seems there are no spells that will stop an entirely unmagical bullet, and as far as we could figure out, no one has invented Kevlar either.

Now, I walk down the cobbled streets, and I worry about how long a two-bit con man can hang on as the most powerful crime lord on a different plane. Tom just smiles and says not to worry about it.

But then he would. He's easy.

SOULMATE

▼▼▼

MARVIN KAYE

POOR wittle me am lonely for a peepy soulmate.

When you catch yourself typing gibberish like that, it's definitely time to knock off writing for the day. Unfortunately, landlords find it hard to understand why the rent isn't forthcoming because you didn't receive your second-half royalty check. Sure, you might try sending this excuse: "Dear Landsire, I'm late with this month's rent because poor wittle me am lonely for a peepy soulmate. Peepy refers to the fact that I'm a telepath." Don't keep a copy. A relative might use it at your incompetency hearing.

Well, cash flow notwithstanding, I couldn't hook another painful image from the right side of my brain, so I typed Control-KX to save the file, waited for the monitor to return to plain vanilla CPM (yeah, yeah, I still work on a Kaypro—treat me to an IBM clone or else shut up), removed WordStar 3.3, replaced it with a backup disk and copied the day's work, "wittle peepy soulmate" and all. I semi-combed my hair, slid into my shoes (too frazzled to bother with socks) and tramped over to my other office, Matson's bar at 84th and Broadway.

Candy showed me ten thousand teeth in a smile that suggested I was a favored regular as she poured a double from a bottle of Ballantine whose level hadn't lowered since last time I stopped by. I sipped gratefully, eyes darting here and there in order to ignore my own tired reflection in the obligatory mirror behind the bar.

That's how I saw her: a petite brunette with heart-shaped face sitting in Siberia, a table in an alcove where you might die of old age before the waiter recalled that you still existed, which you wouldn't by the time he remembered. She was nursing a half-empty glass (I'm a pessimist) of cognac and a demitasse of espresso to clear her palate and she was writing with a ballpoint on a cocktail doily. Her arm rested on a pile of already-scrawled-on napkins.

A *fellow writer?* She looked up and smiled at me as if she'd heard. I grinned and thought about introducing myself. A *soulmate?*

"She's so weird," Candy the bartender said. "That's the third night in a row she's been in here doing that."

"What's weird?" I shrugged. "I get great ideas midway through my third Ballantine. Only I can't figure them out the next day. Just as well. Sober, I'd probably find out they're incredibly stupid."

"They can't be any dumber than *her* stuff," Candy argued. "Wait, let me show you—" She turned and rummaged through a drawer beneath the cash register. Candy rummages beautifully; I told her to take her time. She rooted through the drawer, then looked up, bewildered. "Natie, it's gone. I swear it was in here."

"What?"

"Something she wrote last night, craziest crap I ever read. She dropped it. I stuck it in here. Now it's gone . . . like magic."

"You remember any of it?"

She laughed. "Word-for-word—" But before she told me, I peeped her and read it. I turned to the woman, peeped her, too, then dealt six bucks on the counter and headed for the door.

"Hey, Natie, where you going?"

"Home," I told Candy.

Well, would you want to get involved with a witch who sends messages like "Poor wittle me am lonely for a peepy soulmate?"

You *would?* Me, I'd feel cheaper than a copy of Strunk & White.

STILL LIFE WITH CROCUS
▼▼▼

MARY A. TURZILLO

GLENNA savored the citric scent of spiced tea, a sweet scent, like revenge. A moist breeze from the window ruffled her manuscript as Harper dropped it on the breakfast nook table, knobby fingers uncurling in distaste.

"I don't like it," said Harper, "The plot is boring, trivial."

She snapped, "Infidelity? That's trivial? And a murder?"

Harper squinted at her. "A murder? Did I miss something? I thought the husband died in a car crash."

"I meant, accident." Glenna, thirty years a house-proud matron, scowled at the leaky crocus pot to hide her anger. Harper was dense. Still, she had taken years to find her gift, so perhaps her old writing buddy would never notice it.

"Maybe I'm wrong. Retype it, send it out." He wrapped a gnarled hand around the mug.

"No, I'm sure you're right. More tea before Tony comes home?"

"Thanks. And more banana bread." Harper stretched, his bony frame filling the breakfast nook, then folding like a broken umbrella. "You have talent. But in this one, the heroine discovers her husband cheating. He gets creamed when his car is broadsided by a truck. So what? That's not a plot, Glenna. No causality."

"Did you feel glad when the husband died?" Glenna plunked fragrant banana bread on Harper's plate.

"Sure. The way you twist villains, you'll sell."

"But not to religious markets."

"Look, I make pin money. Ekes out my disability check. But if I know editors, this won't sell."

"Gee, Harper. Some of us are just more talented."

"Don't be like that."

"Sorry. It shouldn't mean that much to me."

"Got to go." He stuffed the banana bread in his mouth, grabbed his cane, and left. From the window, Glenna watched him hobble away through the cool, bird-haunted spring air.

"Be that way," thought Glenna.

The leaking crocus pot had stained her manuscript. She pulled a tablet from her portfolio. A poem. A poem for her day of vengeance.

Half an hour later, she had a draft.

> *Crocus,*
> *You harbinger of*
> *spring's birth. No wonder,*
> *spring is harbinger of*
> *your death.*

Perhaps she would show it to Harper. But not to Tony. Tony was deaf to subtlety. He had referred to her, early in the marriage, as "wifey." Then, she had hoped he might improve. Now she knew better.

Almost five o'clock. She decided to see how things were progressing.

She dialed.

"Monticello Insurance." A new receptionist, whose voice Glenna didn't recognize.

"Hello, is Tony Charnwell there?"

"Mr. Charnwell left for the day. May I take a message?"

"What time did he leave?"

Long pause.

"Nobody seems to know. May I ask who's calling, please?"

"Nobody. Just a former customer." Yes, a customer. Tony had sold her a bill of goods for thirty years.

She made more tea. Her head started to ache, as it did when those other stories had started to really get going. Harper was such a fool. Didn't know what he was talking about. Thank God.

She drank the spiced tea slowly, then dialed a different number. Her hands shook. Maybe she needed a nip of something in the tea.

Five rings, six, seven. On the tenth ring, a syrupy contralto answered, blurred, unhinged, as if summoned out of an altered state.

"Hello?" the woman said.

Glenna said nothing.

"Hello? Listen, this isn't scaring me. I've called the phone company. You stop calling. You hear me? Just bleeding *stop*."

Glenna smiled slowly. Wouldn't be long now. Was that Tony's raspy breath in the background, or just imagination? Her hearing was very sharp. She was sure he was there. It was Wednesday afternoon, after all. Tony was a creature of habit.

After a long time, she hung up.

She gazed out the window at the neat yard, thinking of her years here with Tony. She had planted those tulips just beginning to send green dagger-tips through the topsoil. She had put in that lilac, that forsythia. Just twigs when she put them in, and look at them now. Damned if she'd move from this house just to get rid of Tony.

She sipped her cooling tea, bitter, grainy at the bottom with crumbs from the banana bread, and moved back to the breakfast nook. Any time now. She propped her elbows on the table and examined the crocus. Not thriving. The leaves seemed withered and rubbery, the petals browning on the edges. Not well at all, poor thing. She glanced at the poem and, in a sudden move, stuffed the legal tablet back into the portfolio with her story.

The crocus, unlike Tony, was innocent, but she had to prove

to herself that it was *her*, not just coincidence. Too bad. It was a nice crocus, except for being in a leaky pot. And that was hardly its fault.

The doorbell rang. "Tony," she whispered. After a moment, she pulled herself to her feet and answered it.

"Mrs. Charnwell?" the man said. He didn't look like her stereotype of a policeman. Too thin. She'd have to remember him for a story sometime. "Mrs. Charnwell, there's been an accident."

The policeman went on and on. She had trouble composing her face. What was she supposed to be thinking? How did one act? Of course, she had to pretend to be surprised.

To her astonishment, real tears sprang up. Real grief.

But she had been forced to it. If Tony had made a fuss and contested a divorce, maintained that the house had been his before they were married, where would she be? How would she survive? She would miss him keenly, though of course she still detested him. A tragedy, yes, but a necessary tragedy.

And if she had not caused it, why then that other thing, the Wednesday afternoons with the contralto-voiced woman, that would not be true. And she knew that *was* true.

The policeman stayed such a long time, talking, trying to explain. Uncomfortable with grief, he could not let it be.

Tony's car, he said, was undrivable. It had been towed. Did she want a ride someplace? To her children? No, there were no children, she answered. To friends? She almost laughed. Imagine throwing herself into Harper's arms, pleading for sympathy in her bereavement. Heaven forfend. Harper would be mortified.

After a long time, too long, the policeman allowed that she was comforted, and left.

She swirled the dregs in her teacup and filled it with water again. The microwave chimed softly; she drowned the fresh bag. Slowly, without haste, and without dwelling on what was not her fault in the eyes of the world, she settled again in the breakfast nook.

She would write more stories, of course. Maybe one about Harper, in which his arthritis was miraculously cured and he wrote a best-seller. Or one in which he was convicted of plagiarism and fell downstairs in the dark.

And maybe she would write one about herself, about winning a Newbery, a Pulitzer, or a Malice Domestic. She'd have to be careful, of course.

But then, who would suspect?

▼▼▼

The crocus had been lavender, veined with dark purple. No, Tony had not given it to her. She had bought it herself, at the grocery. Pretty thing. Healthy, an hour ago. Before the poem.

And now, like Tony, it was quite dead.

CHAVI CHORI
▼▼▼

JOHN KAIINE

I

SHE sat in her corner. With splintered bone for a needle, she stitched.

The cave was dank, stinking, but to these things, she paid no heed; for a spider wove its web about her heart, and with the passing of days, like the flailing beast in the trapper's net, it got tighter every slow second.

She sat in her corner, chewing the cooked meat. It was a lie that she ate them raw and that she sucked their bloody bones dry. Another tale about her, one more ghost story to scare the young at bedtime. The endless chorus down the years: "Don't ye get going near no woods, or Chavi Chori 'ill get ya' "

"If ye be naughty, old Chori 'ill skin ya alive' "

No, Never alive.

Never once alive.

Always dead. Still.

She knew the hated names they called her—"Old Annis," "Shadow Skinner," "Pup Scratcher," "The Angel of Maggots" . . .

she knew them all. And the name the Travellers gave her—"Chavi Chori," Child Stealer.

With a fine necklace of finger bones and incisors strung around her crooked neck, and cave wall lined by patterned patchwork of children's skins turned inside out, she knew only one name.

"Pain."

II

And here they sit, chewing on bones of part roast pig. The men drunken, seeped in sweat. The women cackling in their pissy fish stinks. Here this night the village gathered to the fire, making merry. Another forgotten festival: the slaying of a woods animal and ritualistic spillage of the blood about the roots of the rowan or oak as an offering to the gods for safeguard from spirits and the granting of good harvests in fields and their women's bellies.

Huddled together circling the watchfire, wreathed in furs and skins of beasts keeping August and its demons at bay, they gnaw on the baked black bread and finger their charms. Kingfisher skulls, pieces of coral, and Snakestone fossils. Talismans strung together as are the legends—passed down the line of blood and ale of their people. Tales told at fire, at any gathering, like tonight, when a voice is raised and the Old Man—the Keeper, neglected but revered—coughs clear his throat and begins with the yarn of the Fisherman . . .

There was once a Fisherman who was said by many to be the meanest, close-handed man in all the land. Now then, it were a Sun's Day, an' this Pinch-Gut Fisher took himself out to catch him some fish. The day slowed by till he caught him only one fish. Some say it were Mackerel, others say Salmon, a biggun anyways. He took it back to his hovel an' he gave it to his wife, telling her—"Use whole fish, bones, skin, eyes, the lot." Now she, mithed with her miserly hubby, did just that. Using the whole fish, bones, skin, eyes an' all, crunching the lot up, she baked him cakes of fish, an' served it up as his feed. Well, he gozzled it all down, he did, not wasting a crumb. She laughed. She'd gotten her own back on him after all them long years of his stinginess an' greed. The only thing he'd ever given her was a son, an' a daft one at that.

After his feed, he asked her what she had done with the bones an' rest of fish. Had she dried them out for use as needles or tools? Had she smoothed out the skin an' fish eyes for a cure-all? But like a Fool, she just grinned. Later that night, when moon was full an' tide high, that mingy Fisherman fell on his back moaning of an ache in his belly, an' his wife, poor woman, fearing she had done 'im in, just didn't know what to do.

He cried, "A Thing be in me, be living in me!"

Well, she took to her heels, ran away, blathering that "The Devil had got 'im, an' were coming back for 'er!"

Later, she returned with her son, found the Fisher dead as wood with a fish head popping out his mouth. Now, the son, he was slow, but had the Knowing, an' he pulled it out, an' there was more of that fish, a whole body, just aflipping an' aflapping about. Now the Mother, she was screaming like a Banshee on heat, saying, "I've killed 'im'" Well, the boy, 'cos he had the Knowing, he picked the fish up an' ran with it all the way to sea, an' there, he throws it back in, watched it swim away.

When he got back to hovel, his Ma was whining, mad. An' he saw that she stood in a puddle of water. Mind, this much is true, he bent down to look at the water, an' to see where it came from, an' from his father's mouth it came. Spilling out. Water ev'rywhere, water. Fresh sea salt water.

III

A young girl screams with the end of the fable. The men, bawdy in their sottishness, laugh and jeer, calling her "Soft Heart" and "Lamb Head" but not one of them, for all their bravado, did not invoke the unspoken benediction and cross himself inwardly.

The Wood Gods stir. A man with a magpie's head shifts, restless, eternal. The girl's scream woke not only the spirits but the village young as well. Teary eyed and sleepy, wanting Mama and wanting to know what was wrong, here they all come. Skinny moths to the flame. Everyone laughs, and the fathers drunk with the brew and maleness hoist up their sons to thrones of knees to let them sip on night ale—leaving the mothers to care only for daughters. And fathers and sons all with proud swagger call for a tale.

"Tell us o' the Beast o' Bones."

"Tell us o' Chavi Chori."

"Aye, tell us o' the Chori."

Now some fell silent. Others wept. And the Story Teller stared in the fire, gobbed, and began—

IV

The sleeproom was a chamber with platform upraised in its center. This is where they were, the family. Huddled under goatskins and patchwork rags. Four boys, two girls, a cousin, and Ma an' Da. Nine grubby shadows. But Ma an' Da stir, titter.

And Ma an' Da are humping, moaning. Groaning.

And in the shadows, in the very heartbeat of the dark, lurks Chavi Chori.

He can't keep stiff, the father. Too much ale. Bent, like a

tree in the wind. The woman at least is thankful of his attentions. Better than any fire, this warmth. And if the mother weren't looking at her man's member, coaxing it with thumb, forefinger, then she would have seen Chavi Chori, child stealer, Angel of Maggots, haunting the bedside of her young, and could have yanked in her youngest girl's foot, sticking out under the nest of furs. But the mother didn't see, just went on jerking, and the beastie came closer, closer still.

The eldest boy woke, saw the child stealer take firm his sister's ankle. Saw too the impossibly long, long arm, saw the other blue-gray hand moving in, gently stroking the sleeping girl's foot. He couldn't scream—just relinquish sanity and stare, chilled.

Chavi Chori caressed, petted the little girl's sole, pawed it gentle in the mournful dark, brushing it to a slight tickle, continuing till the girl stirred, began giggling. The paring couple heaved, shoved away, aware of the giggle, used to it, but aware also, deep within, of a fear older than old, of what was happening and the *true* meaning of this childish laughter. And deeper still within, the thought of one less mouth to feed and another in the making.

Impotent with fear and the dark, deep, deeper within her.

All the brothers and the sister, awake now, all watching. Dumbstruck.

Only the cousin sleeps. Safe—this one. Strong with the strength of the outsider. And the giggle of the girl, now a whimper. The tickling game no longer funny, she cannot catch her breath. Sucking in the warm air, heaving and choking as the Skinner of Shadows continues. Continues with her death-strokes.

The Ma an' Pa, snorting and huffing still, as laughter is replaced by sobs, hurt and pain. The rankle caress is no more than claws scratching, grating away raw skin. Blood sniffling out between child toes.

Four boys and one girl watch their sister dying. Drowning. In asphyxia. She had laughed so much, she had bust a gut. Her tiny gut and lungs, broken. Now the final thin whisper of air leaves her swollen body—and for requiem, a shout of carnal jubilation, like a horse breaking wind. And a sickly thump, as the carcass is dragged, raw-foot-first from the bed. And the dead head hitting the floor.

The Angel of Maggots draws into night, a dog with sack of bones, and in the morning, the mother's quick regret, and their seven tears cried, but soon forgotten.

V

Some had heard the tale before, and were still frozen by it. Mothers snatched up their young, hurried them off to bed again. Watchflames would burn bright tonight.

The menfolk, shamed of face but bemused, keep their places at the fire with the drink to prattle and chatter and lie with stories of the Pup Scratcher, Chavi Chori.

Ale loud, a young man speaks up, a tale heard from travelers: "There was this rich house, satin on the floors, goose feathers in the pillows an' in the nursery, there was a little boy an' the Beast, the Chori. Now, the Devil, she wants some fun. So she whips out a feather from the pillow an' starts titillating the boy's nose with it. Well, the young fella, he wants to sneeze, but he can't, an' he gets to choking, an' breathing in's all he can do. 'til he's all bloated, an' something goes *snap* in his head, an' out of his nose comes all this blood an' snot an' bits of brain an' . . ." A boot, thrown, hits him hard on the head. His audience had not favored his yarn, thinking it too much like the previous one. However, much fun was gotten from the boot and its target. The young man stifles back tears and swigs fast down his ale. Strong still. When the Keeper quietens all with a word—

"Milk."

VI

Far aways back, when old was young, before gods had names, the Chori haunted this place. My mother's mother told me of a poor blind woman—cursed she was for looking at another's man—an' she were with *his* child, an' the child were born all weak an' scrawny. Now then, the sightless Mama gets to feeding the bairn at the breast. An' the little babe, it were suckling her one night, one ice cold night, when Old Annis, the Maggoty Angel, Chavi Chori did poke 'er head 'round the door. An' the eyeless woman could only hear the wet pawing of the beastie, but thinking it to be a cat or dog, she paid no heed. An' the beastie— the bastard beastie—it held the baby's face into its mother's breast, an' the milk were going all over, down poor little bugger's mouth, up its nose, in its eyes. It were drowning.

The bitch drowned the nipper in its own mother's milk.

An' the no-eye, she were singing a melancholy about another man, couldn't hear, couldn't see. By Gods, she didn't know.

Anyways, she woke in morning, found child all cold, stiff. Some says as she went mad, others, that she saw again, just long enough to take up meat blade an' hack 'er own head off!

VII

A glug of ale and the final word: " 'Tis why, whenever there's a blind one born, we kills it straight off, strangles it with its own cord an' bury it with no marker."

The men were afraid now, for they knew of this custom, but did not know why. And all around, unmarked mounds of earth with eyeless bundles in, not knowing they were dead, unable to see their own ruin.

A wood's spirit, a tawny owl, swoops and screeches, catching a night mouse. Its cry unnerves the young man of the sneezing tale, sends him squealing toward his hut—the arse hanging out of his britches and his ale left to spill into an unmarked mound which was his seat.

They find this funny, and use their laughter like fire, to keep the fear away.

Draining last swigs, they belch and fart out the wind and foul smells, deciding to end their evening on this cheery act.

Sod and kindling are thrown upon the fire, securing its warmth and light for another night, when a murmur erupts, and more scared laughter. A story, though, more of an afterthought: A joke about a child, a boy who was fond of wanking, who was told by the Holy Man that, "If he kept on, his piece would fall off!" So anyway, the boy stops awhiles, but couldn't hold out any longer, 'til in bed one night, he's wanking away, and . . . Op! Off it *comes* in his hand. . . .

Silence, and a moment for eyes to meet, for heads to nod at recognition of the word play. "Ha ha ha," from every grubby mouth.

Their laughter like fire: Loud, bright. Too harsh.

And all around. . . .

VIII

Dark. Dark like lung blood. And in this darkness, a child, a boy. Taka.

And Taka is asleep, all snugged up, safe in his uncle's hut. The boy's mother was killed a week since. Eaten by wolves. Her brother, Bal, took the lad in, gave him food, shelter. A chance.

And Uncle Bal is safe enough, with heavy head beneath blanket of rag, thinking twice before tossing off, and keeping his stinking feet well under the bedclothes. He toys with thoughts of having some "sport" with the young boy to let him earn his keep. Some warmth at least. But there would be time enough for that later. Hard, drunk, he sleeps.

Taka dreams of his mother again. Her kisses and her big, blue eyes. He wakes, for there she was, at the bedside. Through teary eyes he sees only her face—her beautiful face. Smiling, she bends to kiss him on the mouth. It is warm, the kiss, pleasant as July. So pleasing that little Taka sighs—but that is all it takes, for the beautiful blue-eyed mother to close her mouth softly around her son's, and with a breath as soft as fleece and as tender as youth exhale. Taka struggles, but the blowing in his mouth sings to him. Sings, "I weren't eaten by no wolves, 'ere I am, can't ya see me?" Cool air fills the lad's lungs. Inflates him like a blown pig-bladder. The kiss of his dead mother puffs his insides out.

Taka, the blood bubble, burst.

Dead, but happy, Taka.

Chavi Chori was no longer the mother. She had faded, as had the child's insides. Cradling the infant, she takes him from the hut out into fire-brave night. She is the color of cold sorrows, the azure of years, the gray of regrets. She is the color of night: "Denial."

IX

Old Whore—Night—had picked off her scabs, fingers herself now with moonbeams and starlight. Spills her flavid drops of bad to the Below. To the seas these vile juices fall, causing waves and beasts to crash upon night-fishers and their catch. Spilling into villages, waking peasants with demon dreams of a stolen youngster killed by a mother's kiss. Spilling too into woody lands, where they send a shadow skittering 'tween paths—a shade with thieved corpsy sibling.

The Old Whore Night is too enriched in her luxurious coming to spy the Angel of Maggots—the blue as sin Chavi Chori—sloping to her hidden hole with shame and child remains.

Tidal waves and tempests. The slut Night comes: a climax of hurricanes, of avalanche. Wave after wave of darkness, destruction.

The Whore Night comes.

And after the storm, a thin shower of rain and rats' blood.

Raining, raining, raining.

The rain of the Whore Night, coming down.

X

Through rents in loose cave walling came the slender parade of sunlight. And there the congealed curd of the boy—the skinned flesh, splayed out on a wooden frame. And the grieving Chori, fast awake in her corner.

Remnants of rain piddle in, drip drops of teary shapes, some mourning at least.

The blood on her hands (claws) is the only memory she needs. There was a village, a storm, rain and the arrival at the cave: The boy was peeled like a fruit, skin unyoked from the body, and prepared, cleansed, a mewled prayer said half out loud. Next, sleep, and the almost repose of the Maggot Angel. Awake now, and this—the raw carcass lying on a slab, the shroud of skin outstretched upon the frame.

And the Map near complete.

And her—the bent blue body, the dry tearful eyes, that glimpse the carrion below. The same old hate she is powerless against or with. Unable. She rises, stretches, a creaking sound, and the taking up of the cleaver, with a sigh, brought sharp down, once, twice, ten times, chopping up the pared, gorish shape.

And the Map near complete. . . .

Into the cooking pot the hacked bits go, bobbing about like grisly ducks. She lifts the caldron with ease, hooking it over the ardent hearth—for this is her meat breakfast, her brunch of bones and wretched high tea. Nothing else can she eat, save the innards of the young.

She cries without tears, the Shadow Skinner, moving as one with misery from the pot to the Map.

The Map. Seventy, nearer eighty, stolen children's skins turned inside out, making a fleshy patterned mosaic, stitched together by hair with a sharpened finger bone. Skins marked by God's hand with designs and vestiges, drawn out taut upon mucid cave wall.

The Map. A chart in a score of parts, painted upon the insides of little children's skins. It shows paths, hamlets, countries, seas, and beyond. Showing the way to true happiness. Peace.

Shows the way to Hell.

The Map. Five decades of toil, collecting only the skins carrying the internal engravings and directions, selecting, at the age of five or six, the chosen child. For this age it must be. Any younger and the inner painted design is not yet *prepared*, all too restrained, quashed together. Any older than six, and the tracings are stretched, snapped, unintelligible. Useless.

She has returned to her cave on hated occasions with a child, all stiff and less of life, and on disrobing the rashers of pink wrapping, has discovered not a portion of the Map as always, but Biblical writings from the book of Ezekiel or Isaiah. This was God's jest.

A cruel joke.

A scant number of "pieces" are still missing from the Map. Mostly segments of the edge, although not needed, only showing a line or trace of hill or coastline. One central section is not yet in position, not yet tacked up with the others. Still drying from last night, still being stretched into shape.

Strange, one sheet of the chart, a singular reverse boy skin, with a hole in its middle-most. A hole worn away by too much self abuse.

The Map.

She runs a talonious paw smooth along the inky blue line of a river, follows its penned route through hills and valleys. Is as one with its every contour, its every fold and line. As surprising as a lover, as familiar as the shadows.

This is *her* child. Her life and death.

Rain fragments in, pissing down walls of filth, seeping under the Map, staining its joints, loosening mane stitching.

Blue as sin, the Witch, tracing paw on loving blue line, transcending to its mental vista, following on into stranger territories, finding herself in the darkness before dawn, splashing in dew and small suntides, finds herself traveling the sketched roads, beyond the woods and the villages of ignorance, discovering mountains of ice and cities of lake. Empires of bone and cathedrals of blood. Moving on through crooked paths of charnel houses, asylums and great deserts where the seas meet, freeze and turn to chalk white dusts. She travels the wilderness where only the black bears roam. On through battlefields where the Magician, Death, juggles with life. Through lands like abattoirs, to palaces of shadow. And finally, through years of long searching, arriving and descending into a strange, new land, finding peace, tranquility.

A world, warming.

Finding a carved open doorway, and flute song, calling her inward, down.

Calling to Old Annis, beckoning with words like waves, crashing upon the rockface of joy, like the sea and its soft waters meeting . . . opening wave after wave, calling, with happy gullish voices all around.

Calling . . .

Hot waves from the boiling pot hiss and spill over into the sizzling hearthstone, scalding the cook flame. Steam fizzing up.

She is caressing the Map still, then sees smoke and a return to savage reality. Boy meat slopping in the pot, the carving, skinning

implements strewn upon the deck, the tiny tides of blood and
boiled water. Childy scalp pigtail decoration. The lifetime's gathering of the Map, and the question, "What scares Fear?" Life.
Life scares Fear, scares the Maggoty Angel, has made her sane
with the madness of it all, and her sanity rages now, howling,
tearing down the chart of skins, ripping through its weaved, fleshy
cloth. Foaming, snarling, she razes the caldron, scatters boy stew.
She claws with fury the dire trimming of finger bone necklet,
slams it under clubbed foot. Screaming, tearing at her own blue
self, cutting deep, but swiftly healing, for she cannot die, only
one way out. The doorway into waves. Hell.

Hopeless, useless. On knees now, in blood ripple water, rend-
ing the rag of skin and frock of slops. But no tears, for tears, like
death, are not a part of her design.

God's jest. . . .

Through rents in loose cave walling, came the slender parade
of sunlight. She sits, a torn heap, pressed to wet corner, cradling
Map of tattooed child skins, as if it lived, breathed. Suckled.

She sits in the corner, chewing the cooked meat, and she
knows the names they call her, knows too, the stories and fables.
But they are wrong, never once drowning in milk, or death by
sneezing. Just bad lies told by scared men.

And what scares Fear?

XI

"Nothing scares me!" says the boy with the blunted dagger.

"That's my son. Afraid of no thing or no man, be it live or
dead."

The traveling aristocrats have their motley fool dance and
weave about the boy as a monster, or ghost. The Baron's son
thrusts and parries with his father's gift: a golden blade, jewel-

handled, worn down at its point. The boy was used to gifts, had many toys and clockwork fancies. Wants for nothing today, as like any day, as he and his family journey through the forest en route to the other land.

"That's my son." The corpulent Baron halts the procession of carriages, wagons, calls the servants and other overdressed relations around, lifts his boy from the grass and green, to hold him aloft by the waist, above his head. Giggling, the child raises his smooth knife like the headman's axe. The slaves trail behind, stop and wonder what's happening now. The food wagons are at a standstill, slopping out the grub for the Gorbelly Baron. Dog handlers draw around, whistling over the wolf-hounds.

All about, encircled. The jovial Baron, big of heart and head, silences the lot; his bored, pearled wife, his sister's serfs, watch him clamber up the wagon. The buffoon in patches blows a mock horn for attention, as the fat bastard Baron slobbers out his glee-proud words.

"This is my son, he is afraid of no thing, or no man, no ghost or goblin, no assassin's dagger. He is worth ten of any of you. And I'd gladly kill anyone of you to safeguard his life. You remember that. He will sit in my seat one day, will wed a princess, will sire fine sons, and all this land will be his. He is my son, the son of my loins and heart, and as strong as that can make him. Be sure to serve him well. One slip—beware. Bruise his foot, and I'll flay your back. And you, woman"—he indicates the young wife—"you be his servant too. He is born to rule, and you, all of you, are here only to obey.

"Long life to my son!"

There is no dissent. Only silence. The Fool farts and scratches at himself, but nobody chooses to see or hear. Only the happy boy wants his attentions now, wanting one more game.

All smiles, the Fool. And all disgust.

The trail continues, the boy and patchwork flunky, darting in and out of the carriages' path. The boy and the beast, playing at ghosts.

Downwind, and the scents are carried. The odor of boy skin, and insides.

Chavi Chori bathes in the be-dewed, clear stream, abluting her gibbous blue self, and sniffs suddenly, snuffles at the air. For the breeze has sent her downwind, an ending.

She tugs on her slops, awkward, crouches low. Can smell a drawn fortress and an inky mausoleum of stone, can smell the flesh outstretched, joined with the rest.

The breeze has sent her an end. A fraction of the Map, showing a doorway, leading *down*.

She can smell the sickly Fool and his malicious fashion. A blunted dagger and hunting dogs. They are approaching, getting nearer.

Leading down. . . .

She can smell the sea.

SOURHEART
▼▼▼

NINA KIRIKI HOFFMAN

EDMUND parked the rattletrap Volvo station wagon beside a narrow road in the Sierra Nevada foothills and turned off the engine. Westering sun reddened the iron-pink earth of the road cut, and the air out his open window smelled of pine.

Something up the slope among the evergreens had tugged at the place near his heart, his listening spot. In recent years, he had attained the third stage in his witchhood. The first stage, when he became a witch suddenly at sixteen, had been denial and disbelief; during the second stage, which set in soon afterward and lasted for years, he had asked how can I use this? In the third stage, he asked how can this use me?

The answer lay in listening. When he listened to the fainter cues beyond his own desires, he heard promptings. Following them led him in strange directions.

He touched the cloudy quartz globe on the dashboard, felt vibration in his fingertips. He held out his hand above the seed pods, dried leaves, pine needles, and feathers that made his dashboard into an altar. An owl feather drifted up to touch his palm, then settled down among the others—crow, towhee, duck, jay, eagle, goose—some illegal to own, all gifts the ground had offered him as he walked through wildernesses.

Owl. Night energy, hunting energy. What he had wanted was green energy, a place to connect with Earth, cleanse the stains of contact with too many people and too many dark thoughts. Cities made him edgy, but sometimes the trail led him there. This time he had gone for his own reasons, to touch bases with his younger sister Mary, her husband, and her three children. They lived in San Francisco. He had spent two months reminding himself what human contact was like, and much of it had strengthened him, but some of it had made him feel strange and ungrounded. He was ready for a mental shift.

Owl. Here was the offer of shared energy, but the energy was restless and dark.

He sat back and closed his eyes, resting his hands in his lap. He drew in breath, held it, released it slowly. "I give up what my will is; I accept what you offer," he muttered three times, and opened his eyes.

He rolled the window shut, leaned over and pushed down the button locks on all the other doors, and climbed out of the car, locking the driver-side door behind him. The city influence was still strong within him. He opened the tailgate and picked through a jumble of wrack until he found his favorite dowsing rod, then locked the back door and put the car keys inside the back bumper.

Sitting on ground matted with fallen pine needles, he stroked the dowsing rod, murmuring to it, "Please work with me; lead me where it is right for me to go; let us discover whatever waits for us here."

The rod pulled at his hands, and he answered the pull, rising and wandering under the pines, breathing in the scent of warm needles and pine sap, aromatic in the late afternoon sun's heat, each step of his moccasins crushing and kicking up the spice of the fallen. Following the dowsing rod's pull, he climbed up a rocky escarpment and entered a thick stand of Ponderosa pines and Douglas firs. At the edge of a clearing surrounded by a ring of rocks, the tip of the rod dipped groundward.

A mixture of strange energies whispered to him from the clearing. In its center blackened stones ringed a firepit; the scent of wood transformed by burning lingered in the air, blending with a rank human smell and the echo of vanished drumbeats.

Edmund stepped where the rod pointed, a place less walked on than any other spot in the clearing. At first he felt nothing from the Earth. He knelt, setting the rod aside, and pushed his fingers through the pine needles and mold into the rich soil below. I am here, he thought, I reach for you, I release you, I welcome you.

For a long moment he felt stillness, and wondered if he had misread the pull of his dowsing rod. Then he felt a sensation like the tearing of a dried leaf, and a core of energy flowed up from the Earth, green and welcoming as a cool spring on a hot day.

Edmund slipped out of his shoes and socks and worked his toes down under the layer of pine needles, then stood silent, opening himself to the green.

"Welcome," he whispered, "welcome into me, welcome through me, welcome as you leave me; I offer you these stains, I offer you what you want from me, I thank you for connecting me with the Lady." Green washed through him like warm water.

"Hey!"

So deep he was, feeling the green, opening to it, feeling it scrub away the oily psychic dirt, that he did not hear the woman's voice at first.

"Hey! Hey, what are you doing on my property?"

When she poked him with the business end of a rifle, he felt it, and brought his awareness up into his head, looking out of his eyes. Hunting energy, owl energy. He had known the green was not the only thing he would find on this mountain.

"What are you doing here? Think I don't know about you all, all you stupid men, sneaking up here, invading my space, taking without asking, think I won't do anything about it, like the other women you've known all your lives? You got another think coming!" She prodded him with her rifle. "Arms up, high!"

He lifted his arms, stretching them as high as he could. Sky energy, I salute you. The green energy was still flowing through him; he felt cleansed. Gently, with thanks, he disengaged.

He looked at the woman in front of him. She was much shorter than his own six foot three. The squint lines at the edges of her gray eyes were graven deep as the cracks in sun-baked mud. Winter-gray strands wound among the glossy brown of her tightly braided hair. Her small frame was lost in a layering of light blue workshirt, black T-shirt, green sweater tied by the arms around her waist, baggy jeans with frayed cuffs that ended above the toes of worn hiking boots.

She squinted at him. "Trying to figure out what you can get from me, bastard? Nothing. Nothing. I'm through giving anything to self-involved idiots like you."

He stretched his fingers to the sky, curled them, flexed them, waiting for the next direction.

"I know what you call me. Witch. Witch. I know you have your stupid quests. That idiot guru of yours sends you up here to face me. Make me stand for your hateful mother. Think you accomplish something coming up on my mountain, stealing a stick or a stone from me for some kind of trophy, go off and display it to your little group of yuppie warrior friends. Knew if I waited long enough I'd catch one of you bastards alone."

"People come hunting on your land without your permission?" he said.

She straightened when she heard his voice. Most people did. His best friend John had told him years ago that there was music in his voice, though Edmund couldn't hear it himself. She swallowed. "Not people," she said, after a moment. "Men."

"Men come on your land," he said. The well of green beneath his feet flowed full, inviting. He glanced around the clearing, realized that the stones around its edge had been placed there, that this was a place where Earth energy and human intention had met for centuries. Below the whisper of recent drumbeats and chants were older communions.

"I didn't know this was a private place," he said. "I'm sorry. Is there any way I can repay you?"

Her lips pinched, and she took a step back. "Think you're pretty cute, don't you?"

He smiled at her, turning his hands above his head, sky energy caressing his palms.

"What have you got you could give me?"

"Labor."

"What sort of work do you do?"

"Hand work, wood work, craft work, garden work," he said.

"Cooking? Cleaning? Scrubbing?" At last she smiled.

"Sure," he said, wondering if owl energy could be disarmed by housework.

"That'd be a sight," she said. "Might be payment. You have any weapons?"

He glanced down at himself. He wore a loose white cotton shirt; the tan pants were tighter and had no pockets. "I have a stick," he said, nodding toward his dowsing rod, which lay next to his moccasins and socks. An oak tree had given it to him.

"A stick," she said. Keeping the gun aimed toward him, she edged around and knelt to pick up the dowsing rod. "Ouch!" She shook her hand, leaving the rod on the ground. "That thing boobytrapped?"

"I don't know," he said, staring at the rod.

"It stung."

He rubbed his hands together over his head, then lowered his arms. "Let me look," he said, holding out a hand to her.

"Hey! Get those hands up!" She gripped the rifle with both hands.

He raised his arms again.

"Start walking." She gestured toward a thin trail on the other side of the clearing.

Edmund glanced at his moccasins, then decided he was better off without barriers between himself and the Earth. He walked.

▼▼▼

Her house backed against a slope, rocks fitted together and cemented with mud mixed with moss, the roof overlaid with branches and lichens and melting into the Earth. A stovepipe poked up from the roof. Two small dark windows showed nothing of the interior. The plank door between them bore a shiny padlock. She lowered her rifle and wrestled the lock open, then cast him a dark look. "Never used to have to lock up."

He thought of locking his car before he came up the mountain. City energy.

"You better not take anything from me."

He said, "Nothing you don't give me."

"Ha!" Her voice was bitter. She stood on the threshold of her house, staring at him from under her brows for a while. "Okay," she said at last, "you can put your arms down. But don't you try anything. I'm not afraid to hurt you."

"I understand." He didn't understand. He had never met anyone as angry as she was. He didn't spend very much time with people, though. Maybe there were a lot like her and he just hadn't run into them yet.

"The dishes are over there," she said, pointing inside the house. "Think you can get them clean?"

He slipped past her into a close darkness that smelled of fire and sweat and decaying food.

When his eyes adjusted he saw piles of soiled ceramic and tin dishes stacked on a counter beside a large enameled basin.

"I purely hate doing dishes," said the woman.

He went to the counter. The water in the basin bore a soap scum on its surface. He dipped in a finger. The water was cold and greasy. He looked around, spotted a woodstove with a scorch-bottomed enameled coffeepot and a small pan on it. The stove was cold too. He opened it and found a glut of ashes with a few charred sticks of stovewood on top.

He glanced around the house. What light there was came from the open door and the two small windows. A bed stood against the back wall, a frame with strips of leather nailed across it, dark blankets thrown over it, a clutter of rags scattered across the floor near it. A wooden table and a chair stood below one of the windows, the table bearing a sketchbook, some colored pencils, and books stacked beside an unlit kerosene lamp. Shelves stood against other walls, cluttered with dark things. Herbs hung from the eaves. A breath of cold damp air moved past him; he looked toward its source and realized a rug on the back wall concealed a passage deeper into the mountain.

On the back wall opposite the door, where the late light fell full upon it, a black paper circle hung, with a heart the green of sour apples in it. Against the green glinted two small half-moons of gold. Of all the things in the room, this green heart gave off the most energy, a haze of bitter anger.

Biting his lip, Edmund opened to the other energies here, and what he felt was: under siege.

"May I start here?" he said, touching the stove.

"Sure," she said, grinning. Still hugging her rifle, she went and sat on the bed, which produced a symphony of squeaks. "Just go right ahead."

"Is there a tool?"

"You got your hands, don't you?"

He looked at her a moment, then took his shirt off and laid it on the ground below the stove. Gently he pried the ashes and the skeletons of former fires out of the stove and onto his shirt, sinking a little under the surface of life so he could talk with the ashes, ask them not to jump up in clouds, listen to their tales of the wood they once had been, reassure them that they could return to soil and rise as wood again. The stove's iron spoke with him too, saying it would give up these ashes if he promised it new ones; it wanted a fire in its belly.

Something cold poked his spine. He surfaced, looked up.

"You tetched?" said the woman.

"What?"

"There's nothing left in the stove. Darned if I know how you did it, but it's washday clean inside; won't do you any good to keep rubbing at it."

"Oh," he said. The ashes lay in a compact heap on his shirt, and the stove's interior shone. His hands were smudged and gray.

"So—you tetched?"

Tetched. Touched. He thought of the touches he had learned to know, the caressings of energies, the gentle guidance from powers he was trying to tune in to better.

Was he touched? He nodded yes.

She sat down cross-legged on the floor a little way away, the rifle across her legs. "You aren't like my ex, are you?" She glanced up at the green heart on the wall. She fed a thin flame of anger to the heart, a sort of talismanic worship he had seen before. He realized that the gold moons were the halves of a wedding ring. She looked back at him, coming out of her brief trance. "One of those yuppie weekend warriors?"

He frowned. "I don't know what that means."

"That get out in my woods and drum and howl at the moon and yell about their warrior forefathers and their manhood and scamper around on all fours naked and painted up?"

"What?" he said, trying to imagine it, and, imagining it, unable to suppress a smile.

"You're just some fool wandered up here."

"I didn't know it was your place."

She sighed. "And all you wanted to do was stand in the fire circle like a fence post?"

"Mm-hmm."

"Nobody sent you up here to face the great Woods Witch and conquer her goddess power and her mother power and her lover power and steal the key from her to prove you're ready to go on the manhood quest?"

"Conquer?" he said.

"That's what they say. Sometimes I sneak up at night and listen."

He gathered the edges of his shirt and lifted. The ashes stayed in a neat pile. He rose. "My rod brought me here."

"What?" She sprang to her feet. "Your so-called magic wand?" She stared at his crotch, her face sour.

He laughed. "My stick, the one we left in the circle."

"A stick? A forked stick. I don't get it."

He walked out of the house, wandered to a stand of trees, knelt and spread the ashes among the pine needles. Thanks for living and dying and changing, he thought, patting the soft gray. He put his smudged shirt back on.

She had followed him. "I don't get it," she repeated.

"A dowsing rod," he said.

"Like they use to find water or oil?"

"Right." He dusted off his hands and stood. "Do you have a wood pile?" He had seen a small pile of kindling and shavings near the stove, but no logs.

"This way," she said, pointing with her rifle to a place behind her house. He followed her past a screen of trees and found a clearing she used for a wood lot, with a chopping block in the center, and stove wood piled neat between two trees, half hidden under a green-gray tarp. He gathered armfuls of wood and headed back inside.

He laid a fire in the stove, then touched the wood and invited fire to feast, just as she said, "The matches are—" and stopped. "How'd you do that?"

He smiled and closed the stove, adjusting the vent in the door to draw air. The coffeepot was empty. He took it off the stove.

"Water?" he said, lifting his eyebrows. He got the basin from the counter.

She licked her lip. Her brow furrowed. Her eyes shifted toward the rug covering the passage, then back.

Water had whispered to him on that quick breath of breeze from the mountain's heart, but he could tell she wanted to keep her spring a secret. He said, "I'll use this."

"But that's dirty."

He carried the basin outside and talked to what was in it. Sitting on a space of packed earth where nothing grew, he thought, *Everything that is not water, please come out.* He tipped the basin slightly and watched as soap scum and grime gathered along the lower edge. *Water, please stay.* He tipped a little further and the impurities poured out. *Thanks. Blessings.*

He took the basin back inside, poured as much water into the coffeepot as it could hold, and set it on the stove to warm. The rest he left in the basin. "Do you have a trash can?"

She was staring at him. She had watched him playing with the dishpan, had seen something happen that she didn't understand.

"A waste basket?" he tried.

After a moment she shook her head and brought him a brown paper grocery sack. He sat on the floor with a stack of dirty dishes in front of him and pried what caked-on food he could off them and into the bag. The light coming in the door and windows dimmed as night gathered. The woman lighted the kerosene lantern, then brought her chair closer to the stove.

When at last the water on the stove steamed, Edmund poured it into the cool water in the basin, mixing in soap flakes she offered him. He washed dishes. She sat in her chair and watched.

When he had finished, having stacked the drying dishes into a braided tower that left most of their surfaces open to air, he turned to her and said, "What else can I do for you?"

"I think that's plenty," she said. In the cool darkness the lamplight touched her hair, leaving her face in shadow.

"Are you sure?" He opened to the energies, asking if he had accomplished everything he had been sent up the mountain to do.

A scent came in the open door. A rank human scent, an aura of city wildness.

"Look," said the woman, "I was mistaken about you. A person comes up my mountain and just wants to stand on it, well, that ought to be all right. You've done more than enough for me. I can tell you got no harm in you. You go on along now."

He walked to the door and looked out into the night. Trees were dark jagged silhouettes against a lighter sky pricked with millions of stars. He reached up to the stars, opening to ages-old light, and listened.

"I'll walk you down to the road," said the woman. "Wouldn't want you to trip in the dark."

Something moved across the pine needles, the whisper of shoes. Something smelled of a violence beyond any scent the woman's rifle had produced.

Night, I am here, Edmund thought. Earth, I am here. Air, I am here. I am open to you. Lead me.

Through his bare feet he felt a gathering of mixed energies, dark blue and flame red, rising up and spreading along under his skin, rippling through all his muscles, tingling.

—It is on us it is in us it is against us—

—want it off us—

Light wavered in the house behind him, casting his own long dark shadow on the ground before him. "You got to move so I can get out," the woman said, touching his back with her bare hand for the first time.

"No," he said, his voice coming out odd, thicker and deeper—doubled, tripled, other forces augmenting it.

"What?" She sounded startled. "You need light—"

Blue-gray radiance gloved his left hand, growing steadily brighter, lighting up the clearing in front of her house.

"Something's out here," he said. "Stay behind me."

"The key. The queen keeps the key under her pillow," said a flat hissing voice out of the darkness. "I must steal the key."

The woman's hand gripped Edmund's shirt.

"To let the wild man out," said the whisper.

Edmund raised his hand like a torch. Clutching the trunk of a tree across from them stood a man dressed all in black, with black streaks painted under his eyes.

Hunting energy, night energy: owl energy.

"The queen. The witch. The bitch. Won't give me the key, won't let me find my golden ball."

A memory of Edmund's almost-normal childhood rose up to confuse him: key? ball? A list from a scavenger hunt? The front of his brain could make no other sense out of the mumblings, but the night-blue energy inside him answered, its voice deep and wild: "Your key is not here. You left it in the city."

"You lie. The witch has it." He released the tree and took two steps toward them. "The witch has it, keeps me locked up inside myself. Won't let me loose."

The woman's hand tightened on Edmund's shirt, pulling at him. "I know him," she whispered. "He used to be my husband."

"She took my wildness away and used it herself!" screamed the man in the woods.

"He took everything I had in the divorce, except the mountain," the woman muttered. "I was glad anyway, because he was getting too weird to live with."

Edmund closed his eyes and dropped into a deeper listening mode, asking: what is it you want me to remove?

—*The screaming thing,* murmured the world. —*House thing lives with; screaming thing presses down, caps the well.*

Edmund remembered the membrane that had sealed the green energy underground instead of letting it well up in the fire circle.

"I need my wild man," said the man, coming toward them.

Smoky red light gathered around Edmund's right hand. "Your wild man is not here," said a ragged voice from within him.

"She has him. She's eaten him. She's using him. I have to let him out of her." He stopped a few feet away and tugged at something on his belt. He freed it and held it up. Red light glowed along the metal of a knife.

"No," said Edmund and everything in him. He walked to the stranger.

The knife came up, aimed at Edmund's chest.

Metal, remember the fire that forged you? Edmund reached out with his red hand and touched the knife. It glowed red, then orange, then white hot, and melted into hissing drops that splashed on the ground between them. The man dropped the bone hilt, shaking his hand.

"Go away," Edmund said.

"Not without the key," whispered the man.

Edmund reached down into the pool of cooling metal with his red hand, plucked a key out of it. "Here it is. Threats and violence. Go home and unlock. Your wilderness is closer to home." He pressed the key into the man's hand.

"That's not right," said the man. "I can't be given it. Not by a man. I have to steal it from my mother."

—*Talking does not work,* the world murmured, and flexed Edmund's muscles. He gripped the man's shoulders, one in a fire-red hand, the other in an ice-blue one. He turned the man and aimed him down the mountain, then walked, pushing the resisting man before him.

"No," the man cried, jerking his shoulders. Small smoke rose up from the one Edmund gripped in his red hand. Deep inside, Edmund felt alarm: he never meant to hurt anyone. But he had given control of his body to these powers, who had different priorities.

The blue and red light from Edmund's hands showed them a path to follow, and they made it down to the road, where a black Lincoln Towncar was parked behind Edmund's Volvo. The man had struggled and fought all the way down the mountain, but the energies inside Edmund would not be denied; they crushed resistance. Behind him came the woman's footsteps, faint on the pine needles.

Edmund turned the man to face him, pressing him back against the car. "Listen," Edmund said in the tripled voice. "The woman does not have your wild man."

The man's face bore traces of tears. "You are the wild man," he whispered.

Mazed in a web of symbols he didn't understand, Edmund shook his head, but the others inside him spoke. "You do not come to find me in this way," said the ragged red voice. "Not with theft and deception and intending harm without need. You come to me when you are ready to listen. Then you sit and wait and invite me, and maybe I will come. Not from the woman. From the Earth."

His blue hand reached for the passenger door of the car, and it opened at his touch, its lock clicking. He pushed the man inside, shutting the door after him. He leaned both hands on the car. Energies spoke to the car: hold him safe, take him home, away from here, shaped metal that once lay inside me, energies I once cradled.

The car's engine started. Edmund straightened, letting go. The car's headlights flicked on, scything through the darkness, and it pulled out into the road and drove away.

"What," cried the woman, "what? What?"

The light faded from his hands. The energies warmed him, stroking him on the inside, before they fled out his feet. He turned toward her in the new darkness, his hands down at his sides.

"What are you?" she whispered.

"Not an easy question," he said, his voice toned down to normal.

"Voices came out of you," she whispered, "voices I've heard in dreams."

"It was the mountain talking," he said. "Night and the mountain."

"How can that be?"

He smiled down at her through the darkness, even though he knew she couldn't see his face. She would hear the smile in his voice. "That's what I'm doing now; that's all I do, is listen. Sometimes the conversation comes up inside me."

"You were listening when I first saw you." Her voice was quiet and steady.

"Yes."

"To something most people can't hear."

"Most people don't stand still long enough, I guess."

"Like Brett." She sighed. "So it had to talk in a voice he could hear." Her hand came out of the darkness and gripped his. "Thank you. Thank you. What if you hadn't been here?"

"You would have had your rifle ready."

"Yes. Thank you for being here. Are you hungry? I'm not much of a cook, but I could make some kind of soup."

He couldn't remember when he'd last eaten by mouth. Powers sometimes filled and fed him. "Sounds great," he said.

"And I got something else I need to burn," she muttered. "That heart. Maybe it's the key he was looking for. Don't want it in the house anymore."

She stood in the silent darkness for a moment, then said, "Can you make your hands light up again? I left the lantern up in the house."

"Not without provocation, I don't think."

"Put your hand on my shoulder, then. I know my mountain; I'll lead you."

They were halfway to her house when she broke the silence again. "Your voices say anything about yuppie warrior scum?"

He laughed. "I don't know anything about them."

"Could you be here next full moon? That's when they come. Bet they'd scare away pretty easy."

"I'll listen," he said. "If the mountain asks me, I'll be here."

THE SWEET SMELL OF
SUCCESS
▼▼▼

PACO IGNACIO TAIBO II
TRANSLATED BY WILLIAM NEUMAN

1. WHAT'S WRONG WITH YOU, MARCIAL?

FROM Chihuahua all the way to Ciudad Juarez, the whole damn way, his hands smelled like a corpse. They stunk like a dead man. It didn't matter what he tried. Dousing them with orange blossom cologne from Sanborn's, washing them in tequila, the smell wouldn't go away. Out of pure desperation, outside Villa Ahumada, the ugliest town in northern Mexico, he even tried pissing on his hands. They stunk as bad as ever.

The worst thing of all was that nobody had died. There wasn't any corpse. The smell definitely seemed to be coming from his hands, but just to be sure, he pulled into a filling station in the middle of the desert and looked in the glove compartment, under the back seat, and even in the trunk. There was nothing there. No dead people, not even a dead cat. Nothing.

When he reported in to his group leader, he was careful not to say anything about the smell. They'd just think he was going soft on them, some little pantywaist fag who couldn't cut it in the judicial police. In other words, 100 percent replaceable.

His boss looked him over slowly, from top to bottom: the unruly hair sticking out from under his Dodgers cap, the embroidered vest, the enormous belt buckle on his dungarees, the scuffed cowboy boots. Then he sent him off to a nearby ranch to check the serial numbers on some farm equipment. The rancher had supposedly bought the machines off a local dealer who hadn't been paying off the right people.

It'd been more than two days since Marcial had gotten any sleep, thanks to a job that hadn't turned out quite right. And on top of everything else he couldn't get his mind off the strange smell coming from his hands, so the whole thing at the ranch got off to a bad start. Following his usual routine of making accusations first and investigating later, he accused the rancher of using the combines to harvest marijuana. He raised his voice, threw a jug of water and a plateful of tacos onto the floor, broke the rancher's wife's jaw with his gun butt when she spoke out, and finally threatened to shoot the man's two sons if their father wouldn't tell him where the dope was. One of the kids shit his pants, and then the rancher attacked Marcial with a kitchen knife. Marcial, of course, was obliged to blow his face off. . . . It was a total disaster.

His hands still smelled like a corpse on the way back. He went by the office, but his boss was out. Still, he must have looked like the walking dead, because they sent him home to get some sleep. Back in the Hotel Sarita, in the red-light district in Chihuahua, where he'd been staying for the last week, he spent the first half of the night scrubbing his hands with Mister Clean, Lemon Fab, and Lavamatic, to no avail. The only noticeable effect was that the vapors from the cleaners got him drunker than if he'd swallowed a whole bottle of brandy. He hadn't been that drunk in a long time, and he couldn't get the bed to stop moving. A pink-robed Christ stared at him from the wall, swinging back and forth in time with Marcial. Christ on a trapeze. At four in the morning, as he puked his guts into the toilet, he thought he heard his name on the television, on a late-night gringo game show rerun. That made him more afraid than ever.

He had breakfast with his boss in a restaurant called Las Cazuelas, huevos rancheros for the boss and three black coffees for him, while he reported on the mess at the ranch with the supposedly illicit combines and the nonexistent pot plantation.

His boss patiently explained to him that there are times when things turn out well and other times when things turn out poorly. That's how it is, sometimes you're on and sometimes not. But he stopped in midsentence and asked: "What the hell are you smelling your hands for all the time, Marcial? They smell like shit or what?"

To change the subject, Marcial volunteered to do a job in one of the city's outlying neighborhoods, keeping an eye out for a certain Demetrio, who was said to be a half-brother of El Ronas, who was being sought for the murder of a cop in Nogales. It was a late-night job that no one wanted, in a part of town that got cold enough to freeze a duck's ass at night. The boss looked at him sideways, with suspicion.

At his wit's end, Marcial Cirules Marulan—federal judicial police agent, thirty-five years old, mother's name Elvira, father's name Gaston, a native of Tepic, Nayarit, marital status divorced—pulled into a service station on Avenida Revolucion and pumped gasoline directly onto his hands. He gave such a black look to the attendant that he didn't dare to say a word. He rubbed his hands furiously, and then dried them with a rag he got from a skinny kid hanging out by the pump.

He gave the skinny kid a thousand-peso tip, but the smell wouldn't go away, so he pulled out the gold Ronson lighter that he'd stolen off a dead man killed in a robbery, and lit his left hand on fire. It didn't burn too much; he'd managed to clean most of the gas off with the rag.

He left the gas station half an hour later in the back of an ambulance. Besides the burned hand, he had a broken left shoulder bone and two broken ribs. While he was lying on the ground, crying with the pain from his burned hand, somebody came up from behind and started kicking him. He never saw the guy's face. He must have owed him some money or something.

His boss didn't even want to look at him when he reported back for work three weeks later. "Get out of the way, asshole. What are you staring at?" was all he said.

They gave him nicknames: Hot Hand, Black Hand, Angel Hand. They said he burned his hand trying to stifle the yawn of a fire eater. Or that it was the product of compulsive masturbation. He pretended not to notice. He was already upset enough over his hands smelling like a shitty burned-up damn corpse. He walked around all the time now with one of those little drugstore inhalers stuck in his nose. If anybody asked, he told them he had asthma.

2. THE BRUJA

If she left the TV on all the time, it was because she was lonely, not because she used it to conjure ghosts. She didn't believe in stuff like that. Anyway, it didn't use up much electricity. Less than an iron, from what she'd heard, or an old refrigerator, or a space heater.

She never paid much attention to what was on. After a few months she'd get tired of seeing the same faces, the newscasters, the soap opera stars, the sitcoms, so she'd just change to another channel. She hardly listened to what they were saying. Most of the time she kept the sound down, so as not to bother her neighbors, especially at night.

One day she asked herself: "If I have it there to keep from feeling lonely, what's the point of leaving it on when I'm not at home?" And she answered herself: "So that there will be less loneliness when I come back."

It wasn't for her witchcraft that she left the TV on all the time. To make magic, one needed steady images, things that weren't always moving and changing: drawings, photographs, newspaper clippings, birth certificates, grade school diplomas. At least that's how she did it. She couldn't get anywhere with things that moved all the time.

Helena worked as a bank teller during the week, and she took care of the children of gringo tourists at one of the big hotels on the weekends. She more or less made enough to get by on, even with things as bad as they were. And it kept her busy between boyfriends. Witchcraft for her was—how to put it?—a way to pass the time, a hobby. But she couldn't have too many spells going all at once, or they didn't work. She had to concentrate in order to make them stick. Lately, although she only had four projects on her hands, one of them hadn't been working out right. There was the one to keep the dog from barking, the one for seducing the manager's brother, the one to make the judicial policeman's hand smell like a corpse, and the one to get lots of money for Dona Elisa, the woman who owned the little store on the corner.

Maybe the last one wasn't working out right because it was too abstract, too ambiguous. What was that supposed to mean, "lots of money?" So she was thinking about changing it a little, like maybe to have everyone who entered the store pay for their purchases with ten-thousand-peso notes, mistaking them for five-thousand-peso notes. But there was always the risk that Dona Elisa would correct them and give them the proper change.

She was also having a little problem with accuracy. For instance, the dog had stopped barking for a while, but lately it had started baaing like a sheep. And one time the manager's brother had suddenly unzipped his pants in front of her and he had to be restrained while it was explained to him that he couldn't just get it on with one of the tellers in the middle of the Reforma Branch of the Banco Internacional at eleven o'clock in the morning, and with fifty customers watching. The one with the cop seemed to be working well, however. Whenever he came into the bank lately he was wearing gloves, and he was always rubbing and scratching his hands.

So if it was working so well, why did the dwarf want her to change it?

3. WHAT THE DWARF WANTED

"Can you make it so that other people can smell it too? Can you make it so that they can smell it even from far away?" asked the dwarf.

"I don't think so . . . No, I don't think I can. No, definitely not," said Helena. "He's the only one who can smell it. It's better that way, don't you think? How can you get rid of a smell that no one else is aware of? What can he do? Go to the doctor and say, 'My hands smell like a corpse.' And then the doctor doesn't smell anything. . . ."

Helena sat combing her long black hair. Without her thick glasses she was spectacular, a real beauty. "Why didn't she do something about her nearsightedness?" wondered the dwarf, as he watched the brush sliding up and down her back. "She could go to Cuba and have an operation. Or just conjure it away."

"You're just a second-rate witch," he told her.

Helena saw where he was coming from and she answered the unasked question, just as she had so many times before: "No, I can't make you grow taller. I might be able to make it so that other people see you as taller. Maybe ten or twelve centimeters. But that's all. . . .

"That's not good enough."

Helena smiled at her reflection in the mirror.

4. TAKE IT EASY, MARCIAL

Late at night, the smell seemed to seep from his hands and fill the entire room, impregnating the walls, the bedclothes, the TV screen. Around dawn the smell eased up slightly and he could get some sleep.

Who had he killed that the smell of the man's dead body had stuck to his hands, he would ask himself when he woke up. He'd killed at least a dozen people that he knew about for sure, more if you counted the ones who might have died a week later with a bullet in the leg, hiding out in the mountains, where he didn't have any way of knowing what had happened to them. He'd killed three women, and one old lady, a Tarahumara Indian, and the manager of a cheese factory. He'd killed just for the sake of killing, because a tough guy's got to kill someone every now and then just to show people that he can do it, to keep up his reputation. He'd killed people in drunken fights, and he'd killed people as part of being a cop. He'd worked as an enforcer for a druglord, and he'd killed people by accident. It was his job, wasn't it? So why the hell had one of the dead decided to come back to him now, in this way? With his smell. It was only luck, after all. They could have killed him just as easily as he killed them, couldn't they?

When he showed up again on Monday to report to his boss, after a weekend filled with lonely demons, his eyes darted nervously around the room; they were ringed with black bags, and his hands shook.

"What the hell is wrong with you, Marcial?" his boss demanded, watching him guardedly.

Marcial wondered if his boss didn't have the same problem as he did, but had just grown used to it. He'd killed more people than Marcial ever had; he'd done things a whole lot worse, and for a whole helluva lot longer. Maybe the boss smelled like a corpse too, but he'd just gotten used to it, so that he didn't even notice it anymore.

He sniffed cautiously.

"What the hell are you smelling me for, you idiot? What are you on anyway? Are you doing some kind of drugs?"

Marcial shook his head no.

"I've got the cold. The flu. It won't go away."

"You keep this up and you're out of a job," the boss said. He stared at him attentively for a minute, no longer sure he could still be trusted.

"I want you to go keep an eye on the Hotel Luna, and if you

see this guy, arrest him," he said, throwing a photograph onto his desk. "No funny business this time. Don't get out of line. Just bring him in. He owes some money to a friend of a friend. . . ."

The dwarf was in the office doorway, as usual, doing what he normally did, shining shoes. When Marcial went by, he gave him a sharp kick in the back with the toe of his boot. The dwarf only smiled.

Marcial went to the Hotel Luna, waiting for his man to show up: a tall, well-dressed, gray-haired man. After taking a couple of turns around the parking lot and lobby, he finally found him in the restaurant, eating breakfast. He walked right up to him.

"Excuse me, sir. Could you come with me," he said, showing his badge.

The man looked at him hard. "Tell your boss that when I want to see him, I'll go see him, and not to try and screw me around."

The stench rose up overwhelmingly from the hands that Marcial had prudently hidden in his pockets. That could be why, instead of trying to reason with the man, he took his right hand out of his pocket and hit him as hard as he could in the face. The man's head snapped back, and he spit out a tooth, along with a mouthful of eggs. He stuck his hand inside his jacket, and before he had his forty-five halfway out, Marcial put two bullets through his head.

The rest of the people in the restaurant threw themselves to the ground. Somebody screamed. Marcial looked around him, the blood flowing from the shattered face, the overturned table. He walked away without knowing where he was going, until he found himself in the kitchen. Everything smells like a dead man now, he thought, looking for a way out. Maybe the smell would stay behind him there. Maybe it wouldn't follow him around anymore. Someone was throwing up in the hotel patio. Marcial smelled his hands. The stench of death was stronger than ever. He went into a small garden in front of the main entrance to the hotel. He picked up a machete that was stuck into the ground next to a rose bush, and, resting his left hand on the trunk of a blue Ford, he cut it off with one clean stroke.

5. THE BRUJA

The witch put on a green miniskirt and a turquoise blouse and went out, determined not to be fazed by the shifting heat. It was 110 degrees in the shade.

The dwarf was waiting for her at the door to the bank.

"The son of a bitch is dead."

"Oh well," she said. "We all have to go sometime."

The dwarf smiled slightly. "So what's next?"

6. THE SMELL OF DEATH

The chief of the Judicial Police for the state of Chihuahua had himself killed seven innocent people in the last three years, besides making half a million dollars working on the side for a group of drug runners from Houston, and as he walked out of the governor's office, he became aware of a strong smell. Like the smell of a corpse. He'd spent the last half hour explaining how one of his agents had killed the chief of the state police of the next state over. The smell drifted up to his nose in a fetid wave. He looked around him before getting into his pickup, without finding anything unusual, but the smell only got stronger when he turned the key in the ignition. He turned on the air conditioner. It was his hands. His own hands. He thought back, but he could only remember having shaken hands with two people. The governor, and the governor's press chief. Had those assholes given him something? He took his hands from the steering wheel, cupped them around his nose and breathed in. They smelled like a dead man!

THE WITCH'S DAUGHTER
▼▼▼

LOIS TILTON

THERE was once a witch who had lived alone in the forest for many years, but by her arts she did not age, so that she appeared neither young nor old, neither beautiful nor ugly. Yet as time passed, she came to feel the weight of her solitude, and so she wished for a child to share her days.

Thus it came to pass that she gave birth to a daughter she named Mellilot, for she was as golden and as sweet as honey. The witch raised her daughter and instructed her in her own arts, so that by the time the girl had entered her eighteenth year she knew the names of every herb and plant that grew in the forest and their properties, to kill as well as to heal. She could scry out distant lands in a bowl of liquid silver or the water cupped in the palm of her hand. She could take the form of beast or bird. She could compel the elements of earth, air, fire and water to do her will.

In all that time Mellilot had lived alone with her mother in the witch's house and had never encountered another living person. But she had heard of love, for many of her mother's books spoke of it; there were spells to summon a lover, spells to win one, spells to warp love and turn it into hate. These the witch refused to teach her daughter. She had nothing but scorn for love; she called it a delusion and a snare for the foolish. But alone in her garden, hidden from the world, Mellilot longed for love and waited for the day it would find her.

One evening she walked in her garden while the moon rose full and the night-blooming flowers exhaled their fragrance. The apple and pear trees bowed down low in front of her, their branches heavy with fruit. The roses turned their thorns away from her fingers. Succulent mushrooms rose from the earth at her feet. But there was a discontent in Mellilot's heart and her existence was as dust and ashes to her. She was seventeen.

In the corner of her garden wall there was a deep shadow, and from it a figure suddenly stepped. He seemed to be a young man, and he was dressed all in black: in velvet and in fine, soft leather. His hair was dark, and his eyes in his pale face were black wells leading deep into nothingness, for he had no soul. No ordinary mortal man could have made his way through the tangled forest that concealed the witch's house from intruders, but this was a vampire, and the sweet warm yearning scent of Mellilot's blood had drawn him to her.

He stepped forward from the shadow into the moonlight and bowed to the maiden. She gasped slightly, and her innocent blue eyes opened very wide. "Who are you? How did you come here? How did you find this place?"

"What does it matter? I am here. I have found you." And very gently the vampire reached out for her hand, very gently he brought it to his lips. "Your skin is so cool."

"But not as cool as yours," she breathed, and her heart beat slightly faster.

He raised a fingertip and touched it to her cheek. "Your face is so soft, so white—like cream."

"But yours . . . is like pure marble." And her heart beat faster still.

He lowered his face and buried it in her hair. "Your scent is of honey and flowers."

She said nothing in return, for about him was only the faint, cool odor of the earth. But she feared no harm. She could see no evil in a face with the cool marble beauty of an ancient god.

He took her soft hand in his, and they walked together in her garden under the moonlight. She looked into the black depths of his eyes and thought she was falling into them. The cool touch of his hands on her body made her burn.

When at last he lowered his mouth to the creamy soft skin of her throat, she shut her eyes and held her breath in longing. Her pulse fluttered just beneath her skin, just beneath his lips. And when he pierced her, the hot sweetness of it made her gasp aloud.

He held her in his arms when he was finished; he lowered her carefully to a bench and brushed her hair back away from her suddenly pale face. He lifted her hand and touched it with his lips, and she sighed with tears in her eyes. "Oh, must you leave me now?"

"If you wish it, I can return. Tomorrow night, and the next. And then you will leave this place and come with me to be my bride, forever."

"Oh! Yes!" she cried, but he put a gentle finger on her lips to silence her.

"Now is too soon. Only wait for me. Be here in your garden tomorrow night, and I will come to you."

"Yes!" But he was gone, as silently as he had come, fading back into the shadows.

The next morning when the witch's daughter woke, there were two small unhealed wounds on her throat. She put her hand to the place and sighed again, remembering. Then she wound a silk ribbon around her neck to conceal the marks from her mother.

The witch frowned at the sight of her only child. "Daughter, you look so pale!"

"Oh, I can hardly eat or sleep! My life seems so barren and I can only think of love!"

"You think of love because you are young and foolish," the witch replied. "You'll know better when you are as old as I am."

Mellilot paid no heed. She could only think of her lover, of his cool white hands on her body, of the marble-pale chiseled beauty of his face. So eager she was to see him again that she went to her mother's liquid-silver scrying bowl and stared into it, whispering the spell to summon up his image. But all she could see was darkness.

As evening came near again she walked in her garden, sighing, waiting for him to return as he had promised, waiting for his touch, for the moment when he would pierce her throat and her whole body would tremble with the hot, sweet thrill.

As the shadows grew deep the vampire appeared again. "You waited for me."

"You came for me."

"And I will come for you again, until you are entirely mine. Oh, you are as beautiful as I remembered!"

"I cannot wait to be your bride!"

"We will lie next to each other, side by side, forever," he promised.

His kiss was cool on her hands, on her lips, but it was hot, piercing hot on her throat. "Take me with you now," she begged when it was over.

He shook his head. "I must come to you once more before you can be completely mine."

"Tomorrow then?"

"Tomorrow." And with the daybreak, he was gone.

That morning when Mellilot dressed, she wound a silk scarf around the wounds on her throat. This time the witch gasped at the sight of her child. "Daughter, I'm sure you must be ill, you look so pale!"

"Oh, I can hardly eat or sleep! My existence is like ashes, and I can only think of love!"

But the witch was not so easily deceived. She gave her daughter an herbal draught to strengthen her blood and watched her closely all the day long, so that Mellilot did not dare try to scry out her lover's image except once, for a brief instant, in the cup her mother gave her. But all she saw there was darkness, as if she had looked into a grave.

All day long she walked in her garden, waiting, waiting for the night. But when the vampire stepped out from the shadows and she ran to throw herself into his arms, suddenly the witch was there between them.

Her wrath was terrible. "So *this* is the lover of your dreams!"

The vampire stepped forward to reach for his bride. "She is mine!"

"No," the witch insisted. "Not yet. Not ever." As she spoke, the vampire collapsed to his knees; his body shrank rapidly. In a moment he had been transformed to a small black bat that fluttered helplessly among the trees of the garden.

Mellilot cried aloud. "No! This is my promised bridegroom!"

"And then your bridal bed would have been a grave!"

But the witch's daughter would not listen. She stared in anguish at the small darting form of the bat among her trees. "I cannot bear to live without him!"

The witch in her anger lost all patience. "Then have him! And have nothing of mine so long as you have him!"

With those words, the flowers of Mellilot's garden turned suddenly to nettles and briars, the fruit trees to thorns. The forest closed in around her until she could no longer see the house where she had been born. "Mother!" she cried, but there was no answer. In terror, she stammered the words to open the way through the trees, but nothing happened. One spell after the other, and all of them useless, her powers gone. She was abandoned, lost in the forest with no way to find her home again.

But not alone. Above her head the bat chittered in the branches, as forlorn and lost as she was. Mellilot reached up to him, and at last he came to her hand. He was so small he could hang from her finger. She stroked the velvet-soft black fur. "At least we are still together. I know the spell she used, and it can last no longer than seven years. If we were to be with each other forever, surely we can wait so long!"

As if in answer, the bat sunk his needle-sharp fangs into her finger, but they were so small they barely pierced the skin, and he took only a single drop of her blood. Mellilot wept. She would have willingly given so much more to have him in his own form once again.

When he was done, she placed him next to her breast and tried to make her way out of the darkness of the forest.

▼▼▼

The years that followed were hard ones. Mellilot had known nothing of the harsh world outside her mother's gate, nothing of hardship, hunger and thirst, nothing of cruelty or meanness. When she emerged from the forest she encountered all of these things, besides the hot choking dust of the road in summer, the bitter cold snows of winter.

In the first village she entered, men saw her beauty and seized her, tearing away her clothing, for she was alone with no defender. Her spells of ward and protection had no power. Afterward, when she ran weeping, seeking aid, the goodwives of the place reviled her for a wanton harlot and drove her away with blows and stones.

After this, she learned to conceal her face beneath her cloak and hood. But even then her innocence made her a target for dishonest merchants and thieves. Before long she was reduced to wearing rags, her honey-colored hair was dulled by the dust and grime of the road, her creamy skin worn harsh by the relentless sun. After a while she had no great beauty left to conceal and no cloak to cover it.

She survived only because her memory of herb-lore had not been lost along with her witch's powers. She trudged through the forests and fields picking leaf and flower, root and seed, drying them, grinding them to powder and paste in a rough stone mortar. The villagers were often ill, and they valued her remedies in times of sickness and need.

But these people feared witches and much more: the vampires who brought death in the night, shape-changers, demons, the walking dead. They were a furtive tribe who locked their doors shut at night and suspected any stranger. To their minds, an herb-woman was only one step away from a witch. They would come to her for cures for their fevers and aching bones, but let there be an unexpected death in the village, a child born with a blemish, a stillbirth among the herds, then they would think of curses or poisonous draughts, and sooner or later one among them would see the herb-woman and whisper the fatal word: *witch!* Then it was never long before the first one among them would reach for a stone, and a moment later the rest.

There was even more danger should one of them catch sight of the bat that nestled in the daytime at her breast and fed on her blood at night, for what could it be but a witch's familiar, a demon in bat's form? Oh, if only it were so! Mellilot's mother had taught her a little demon-lore, but she had always considered summoning the infernal beings too great a risk. Now, what her daughter would have given to be able to take such a risk, to set a demon on her tormentors!

As if the bat were capable of doing any harm. With his tiny, needle-sharp teeth he could only extract the smallest amounts of blood, a drop at a time. As was natural for any of his kind, he could not stand the sunlight, and Mellilot wore a small leather sack on a thong around her neck where she kept him safe during the day. At night he emerged to feed, to fly, but never far from her. She took his constancy as devotion. Her own devotion never failed. Throughout all of her trials, all of her hardships, she never considered abandoning him. He was her only consolation.

"Nothing has changed, not really," she would whisper to him, stroking his soft fur. "When you have your own form again, everything will be the same between us. What are seven years, when we have an eternity of nights to look forward to together?"

The witch's daughter was no longer the young girl who had lived in her mother's house, innocent of the outside world and its evils. She knew her lover's nature now, what it would have been to be his bride. The knowledge had not changed her resolve. She had seen how he existed, and she was still ready to share that existence with him—forever, now knowing what "forever" really meant.

She held the bat cupped in her hand, briefly stroked his fur against her face. But he struggled and fluttered in her grip and made an impatient chittering sound. His bones were so small, so delicate in this form. She set him on her shoulder and he pierced the whitely scarred skin of her throat, making her sigh with long-remembered pleasure. This pinprick was nothing to the sweet rush of the blood running hot from her veins like honey. To know it again was her greatest desire.

So seven years of hardship passed. And on the last evening of those seven years, when the sun had set and the shadows deepened and Mellilot held her lover in her hand, he stretched out his wings and rose fluttering into the air. A moment later he stood in human form, dressed all in black velvet and fine leather.

She exclaimed aloud in joy, flinging open her arms to him, tearing open her rags to fully expose her throat. "Oh, my love! Come to me now, now! I've waited so long!"

But to the vampire, seven years had been as nothing. When he looked at her now, there was no warmth on his marble-pale face, and when she gazed into the darkness of his eyes, the depth of nothingness there made her pause with a sudden shiver running the length of her spine. "You remember your promise? To make me your bride?"

His face seemed even more white, more cold as he sneered, "You were beautiful then."

His lips drew back from his fangs, he took a step toward her, and she reflexively made a warding gesture. So many times in the last seven years she had unthinkingly made such gestures, with no effect but to make the villagers stare suspiciously at her and reach down for a stone to throw. But now the vampire drew back sharply, hissing as if he were pained. "So. You are her daughter, after all, Witch."

But he made no attempt to touch her again. Instead, he stepped into the shadows and was gone.

Mellilot stood numb, in shock as all the dreams and desires that had sustained her for seven long, terrible years shattered and crumbled into bitter dust. She had seen it in his eyes at that instant, in the black emptiness: he had never loved her, he was incapable of love. Once, he had wanted her beauty, would have preserved it forever; but now it was already faded because of her hardships, and he had wanted nothing from her but her blood.

He was gone. He had rejected her, abandoned her.

Mellilot began to shake with grief. She threw herself onto the ground, weeping in empty desolation. It was only when her pain began to turn to anger and her tears finally dried that she realized what she had done in warding the vampire from her, what he had called her: *witch*. Trembling, she wiped the tears from her eyes. There was an echo in her mind, as if she could hear her mother's voice: *Have nothing of mine so long as you have him!*

Yes, she was once again her mother's daughter, her own curse lifted, her powers restored.

Nearby was an abandoned, disused well. She drew up a bucket of water. Most of it sieved out from the cracked staves, but enough remained for her purpose. She knelt down, settled the surface with a movement of her hand, and stared into the water, looking down beyond her reflection, into a center that grew wider, wider . . .

Her mother's face met her eyes. *Daughter. So, I see you have finally learned what manner of being you thought you loved.* Mellilot did not hear the witch's words, but she could read them on her lips. At first she wanted to protest, "No! I did love him." But all she said was, "He is gone. He left me."

Forget him. Your home is waiting for you. The way is open now.

Mellilot's face clouded with a frown. To go back, to her mother's house? To the straight white bed of her childhood, to the garden where she had walked in the moonlight and dreamed of love, knowing nothing of its bitterness? "No, Mother. There is too much of the world here that I have not seen."

The witch nodded. *You are older, daughter. And wiser now, I believe. You can learn much in seven years.*

Mellilot nodded. "Yes. I think I have learned. You have taught me . . . much." She rippled the surface of the water with her hand, and her mother's image disappeared.

Then she looked back into the water remaining at the bottom

of the bucket. This time, she saw her reflection staring back at her. It was true, the seven years had worn away all her beauty. Her once-creamy skin was now coarse, darkened, with hag-lines at the eyes and mouth. Her hair was dull and tangled. *You were beautiful then.*

But the witch had taught her daughter well. Soon Mellilot looked again into the water, and this time she saw honey-colored hair fall in curling masses down her back. Her skin was again as white and soft as cream. Only her eyes, which had been as innocently blue as a summer sky, were now the color of ancient glacial ice. She smiled at the reflection and rose to her feet.

The well stood near the edge of a meadow. As Mellilot crossed it, a peasant looked up from his mowing and gaped to see her there. She remembered this man. She had sold him a poultice a few weeks ago to draw the swelling from a carbuncle on his neck. Several days later he had been among the ones with stones. Now she stopped and pointed a finger at him. In an instant his face had erupted with red, suppurating boils.

Laughing, Mellilot continued toward the forest, where the paths among the trees opened before her, leading wherever she would go.

BROOMS WELCOME THE DUST
▼▼▼

STEVE RASNIC TEM

THERE are many stories told about Halloween. Although this one all started before Halloween, it's pretty much a story about the day after. I was twelve, my sister Myra thirteen.

Brooms know about plans gone bad, Grandma used to say.

Every year, beginning the week before Halloween, Myra and I would start our yearly fight over costumes.

"Ray guns aren't supposed to have triggers on 'em," she said in that little witchy, cracked voice of hers.

"Huh?" I've seen my face in its absolute bafflement mode—it's somewhere between incontinent dog and cat-trapped-in-the-dryer. I must have looked pretty stupid to Myra. But what did *she* know about ray guns anyway?

"Ray guns don't have triggers." There, she said it again. But I still could not understand her.

"Why *not?*" I asked, unable to keep the little brother voice from escaping my mouth. "How else would you fire 'em?"

"Buttons. The pushin' kind, not the fastenin' kind."

"Oh." I tried to keep acknowledgment of her greater wisdom out of my tone. I did not think I had succeeded. I had to admit it made pretty good sense. Buttons were a lot neater. Buttons. Damn. "All I got is my cowboy gun. Painted up metal blue and these red and white fishin' ball things glued on to hold the atomic rays. I can't break the trigger off; metal's too hard."

Myra wrinkled up her face into her smart thinking expression. She knew I knew she was smart, all right. Suddenly she raised her right forefinger the way she had seen someone do in a movie once. "I know! The attachments for Mom's old vacuum cleaner are someplace in the garage. I bet one of those would make a neat-lookin' ray gun!"

She was right, of course. I finally chose one of those narrow nozzle things for corners. After jamming a rubber ball into the back end (I still needed a storage unit for the atomic rays) and affixing an old clamp just in front of that for a handle, it made a nifty ray gun. Myra gave me one of her black checkers to glue on for a button. I would have much preferred a working button, but that was as good as we could manage.

Now that Myra had improved my spaceman's costume a hundred percent (she had no comment to make about the metal plates tied to my head or the wide rubber tubing wrapped around my neck), I felt I owed her reciprocal aid. Since I was a little brother, that aid took the form of criticism, of course. "That broom's not gonna work."

Myra looked mad and started toward me. I backed away. "What do you mean? It's a broom—all brooms are the same."

"Not a witch's broom. Witch's brooms are special."

Myra looked down at herself. It was that word "special" that had gotten her. Her witch's costume was the best thing she had ever done—she knew it. She'd made it mostly out of old clothes and things she'd found in the attic. Blacks and grays. An old gray piece of curtain that looked a little like a net on her shoulders and pulled up over the back of her head. A woman's black velvet dress that fit her almost perfectly—Mom just had to make it a little smaller in a few places. It had been a woman's dress, all right, but so small I thought it must have been a dwarf woman's or something. Black slippers on her feet—damp had discolored them here and there, making them look silvery in spots when the light hit just so. And this big black thing streaked with brown and green and gray over everything like a cloak or maybe a coat that had driven itself crazy—that was the best thing, the most brilliant thing about her costume. Mom said it used to be a chair cover a long time ago and after they threw it out Dad had retrieved it to put on the floor underneath where he was painting. It was an old thing, worn and full of dust and full of holes and with old fringe hanging down like it was rotting off. I never would have expected Myra to touch such a thing, much less wear it.

But Myra always had a sense for what worked, and she didn't hesitate to act. Grudgingly, I'd always admired her.

Now she was looking at the broom as if that sense had betrayed her somehow, let her down. "It's too new-looking," I said, although now that she'd really looked at the broom I knew she needed no explanation. "It's even got the company's name burnt into the handle. Witch's brooms aren't made in some factory."

She looked up at me. "Grandma's broom would work."

I just stared at her. I knew which one she meant. Not the one Grandma used around most of her house—the front porch and the sidewalk and even that little wood-floored hallway that led from her kitchen to the living room. That was the broom Dad had bought her at Carter's Hardware and it wasn't much different from the one Myra was holding now.

Myra meant Grandma's *kitchen* broom.

Brooms know all about bad feelings. Grandma used to say.

Grandma's kitchen broom looked ancient, as if it had been left on a trash heap for decades, or hidden away in some corner of the garage, motor oil soaking into all its bristles (what Grandma called its "corn"), then finally, impossibly, drawn up the handle like water rising inside a plant. It had obviously been handmade, and not all that well—its rough-cut stick not completely straight, its stitching uneven and too high up the handle so that the corn seemed loose in its socket. Dirt and grease held it together, and I'd always imagined it must have put more dirt down than it picked up. As long as I could remember it had sat in its corner near the stove and the back porch, dreaming in its dust.

"She'll never let you borrow it," I said, already feeling uneasy.

"She probably never even uses it. She's got that new broom and I don't think she even uses that one very much. Her house is *filthy*."

"She doesn't like kids much," I said, wishing I hadn't brought up the broom in the first place.

"She won't even know it's gone," Myra said, heading toward the front door. She stopped and looked back. "You coming?"

I looked down at my poor excuse for a ray gun, then sadly put it on the table. Even then I had a good sense of the inevitable.

▼▼▼

Brooms know about children, Grandma used to say. *Brooms know where they hide their secret toys, the ones grownups will never see.*

Grandma's house was near where they were building the new highway, surrounded by empty lots full of high weeds. Everybody else had to sell and leave, but not Grandma. I didn't understand why at the time, but nobody was ever able to make Grandma do anything, not even the city. Even back before the new highway went in, people would complain about how her place was an eyesore, but nothing was ever done.

She wasn't really our grandmother. I never knew exactly what she was. Our father had helped her immigrate, sponsored her in some way. And occasionally we'd have to visit, and it really did always seem like a *have to* case, even for Dad, not a *want to*. God knows, never a *want to*. Grandma made us all uncomfortable.

Once or twice when he'd had too much to drink, Dad would mumble something about how his family in the old country had "this debt to pay," and somehow that involved the old woman. That was as much as I was ever able to get out of him.

Myra led me deeper and deeper into the tall weeds. This late in the year they were stiff and dry, and it hurt when they slapped you in the face. Soon I was near tears, but of course I couldn't say anything. Myra paid no attention to me, intent on working her way along some path only she seemed to know about.

I had no idea where we were going—if anything, we seemed

to be going away from Grandma's house. The weeds were too high for me to see over. I could feel rocks and bits of hard vegetation working their way into my shoes and inside my socks. My socks were covered with bristly seeds and my ankles ached. I felt like a fool.

Myra stopped and urged me forward. Reluctantly, I obeyed. I started to complain, but Myra put her hand over my mouth. "Shhhh." Her hand was dirty from the weeds; it tasted salty.

We were at the back of Grandma's house. At least I assumed that was what I was looking at. Several large metal drums, like the kind they use to contain industrial waste, were stacked near the rusted screen door. One of the drums was cracked near the bottom; a slightly luminescent blue powder had spilled out. Containers of all kinds were scattered over the brown grass and weeds: barrels and washpans, enormous glass bottles and hundreds of Mason jars, crates and metal cans and old grass sacks. Here and there were rusted pieces of equipment I did not recognize. And furniture of all eras, antique to modern. I wondered where she'd gotten it all.

In the midst of all this junk were several planters filled with vegetation I had never seen before. Part of the crop bore huge, deformed-looking seed pods. Two ancient dress forms leaned precariously over the planters. They were draped in long flowing coats and necklaces of junk and small animal bones. Old clock radios had been placed on top for heads. Scarecrows.

I was so entranced by all this I hadn't even noticed that Myra had taken me by the hand. Now she was leading me through the junk, past the scarecrows, past a moldering stack of *National Geographics* and three stuffed raccoons frozen in savage, threatening postures, until I was nose to nose with the red, rusted screen. I was so anxious through all of this I continued to let her hold my hand.

"She's at *home*, Myra," I whispered. "She's *always* at home."

"She sleeps most of the time. Dad said."

I knew she'd been sick. She'd been sick a long time. Myra and I hadn't actually seen her for nearly a year.

The screen door drifted open. I looked at Myra; she seemed calm-as-you-please. Right then I could have almost hated her. She took me inside the back porch.

It was as bad as the yard. Moldering piles of magazines and newspapers, bottles half-filled with unrecognizable glop, boxes and crates stuffed with unimaginable junk, debris all over the floor. "What does she need a broom for?" Myra said, giggling. I punched her shoulder.

Before I could stop her, probably more stubborn because I'd punched her, Myra pushed open the door to the kitchen.

It was pitch-black inside. Grandma had all the curtains pulled. Somewhere there was a steady sound like a large clock, but muffled, hushed, as if it were underwater. Somewhere else there was a soft, rhythmic squeal, like a mouse being tortured. An alternatingly sour and sweet smell played with my nostrils, then stung them. "Let's get out of here," I whispered to Myra. I couldn't even see her.

Out of the darkness she punched me in the chest. "I can see the stove," she whispered back. "Look to your right."

I turned. My eyes strained until they felt as if they were growing stalks. After a moment I could see a whitish, blocky shape there. The stove. I tried to work my way around to the corner where I knew Grandma always kept her broom. That corner seemed even darker than the rest of the kitchen.

Something furry grabbed onto my ankles with tiny needles. I bit my lip and kicked. Something soft struck metal and skidded.

"Get it and let's get out of here," Myra whispered behind me. For the first time I could hear fear in her voice.

As I reached into the dark by the stove, touching web and soft streamers, touching damp and something crumbling to powder over my hand, something crawling down my arm, then finally touching something hard, something wood, I heard a rumbling toward the front of the house. I turned immediately, and knocked Myra down.

Steps boomed along the short hallway toward the kitchen. The all-too-short hallway. Myra had begun, softly, to cry. I helped her up with one hand, the other still clutching the greasy, gritty wood. I jerked the door open, my own breath like a series of explosions that spread up into my head, making it hard to hear. When I hit the rusty screen door, it fell apart around us, screen and wood and all. A piece grazed my forehead, and a finger of warm fluid slid down into my eye. Behind us I could hear a low moan building into a scream, a screech, a howl.

I began to cry too. We knocked the scarecrow forms over into a planter. One of the deformed fruits exploded, showering us with bright red seeds. We kicked bottles and boxes aside, racing for the weeds. The weeds had been raking my face for some time before the demented cries behind us began to fade.

Myra was crying harder when we reached the road. I looked down at myself and started to shake. I dropped the broom and did a little Saint Vitus' dance, brushing frantically at the dozens of shiny black spiders scrambling over my chest.

Brooms know the quiet thoughts a spider weaves, Grandma used to say.

▼▼▼

Halloween night Myra decided not to take Grandma's broom. I wouldn't hear of it. I cried and shook my fist at her. After all we'd been through, I couldn't believe it. "I'll tell," I threatened. She stared at me sullenly. "I'll tell about all we did. I'll be in trouble, too, but at least you'll get it. It was *your* idea!" I took the broom from the garage where we'd hidden it, wiped off the dust and webs, then shoved it into a bucket of warm water to soak some of the dark grease out of the bristles. After a little while it didn't smell so bad anymore. Myra finally took possession of it, reluctantly, trying to hold it at least a foot away from her as we headed out on the sidewalk in full costume.

I have to admit I had a pretty good time that Halloween. Even better than usual. Maybe it was because of the bad scare I'd gotten at Grandma's. All the silly costumes: goblins and ghosts, and maybe a dozen short, babyfat witches—which bugged Myra pretty bad, I guess—pulled the weight of that day right off me. I wanted to run and laugh, scatter my candy up and down the sidewalk, go soap some windows, scatter pumpkins from one end of town to the other. My ray gun turned out to be not such a good idea after all. The "button" came unglued and the clamp/handle kept slipping off, sending the vacuum cleaner nozzle flying through the air. Several times I had to stop and search people's darkened yards for it. But I didn't care. I felt free.

Myra was another story. I hadn't heard her laugh since we'd left the house, and normally she enjoyed Halloween even more than I did. She hadn't even said anything when Mrs. Jessup dropped a whole handful of peanut butter logs into her bag, and those were her favorites. Sometimes she didn't even go up to a house—she just waited for me back on the sidewalk. She clutched Grandma's broom with the tips of her fingers, letting as little of her skin as possible touch the handle. Holding it like that must have hurt her arm something awful. She walked stiffly, like she was in pain. Several of our friends complimented her on her costume, but she didn't say anything. Maybe because they all said the broom was the best part, that it looked like a *real* witch's broom. I was beginning to feel sorry I'd ever made her take it along.

"Hey, witchy!" someone shouted in the dark behind us, and jerked Grandma's broom backward out of Myra's hand. I spun around. It was Billy Abrahms, the biggest jackass I knew.

"Give it back," I said, lowering my voice so maybe he wouldn't know who I was under the costume.

"So shoot me with that vacuum cleaner!" he cackled. Then he took off down the sidewalk, straddling the broom like a stickhorse.

"Let him *go*," Myra said.

"Do you want to lose Grandma's broom?" I took off after him. After a moment I heard her following at a broken run. Until then I hadn't thought about actually returning Grandma's broom, actually having to go back to that place. Until then I hadn't realized I was scared *not* to return it.

Billy was older and bigger. After removing the broom from between his legs he was rapidly pulling away from us. Far enough away, in fact, that he felt he could play. He held the broom horizontally like Little John's staff, forcing every kid ahead of him to abandon the sidewalk. Now and then he would veer just enough to take a swing at some jack-o'-lanterns, sending their glowing faces tumbling into darkness.

This went on for several blocks, and now some adults were chasing Billy too. Maybe people whose pumpkins he had destroyed or whose kids he'd pushed out of the way. But Billy kept laughing and hooting, leaping up with the broom now and then as though he were preparing to take off.

And, I swear, just for a moment, he did. Suddenly Billy cried out and I saw him clutch at the broom. The broom rose with a hop, taking Billy a couple of feet off the ground, then back down again.

"Jeezus!" Billy yelled, staring at the broom. The rest of us just stopped where we were. The adults, I knew, were already working out logical explanations in their heads, how Billy had just jumped and seemed to hang there for a moment, and how good athletes—high jumpers, maybe—seemed to be able to do that, too. It was all just an illusion. A couple of them yelled at Billy about how his parents were going to hear about this; then they went back home.

They weren't there when the broom suddenly seemed to bend in Billy's hand, then ripple into a W-shape like a snake with a huge flat head. Like a cobra, maybe. The other kids ran away. Guess they'd had enough of Halloween for the time being. Myra and I just watched, hoping Billy would let go of the broom, but not sure what we'd do if he did. He stood frozen as the broom slid over his chest and curled over one shoulder, the tip bobbing around his head as if to kiss him. Myra was crying a little. I guess Billy would have, too, if he hadn't been so scared.

Suddenly the broom straightened out again with a loud crack, twisting Billy's hand and whacking him on the side of the head with the hard bristle-end. Billy yowled and jumped out of the way. The broom lay dormant on the sidewalk between us.

I waited for Myra to pick it up. I think she was waiting for me.

Billy snapped out of his shock and howled with a rage fueled, no doubt, by absolute terror. He started frantically kicking fallen leaves on top of the broom, then picking up great handfuls and dumping them on the pile. I thought he'd gone crazy. Once he'd completely buried the broom he ran over to Johnson's porch and stuffed his hand into the back of the jack-o'-lantern. I couldn't figure it. I had this mental picture of Billy dancing around with this big, glowing jack-o'-lantern over his fist like some demented ventriloquist's dummy. Then I saw the candle inside tipping over, the pumpkin beginning to burn, Billy's hand on fire and Billy continuing to dance . . .

"Billy!" I screamed.

But Billy wasn't in trouble at all. Billy was walking over to the pile of leaves with the candle in his hand. Before I could reach him the pile was already blazing, the dry leaves going up in a series of pops and cracks like gunshots. He stood back, his face glowing from the fire.

The pile rose up a few times, just three or four inches, and occasionally something twisted, even groaned, inside—like a man dying under a burning blanket. After the leaves burned away, the broom looked like charcoal arranged into a broom shape.

Brooms know what Death dreams about, Grandma used to say.

▼▼▼

The day after Halloween I got up early and spent most of the morning in the garage. What remained of Grandma's broom was leaning up against the wall. Myra and I had gotten some rags from a trash can and wrapped the broom in that. We were afraid of getting whatever it was inside the broom on our skin. After wiping it down good with those same rags, it didn't look much better—most of the bristles had fallen out, the stitching had burned away, and the blackened stick had chunks missing here and there as if something dark and mean had been taking bites out of it.

I'd sneaked Mom's good broom out of the house with the

thought that maybe I could snip some of the bristles out of it for replacements. And maybe a good solid branch could replace the stick. Obviously, neither was going to do much good. The broom looked like an old lady retrieved from her cremation, black and flat-chested.

My broom . . .

I looked around. I'd left the garage door open a foot or so to allow extra light in. But there was no trace of *her* feet in the opening. If Myra was playing tricks I was going to kill her.

My broom . . .

I twisted back; my spine suddenly felt electric. I stared past the destroyed broom to the back wall where Dad kept his tools. A small window was set into the middle of the wall, surrounded by heavy framing. But no face there.

Brooms are Death's only friends. Brooms know the dust of millions.

Twin crescents of shiny emerald grabbed my attention. Two dusty green bottles full of nails sat precariously on a two-by-four to the left of the window. Her eyes. Sagging diagonally above these were several rusted strands of chain. Her hair. And below: the twin rows of wrenches of varied sizes, hanging from a shiny steel rack. Her enormous, uneven teeth.

I backed away, feeling the skin on my arms tightening, beginning to itch. Then my arms, my hands began to shake. I tried to make myself look at her face in our garage wall but my neck stiffened and fought me. I thought I was going to throw up.

Does your father know you are a thief?

I wanted to say it was Myra's idea. I wanted to say it was all Myra's fault, that she had planned the whole thing. But I knew I could not.

Did you know your father might have to pay for your thievery?

"No! I . . ." I glanced over at the destroyed broom, desperately wondering if I could still offer to fix the thing.

That broom is dead. That broom is no more.

"No! I can fix it! There's still something here to fix." I walked over to the black shape of the broom. But there was no broom anymore. Just a dark stripe of shadow and dust balls scattered around my feet. The air smelled like charcoal.

Brooms welcome the dust. Dust welcomes the broom.

"I'm sorry." It was all I could think of to say.

Brooms value neither psychology nor apology.

"It's all my fault. My dad and mom, and Myra, too—they didn't have anything to do with it. *I* stole it. Me."

A dry chuckle moved rapidly through the dust that filled the garage. *Brave little man.*

"What are you gonna do with me?"

Why, I still require a broom. And I cannot go there myself.

"There? What do you . . ."

Poor Town. Jay Street. There is a man by the name of Johannsen.

"But how do I . . ."

You cannot buy or ask for a broom. It must be taken. You are the little thief, so you know how to go about it. Johannsen is poor. He knows what it means to be robbed. So do not feel so bad.

The dust closed in around me. Suddenly I couldn't breathe. I fell to my knees and slid under the garage door, slamming it shut behind me. The metal handle was warm to the touch. Loose roof shingles rattled beneath the sudden warm breeze.

Brooms know what it means to be left alone, Grandma used to say.

▼▼▼

My initial plan had been to keep Myra out of it this time. But she'd seen how upset I was as I prepared to leave the house, and I guess I needed to have someone verify that I hadn't gone off the deep end, and of course she was the only one who could. So I told her everything that had happened in the garage. She nodded here and there, calmly, as if it had been the most normal thing in the world. But of course she hadn't had a conversation with a set of talking wrenches. Maybe I was wrong; maybe I was being a coward. But she certainly seemed as able as I to handle whatever was to come. Besides, this quest of Grandma's might require two.

"Poor Town" wasn't really the poorest section of town anymore. Traditionally, it was the place the immigrants lived when they first moved here, before they'd started climbing that American ladder of success that was to take them to more pleasant, upwardly mobile neighborhoods. But there were always a few who stayed and kept their money there—although there might not be any evidence that they ever spent any of it. Each successive wave therefore left its own particular layer of silt, until the area was quite a hodgepodge of the arcane and the eccentric. Not well-to-do, certainly, but no slum area either.

Of course, I didn't understand any of this at that age. All I knew was that the area was *strange*, and a lot of adults said it was outright *dangerous*. Later I would recognize this for the unreasoning prejudice it was. Back then, however, I wouldn't have been surprised to come face-to-face with Satan himself in Poor Town.

It took Myra and me a long time to find Jay Street. We had a city street map we'd lifted from Dad's desk (I couldn't help wondering if I had, in fact, become nothing better than a common thief, so perhaps I *deserved* facing Hell in Poor Town). But Jay Street wasn't on the map. We had to ask.

"You pick somebody," I told Myra. She looked at me, puzzled. "I don't trust myself."

The first person she tried to ask was a bearded man in long flowing robes. He was singing in another language. When Myra spoke to him he sang louder and walked on past.

She had a little better luck with the next fellow: an old white-haired man in shorts and knee socks. I couldn't understand why he didn't look cold. He spent several minutes explaining in broken English how to get to Jay Street from where we were, bowed to us both, then went on his way. We looked at each other, not having understood a word.

Then a lady in a tall fur hat stopped and asked us, in good English with a slight accent, if we needed anything. She wrote down a few simple directions on the back of a card and handed it to Myra. It took us only a few minutes to get there, even stopping now and then to gaze at the odd architecture—gingerbread and colonial and even log—all jammed one wall against the other.

Jay Street turned out to be only one block long, wedged between two virtually empty streets. One side was filled by a solid wall made up of several different kinds of brick and stone, the backs of the buildings that faced the next street over. But no windows anywhere in the wall. On the other side was another, shorter wall, with a gate in the middle. Through the ornamental iron we could see a small cottage surrounded by trees. The perspective seemed to be slightly off, as if the tiny house were very far away.

"Good thing there's only the one house," Myra said, "since she didn't give you any house address for this fellow." She pushed ahead to open the gate, which was fine with me.

The area inside the wall was lush with all kinds of vegetation, including some varieties I'd never seen before. Of course, I hadn't been *anywhere* yet. Except for Grandma's.

We made our way to the sides so as not to approach the little house head-on. As we got closer, we could see that, as well-kept as the vegetation seemed to be, the house looked terrible. One outside wall was discolored with a reddish-brown stain. If the house had been metal, I might have thought it was rust. Part of the roof was gone. The windows had been replaced with some sort of plastic. And the door was broken, held to the jamb by a graying loop of rope and a huge nail.

And, as we got closer, there was the distinct odor of garbage— rotting fruit, soured milk, decayed meat—and, I realized, of excrement.

A thin brown shape bobbed around the corner. We dived behind a bush. Myra moaned; she'd scraped herself on a sharp piece of discarded can. Blood welled up under the shaved pieces of skin. She bit back the tears.

I stared at the little brown man. He was ill-shaven and showed his ribs through a tight red shirt. His khaki shorts were so much too big for him that I waited for them to fall down. He had long arms out of proportion to his torso and legs.

And he had sores. At first I thought they might be large moles or liver spots. But when the light hit them just right, I could see them for what they were. Dozens of them on his arms, legs, face and hands. Small red ovals with a subtle halo of blue discoloration around each one.

Brooms know about suffering, Grandma used to say.

After he went inside, I pulled Myra up to a crouch. "He came from somewhere behind the house," I whispered, and we moved slowly in that direction.

The thick carpet of vegetation cracked like eggshells beneath our feet. It seemed to be a spongy green surface layer over dead or dying plants underneath.

As we rounded the house we came to a miniature forest: hundreds of thin, more-or-less straight saplings planted only a foot or so apart. With small, strawlike heads. No fruit or flowers on any of them.

"What are they?" I asked. Myra put her finger to my lips and pointed to the house. I could hear the front door knock against the jamb. The little man was coming back. We squeezed between the short trees, back into the shadows.

He was rubbing his arm with a towel, his face constricted in pain. Tears squeezed out of his eyes and settled on his prominent cheekbones. He walked up to one of the trees ahead of us. I found myself leaning further back into the shadows, afraid he was going to see me. Myra clutched my arm so tightly I thought I was going to cry.

The little man removed the towel from his arm. I held my breath. The small circular wounds on the uncovered arm looked fresher. Several held drops of bright blood on their surface.

He pulled out a short, trough-shaped knife, like an apple-corer, and dug it into one of the old wounds. Then he held the bleeding wound up to the top of one of the trees and pressed it firmly against the wood, which was golden in the sunlight. The little man winced, then his face relaxed. I could see the blood dribbling down the length of the tree-shaft, soaking into the wood. As he bled, his face appeared to be slowly carved, fatigue gradually adding narrow dark lines to his face, one at a time, his color fading, until he began to look like a cardboard cutout, a black and white sketch hanging from the tree, waiting for the wind to blow it away.

"Brooms." They're *brooms,*" Myra said into my ear.

Brooms offer themselves as Christmas trees for the poor.

One of the man's eyes opened and stared right at me. I was shocked by the bright green of it against the black and white of the roughly sketched face. He removed his arm from the tree—from the broom—still bleeding, and backed away. The broom swayed toward him as he left, its bristles suddenly alive and restless. The rest of the broom heads in the miniature forest likewise began to sway.

"We won't hurt you," I said, stepping out from between the brooms. "Grandma sent us. For a broom."

The little man nodded. Then reached behind him. He held up an axe with his bleeding hand. Myra screamed.

I stepped back. Without changing expression the little man dropped the axe at my feet. I picked it up immediately in case he decided to attack. But he didn't move. Just stared at us.

"Believe me," I said nervously. "We just want a broom. Well, not that we really *want* the broom. We just *have* to get one for Grandma. Or something terrible may happen to us, or our mom and dad."

The little man lay down at my feet and closed his eyes.

"I think he thinks you're going to kill him," Myra said.

"No, no," I said in exasperation. The little man remained motionless on the ground. "Hell!" I said, turning. I swung the axe at the base of one of the brooms with all my might.

It split off with a shriek, trickling a little pink fluid into the ground. The other brooms shook madly, releasing their bristles into the air like porcupines. I dropped the axe and grabbed the broom, which was still somewhat slick with the fluid.

"The little man . . ." Myra said softly. She had bent over him. She tried to lift one of his arms, but it was hard and stiff. "He's *dead*," she said.

Brooms are headstones for the poor.

The broom started to move in my hand. Its head swung back and forth, the bristles loose and slapping me in the face. With my free hand I grabbed Myra's arm and pulled her toward me. She, too, took hold of the broom. It snaked and beat, spun and rippled, but still we held on.

Its bristles grew suddenly longer, wrapping around both our shoulders. The stick grew fatter, longer, and pieces of it shot out, became arms, legs. I kept turning my head, trying to get the bristles out of my face. Suddenly I was staring into small red and black eyes, pig eyes, Grandma's eyes. "Myra! Get away!" I shouted.

But we were already off the ground, vaulting the wall. Turned upside down I could see the rooftops of Poor Town beneath us, spinning away like tossed playing cards. I held on to Myra as tightly as I could and we both held on to the hideous rocketing mass of flesh and straw and wood and noise the broom had become.

Entire treetops were thrown past us in a sudden flurry of leaves. The cold air ripped through my clothes. My arms were so numb I could no longer feel myself holding Myra, and when I tried to call out her name, my voice was torn from me and thrown away.

I closed my eyes then, and tried to imagine my sister, and my sister and me holding each other.

Somewhere Grandma was saying, *Halloween is for brooms,* and, *Brooms are in memory of the dead.*

▼▼▼

Myra was pulling me to my feet. At least I thought it was Myra. I was groggy; it could have been anyone. Even *her.*

"Looks like she dropped us here," she said.

The front of Grandma's house came into focus. "Out of the sky?" I asked.

"I . . ." Myra stopped, shook her head. I put my arm around her. "Did we kill that little man?" she asked.

I shook my head. "No. She did, but because of us, I guess. Showing us what Halloween's about. Or something like that. I don't know."

Brooms know the secret lives of insects, mice, and children, Grandma used to say. *And when the dead speak, only a broom is there to listen.*

CLOSE

▼▼▼

ADAM-TROY CASTRO

HE wakes to the softness of her skin and the rustle of her breath and his usual morning-after obsession with getting away.

She's still asleep, of course. They always are. He learned early in his sexual career to wake up first. That way he can untangle himself from their arms, slip away, and vanish from their lives long before they even realize he's gone. It's a gift he has, just like sensing the night before who they want him to be and what they need him to say.

There had been times in the past when he'd fled so quickly that he didn't even bother to reacquaint himself with their faces. Not this time; this time, as it happens, he's awakened facing her. She's not beautiful. She's a little too wan to be beautiful. She isn't even all that pretty, to tell the truth. He wishes he could remember what attracted him to her.

She stirs. He realizes he'd better hurry.

He starts to pull away, already thinking of all the more important things he's going to have to do today, when he freezes. He hadn't realized it at first, because this routine has become a little automatic over the years, and because he was still a little dulled by sleep, and because their bodies are so well concealed by the sheets . . . but this time the tight embrace of the night before has lasted all the way until morning. This time both his legs are tightly clasped by hers. This time his left hand rests on her thigh, under the possessive touch of her right hand. This time his right hand, lying palm up on the bed, has been reduced to a pillow for her head, pinned by her soft cheek and buried by her halo of long blond hair. He can't possibly move an inch without waking her up.

And just as the problem sinks in, she drops the other shoe by opening her eyes.

They're impossibly blue, so blue he's honestly surprised he doesn't remember them from the night before. He hasn't seen blue like that since his last trip to the Caribbean.

She whispers: "Hello, Philip."

He mentally castigates himself for telling her his real name. "Hello."

"You were wonderful last night."

He doesn't say *you were wonderful too,* because she hadn't been. It's been years since a woman's succeeded in fooling him into thinking she was wonderful. Near as he can recall, this one had just been typical. "Thanks."

"You were everything I've ever wanted."

"Thanks," he says again.

Her brow knits. "Something's wrong. I've done something to upset you."

"Nothing's wrong."

"You're married."

The mere idea of ever entering into such a ridiculous contract gives him the chills. "No, I'm not," he says.

"You're not sure you love me."

"Don't be silly," he says.

He speaks the words with genuine annoyance, but as soon as they leave his lips he wishes he has some way of taking them back. It's absolutely the wrong thing to say. Usually, when he tells a woman not to be silly, he means it literally, without the underlying affection sometimes implied by the words. But in this context it sounds like he's telling her not to worry: that he does love her, and that she's silly for doubting it.

She turns her head just enough to kiss him on the wrist. "I knew you did. It couldn't have been that special if you didn't feel it too."

He's beginning to feel a sick panic. She's already shown she knows his real name—what else has he unthinkingly told her? His phone number? His address? Has he actually promised her anything? He opens his mouth, closes it again, swallows, and says, "Well . . ."

"I always wanted that kind of love," she says. Her eyes unfocus then, looking at something that probably can't be seen by entirely sane eyes. "Even when I was a little girl, I knew that was what I needed. I needed the kind of love they write about in poetry. The kind where two beautiful people who have never met before forge an instant connection just by looking at each other from opposite ends of a crowded room. The kind of love that makes a woman feel complete, that makes her want to hold on and on and never let go. I've devoted my life to finding that kind of love, and I've never ever come close, until now. What about you, Philip? Have you ever loved anybody else?"

"No." It's the literal truth, but even so, his voice sounds strangled. "No, never. Look, uh . . ."

"I knew it." She closes her eyes and smiles, radiating so much pure bliss that his skin burns from the sheer heat of it. "It had to be. It wouldn't have worked otherwise. But I needed to hear you say it."

There are about a million things he can say right now. He can tell her she's crazy, that she means nothing to him, that he wishes he'd never met her, that in fact her gooey illusions and romance-novel clichés make him want to gag. But just as he starts to say it, something she's just said catches up to him. "What wouldn't have worked?"

"That's right. You don't know." She giggles. "Oh, Philip, you're going to be so proud of me when you find out."

His heart, driven by a totally understandable burst of terror, thumps so hard he's afraid it'll burst a hole in his chest. He doesn't want to know what she's talking about. But he has to ask: "What?"

Her smile becomes coy. "Guess."

"I don't want to guess! Just tell me! What wouldn't have worked?"

"The wedding spell, silly."

He gapes at her.

Her voice becomes infinitely patient. "It's like I told you last night, when I showed you all my books and potions: there's a special magic between us. It bonds us together, makes us complete. What else did you think I meant, darling?"

He tries to pull away then . . . tries to hurl her away from him, leap off the bed himself, and flee out the front door, naked if necessary.

He fails.

When he tries to lift his left hand from her thigh, he only succeeds in pulling her body closer to his. When he tries to pull his right hand out from beneath her face, it also refuses to leave her, succeeding only in dragging her head toward him. He panics and tries to kick her away, but his legs refuse to cooperate, remaining tightly bound by hers.

He only stops trying to escape when his struggle knocks the concealing sheets from their bodies, revealing the true nature of their union. Wherever he touches her, or she touches him, the skin flows gently from one lover to the other, without even showing a seam. The skin of her thigh just rises up to become the skin of his hand, and then his wrist, and then his arm, and then the rest of his body, the same way the skin of his right hand becomes the skin of her right cheek . . . the same way the coarse hairy skin of his legs just blends into the soft silky skin of hers.

She mistakes the look on his face for joy and beams: "See, I told you. We're One now."

That they are. The beast with two backs, rendered literally true.

She blinks, suddenly unsure. "I love you, Philip."

He does the only thing he can do. He says, "I love you too," and tries to sound like he means it, without revealing that for the life of him he can't even remember her name.

DESIRE
▼▼▼

LYNN CROSSON

THE last rays of sunlight were filtering between the slats of the window blinds when I awoke. I stretched my arms and legs; slowly the shadows deepened and the furnishings became dark, indistinct shapes. I knew it was going to be a good night.

At full dark, I rose and put on my favorite chemise—deep blue silk. Garrett will find it irresistible, I thought. Pushing up the window, inviting the evening air into the room, I noted how wonderful it felt to be back in control. I forgave myself for nearly letting my conscience chase this one away. Garrett was a fine catch. A *fine* catch. He'd not escape.

Humming, I gathered the pieces of Garrett I'd already collected: the photograph, the poem, the letters, the answering machine tape, the vial of his semen (so cleverly collected that night, he never knew). I put them all in a velvet pouch, hugged it to my breast, whispered a prayer, and carried it downstairs to the shrine. To Garrett's drawer.

The far wall of the basement was completely dominated by an old library card catalog cabinet I had salvaged from an antique shop and customized to my own needs. Each of the seventy-five drawers had been painstakingly sanded and stained a rich mahogany that now gleamed in the light from the single bare bulb overhead. I ran a finger lovingly over the lacquered surface, admiring my handiwork.

My eye was drawn to Garrett's drawer, in the center of the third row. Just last night, I had carefully painted his name in gold on its front panel. He was number thirty-seven. I hooked my finger through the polished brass handle and pulled. The drawer whispered open, releasing the pleasant scent of wood and lacquer. Placing the velvet pouch inside, I let myself recall the night we met.

▼▼▼

The moment I saw him I knew we were both in trouble. The room was crowded, but all I saw was his face: eyes my favorite shade of blue, skin perfectly bronzed, hair tousled and brown. A moment later, I heard my own voice asking Roger, "Who's your friend?" And a moment after that, I knew his name was Garrett and I knew how his hand felt in mine.

The routine commenced automatically; was there once a time when I had at least *some* control over my behavior? Now, the calculated cant of my hip, the toss of my hair, the flashed smile, are all rote. Garrett was aloof—so much so that I thought he was not interested, thought we were safe. The party continued around us for hours, noisily, unnoticed, and for hours I flirted, encouraged and, ultimately, seduced. As we rose to leave together, I noticed Roger's expression: eternal consternation. He wondered why he was never the lucky one. He had no idea how much he really meant to me.

In the car, heading for my house, I kept my eyes on Garrett's headlights in my rearview mirror. He was still following—*good*, said the bigger part of me. The smaller part whimpered for mercy.

Then, the crunch of gravel as we pulled into the driveway, the satisfying slam of car doors, the jangle of keys, and we were inside.

In the kitchen, I handed him a beer, and opened one for myself. "The only air conditioner's in the bedroom," I said. "I don't mean to be too forward, but it *is* a lot more comfortable in there."

With a shrug and a crooked little smile, he followed. I twisted the rod on the blinds, letting pale moonlight stripe the room.

"What about the neighbors?" he asked, peering through the window at the house next door.

"Let them get their own date," I said, and gestured for him to sit on the bed.

He made a chivalrous stab at conversation before making his move, tracing my arm with his fingertip and leaning forward to kiss me. Inside, I felt a self-satisfied purr spreading like poison. I attempted to halt the sensation, unsure which side of me should be allowed to dominate. When his hand found my breast, it was no longer a matter of choice. Ever the victim, I gave in to the inevitable.

Time stretched and compressed as I reveled in the feel of his cool skin warming against mine. Slowly, we explored each other's bodies, his so tanned and hard, mine so pale, so soft, so unresisting. His tongue teased my neck, caressed my nipples, moved down my belly, delighting me.

When he entered me, I drew him in eagerly and whispered an urgent plea, "Kiss me, Garrett!" Our lips met, mouths opened, and I drank; I fed the power.

Later, we slept briefly, Garrett's arm draped possessively over my ribs. The sun rose and my eyes opened. I must not have been fully awake when the moody little *what-have-I-done* groan escaped my throat, but then I smiled at his sleeping form. *Mine, now.*

Still later, after coffee, a kiss, and an exchange of phone numbers, Garrett got into his car and pulled out of the driveway. I watched from the door until he turned the corner, then went back to bed. As always, I slept until nightfall.

It was fully dark when the phone woke me. It was Garrett.

"I miss you, Chloe."

"Yes, well, you too, Garrett."

"Visit me," he pleaded. "Soon."

"We'll see. I'll try."

"I didn't want to leave. I hated it all day without you."

"It's only been a few hours," I said.

"I know. I've, uh, written you a . . . poem."

"Oh, please, Garrett, that's so sweet, but don't do this. It's
. . . well, a little overwhelming. You understand what I'm trying
to say?"

"You're saying you need space; I understand. Okay, then call
me when you feel like it. Call me?"

"I'll call you."

An hour later, the phone rang again. Garrett again, of course.

"I'm sorry," he said. "I know it's only been a few minutes,
but I just had to hear your voice again. You're all inside me,
Chloe. Your scent is all around me. I just can't think of anything
else."

I laughed nervously, giving him his last chance to escape.
"I'm flattered, really. But I'm also a little scared. I mean, I know
we slept together, but we really don't know each other. There's
a lot you don't know. Maybe it's best we give this some time."

"You're right, of course. I'll put the poem in the mail to
you."

I was shaking when I hung up. I'd hooked him—nothing new.
Oh, how I hated this part. How I loved this part.

▼▼▼

The poem was lovely. They always are.

After two lengthy telephone conversations in two days, I let
the machine answer the phone. By the end of the week, the tape
was filled with Garrett's voice. "Just pick up the phone, Chloe,"
he pleaded again and again. "Stop hiding. I love you!"

He loves me. He loves me, he says. Part of me is always
amazed at my own power.

I never really thought I was particularly attractive, and neither
did the boys I knew in school. My nose is a little too big, my
chest too flat, and I'm not at all graceful, always bumping into
door frames and furniture. Playground and lunchroom jeering
made me blush, but it was seeing the other girls kissing their

boyfriends at the bus stop, and then smiling triumphantly, antago-
nistically at me that got to me the most.

I don't recall when the power began to grow in me, but when
David fell in love with me *at first sight*, I knew my life had
finally taken direction and meaning. The heady sensation of in-
spiring passion in a man, of feeling his breath in my ear, full of
desire, devoid of reason or control, was the most satisfying experience I could imagine. I thought at the time that I could have
been content with just David's love. But he left me; said he felt
like a zombie after five years with me. Said he couldn't continue
a life consumed by thoughts only of me while his money, his
aspirations and his creativity faded away. Watching him walk away
that day, I'd cried. I'd begged him to stay, said I needed him.
Then I'd collected all of his letters and every other bit of him I
had around the house and put everything in a box. I'd tied the
box with a red velvet ribbon and placed it lovingly on a shelf in
the basement.

His girlfriends have all called me in the years since then.
They want to know just what the hell I've done to him. They
say he can't get past his obsession with me, even though he knows
he can't live with me. My heart sometimes goes out to them.
They don't have David. They have a husk. Mostly, though, I
think it serves them right. For laughing at me at the bus stop. *I
have David—and Garrett. I can have any man I want.*

I've always had to fight with these damned moods, though.
That annoying little voice in the back of my mind that tried to
discourage Garrett nearly blew it for me. Lucky thing he was
already solidly mine. Let my conscience throw as many rocks in
my path as it likes. Its time is through. This is not about conscience anymore. This is about obsession. And obsession is not
something one simply gets over.

▼▼▼

*Slowly, my thoughts return to my immediate surroundings. The
shrine is a spectacular testimony to my power. I reach for another
drawer handle, slide the box out a few inches. David's essence*

*drifts out, caressing my face. I close my eyes, murmur hello to my
dearest lover (thought you could leave me, did you?). Reaching
into the drawer, I close my fingers around his letters, feel him seep
into my palm.*

No! Close the drawer, now!

*Another drawer opened, Dennis. And another, Rudy. Ah, yes,
they all rise up to greet me, to love me. To make me whole. I
breathe them in, feel their energy humming under my skin. That
pathetic, guilty little voice recedes to a memory.*

*Only slowly can I pry myself away. I must get ready. Garrett
will be here in less than an hour.*

▼▼▼

My heart leaped as the doorbell sounded. I tied my black silk
robe over the chemise, loosely, and hurried to the foyer. Smiling
my best hungry welcome, I opened the door.

Roger, not Garrett, peered self-consciously at me from the
stoop.

"What are you doing here?" I asked, surprised, pulling my
robe closed at the neck.

"I was passing your house and saw the lights on," he said. I
was going to ask if you had a few minutes, but you look like
you're ready for bed."

"Well, actually, I am rather tired, Roger. Some other time,
maybe." *Hurry and get out of here, damn it!*

"Of course. I'm sorry, Chloe. You know how I feel about
you, though, don't you? I just really wanted to ask you what I've
done so wrong these last two years? Would that take long to
explain?"

I sighed and shifted my weight impatiently. His presence
somehow always managed to make my power falter. The little
part of me loved him, I guess, but he made me face my conscience, and I truly hated him for that. "Come in, Roger," I said,
waving him over the threshold. "You know you're my best friend
in the whole world, dear. Would you really want to risk that for
some impetuous one night stand?"

"You know I'm not talking about just sex," he said. "I'm in love with *you*, Chloe. I have been from the moment we met. I know I'm a walking cliché about all of this, but we're so close; why aren't we perfect for each other?"

It has to be overflow. I'm stronger than I give myself credit for. Okay, I'll label a drawer for him next, since I seem to be on a roll. I never intended to take this route with him, but . . . "Roger, I'm sorry, I truly am, but I'm just too tired for this conversation tonight. Why don't you come over later in the week for dinner? We could work it all out then, okay? Maybe I've been blind. Maybe you'll show me the error of my ways. Call me tomorrow, will you?"

"All right," he said glumly. Then, brightening, "A kiss before I go?"

If not for his peculiar effect on my judgment, I would have taken Roger a long time ago. I'd always appreciated his broad chest, dark eyes, and tall, commanding stance. Perhaps he *would* make a suitable addition to my collection. I stood up on tiptoes to give him a friendly little peck on the cheek. He surprised me with an imprisoning embrace and a kiss so full of passion, I could not resist drinking it in. My hands came up to caress his face. I opened my mouth to him, felt his essence almost willfully leave him and enter me wherever we touched.

I was dizzy with the sensation when Garrett's car pulled into the driveway. The headlights flashed across the windows; not even Roger could miss it. He broke the kiss and turned. His eyes widened. "Who's that? You didn't say you were expecting company."

I stepped away and attempted a demure downward glance. "What did you want me to say, Roger? A lady has a right to a little privacy, don't you think?"

He brooded on that as Garrett came up the front steps and, seeing the front door open, pulled at the screen door. "Hello?"

"Come in," I called. Garrett entered, a bottle of wine in the crook of one arm. When he saw Roger, he simply gave me a surprised look.

"Hello, Garrett. Roger stopped by unexpectedly. He was just

leaving though, weren't you, Roger? You'll call me tomorrow, won't you?"

"You bet I will. You don't get off the hook that easily. Good night." Suddenly he reached out. He pulled me to him with one powerful arm and kissed me again. *Hard.* A small voice inside cried out to him for help.

Before I could react, Garrett grabbed Roger's shoulder. He whirled him around and punched him in the face. Roger stumbled backward, a startled look on his face.

"Wait!" I yelled uselessly.

Roger raised his hands, palms out in a halting gesture. Garrett stood huffing in anger. "What the hell do you think you're doing?" Garrett demanded. "I heard Chloe ask you to leave. Get out, now!"

Roger gingerly touched his jaw. "Put your cocky attitude away, pal. You've known her less than two weeks, and you'll be out of her life in two more. I've seen it dozens of times. You're as good as gone, but I'll be here when it's over."

"That's a hell of a way to talk about a lady in her presence, you asshole."

With an exasperated wave over his shoulder, Roger headed for the door.

"Roger, wait!" My voice sounded far away.

Roger turned.

"Don't leave me," I said. "I need your help. I need *you.*"

Garrett took my hand. "Chloe, we don't need his help. We have our own plans." His voice was shrill, frustrated.

But my other hand reached out, trembling, for Roger. I felt my face twist with the jumbled emotions warring for control.

Roger was at my side in an instant. He pushed Garrett back and took my hand. In that moment, torn between love and hate and fear, I shook with anger and sobbed with relief. He held me, whispering soothing words.

"Don't leave me," I heard myself cry. "I'm in such trouble, Roger, I can't begin to tell you."

"Shh," he said. "Shh. It'll all be okay. Shh, now."

Garrett shifted uncomfortably. "Chloe . . ." he said softly. Head down, a tear on his cheek, he turned for the door.

I swallowed. "Oh, Garrett, no. Stay, please. Let me explain to both of you. Maybe that will help me get control of my life again."

"Explain what?" they asked together.

"Come with me to the basement. I'll show you."

▼▼▼

Leading the two men down the stairs was a peculiar experience. No one had ever seen the shrine except me. I trembled with conflicting emotions, certain that this was my moment of liberation from the selfish, greedy woman that lived within me, and at the same time weak with desire to feel Garrett's hands, Roger's mouth on my flesh. They flung questions at me and I gestured them to silence. The single bulb cast a familiar dim glow. My guests approached the shrine tentatively. When they were close enough to read the names on the drawers, Roger gave me a questioning look.

"Hey!" Garrett's voice was slightly muffled in the damp air. "This one has my name on it. What's the deal, Chloe?"

Tearfully, quickly, I tried to explain the madness that had been my life for the last decade. They listened impatiently while I told about all the men I had left to continue their lives unable to do much except love me in vain. Men who might well be better off dead, if their existence could be called living. Roger and Garrett were understandably confused. It was difficult to make it clear just how horrifying it was to hold the fate of these men in my hands.

Pride kept sneaking into my voice.

Roger took my hand. "Honey, I had no idea. We'll get you some help. Come on, let's get out of here; this place gives me the creeps. We'll discuss it upstairs, okay?"

"What's in the drawers, though?" Garrett asked, and he pulled open his own before I could protest. As I shouted for him to stop, he pulled open David's drawer, and a few others. Despite Roger's steadying embrace, I felt the power rise again inside me. I clung to him and whispered. "Help . . ." and as he turned his face to mine, I kissed him as though it would be my last.

If it seemed inappropriate to Roger that I would display such passion at this moment, he did not show it. His hands pressed firmly against my back, holding me to him. His mouth opened and our eager tongues met.

Garrett, his back to me, continued to open drawers and lift out the contents for inspection. With every whisper of wood, every rustle and tap of brass, the power within me grew stronger. The purr beneath my skin, the heat in my veins quickly progressed from an exhilarating rush to a mildly alarming pain. I wondered what was happening and tried to break the kiss, but found I could not bear to let our mouths separate. Roger's very soul seemed to be pouring into me. His eagerness suddenly became distress. His arms left my back and flailed, but my hands gripped him to me. There was a roar in my ears and I could think of nothing but Roger's kiss, Roger's life. Marveling at my strength, I kept his head in my hands, his mouth to mine as he struggled and tried to protest.

Then Roger grew limp and feather-light in my hands. His lips slackened and his struggling ceased. Delirious and bewildered, I released him. He dropped to the concrete at my feet, little more than flesh-covered bone. I had taken much more than his essence; I had killed him. A tiny voice somewhere inside me cried in anguish. I barely heard it in the cacophony the power made in my head. Looking at Roger's pathetic remains, I knew there was nothing more I could take from him; yet, I still hungered.

I smiled, my eyes finding Garrett. He stood staring, obviously horrified. My thoughts whirled and then settled. I began to understand what was happening. Behind Garrett, I could see all thirty-seven drawers open. I never opened more than three or four at a time. The essence of thirty-seven lovers enveloped and overwhelmed me. I fed the power, but it would not be sated.

Rooted by fear, Garrett stammered incoherently, eyes wide. I raised a finger and beckoned, "Come to me, my love."

He shook his head, but his feet moved, carrying him toward me. His face registered terror that dissolved into love. I held out my arms, anticipation quickening my breath. Our fingertips touched and I drew on his energy, heat coursing up my hands and arms. Another step brought his face inches from mine.

I held his hands tightly and leaned forward. *"Please,"* Garrett managed weakly just before our lips met. My tongue teased his, barely touching. I doubted he appreciated the subtle gesture, but I wasn't doing it for him. The power fed, this time creating a thrilling, electric sensation as Garrett's life surged into me. His body shook violently, but he amazed me by exerting enough control to raise his arms and embrace me. My fingers grasped at his hair; the passion had never been stronger. He squeezed the hardest just before he slumped, lifeless, to the floor.

▼▼▼

In the moments that followed, I felt deserted by the power. The heat was gone, along with the roar and the purr. Crying, I lunged for the shrine and slapped each drawer closed. Garrett was a stranger, but Roger had been a *friend.*

I finally stepped back to the two piles of leathery bones. "Roger . . ." I pleaded and bent to touch his fleshless cheek. "Don't be dead. It was an accident."

Roger did not move. I sat down beside him and gathered him in my arms. I cringed when one of his hands slipped to the floor; then I cradled his skull more carefully.

"Roger, I'm so *sorry.* It was the power, not me. Come back, Roger. You're my best friend in the whole world, you know that. I would never hurt you. I'll never let the power in again, I promise. I'll destroy the shrine, I'll find a way to work it all out. But I can't do it without you." I kissed his chin, the teeth where his lips should be, his forehead. "Come back, Roger. Come back, *please.*"

I sat rocking him, my head back, crying for what must have been hours, but he never moved.

IN THUNDER, LIGHTNING
OR IN RAIN
▼▼▼

STUART M. KAMINSKY

"WE don't have a hell of a lot of time here, Doc," the old man said, removing the bicycle clips from his rain-soaked pants.

Carl Lenz sat back behind his desk and looked at the old man who tucked the clips into the pocket of his frayed denim jacket and said, "I was thinking the same thing."

The old man, who had identified himself as Max Horner, had appeared at Lenz's door less than five minutes earlier. Carl hadn't heard the bell or the knocking. His wife had nudged him and whispered,

"Carl, there's someone at the door."

He felt her nipples against his back, groaned comfortably and tried to ignore the insistent reality of the banging door.

He opened his eyes and found the red numbers on the bedside clock telling him it was just before two in the morning.

"Morrie," he whispered hoarsely, sitting up.

Connie reached over and touched his naked thigh, her fingers moving between his legs.

"Come back soon," she said softly. "I'm awake now."

He sat feeling her hand slink away, her moist mouth on his bare back. And then another knock, louder.

"I'll get rid of him," Carl promised.

"Good," his wife whispered.

Carl had fumbled for his robe, put it on and tied it, trying to come awake. If it weren't for the demanding knock, Carl could have more than accommodated his wife's suggestion. They had been married for six weeks and Carl had begun to worry about keeping Connie satisfied. He was only forty, but she was ten years younger and apparently always willing and usually eager for his body.

"Coming, coming, coming," Carl muttered as he made his way down the stairs.

The knocks were more frequent now, more frenetic, and behind them he thought he heard the sound of falling rain.

"Morrie?" he asked through the closed door.

"Morrie?" came a man's voice from beyond. "Hell, no. How 'bout opening the door, Doc? I'm dip-tar soakin' out here and time's running out.

Carl looked through the small window in the door and saw a tall, thin old man with curly white hair looking back at him. Rain was beating down. The path was wet and glistening in the glow of the porch light. The man on the other side of the door looked reasonably fit. Carl Lenz was in good shape and reasonably confident of his body, particularly when the potential threat was an apparently unarmed old man. Beyond the man, propped against the black metal railing to the left of the stone steps, was a bicycle.

Carl opened the door.

"Horner," said the old man holding out his hand. "Max Anthony Horner, pedaled down from Providence, took half the night. Truck almost hit me a few miles back."

Carl took the extended hand and felt even more confident. The handshake was firm, but there was a slight tremor and the enlarged knuckles that signaled arthritis.

"Come on in, Mr. Horner," Carl said, pushing the door closed and cutting off the sound of steady falling rain.

"Obliged," said Horner looking around.

Carl put on his best I'm-listening smile, hands in the pocket of his silk robe, and looked at the man.

"What can I do for you, Mr. Horner?" he asked.

"Wrong question," said Horner running his tongue over his uneven upper teeth. "Wrong question. What can Max Horner do for you is the question of the night. Nice house."

Horner looked around in the dim light of the reception area. The house was old, an eighteenth-century farm that Carl had rebuilt; well, he had supervised its rebuilding. Lenz's nearest neighbor was the man who had sold him the farmhouse, Morris Geckler, a former patient. Geckler had asked remarkably little in cash for the farm, but it had become clear soon after renovation began that Morris Geckler now assumed he had free psychotherapy available to him at any hour of the day whenever the Lenzes were in town.

"Can we talk somewhere?" said Horner, rubbing his hands together.

"Is this going to take long, Mr. Horner?"

"Probably. Up to you. I tell my story quick as I can. You listen and make up your mind. I got reason to hurry. Good reason."

The skies had raised the stakes beyond the door and the sound of heavily falling rain hit the windows. A clatter of metal against stone let Carl know that Max Horner's bike had fallen. Horner didn't seem to notice.

"This way," Carl said, moving through the open door at his right. Horner followed him.

Carl turned on the light and closed the door behind them.

"Cozy like," the old man said, and took two steps toward the black leather chair across from the desk.

"How about . . . ?" Carl said, moving behind the desk.

"About? Oh, the chair. Don't want it wet. Got you, Doc. Nice chair. Nice room."

"Used to be the living room," said Carl, sitting behind his desk. "Now . . ."

"Office," said Horner, moving to a straight-backed wooden

chair and sitting. "Nice. Kind of work away from work. Do most of your writing up here?"

"Most," agreed Carl. "Would you like a drink?"

"No time," said Horner. "Mind if I close the drapes?"

There was one large bay window in the room. Beyond it lay the yard with its gentle slope leading to the woods fifty yards beyond. There was nothing to see now but the rain hitting the window.

"No," said Carl.

The old man rose, moved to the window, peered out into the darkness for a moment, and pulled the drapes closed. Then he turned and faced Carl.

"Read your book," the man said, putting his hands behind his back and facing the desk.

"Which book?" asked Carl.

"All of 'em, cover to cover and back again. Last one is the one though."

"A *Longing of Witches*," said Carl.

"That's the one," Horner said. He returned to the wooden chair and sat slowly.

"You bicycled from Providence in the rain to tell me how much you like my book?"

Horner laughed, a nervous old-man cackle of a laugh.

"Knee slapper," he said. "Don't get me laughing here, Doc. Not a laughin' matter, and laughin' gets me achin' on a night like this. Chill, you know. Old bones. Old bones."

"Sorry," said Carl. "I'll try to be more serious."

Thunder cracked far beyond the woods toward the ocean. There was a fireplace in the corner. When the old man left, Carl decided, he would get the fire going and bring Connie down to make love in the heat on the soft bearskin rug. If he started the fire now, the old man might take it as a signal that Carl was ready to talk till dawn.

And then Carl realized that if the storm kept building, he wouldn't be able to send the old man back into the night. He would probably have to put him up in the attic bedroom.

"Your book's okay far as it goes," Horner said and turned his chair slightly so he could take in both Carl and the draped window. "Owes a lot to Ernest Jones."

"I acknowledge that in the book," said Carl. He leaned forward, folded his hands, and placed them on the dark polished oak of his desk to examine this ancient scarecrow of a man who came in the middle of the night to discuss Ernest Jones.

"You got it right why people want to be witches, warlocks, such like that," Horner said, pointing a long arthritic finger at Carl. "Hell, who wouldn't be tempted to make other people do what they want, sex and all, power of life and death, live for hundreds of years taking over other people's bodies. What you got wrong is that not all people who think they're witches are nutcase loonies, Doc."

Carl could see where this was going now. He began to formulate a plan for tucking Horner away for the night and locking him in the attic room till he could drive him back to Providence in the morning.

"You mean there really are witches," Carl said while he surreptitiously checked the old schoolhouse wall clock over the fireplace with the expertise of the experienced therapist.

"Heard this one before I guess," said Horner, looking around the room and shaking his head.

"Frequently, Mr. Horner. Almost all the people I've dealt with who have this fixation think either they or someone else is a witch, vampire, werewolf, or whatever. It's the rare one who thinks there's something wrong with his or her belief."

Horner was shaking his head through Carl's brief speech. he jumped in as soon as he could and said, "We don't have time here for what-ifs and who is and isn't nuts. They're comin' for me. Can't be too far behind."

"Who's coming for you, Mr. Horner?" Carl asked.

"Who's coming? Why the goddamned witches, that's who. Coven up near Providence. Few from as far away as Maine. Been fighting them all my life. My father before me and his mother before him. Way before Salem. Back in Wales. They're strongest when it's raining. Big storm. Harness the energy. Do their stuff."

Carl did his best, which was professional and damned good even at two in the morning, to make it appear that he was giving the old man the benefit of the doubt. It was a tight line to walk, but he had walked it before. Don't buy the argument. Remain open-mided but skeptical.

Then, above the rain, he heard a knock at the office door, and Connie entered wearing her matching silk robe. It was partly open at the neck and when she saw Horner she pulled the front of the robe closed.

She looked pale and quite beautiful. Her short, straight dark hair fell sleepily down her forehead, partly covering one eye.

"Are you almost done?" she said.

"Almost," answered Horner cheerfully before Carl could answer.

"Mr. Horner and I will be done soon," Carl said.

Connie said, "Soon."

"Soon," Carl repeated. "Mr. Horner, and I are fine."

Connie stepped back and closed the door behind her.

"Lovely lady, the misses," said Horner.

"Thank you, Mr. Horner," said Carl. "We're in agreement on that one."

"But not on the witches?" asked Horner, stretching out his legs. A joint cracked. "Age does that. Sorry. Okay, I'll get to the point. They know I've come for you. Gettin' old. Need new blood to help fight 'em. And you're this close to believin' 'cause you got the background. I studied you."

Horner had moved his hands almost together to show how close Carl was to believing. Carl thought the distance should be much, much greater between the hands if they were truly to represent how close he was to believing in witches, but he nodded.

"And they're coming after you because they know you're going to recruit me to carry on the fight against them?"

"Somethin' like that," Horner agreed, running his hand through his hair and closing his eyes.

"Part of it's that they found me just a few days back," said Horner. He opened his eyes and looked toward the draped windows. "I was hiding pretty good, pretty good if I do say so myself, and between you and me, Doc, there's nobody else gonna say it."

"And . . . ?"

"They mean to kill us, Doc," he said. "Pure and simple."

"Kill us?"

"Dead. Come right through that window or the door maybe. Shoot us dead."

"Shoot?"

"Crossbows," said Horner calmly. "They use crossbows. Tradition. Ebony bolts."

"Because . . . ?"

"You mean, why are they gonna kill us, not why are crossbows traditional?" said Horner, biting his lower lip and looking down at his gnarled hands.

"Let's start there," said Carl, leaning back and leaving his hands open. He now had the feeling that the old man might, just might, get a bit violent as he went on.

"It's sort of my fault gettin' you and your wife involved. No, not just sort of, it is my doin'. I'll own up to that right now. But done is done, right?"

"Done is done," agreed Carl. "If this coven is right behind you, why aren't you more worried?"

"I am worried. I'm so damned scared I'm near heavin' up what little I got in my stomach." Horner got up and moved to the window. "I'm scared, but I'm not panicking. Big difference."

Carl watched the old man reach for the drapes and then change his mind and turn around.

"I've been at this a long time," said Horner. "There're things to do to get us through the night, through this storm. Daylight comes, they'll back off and we'll have time. Now we better get goin'. I'll move the chairs and rug back so . . ."

"Hold it," said Carl, getting up.

Thunder rattled close by.

Horner, who had begun to move a chair, paused and looked at him.

"Right," said Horner. "What the hell am I thinkin' here? You're not convinced. No point tryin' to force you."

Horner took three long steps to the door and switched off the light.

The room went black.

"Put the light back on, Mr. Horner," Carl said calmly.

"Don't panic on me here," Horner said. "I'm just tryin' to make my case."

A crack of lightning hit nearby, bringing a burst of light that penetrated the closed drapes and illuminated the face of the old man across the room. The face was pale, eyes deep in their sockets, white hair in shock.

"The lights, Mr. Horner," Carl said, coming around the desk, confident that he knew the room better than the old man.

"Go to the window, Doc," Horner said softly. "Just you humor me. I'll stay right here."

"I . . ."

"Ain't gonna hurt, Doc, for you to look out the window."

"I look out the window," said Carl, moving toward the window with his back to it, "and you turn the lights back on and leave the furniture alone."

"You give a good look and I turn the lights back on. You got it."

Carl wished he was wearing something more than the silk robe. His gray suit would have been better. His sweat suit would have been acceptable.

Thunder cracked again and Carl reached for the drapes.

"Just a little. 'Nough for you to see."

Carl pulled the drape back no more than two inches and looked out into the darkness and rain.

"There's nothing out there, Mr. Horner."

"Give it a chance, young man, give it a chance. They should be comin' any minute. Should be signs of 'em."

A slight rumble and a nearby crack of lightning shook the windows. Carl let the drape fall closed. He turned around and faced the darkness.

"You saw something," Horner said confidently.

"What's going on, Horner?"

"What'd you see?"

"I don't know."

"They're coming from the woods, right?"

"I think I saw some figures near the trees."

"Hooded figures," said Horner. "One of 'em carryin' somethin'."

"Look . . ."

"No, Doc. Best you take another look, satisfy yourself it wasn't some mirage or somethin'."

Carl turned and opened the drapes again. He waited. Waited. The nearby thunder. The pause. The crack of lighting. And no doubt. There were figures. Four. Five. Maybe six of them. Hooded, one of them carrying something, moving slowly, carefully, their robes just touching the top of the grass.

He let the drapes close and turned. The lights came on. Horner was moving as quickly as his body would allow. He grabbed the chair.

"What you think, Doc? I'm givin' you a cock and bull or the gold eagle?"

"Hold it," said Carl, moving forward and grabbing the old man's wrist. "There are people out there. And they are heading toward the house. That doesn't prove . . ."

"Don't see you got much choice here," said Horner, looking down at the hand holding his wrist. "People dressed in robes carrying crossbows coming toward your house. I'd say they mean us no good."

"Shit," said Carl. "I don't . . ."

Carl let go of Horner's wrist and moved back to his desk to reach for the phone.

"Do you no good, Doc," said Horner, putting the wooden chair near the window. "They see the same movies you do. Phone lines'll be cut. Besides, by the time you got help, it'd all be over and you, me, and the misses would be dead and dragged away."

Carl picked up the phone. It was dead. He stood holding it and watched as Horner pushed the leather chair across the room and threw the bearskin rug over the desk.

"Give me a hand here. It'll go much faster," said the old man.

"I don't know who those people are, but we're getting my wife and getting into my car and getting the hell away from here."

"They got to your car by now, Doc. First thing they'd do, even before the phones."

Horner was looking at the space he had cleared in front of the fireplace.

"Nice floors, good wood. Maple," said Horner. "Best get the lady now."

"Wait . . ." Carl began.

"No time. Unless you got a gun, but I know you don't believe in usin' 'em. Said so in your book, the one about violence and TV. Trust me and we'll make it through."

The two men looked at each other now. A beat.

"I'll get my wife."

Carl moved quickly past Horner and ran up the stairs.

"Connie," he whispered into the darkness of the bedroom.

"What?"

Carl made his way across the room to the window and looked out across the field, squinting into rain and night. He urged on the lightning, willed it, wished it, but it didn't come.

"Carl?" Connie said behind him.

Carl saw or thought he saw something move outside. Near the shed in the glint off of rusting metal.

"Con, put on your robe and come downstairs, fast."

"What are . . . ?" she began and he heard her moving out of the bed.

"No light. Don't turn on the light."

"No light?" she asked, sitting up and reaching for her robe.

"Trust me."

"It's the old man. What's he doing? Does he have a gun?"

Carl went back to the bed, found his wife and began to guide her to the door.

"No gun, Con. I'm not sure what's going on, but there are people out there."

"Out? On our lawn? Who?"

They were in the hall now, on the landing next to the bathroom. The night light downstairs illuminated Connie's face as she stopped and looked at her husband. She was beautiful in any light.

"There are people out there who think they're witches," Carl said as calmly as he could.

"Carl, are you sleepwalking?"

"Con, there are people out there."

"Oh God, crazies. Your book."

"My book and Horner, the old man downstairs."

He took her warm, small hand, and hurried her down the stairs and into the office, where they found Horner on his knees, a bottle of dark red liquid in his now red-stained hands. Horner had moved the chairs. The rug, Carl saw, was draped over his desk. The old man was putting the finishing touches on a yard-wide five-pointed star he had painted on the wooden floor. He put a cork in the bottle and pulled a leather bag, ancient and dark, from the pocket of his denim jacket.

"What the hell are you doing?" Carl shouted.

"Pentagram," said Horner. "I've done better. Done worse too. 'Pends on how much time I got."

Carl looked at his wife, who stood wide-eyed, mouth partly open, looking at the floor.

"Blood of the lamb," Max Horner said.

Above the sound of driving rain, Carl heard the handle of the front door turning.

"Stand over there," Horner said as he poured white sandy grains from the bag. "Inside the pentagram. Right there."

"Carl," Connie said, looking at her husband.

Something rattled the window behind the drapes.

"Best step over here," said Horner, pointing to the space on the floor. "Makin' a halo around you with holy powders from the Holy Land. They can't touch you inside it."

"Wait, now just wait," Carl said, holding up his hands as the old man completed the circle of sand around the five-pointed star of blood. "Did they have you in a hospital in Providence? Did you get out of a hospital . . . ?"

Horner shook his head no and said,

"You think maybe I'm some kind of escaped nut and those people out there are a squad of keepers with straitjackets and stun guns, somethin' like that?"

"Something like that," said Carl, holding Connie close to him.

"Pull back the drapes, Doc," Horner said with a sigh. "It's a risk, but can't see no way I can force you."

Carl eased Connie's hands from him and moved to the window. He took a deep breath and pulled back the drape. On the other side of the rain-streaked window stood a figure in a dark robe. The hood of the robe covered the figure's face. And in the hand of the robed figure was a crossbow. Carl Lenz let the drape close, stumbled backward, and took his wife in his arms.

"I don't understand," he said, looking at Connie and then at Horner.

"Nothin' more to understand," said the old man. "Just time to do."

A pane of glass in the bay window broke. A crash of metal against wood sounded from beyond the closed office door in the direction of the front hall.

"Carl," Connie whispered, her voice cracking, her body trembling. "Let's just do what he says. Please."

She took her husband's hand and stepped into the circle of sand at the center of the pentagram. Carl followed her as Horner stood back and checked his handiwork.

"I think I got it all," Horner said as the sound of breaking glass and wood resounded behind him. "Take off the robes. Throw them outside the circle."

"What are you talking about?" Carl cried, holding Connie close to him. He could feel the rapid pounding of her heart.

"Bridge. They can use it like a bridge. Anything. Clothes, jewelry, any such like. Hurry."

Carl hesitated.

"I don't think . . ." Carl began, and then stopped.

Horner had pulled a small, shining gun from the pocket of his denim jacket. The gun was aimed at Carl's chest.

"No time to argue here," said Horner.

Connie took a step back, took off her robe, and flung it toward the bearskin on the desk. She was panting in fear, trying to catch her breathe. Carl tore off his robe and threw it beyond the circle. He held Connie again now, skin-to-skin, breast-to-chest, feeling her heart beat, tasting her breath.

The sound of a thud and a crunch of wood came through the closed door.

Horner moved quickly, a pocket lighter in one blood-red fist, the gun in the other.

"Stay close together and close your eyes," he said.

Horner's down-home accent seemed to have disappeared, but Carl had no time to examine the observation.

"What about you?" asked Carl.

"You'll just have to carry on for me," said Horner with a cockeyed smile. He flicked the lighter, and knelt to set the sand afire. The flame moved serpentlike around the circle, sending a blazing wall around Connie and Carl Lenz.

"I love you," Carl whispered. He closed his eyes as he heard a body crash through the bay window and the office door crash open. The heat was searing.

Connie whispered something back, but he couldn't make out the words. She shivered in his arms. He held her close and kissed her, soft, warm, and deep. He felt a sudden jerk inside and tried to open his eyes, but they refused to respond. Voices surrounded him and the heat was gone. The heat was gone, but he felt suddenly stiff, aching.

Carl Lenz opened his eyes and saw three hooded figures in front of him, he heard the crackling of flame behind him. Cold wind billowed the drapes in front of the broken bay window.

Carl turned to the sound and heat of the flames, and reached out for Connie. Across the room in the circle of flames, in the center of the five-pointed star, he saw himself, naked, clinging to

Connie, kissing her. He saw himself turn, and the face he had seen every morning and night in the mirror smiled at him.

"No," screamed Cârl Lenz, looking down at his gnarled, bloodstained arthritic hand holding a gun. "No."

Carl moved as quickly as he could toward the flaming circle, and raised the gun toward the body that had been his. He felt a sharp pain in his back, a piercing pain that sent him sprawling into the desk. His fingers found Connie's robe on the bearskin as he dropped the gun. Carl Lenz in the body of Max Horner rolled toward the hooded figures. One of them held a crossbow. There was no bolt in the bow, Carl knew the bolt was embedded in his back.

Carl tried to speak. Blood blocked his throat. He coughed and raised a hand toward Connie. Carl felt the life in this body ebbing as one of the figures took off his heavy robe. Beneath the robe was a man—not a young man, but a bald man with a middle-age belly. The man threw his robe on the flames and stamped them out.

Carl watched the man help Connie and the creature who had taken his body step out of the circle and look at him. The creature in his body held Carl's wife close to him.

"Who are you? What is this?" asked Connie. A second figure, a thin woman in glasses with her hair tied in a bun, handed Connie her robe.

"This man," said the being in Carl's body, pointing at Carl. "He came here, pulled a gun, made us get in that circle. What's going on? And who the hell are you people?"

The third robed figure in the room slowly, somberly, reloaded the crossbow with a black bolt. In the doorway to the office stood another hooded figure with his hands folded like a monk in flowing sleeves.

"We're members of the Order of St. Robert," said the woman as she handed the man inside Carl's body Carl's robe. The man put on the robe. "Our order is dedicated to finding true witches and warlocks and destroying them. That man," she said, pointing at Carl in the body of Max Horner, "is a warlock. It is the night of confluence, the thirteenth of April. If the heavens and hell collide and thunder, lightning and rain prevail, a witch or warlock can take the body of another and discard his own."

"I don't believe this," said Connie, looking with disgust at the agonized dying body of Max Horner.

Carl tried again to speak. Tears came to his eyes as the man in his body put his arm around his wife and kissed her comfortingly above her ear.

"No," Carl managed to croak from the floor. "I'm Carl Lenz."

The bald man and the thin woman turned to him.

"He's gone crazy," said Connie. "You're all crazy. He's no witch. He's just a lunatic. You're all just lunatics."

Connie put her head against the false Carl and wept as he held her tight. The bald man and the woman looked at each other and nodded.

"Inquisition," said the woman, turning to Connie.

"Inqui . . . what are you . . . ?" the man in Carl's body said incredulously.

"He may be telling the truth," said the woman. "The pentagram was drawn. The flame was lit. He may have had time."

"To do what?" asked Connie.

"To take one of your bodies," said the man.

"Take my body?" asked the false Carl, pointing at himself.

"Or that of your wife," said the woman.

"Inquisition," said the man.

Carl, dying in the body of Max Horner, gasped.

"Doctor Lenz, ask your wife questions only she could answer and tell us if she answers correctly."

"Hold it," said the man in Carl's body. The crossbow rose toward his chest.

The creature in Carl's body looked at the dying Carl, shrugged, and turned to Connie.

"What did you wear on our wedding night?"

Connie looked at the people facing her and then at the crossbow now pointed in her direction.

"Silk," she gasped dryly. "Pink, one piece."

"The last time we went out to dinner," asked the false Carl. "Where did we go and what did I eat?"

Connie gulped, paused, thought for an instant and said,

"Martoni's, last Friday. You had the filet mignon and a Caesar salad."

"This is Connie," the false Carl said with a sigh of exasperation. "And this is ridiculous. This man is dying. I'm a doctor. If you'll just let me . . ."

"Now," said the woman, ignoring him and addressing Connie. "You ask them questions. Do not tell us who is right or wrong till they've answered all the questions. You understand?"

Connie looked at the false Carl, who nodded his agreement.

"I've got to think," said Connie, biting her lower lip. "I've . . . My mother gave us a wedding present. What is it?"

The woman turned to the false Carl, who said, "A crystal vase. It's in the hallway."

Carl, in Horner's body, shook his head and gasped, "No, a quilt, handmade quilt. On the bed upstairs."

"Next question," ordered the thin woman in glasses.

Connie looked at the two men, the one dying, the other her husband.

"My favorite movie," Connie asked.

The false Carl smiled sadly and said, *"The Way We Were."*

Carl, on his knees, blinked away tears and tried to swallow blood and bile; he mouthed, and then managed to painfully cough out, *"Lost Horizons."*

"One more," said the woman. "Time for only one more."

"What did I tell you I want for my next birthday?" Connie said, her eyes moist, darting from person to person around her.

"The French designer dress we saw in the window of Saks," said the false Carl.

"Pearls," Carl tried to say through the puffed lips of Max Horner. Nothing came out. He tried again. Still nothing. Rage filled him. He clenched his fists and managed to spit out, "Pearls."

"Enough," said the woman. "Identify your husband, quickly."

Connie looked at the dying, crumpled figure on the floor and then at the man in Carl's body. Carl blinked once and watched in disbelief as Connie moved into the arms of the body snatcher who had answered every question incorrectly. She kissed the false Carl, kissed him with open mouth and tears flowing.

Carl felt himself being lifted from the ground. He tried to speak but was too weak. He blinked in agony as he was carried toward the door and heard the woman say,

"No one will believe you if you tell about this."

"We won't tell," the false Carl promised.

Carl wanted to howl in death as he saw his wife nod in agreement. And then Carl closed his eyes, sensing only movement and nausea and then the spray of rain and the chill of night as he was carried out. His foot kicked the bicycle Horner had come on only an hour earlier.

"Do not die," a man's voice said in his ear.

"Be very quiet," a woman's voice whispered in his other ear.

Carl opened the eyes of Max Horner and felt rain on his dry lips. Before him, he saw something familiar and yet unfamiliar, and then he realized that he was standing outside his office window, his broken office window looking at the billowing drapes.

"Do not speak," came a voice so soft that Carl was not sure he heard it.

And then he heard other voices, his own voice, the voice of his wife from within the office.

"Too long," said Connie. "Too long."

"As quickly as I could," he heard the man in his body say. "The body was not spent. The signs weren't right till tonight."

"Shhh, I know," Connie said, and there was silence.

The wind billowed the drapes and through the opening he saw himself and Connie naked on the floor on the bearskin rug, mouths together, bodies together. He knew he was about to cry out, but a hand covered his mouth to stop him.

"I took this body in April," said Connie, rising over the body of Carl Lenz, "and you come back to me in April. The circle is complete."

The drapes closed again and low, chanting voices surrounded Carl. The hand came away from his mouth and the chanting voices rose.

Again the wind and the drapes parted. The man in Carl's body looked toward the window and Carl found himself once more gazing into his own eyes. Connie noticed nothing, caught up in her passion.

Carl shuddered. The body of Max Horner shook as death entered his open mouth. Carl closed his eyes as the chanters shouted something harsh that sounded like a long ZZZZZZZZ. The pain in his back departed, replaced by a softness and a feeling of life between his legs.

Carl opened his eyes and found himself looking up at Connie, who was arched backward in ecstasy, a satisfied smile on her face.

She looked down at him as he felt himself releasing in horror and uncontrollable animal heat. And in her eyes at that moment, there was recognition. Though she too couldn't stop, he knew that she knew.

"Connie," he groaned, and she roared in pain as the bolt entered her long, white, beautiful neck.

And the rain stopped falling.

GRIMM WITCHERY

A FAIRY TALE
▼▼▼

JANET ASIMOV

IN the small Kingdom of Corus, royal families traditionally ran to three offspring, all male. This made for a shortage of royal females, particularly since the planet contained only one sparsely inhabited continent and no other kingdoms.

No one, least of all the three royal princes, expected gray-bearded King Coruman to do anything about the fact that he'd been a widower for many years. But he had.

"Zounds!" said Crown Prince Corvol, his black mustaches bristling, "The new queen is younger than we are, too skinny, not blond, not beautiful, reads improving books, and supports the Dragon Conservation League."

Second in line Prince Corst clenched his large fists, erecting the tufts of red hair on each knuckle. "She's only a minor princess on Hellbot, but every royal female from that accursed planet is a witch. Pops says she'll make him live happily ever after."

Corvol blanched. "He'll be King ever after!"

"But he seems happy," said the third son, Prince Charmo, who suffered because he couldn't live up to tradition. Third sons were supposed to be terribly muscular, terribly stupid, full of noble goodness, and entitled to rare adventures. Charmo had long ago given up on fulfilling anything but the goodness, no challenge in the dullness of life on Corus.

"Well, we royal princes aren't happy," said Corvol. "Our stepmother's programmed the food synthesizers with low-fat, low-cholesterol, low-salt recipes . . ."

Corst grunted. "She hexed the plasti-armor I use in tournament practice. I itched until she said I'd stop itching if I took a shower every day."

"She's a menace," said Corvol. "She put a spell on my holovid to lower the volume of music on my favorite bare-bottom dancing shows. I think the bottoms have slipped, too. Let's do something to make Mavis miserable."

"Let's kill her," said Corst, putting on hold his planned assassination of Corvol so he could become Crown Prince.

"I don't think that's a good idea," said Charmo. "If Mavis is a witch, it might be dangerous to try—anything."

"Of course she's a witch. There's no doubt about it," said Corvol. "She casts spells on Pops and dances around their bedroom while he sleeps. I can see it from my windows."

"You mean they never . . ." Corst's eyes bulged out.

"Not that I've seen."

"Papa likes the way he's been sleeping so well since he married Mavis," said Charmo.

"We'll begin with making Mavis miserable and proceed from there," said Corvol. "First we'll find out if Mavis is a virgin."

"I don't think that's a good idea," said Charmo. "If she can cast sexual spells, you might become her next victim. Who knows what she concocts up in that tower room she's turned into a laboratory?"

"Shut up," said Corvol. "Let's get away from Corus for a while. We'll poach a few space dragons and drape the skins all over the throne room. That ought to botch up her witchery and prove to Pops that she's a poor choice as queen."

Corvol and Corst took their favorite hunting ship, which they could manage without a troublesome crew, some of whom might be timid about chasing dangerous space-dragons, or, worse, tearful about killing them. Charmo was not invited.

King Coruman decided to accompany his two eldest sons on their dragon-hunting expedition. He said he was a little tired of sleeping so soundly and needed more exercise.

A few days later, the royal spaceship gave chase to a huge space dragon, tickling its solar sail-wings with bursts of phaser fire. Space dragons are not bright, but they know an enemy when they see one. The dragon was making excellent progress at prying open the spaceship when the two princes upped the phaser dosage.

King Coruman, somewhat prematurely, spoke to his young wife by ship-planet hycom to announce the victory.

"Can't you hear me, Mavis? I said we'll be bringing home a magnificent dragon head for over the dining room fireplace . . ."

"I'll throw up at every meal," said Mavis.

Charmo, who was listening, reflected that for such a small, plain Queen she had a reasonably musical voice. It was probably one of the evil assets exploited by witches.

"Speak up, Mavis," Coruman roared. "Can't hear a blasted thing with—hey, watch out, boys! That's a female dragon, and you've got babies flying out of the carcass into the photon torpedo vents! Shoot 'em out, boys!"

Those were his last words, before the explosion.

▼▼▼

The triple funeral was magnificent, the King's coffin draped with the largest dragon skin anyone on Corus had ever seen. The Corusian salvage team had been successful in recovering not only the corpses of royalty, but that of the royal prey.

Plus one baby dragon, alive and well in a crib Mavis installed in her tower laboratory. While adult dragons can travel handily in the airlessness of space, their young do better growing up with all the air and care needed by a human baby. Or so Mavis said. She seemed to know so much about everything.

▼▼▼

After his coronation, Charmo told Mavis she ought to go back to Hellbot. He'd found himself unduly disturbed by the bodybuilding exercises Mavis had taken to performing every morning in the palace courtyard.

Mavis shook her head, her silky black hair shimmering. "I won't go back where there's a surplus of royal females, all of them witches. I'm a novelty here and the Corusian populace pays hefty fees for the various, ah, services I perform for them."

"Services?"

She blinked. Her dark lashes were longer than he'd noticed before. "Fortune-telling. Simple spells. Potions to heal the sick and grow the crops and insure virility . . ."

"The same potion?"

"Certainly not. And I'm staying on Corus."

"Then you must move out of the palace. You must be gone by the time I return from my quest."

"Quest?"

"To seek True Wisdom, and the Proper Princess."

"In that order?"

"Not necessarily. When I bring back my Queen-to-be, I don't want you in the palace, Mavis. You're a bad example."

"Okay, Mo. Have fun, and bring back a beauty."

▼▼▼

Weeks later, married and landing on Corus, King Charmo was proud to inform his subjects that he had found his Proper Princess and that her name was actually Beauty. The populace cheered when she stepped out of the ship, for she was gorgeous from the tip of her delicate toes to the crown of her magnificent blond head. Even her profile was perfect.

"Congratulations, Mo," said Dowager Queen Mavis. "By the way, I won't be at the banquet tonight, in case you were thinking of inviting me. Now that I've moved and expanded my laboratory, I have so much work to do. I'm busy with a form of witchery called genetic engineering."

Charmo watched Mavis hitch up her blue jeans and stride off

to the back of the palace where there was a mountain Mavis had just finished building with a machine she'd invented. She opened what seemed to be a door at the bottom of the mountain, entered, and shut it behind her. The mountain was smooth, circular, and shone like glass, except at the top, where the laboratory was surrounded by a briar hedge.

That night, after performing his conjugal duties, Charmo kissed his beautiful sleeping bride and sneaked out to the backyard mountain. The door was locked. He touched the mountain's surface. It was genuine glass.

▼▼▼

"Charmo," Beauty said one day, "your witchy stepmother has got to go. I don't like her. The other day she gave me a computerized mirror that says I'm the fairest in the land."

"It's true. Rather nice of Mavis."

"The mirror adds a depraved chuckle. You must get some foreign prince to marry Mavis and take her away from Corus."

"Excellent idea, my love. We'll invite the richest, handsomest, bravest princes in the Galaxy."

Mavis agreed to marry the first royal male to achieve entrance to her guarded laboratory on top of the mountain.

"Without using any sort of antigrav machine or spaceship," Mavis said. She grinned. "I've greased the mountain, and the briars are poisoned."

"Mavis, it's embarrassing. If there has to be a contest, send them for the Golden Apples of Mu or the Chalice of Gu."

"The apples of Mu are contaminated with pesticides and the Gu authorities disapprove of illegal exportation of antiquities. Anyway, Mo, this contest will be more fun."

"Dowager Queens aren't supposed to have fun," said Charmo.

"You're a pill, Mo. I don't know why I like you."

Speechless, Charmo took the paper she handed him. It was a printout entitled, "The Non-Mythological Dragon—Problems in the Conservation of an Endangered Species."

Charmo was still staring at it as Mavis vanished again into her glass mountain.

▼▼▼

"Listen to this, Beauty. I didn't realize that adult space dragons survive space trips by stiffening their scales against vacuum and metabolizing stored oxygen compounds . . ."

"I think I'll go down to the spaceport as royal welcomer for the princes competing for your stepmother's hand."

"How graciously noble of you, my love," said Charmo. "Just don't tell the princes that Mavis is a witch."

"It seems a shame not to warn them."

"But as you said, we must get rid of her."

Beauty nodded. "Of course. The other day there was a fly in my skin cream. I'm sure Mavis sent it there. Furthermore, I've heard that she loaded the palace computer with some sort of magical and dangerous documents. They clearly bewitched you, for you've neglected me many nights."

Charmo sighed. "They turned out to be an in-depth analysis of the Corusian galactic trade problems, with possible solutions. I hope the prince who wins her doesn't find out what he's getting until it's too late."

▼▼▼

A goodly number of royal princes arrived for the contest, all of them younger royal sons who needed a wealthy marriage—and according to the late King Coruman's will, Mavis fitted the bill. Since the visiting princes had to be quartered in the palace, and entertained, Queen Beauty had many things to do.

As Charmo and his queen watched the contest from the back balcony, he said, "Look, Beauty, isn't it fun to watch them slide back down?"

"We want to get rid of her, Charmo."

No contestant made it more than halfway up the mountain the first day of the contest. Charmo had to buck up and console them that night at dinner. Queen Beauty seemed to be consoling one particularly tall, handsome prince who virtually sobbed on her shoulder. Charmo was touched.

When Charmo woke the next morning, Beauty was not in the bed beside him. She was not in the bath, or down at breakfast, where he discovered a document and a note in his gold cereal dish.

The document was a certificate of divorce. The note said that Beauty had taken the midnight spacebus with one of the princes. The one, presumably, so in need of comforting.

Embittered, Charmo went listlessly to the back balcony with his binoculars. He noted that the remaining princes were now wearing assorted diamond studs on their boot soles, wielding spray cans of detergent, and had cans of superdefoliant strapped to their belts. The briar hedge wouldn't stand a chance.

Suddenly a large dragon flew up from behind the hedge, skimmed over the heads of the panting climbers, and sailed down to hover next to Charmo's balcony.

"In case you didn't know, I'm a mutated, talking dragon." Each word was punctuated by a tiny puff of smoke.

"Go away, dragon."

"I'm alive. I'm not an antigrav machine, or a ship."

"So?"

"So Mavis will soon be married to one of those energetic princes. Before that happens, she sent me to ask you a question."

"Well?"

"It is this. Having found, married and divorced your Proper Princess, have you achieved your other goal in life?"

"I can't remember what it was."

"True Wisdom."

"No, I haven't. Do you know anything about True Wisdom?"

"Absolutely nothing, but I have another message."

"Get on with it, dragon." The top princes were now spraying the briar hedge.

"Mavis says that using nonmechanical means of bypassing the contest rule doesn't disqualify a contestant. It merely subjects him to a penalty."

"What penalty?"

"Life imprisonment."

"I've already got that,"said Charmo. "I'm king. Can you carry my weight?"

"Certainly. Hop on, Mo."

▼▼▼

Much later, Charmo said to Mavis, "My love, we will live happily ever after."

She kissed him and said sadly, "But ever after isn't possible, even for witches."

"It doesn't matter. I have the strangest feeling that I've found True Wisdom, yet I don't know what True Wisdom is."

"It's the happily," said Mavis.

IN SEARCH OF
ANTON LA VEY
▼▼▼

NANCY HOLDER

WHEN I was twenty, I fell in love with Allen and moved
into the house where he lived. It was an incredible, psychedelic
fantasy: We were students, so we smoked a lot of dope and listened
to Carole King's *Tapestry* album, over and over and over. Night
and day, it was our mantra, that and "I love you, I love you,
too" until the record got so scratched we didn't really listen to it
anymore; we just remembered how it had sounded and manufactured the songs in our minds.

Just as we manufactured those love words in our minds.

I was astonished when Kathy, who lived in the house with
us—we were students, and five of us were crammed into a two-
bedroom house—Kathy, who had once been Allen's girlfriend,
and still wanted him, it was clear—reminded him that he had
promised, long ago, to take her to San Francisco. He hadn't done
it. Now she wanted to go.

And he said he would.

I couldn't believe it. In my drug-induced torpor, my macrobi-
otic haze, I could not credit that the man who slept in my bed
would actually consent to taking another woman on a trip like
that. I deduced he didn't love me.

But Celia, another woman who lived in the house and who had never been Allen's girlfriend, although she had slept with him a couple of times, explained to me that he was just being Allen. When she went to him and told him I was hurt, he was surprised, and suggested we all go to San Francisco together. We would ride in his green Datsun pickup, taking turns sitting in the cab while he drove. The rest of the time, we would lounge in the truck bed with the luggage.

This mollified me. I had only been to San Francisco once, and that was with my parents, some time before. I remembered how we had driven to the Haight to see the hippies, rolling up our windows and locking all our doors, and I smiled. For what was I now, but a hippie myself?

So we determined to join the party, Celia and I, much to Kathy's poorly concealed disappointment. As we carried our sleeping bags and rickety suitcases to the truck, she looked us up and down, and her eyes narrowed with anger. I wondered if this was such a great idea after all, but I'd be damned if I'd stay home while she took away my man.

It took two days to get there, and much of it I spent lying in the bed of the truck inside my sleeping bag so I wouldn't get sunburned. But finally, we reached San Francisco, and checked into the Y there. Allen and I had one room, and signed in as Mr. and Mrs. (you had to in those days). Kathy and Celia shared the other room. And I narrowed *my* eyes at Kathy, in triumph.

We saw the sights—the Mod Squad go to Fisherman's Wharf, to Coit (we called it Coitus) Tower, to Sausalito. We ate on the cheap. It was so exciting. Being in San Francisco with someone I loved was like a wonderful dream. But it was also partly how I expected life to be: filled with possibilities and amazing events, and better than I had imagined. That was the kind of life college students often led, at least back then. We were middle-class Bohemians, pushing the future farther and farther away as we slowed down our schooling and remained in college—a legacy of student deferments, when school was a refuge from the draft. Buddhist studies, nonverbal communications—the world swirled with discussions and research, all-nighters at the library, and infinite amounts of hallucinogenic drugs.

The only shadow on this entire adventure was the fact that we had had to leave our friend, Richard, behind. Richard was the only one among us who wasn't a student, and who, in fact, owned the house we lived in. He had a job and couldn't get vacation time. Right Wing Richard, we called him, who came home from work every night to get stoned with us and listen to our debates about the Military-Industrial Complex, and who, one night, said, "With all the money I've paid in taxes to send you guys to college, I could've gone myself."

Richard never had a girlfriend among us. We lavished our attentions on Allen. No one slept with Richard, not even occasionally, as all of us had done with Allen. He just wasn't that kind of guy.

In San Francisco, then, as we rode the streetcars and took pictures of each other by the mermaid fountain in Ghirardelli Square, I tried very hard not to think of Richard, and what his absence represented: life after school, and a less-than-satisfying one at that. The end of the pot party, of drifting along to Joni Mitchell and hitching through Europe, and paisley shawls, and summers of love. I didn't want to phone him or send him postcards, but as I thought of him at home, alone, I did both. I called him every night, collect, and every night he took my call.

"We're having a pretty good time," I told him, and wasn't sure if I should play down just how much fun we were having, or if I should go ahead and share it with him.

"That's great," he replied, every night, and he sounded so wistful it made me ashamed and embarrassed.

Then one night I told him, "Guess what? We have Anton La Vey's phone number."

"Who's that?" he asked, and I felt a small burst of anger. I had forgotten that a chasm lay between us, the college students, and him, the worker. He had very little interest in the world of the mind. All he read was pulp fiction, and he was gaining weight, too, because all he did was go to work (civil service, at that) and come home and get stoned. He had no appreciation for the fullness of life. He was the most closed-off person I had ever met, which was why no one slept with him. Truth be told, he was boring. And it was his own fault.

"He's the head of the Church of Satan," I informed him. "A devil-worshiper. He's up here."

"Oh." He didn't care. Shortly after that, we hung up.

But the fact of the phone number had caused a stir among us, the travelers. We had found it in an underground guide book. "Naked women as altars, the Black Mass, the whole bit!" the entry read. We were trying to decide if we should call.

Kathy didn't want to, because, she said, that would mean crossing something else off our list. Yet I sensed the real reason was because I *did* want to. Celia was gung-ho, eager to compare her Catholic-school imaginings about the goings-on of The Other Side. Allen thought it would be a trip.

But we didn't make the call. We were busy from morning until late at night—doing the things on Kathy's list. After all, this vacation was officially for her.

I was pissed, and I knew Celia was, too. But I also knew I was the only one who was *afraid* to call Anton La Vey. What if it were true that he communed with the devil? What if he really were a warlock, as he claimed?

It was a profound experience, fearing Anton La Vey. I was delighted to discover that I believed in the possibility of evil. I was enchanted by my open mind.

"Then *you* call," the others said, probably tired of hearing me talk about it. Kathy handed me the phone. Allen sat cross-legged on the bed, picking the buds from a lid of dope we had scored at U.C. Berkeley.

I hesitated, genuinely nervous. What would I say? We'd like a tour of the Church of Satan? Weren't Satanic rituals closed to all but members? Would we have to take our clothes off? Well, we were used to that. Would we have to drink blood or kill a chicken?

"I can't believe it. She really is afraid to," Kathy taunted me.

That settled it, of course. And secretly, I was almost jubilant about my unease, because that meant that somewhere in me there was a shred of belief in the supernatural, and that made life so much bigger. If magic was real, then so much could happen, could be.

But just as I opened the guidebook to the number, the phone rang. It was Richard.

"Hi, you guys," he said to me. "Just thought I'd see if you were in." And we all took turns talking to him, as if he were our uncle, and I felt relieved that I'd missed my chance for that day—it was past five, and the guidebook said it closed at four-thirty—and sorry about it, too.

We had four days left after that. No one brought up Anton La Vey again. Kathy was making her moves on Allen—sitting next to him as often as possible, coming into our room in her nightgown, feeding him tidbits at restaurants—and he and I started to quarrel. He protested his innocence, but Allen was always innocent. He never had to do anything to get women into bed; they just ended up there. He was quiet, which made him mysterious, and handsome, and I guess that was enough. It had been enough for me.

Yet I could see the interest growing in his eyes. Kathy was an engineering major. He was scientifically oriented, and that gave her an edge. Besides, they had a past. As for Allen and me, we both took German, and I was pretty good in bed. I thought that would secure my position.

But Celia saw what was happening, and patted me sympathetically on the shoulder.

Then, on the day before we were to leave, Kathy and Allen announced they were going to grocery store. Kathy needed "something." What could I say? They went. Celia and I packed, and as I watched the clock, I began to seethe. Damn it, they shouldn't be so obvious. He shouldn't hurt and humiliate me like this. Celia's silence as she watched me struggle with my tears was horribly mortifying.

"I'm calling him, and I'm going to tell him to put a hex on

them," I said. I slammed my suitcase shut and picked up the phone. "Give me the guidebook, please."

"He's just a ripoff artist," Celia said nervously. She had a crucifix around her neck; back home, a statue of the Virgin Mary sat on her dresser. She told me once how the nuns at her parochial girls' school had told them that people possessed by demons could make potatoes fly through the air. Both of us had been stoned, and we'd laughed so hard we couldn't breathe.

But now she was nervous, as I had been.

Defiantly I dialed the number, bracing myself in case it had been disconnected or was no longer in service. No one had phone machines in those days.

It rang. I glanced sharply at Celia. She took a breath, eyes wide, waiting.

It stopped ringing. There was a click, followed by white noise, a surflike, *shushshushshush* in my ear as if I held a shell against it.

I licked my lips. "Hello?" No one spoke. "Mr. La Vey? Anton La Vey?"

There was more white noise.

And then something happened: I felt . . . hot. I tingled. My scalp crawled over my head. My brains quivered. I had a deep, sure sense that someone was on the other end. Someone, how shall I say it? someone who knew me without knowing me. Someone who had connected with me in a way he shouldn't have, burrowed down deep, and invaded me.

I dropped the phone on the bed and brought my fists beneath my chin. Celia looked at me in astonishment.

"What?" she whispered. She reached for the phone.

"No!" I said, but she ignored me. She listened, shrugged, and replaced the receiver in the cradle.

"What did you hear?" I asked.

"A dial tone. Holy moly, what's wrong with you? What happened?"

"I feel so . . . funny." I didn't know how to describe it. "I think someone was there."

"Then they hung up." Celia cocked her head at me. "Did he say something to you? Did he answer?"

I replied, "I don't know," but I was close to lying.

▼▼▼

An hour later, Kathy and Allen were pulled dead from the wreckage of the Datsun. They had turned the wrong way on a one-way street.

After flying through the windshield, they had no faces.

The Y was very nice to us. A doctor came and gave Celia and me sedatives. The staff asked about calling our families, Kathy and Allen's families. We hadn't even told our folks about the trip. Parents were like Richard—too close to another life that we weren't yet ready for. We were like the Lost Boys, determined never to grow up.

In a stupor after long hours of crying, Celia and I lay in her and Kathy's room, dozing through the medication. When the phone rang, I flailed for it automatically, and the fact of the deaths rushed through me again. I panicked, grabbing the receiver. A mistake, I thought; it didn't happen. The news of the accident had been a big joke, a bad trip brought on by the Thai sticks we'd smoked with a couple of Jesus freaks in the Haight—

"H'lo," I rasped.

The line crackled with the *shushshushshush* white noise. My eyes pulled open.

"Hello?"

Shushshushshush.

All at once I burned, deep and hot and hard; my eyes burned, my mouth, my fingers. My stomach, my heart. I was connected again, deep, past bone-deep—mind-deep. Mr. Spock. Beyond what you imagine you achieve when you're making love on acid.

I hung up. I lay in the stillness, wide-eyed, as Celia slept.

A few minutes later, the phone rang again. I cried out, waking Celia, who fumbled for it, got it. Her face lifted.

"It's Richard," she said. She held it out to me.

"Stay there. I'm coming for you."

"But you can't," I said stupidly, thinking that somehow his life prevented it: no vacation, the cost, the time.

"Stay there."

▼▼▼

We waited all the next day for Richard to fly in and make his way to the Y. I realized how ridiculous I had been, with my absurd, almost subconscious fear that my call to the Church of Satan had done anything besides waste a dime. I was in shock, that was it. Until then, life's possibilities had not included death. The life of the mind concluded when your brains were sliced to ribbons by windshield glass. No magic had sent Kathy and Allen down a one-way street. They had sent themselves. Stoned, with Kathy's underpants on the floor, so the police officer told us.

Richard was delayed several times. Some of our parents were also coming, and Celia's instructed her to grab a plane and go home to Greenville, North Carolina. For some hours, I would be completely alone. She seemed only mildly concerned about that, and I was very hurt.

I watched from the window at the Y as her airport shuttle pulled away from the curb. My fists clenched. I hoped she wouldn't get into an accident. It seemed so likely now that Allen and Kathy were dead. Tears rolled down my cheeks. I had loved Allen very much. And Kathy had died with me beginning to really hate her. Love and hate, and they were dead; and I was left with that, and shame, too. And grief.

The phone rang. I tensed. Richard was on the other end, announcing that he was in the lobby. I asked him to come up. I didn't like going down there; people stared at me and asked me how I was doing, and made me feel guilty for being alive.

I sat on the edge of the bed, waiting for him. It seemed to take forever, and as I waited, I grew hot, and dizzy, and I felt so . . . needy. I was reeling. My shoulders heaved as I sobbed; my entire body contracted, and I felt . . . imploded.

There was a knock. I raced to the door and let Richard in.

He took one look at me, and then he threw his arms around me and held me. He rocked me. I cried, hard, and when he kissed me, I kissed him back. He kissed me again. Again.

He said, "I love you. I've always loved you. Oh, God."

Urgency filled me. I tugged him toward the bed. We tore off our clothes and made love. It was incredible; he was by turns gentle and rough, so very eager and amazed. I found myself thinking, *He would never hurt me. He would gladly become whatever I wanted, just to have me.*

As I drifted off to sleep in his arms, his tears on my cheeks, I wondered why all us girls had been so dense. Allen was mysterious and handsome, but he was . . . had been . . . used to being loved. What a jerk. I thought of a hundred things he had done to wound me, before the final betrayal—thoughtless remarks about my appearance, forgetting my birthday, flirting with other girls. Taking Kathy to San Francisco. And I had put up with all of it.

But Richard would never do any of that. He was a prize. My prize, and I probably never would have had him if Allen hadn't died.

I was appalled that I could think like that, but that's what I did think.

Hours later, the phone rang: white noise. *Shushshushshush.* The connection made.

"Mr. La Vey," I whispered, as the tingling and burning streaked through me, engulfed me. "Mr. La Vey." Was he claiming credit? Reminding me of his presence in my life?

I lay sleepless in the bed, until it grew dark. Richard was asleep. I stole out of bed. I had just slept with another boy only hours after the death of my lover. But I looked down on Richard with tenderness, and new affection. Shyness, even. Out of catastrophe, our love was born. That was a twist in the journey I could never have anticipated.

I took a step away from the bed. Overweight, yes. And when we got home, he would read science fiction and get stoned. He would go to work. He would be no different. How had I imagined that I loved him? But I did. I did, and it wasn't like me to love him.

It wasn't me.

I looked at the phone. I started to pick it up. Then I shook my head and began to dress.

As I stepped into my jeans, the phone rose in the air and floated toward me.

Like a cartoon apparition, it bobbed before me, chest-high. The receiver lifted from the cradle; I saw each twist of the phone cord as it drew toward me, beyond, out of focus, Richard's peaceful face. My body shook; I was cold beyond belief. Then I flushed numb from head to toe. I staggered backward with my bell-bottoms around my ankles. I smacked into the door.

The phone followed, stretching the cord from the jack. It dragged over Richard's still form. Oh, God, I thought, he was dead, too. I licked my lips and tried to call to him. I couldn't make a single noise.

Overwhelmed, I closed my eyes and sank to the floor.

▼▼▼

When I awoke, Richard was standing over me, and I was back in the bed. I couldn't speak. My throat ached; I had a sharp, vivid image of the cord around my neck, strangling me.

"Hi," he said somberly. I half sat up, but he stopped me with a gentle hand. I darted my gaze around the room.

The phone sat on the stand beside the bed, innocent and unmoving.

"I have . . . I have to . . ." I said, and he held me, whispering, "Sssh. Your folks will be here soon."

After a time, I convinced him to let me up. He reluctantly agreed. I wondered if my parents would take me away. They didn't know I had been sharing a house with two men. They wouldn't like my living with Richard. They might decide a change of scenery was for the best. Home, where life was lived at the narrowest, where there was no life of the mind at all. Neither of my parents read; their most intellectual pursuit was watching game shows.

What if Anton La Vey knew how much I didn't want to go? What would happen to my parents?

I had to see him. I had to really talk to him, face-to-face. Without the connection he could force upon me.

But the guidebook listed only his phone number. And there were no yellow pages in our room.

With my reassurances and protestations that I was all right, I left Richard in the room. I took the guidebook with me, to make sure I had the correct name for the listing. As if you could forget something like the Church of Satan.

In the elevator, I began to shake. It occurred to me that Richard was a bit of a pushover. I had almost wanted him to insist that I stay with him, or that he fetch the phone book for me. But he had let me go so easily.

Then I shut my mind, lest Anton La Vey know what I was thinking and harm Richard, or perhaps even change him in some way. I would save it all for our meeting. I would tell him I didn't need his help, or interference, to run my life. I had only called him, not called to him. He must know there was a difference.

At the reception desk, the bearded, long-haired clerk tiptoed around me, the survivor, and immediately found me the phone book. He told me my parents had left a message—my phone had been busy—and would be there in two more hours.

I thanked him and carried the phone book to a bank of pay phones, ignoring his offer that I use his. I flicked the pages. Religious Associations? Churches and Synagogues? It must be there.

Yes. I found it. The Church of Satan. But listed by phone number only.

Damn. I paused. I knew what would happen if I called. But perhaps not; maybe if he knew I wanted to talk, he would speak to me this time. After all, had he not offered me the phone? At the memory of it gliding through the air, the blood drained from my face and my knees buckled. I held on to the phone box, hoping no one had noticed. I had to get through to him without any intrusions.

I dialed the number. It rang. It clicked. I waited for the white noise, the tingling, and the heat.

"Hello, Church of Satan," a woman's bright voice announced.

"I . . ." I was so surprised I stopped speaking.

"Hello?"

"Yes." I cleared my throat. "Yes, I would like your address. I would like to speak to—"

"Are you interested in becoming a member?" So eager and friendly.

"I—I saw your name in a guidebook."

"Oh, that underground thing?" She laughed. "Did they finally fix our listing?"

"Fix?"

"They had the phone number wrong. It must be right now, since you're talking to me." She babbled on while I flicked open the guidebook and compared the number with the one in the phone book.

They were different.

". . . services tomorrow evening," she concluded.

I stared at the two numbers.

"Hello? Hello, miss?"

"What—what's the other number?" I asked. My voice was quaking. "What's it for?"

"Oh, it's just nothing. All you get is a dial tone. Now, as I said, Father La Vey is out of the country, but we will have a mass tomorrow—"

I slammed the receiver down.

Anton La Vey. Anton La Vey. Oh, save me, save me, Anton La Vey. Life is too big. It's a fathomless void.

The receiver rose and floated toward me.

I screamed.

I ran.

And no one I loved ever saw me again.

THE SORCERER
EVORAGDOU
▼▼▼

DARRELL SCHWEITZER

WHEN I was ten, a naked, mad boy came into our village, proclaiming the advent of the sorcerer Evoragdou. I remember how frightened I was of that boy, though he couldn't have been more than a year or two older than me. He was so emaciated, so filthy, so burnt by the sun that he seemed less a human being than a piece of driftwood inexplicably come alive.

"Evoragdou," was all he would say, in a kind of delirium. "Evoragdou shall dwell in this place."

In time the women fed him, washed him, gave him clothes, and took him away.

I asked my father what all this meant, and he merely said, "The sun has destroyed his mind."

"Who is Evoragdou?"

"There is no such person," my father said, very sternly. I didn't think he believed what he was saying. He was hiding his own fear.

▼▼▼

Two months later, I wandered out in the night, to answer the call of nature, then to stare at the dark sky and make up stories about what I saw there.

I walked for a ways, across the rickety wooden bridge over the irrigation canal, then between the rows of newly planted grain, careful of my step. The heavens were clear and moonless, the millions of stars like the sparks of some enormous forge, frozen in time. I could never be lost in the darkness, because the Great River was behind me and the desert before me. Besides, I knew my way among the stars.

I was hungry for a miracle. Pridefully, almost arrogantly, I longed to be the special one to whom visions came, who beheld the gods leaning to whisper to one another where they sat seated like vast and looming clouds, *behind* the stars.

It never occurred to me that the mad boy might have had his own share of miracles, that they had transformed him and could transform me. No, I wanted mine. Now.

But instead of any vision of gods, the stars themselves rippled like lights reflected in windswept water, and suddenly a third of the entire sky was blotted out.

Suddenly I was standing on the doorstep of an enormous wooden building, vaster than anything I'd ever imagined could be built. With a yell, I fell back, then scrambled to my feet and ran a distance off to hide in a clump of tall grass by a water channel. There I crouched, wide-eyed, watching, listening as the fantastic house began to shift and change, its timbers creaking, groaning, shuddering, as if a living monster, not a wooden structure at all, were stirring from sleep.

There, as had been foretold, undoubtedly and undeniably, was the dwelling of the sorcerer Evoragdou.

Towers rose like slowly stretching arms. The windows opened, like eyes, black and sightless. A corner swelled outward, becoming a turret with a gleaming, glass dome on top, sparkling in the starlight.

Truly this was as great a miracle as anyone could hope for, but I waited in greedy expectation for something *more* to happen.

Toward dawn, something did: A door opened onto a balcony far above, and a silver-bearded man in a flowing robe came out. What seemed to be a living flame flickered in the outstretched palm of his hand. It was enough to illuminate his face, but I couldn't see the rest of him clearly. He might have worn a fine gown, or rags.

Slowly he turned from side to side, holding up his light as if searching for something.

I crouched very still.

Then he spoke just a few words, which made me very much afraid and sent me scurrying away through the mud on my belly in a ridiculous attempt to avoid being seen. I wanted to cry out, but I bit my lip so hard I tasted blood, and remained silent, as if somehow in silence I could still *deny* what I had heard.

At the edge of the village I got up and started running. I arrived home screaming like the mad boy who had come before.

▼▼▼

That morning, everyone went to see the sorcerer's house, but stood a safe distance away. I returned, holding my father's hand. By daylight it was even more fearsome, its details visible, no longer an ill-defined shadow but a living mountain of wood and brick and stone. Peaked roofs rippled like waves on a windswept lake to form the heads of fabulous birds or horses or dragons, which opened their eyes and mouths and wriggled their shrieking wooden tongues. More windows revealed themselves, some filled with light, some dark, appearing and vanishing like foam in a swift current. Great masses of wood turned before our eyes, revolving slowly like wheels within wheels, a pattern endlessly shifting. Sometimes the house would extend itself, walls and roofs forming a covered way, reaching out like a limb, snaking across the earth, shutters and doors clattering as if trying to speak. The people scattered to avoid it, and the extension would suddenly collapse, fusing back into the body of the house.

Everyone wanted to know what this meant. My father, my uncles, the head men of the village all conferred, speaking among themselves in hushed tones, as if they didn't want to be overheard by whoever was inside. A runner was sent to Thadistaphon for the priests. But he wouldn't be back before nightfall at least.

So we stood and waited. Throughout the day the house shifted restlessly in the hot sun, sometimes seeming to crumble into ruins, then rising up again, more magnificent and strange than before, its facade sculpted into the shapes of leaves and sunbursts and impossible beasts, sometimes into human faces which belched black smoke, then were consumed by flames before they renewed themselves.

Always the people asked the elders: Who had come to us? Why?

The elders only shook their heads and pretended not to know. But they knew. I was certain of that.

I made a serious mistake, perhaps because I wanted to be a hero, or just because I wanted to help. On an impulse, I tugged on my father's hand and said, "Papa, it is Evoragdou, I know it is."

"What?"

Hadn't anyone listened to the mad boy, who had warned us of this thing? Didn't they remember? Why were they deliberately denying the obvious?

"In the house. It is Evoragdou."

"How do you know? No one else is so certain."

I pulled away, and stood hugging my still-muddy sides, swishing one toe back and forth in the dirt. I couldn't meet my father's gaze.

"I just do."

My father seemed both sorrowful and afraid.

▼▼▼

When the priests arrived that evening, *I* was the center of attention. They took me into a shed and locked the door, then grabbed me by the arms and yanked me around and around, from one angry face to another, demanding what I truly knew. Had I gone inside the house? Didn't I know that to speak a sorcerer's name is to summon him? Had he sent me? Was I his creature, a demon shaped like a boy? What did he want here? I screamed. I wept. I couldn't answer. I tried not to tell them anything at all. More than anything else, I wished I'd been able to keep my secret to myself. They beat me with sticks. They said they would lock me in a dark hole beneath the temple in the city and I'd have to stay there forever while the sorcerer spoke out of my mouth, as inevitably he must.

I screamed some more and finally said, "I knew who he was because he said he remembered!"

The priests let go. I fell to the floor and lay still, sobbing, somehow very certain that I had ruined my entire life, that nothing would ever be right for me again.

The priests whispered among themselves, glancing down at me, then whispering some more.

Somehow they were satisfied. They didn't carry me off to the city. Instead, they filed out and left me alone in the shed, with the door unlocked. Much later, when the door opened again and my father and mother stood there, I thought I had won. I hadn't confessed everything. I hadn't told the priests that the sorcerer *had known my name*, that, as he held his tiny flame aloft in his bare palm and peered into the darkness, he had called out, "Pankeré, I know you are out there, for I am Evoragdou, and I remember."

But I had not won. It was Evoragdou who was victorious.

▼▼▼

Nothing further happened for a long time. The priests built a fence around the sorcerer's house, painted all over with signs and sigils and strange writing. Not even they had ever dared to go inside.

Soon multitudes flocked to see this wonder—first more priests, then the rich and high-born from Thadistaphon and passengers off boats that passed along the river, even a few nobles from the City of the Delta. Our village prospered as the people sold bread, palm wine, embroidered cloth, and painted images to the travelers. No two images were ever the same, for the house of Evoragdou was never the same for two consecutive hours, let alone between one day and the next.

But in time, the flow of travelers diminished. The house

merely remained as it was, forever assuming meaningless shapes, offering nothing, threatening no one. The sorcerer never emerged, nor did he speak again, through me or anyone else.

We all recited the legends of Evoragdou; some of them genuinely ancient, a lot more newly invented to amaze the foreigners and earn a coin: of his battles with monsters, his voyages to other worlds, and, most especially, how he ventured into *time* until his past and future were as confused as images in a house full of mirrors. He was the greatest of all sorcerers, we said, virtually a god. But secretly tellers and and listeners and priests alike began to suspect that only the house remained, mindless, like a waterwheel left turning when the miller has gone away, and that the sorcerer Evoragdou was dead.

The priests may have let me go, but certainly I was marked, singled out. Neighbors turned their faces from me. They made signs against me, to ward off bad luck. The other boys threw stones if I tried to come near. The girls ran away.

I think they all may even have been jealous, because I had actually seen what they and the travelers who had come so far longed to see. Certainly I felt so. I hated them for it.

But when no miracles or demons manifested themselves around me, I was allowed to grow up. Two priests returned to our village to live. They took me aside, taught me letters, and probed, very delicately, for news of the sorcerer Evoragdou. Many times I disappointed them, but they never beat me, and I even came to take comfort in their company.

They wanted me to go away with them, to become a priest too, but I would not. Unfulfilled as I was, I heard no god calling me. In the end, the priests arranged a marriage for me with a girl from another town. My parents had died by then. My wife Ricatepshé and I dwelt in the same house I had always known. I worked the same fields. Heaven sent us three sons, but a plague took two of them back again. By the time I was forty, my beard was gray, Ricatepshé's hair was almost white, and we had two children left, Nefasir, almost a grown woman, and the boy Khamiré, who was twelve. We neither starved nor particularly prospered.

▼▼▼

When I was forty, the thing happened for which I had been waiting all my life. I recognized it at once.

Nefasir woke me in the night and led me outside. She was trembling. She took my hand in hers, then pointed across the fields in an all-too-familiar direction.

"I couldn't stop him," she said, breaking into sobs.

"Stop who?"

"Khamiré. He has gone into the sorcerer's house."

▼▼▼

I spoke with Ricatepshé, trying to deny the obvious, the inevitable, for I was very much afraid.

"We must ask the priests for help," I said.

"We have no money. If the sorcerer destroys one child for whatever purpose, the priests will not risk opposing him unless they are very well paid. You know that."

"We'll go to the Satrap."

"You'd never get inside the palace. The guards would likewise demand money."

"Then I will stand in the marketplace and proclaim our plight to all who will hear, until I find a hero who is seeking fame, like Canibatos in the stories."

"Such heroes only exist in stories. Besides, what will Evoragdou have done to our son while you are waiting? Have you thought of that?"

"Then I must go myself. I am the hero. Let the story be mine."

"Yes," she said softly.

So we prayed together for an hour to all the gods whose names we knew, and I purified myself, then put on shoes and a woolen robe as if for a journey, and got out from its special chest my grandfather's sword, which he had bequeathed to my father as his firstborn, and my father to me as his, in case a hero's courage would ever be needed.

Grandfather had been a kind of hero, a soldier in King Wenamon's army during the Zargati wars. I prayed to his spirit too.

Just before dawn I set out, across the fields. Ricatepshé walked with me for a while, clinging to my arm, but let go as the sorcerer's house loomed over us like a black mountain, motionless for once, as if waiting for me. I barely noticed that my wife was gone. I lived only in that instant, concentrating on what I had to do, as I broke through the fence and entered the domain of Evoragdou.

▼▼▼

The transition was more subtle than senses could follow. The house itself reached out and embraced me, though I did not actually *see* it move. Shadows shifted, and without any sense of opening a door or climbing in through a window, I was suddenly inside, surrounded by the domain of Evoragdou.

I groped in utter darkness. The sky overhead was shut out. My hand found a wall. I followed along it to another wall, this one cold to the touch, and alive, wriggling like a tapestry of serpents. I let go in fright and disgust and staggered back, tripping over something, crashing into pots and jars.

I sat up on a creaking wooden floor, amid clay shards, trying not to think about what might have been in the jars. Something scuttled across my hand. I let out a yell.

"Do you desire a light, my brave one?" came a voice out of the air, from no particular direction.

I stood up and drew Grandfather's sword.

Now a dozen or more hands floated in the darkness, tiny blue flames dancing from upturned, bare palms.

"How very foolish," said the sorcerer, "to show your enemy what weapons you have. You lose all possibility of surprise."

I turned, slashing at the drifting hands. They scattered like moths.

"No matter. I knew you bore a sword. I remembered it clearly."

"What do you mean?" I said. "Is this some trick of yours?"

Evoragdou sighed. The tone of his voice changed distinctly.

▼ 282 ▼

He wasn't mocking me any more. He seemed, instead, regretful, melancholy. "It is certainly a trick," he said, "but one I have spent many years trying to puzzle out."

"What is the matter?" Now I mocked him, bitterly. "Can't you *remember?*" Even as I spoke, I was amazed at what I said. I tried to convince myself that I was as brave as Canibatos in the stories, daring to ridicule a sorcerer. But I didn't believe it.

"At least you are clever," said Evoragdou after a long pause. "That must count for something."

"Monster! I have come for my son. Give him to me or I shall find a way to kill you. I swear by all the gods—"

"That is odd. I don't remember you killing me."

"Show yourself, Evoragdou. Come to me *now.*"

"Here I am." His voice came from a distinct direction. I rushed toward him. The lighted hands swirled around me. I tumbled headlong down a flight of stairs, banging knees and elbows, desperately trying to catch hold of something without losing my sword.

When I came to rest at last, I shouted into the darkness. I screamed. I cursed myself and Evoragdou. I pleaded with him to let my son go free. I offered myself in the boy's place.

"Ah, Pankeré, son of Zorad, father of Khamiré, if only it were that simple. But no, you must first come to understand the entire mystery of this place, and of myself. First that. I lay this *geas* upon you."

▼▼▼

It might have been that same morning, or some other, when pale light finally seeped in through slatted windows. I lay where I had fallen, in a dusty, debris-strewn room filled with boxes, jars, bundles of cloth and, more disturbingly, with man-sized, wooden images of beast-headed demigods or demons, creatures so cunningly carved and painted that they seemed to shift slightly as the light and shadow played over them. I waited to see if they would come to life. But finally I prodded one with my sword, then ran my hand over the gilded snout of another. Only wood.

I got up and went over to one of the windows. Fumbling, I discovered a little lever that opened the window slats, and looked out.

Already I was disoriented. I had come in at ground level, then fallen down a long flight of stairs. I should have been in a cellar. But when I looked out the window I saw that I was high up, and, more amazingly, I beheld a landscape like none I had ever seen. Forested hills rolled green to the horizon, where blue mountains rose like stationary clouds. A river forked among those hills and vanished among the trees as the Great River, I was certain, never did.

The wind blowing in through that window was bitterly cold, yet dry, unlike a rainy winter wind.

Risking all, I raised the latch and opened the window, leaning out into the freezing air. I couldn't see the ground below. The house seemed to float in an endless forest like a boat among water-grass.

I drew myself back into the house, bewildered, but by now too numbed by wonder to be afraid. I made my way out of that first room, into a second, which I found utterly bare and brilliantly sunlit—only its windows revealed, instead of any forest or mountains, a placid ocean stretching to the horizon in every direction, its waves lapping less than an arm's length below the windowsills. I reached down, touched, and then tasted the salt water.

So I returned to the first room, which now had no windows at all. The disembodied, burning hands drifted among the wooden beast-men.

"Evoragdou," I called out. "Enough of this. Give me my son."

He made no reply.

I couldn't find the stairs down which I'd fallen, passing instead into a third room, where the floating hands did not follow. Here the air flickered with faint light, like a captive aurora. I stood in the doorway for a while as my eyes adjusted, then shuffled cautiously forward, probing the air in front of me with my sword, until I reached another window.

The latch came off in my hand. The shutter swung wide, this time presenting neither hills nor forests nor ocean, but infinitely receding stars. I clung to the window ledge for a long time, leaning out, somehow expecting, *demanding* that I see more. What? Some vast sky-serpent stirring in the depths? The very gods? Or perhaps the Shadow Titans, who dwell in darkness and whom the gods fear? Possibly a trained sorcerer could discern these things, but I saw only the unflickering stars.

And I shouted the name of Evoragdou once more and pleaded with him to explain himself, to end my torment, or at least let my son go, whatever he would do with me. But he did not speak, nor did he reveal himself in any way. His magical obligation, his *geas*, was embodied in this house, its mystery like a book I could not yet read, unopened on a table before me.

▼▼▼

The heroes in the stories complete their tasks quickly, invading the enemy's domain, performing mighty labors, seizing rare prizes, then returning to the familiar world, or perhaps dying nobly in battle, there amid strangeness. Think of Canibatos when he rescued the sun and moon. Think of Arvaderé and the Bird of Night, or of Sekenre, who descended into the land of the dead. Their stories came to definite conclusions.

It wasn't like that for me. The mystery was like smoke, rising forever.

I spent what could have been days or even weeks exploring the house of the sorcerer, where no two rooms were ever alike, and no room the same after I left it; nor was there any limit to the number of them; an infinity of wood and brick and stone, shifting, appearing, vanishing again.

Through the countless windows, I observed plains, deserts, mountains, rain-filled and impenetrable forests, and even the bottom of the sea where fish-headed men warred among the ruins of green-stone cities. I think I even glimpsed that empty expanse of white sand that was the entire world on the first day of creation, before ever the gods walked there and sowed living things.

This was the first part of my understanding, of the unraveling of the *geas:* that Evoragdou's house drifted through time as well as space. In sorcery, time is but an illusion or a convenience, depending on how you use it. All times are one. A million years are as an instant, an instant as a million years.

Still I searched for my son and called his name, and dreamed of him, then wept when I awoke and did not find him. In my dreams I could hear his voice and feel the touch of his hand, and the weight of him on my shoulders as I carried him when he was small was so real, so intense, that it was a special torment to discover my shoulders empty and myself alone. Ricatepshé came to me in my dreams too, speaking of everyday things: crops and prices, what ships arrived on the river, children and washing, of quarrels with the neighbors and preparations for the spring fair. It was as if I still lived with her, in my own home, in my own country, and all that I experienced in the house, everything I saw through the countless windows, these, *these* were the phantasms, the insubstantial vapors of the mind.

Nefasir appeared, with her husband Takim, whom I had never seen in waking life. Later, they brought their sons, the oldest of which reminded me so painfully of Khamiré, the child I had failed to rescue.

But in this place, what was an instant, a day, a year? Had it been any more than the count of ten since my boy had come into the sorcerer's house? *Had he even arrived yet?*

I learned to think like that, in paradoxes, in puzzles that the farmer Pankeré would have thought merely the ravings of a sun-struck madman.

In my mind, I felt the sorcerer Evoragdou's approval. It is like a lock you're trying to pick, he told me. Now the first tumblers were beginning to fall.

More. There had to be more.

In a room of living automatons, of fantastic clockworks, I discovered a trapdoor beneath a carpet. I turned a key. A metal ape raised the trapdoor. I descended a ladder to the floor below. When I let go of the rung I was holding for just a second, I was unable to locate the ladder again.

My eyes adjusted. Once more the floating, burning hands gathered around me, their flickering light revealing cubbyholes filled with scrolls, extending higher than I could reach, further in every direction than I could walk.

I knew then, or at least dared to hope that I had found Evoragdou's study and library, the core and source of his magic. Here he wove his vast enchantments. Here all locks were opened, all hidden things revealed.

Trembling with excitement, I sat down at Evoragdou's desk. The hands gathered around me, providing enough light for me to see the pages of his books.

At first any reading was a struggle, for my learning had been only what letters the priests gave me. Black, skeletal hands fetched volume after volume. At last I found something I could understand. This led me to another, and another. Click, click, click. The tumblers fell into place.

I dwelt in that dark room for weeks or perhaps months, as the hands brought me food, fresh clothing, and more books. I found Evoragdou's notes in a desk drawer and made annotations with his own brush, my handwriting at first crude and imperfectly formed, but gradually becoming so much like his own that I could not tell the two apart: the universal script of sorcery, an elegant labyrinth of swirls and dots and intricate angles.

I wore his flowing white robe now. I slept on the floor by his desk, still clutching my useless sword as I lay there, dreaming of home, of the life of the imaginary Pankeré who dwelt in a village a day south of Thadistaphon. He was a grandfather now. His daughter's children had almost grown up. His son, Khamiré, was still missing, having ventured into the sorcerer's house when he was small. Khamiré's father, Pankeré, followed him and was lost; and life became a dream and dreaming a kind of life, each enveloping the other, like a serpent endlessly swallowing its own tail.

▼▼▼

Now I set forth from the house through its many doors, on more adventures than may be told, enacting the legends of Evoragdou, both the ancient ones and those we villagers made up to get money from foreigners.

But it was I who rode the winged sphinx through the stars, into the darkness, and confronted the masters of a world of living flame. It was I who caused the lands to tremble, who raised mountains and shaped them into hieroglyphs only the gods could read. I conversed with heads of black stone in a cavern at the Earth's center. Beneath the hills of Bhakisiphidar, I slew the serpent that walked like a man.

At a crossroads, at midnight, I cut down a hanged corpse from a gibbet, speaking the Voorish name as I carved the symbol *tchod* upon its forehead. At once the corpse sprang to ferocious life and wrestled with me until dawn, when, at the sun's first touch, the dead thing's vigor departed. Just before the rotted limbs broke apart and the spirit fled, the thing whispered to me of the College of Shadows, where all sorcerers must eventually attend to gain true and complete mastery of their arts and themselves.

In that college you take a master, learning everything he has to teach and *more*, for the student must kill his master in order to graduate.

These things I did, over months or years or perhaps in the blinking of an eye. When I closed my master in a room filled with fire and mirrors, and leaned expectantly against the door, my hands and cheek burning from the heat, he spoke to me in my own voice and said, "Do you understand? Do you *remember?*"

When he was dead, I opened the door and waded ankle-deep in his ashes. A thousand like myself walked within the flawless mirrors.

"Yes, I remember and I understand," I said to them, and they to me.

Did I? I was seduced and consumed by what I had seen, what I had learned, an even more willing captive of what I had become. *The sorcerer's lust,* Evoragdou had called it once, that madness that engorges the mind, that changes and erases everything the sorcerer might have once been.

So, lustful, swollen with magic, I filed my former self away, like a book in a cubbyhole, in one of the uncountable rooms of my house.

For my house is my memory, ever growing, ever changing, each object, each window, each key in a lock, turning, each sound of groaning wood, each mote of dust another mark or swirl or curve in that delicate yet indelible script which is sorcery, which is the sorcerer's mind.

Once, a peasant broke in, shouting for vengeance, waving a useless sword. My repartee with him was witty, then sad. He demanded that I reveal my secret to him, so he might slay me. Ah, if only it were that simple.

I left him stumbling about in the dark on a mission of eventual self-discovery.

I knew perfectly well who he was. It remained only for him to find out.

This incident too aroused a mote, a speck of memory. My mind stirred. I sat up suddenly on a pallet of straw in a room filled with carven, marble trees. I felt the sudden and subtle pang of an old sorrow.

"Khamiré, my son," I said aloud. "Come to me now."

Bare feet shuffled on the marble floor. I reached out, caught hold of a thin arm and drew the boy to me, weeping, embracing him.

He struggled at first, but I spoke his name again and calmed him. Then we went out onto a porch, and looked out over the muddy flood-plain of the still receding Great River. The full moon shone overhead, and the spring stars.

I dropped to my knees before the boy, holding his frail wrists in my hands. He was so gaunt, so dirty, his clothing no more than a few ragged scraps. I think he had already been on his journey a long time.

"Why did you go into the sorcerer's house?" I asked him. "Why did you begin all this?"

"I came because you called me, Father," he said. "I didn't begin anything."

"No," I said slowly. "I do not think there even *is* a beginning. That is the greatest mystery of all, lives reflected again and again like something seen in a thousand mirrors, but without any initial cause, any solid thing to cast the first reflection."

"I don't understand, Father."

I stood up. I ran my fingers slowly though his hair.

"Nor do I."

We stood in silence for a time, looking out over the fertile earth. "I am not your father anymore," I said after a while. "*Pankeré* is one of many names meaning 'tiller-of-the-field.' How very appropriate for such a man as your father. But *my* name means 'clutter' or 'forgetting' or 'accumulation' or perhaps 'many dreams.' All these, too, fit. My name has many meanings, like hidden rooms. It changes like foaming water, utterly different and yet the same from one instant to the next. It contains everything and nothing. It is not so simple as 'Pankeré.' "

He shook his head. His wide eyes gleamed in the moonlight. Tears streaked his muddy cheeks. "What shall I do . . . Father?"

I lifted him up. He didn't resist. I marveled at how light he was, like a bundle of sticks. Gently, I lowered him down over the porch railing, until his toes touched the newly deposited mud. He sank almost to his knees, clinging to the railing, gazing up at me.

"I want you to go back home," I said, "and tell everyone what you have seen."

"Yes, Father. I will."

"Khamiré, do you know who I really am?"

He did not answer me, but turned away and waded through the mud, his feet making sucking sounds as he struggled toward higher ground. I shouted my true name after him. I told him who I was, once, twice, three times, as loud as I could. The third time only, he looked back at me and screamed like a lunatic, then hurried on with renewed desperation. At last, I saw him in the distance, running in the moonlight, wheeling his arms.

When he was gone, I went back into my house, climbed a spiral staircase I had never seen before, of beaten silver, then emerged onto an unfamiliar balcony, and surveyed what might have been almost the same landscape, but now a plowed and planted field. Brilliant stars gleamed in a moonless night sky.

Near at hand, a few reeds clustered along an irrigation channel. Someone was hiding there.

"Pankeré, I know you are out there," I said, "for I am Evoragdou, and I remember."

A WALK ON THE WILD SIDE
▼▼▼

KARL EDWARD WAGNER

LESLIE Lancaster sat on the edge of the steaming tub, pain-stakingly shaving his legs with a pink disposable razor. He was not quite nineteen, but his fine blond beard was enough of a problem to require use of an Emulsifying Ointment BP to soften it for a close, smooth shave, and later some Savlon antispetic cream to soothe the burn. Towelling dry, he wrapped himself in his terrycloth dressing robe and sat down to make up his face.

Leslie Lancaster's parents lived prosperously in Colorado, and they assumed from his cards that their son was enjoying his summer abroad at a youth hostel in London while taking in museums and art galleries and the Changing of the Guard; perhaps a walking tour of the Cotswolds or wherever to perk him up after his nervous collapse at school. In fact Leslie had sublet a small flat in Crouch End for the summer and was supplementing his monthly allowance in a manner his parents could scarcely approve of or understand.

His hair was blond and straight, and Leslie had had it styled in a pert pageboy that fit well beneath a wig if he chose to wear one. Mostly he left off the wig and relied upon his rather pretty features and his skill with the cosmetics his sister had shown him how to use. Lydia was three years his senior and very pretty, and

Leslie had burst into tears that day when she had come home unexpectedly and found him dressed in her clothes. She had thought their mother had been shifting her things about.

Dad had taken him to football games in Denver, which Leslie found boring and incomprehensible. When Leslie threw up over the carcass of the deer his father had just shown him how to field dress, Dad had called him Momma's Little Girl. Momma was preoccupied with her church work and often remarked that her life would have been far simpler had Leslie been born a girl and could wear Lydia's hand-me-downs. Lydia had wanted a sister and resented Leslie with all the usual nastiness of sibling rivalry.

When she found him dressed in her clothes, the two held one another and cried much of the afternoon.

After that, she took him shopping for a feminine wardrobe of his own and taught him how to dress up.

Lydia was starting law school now. Leslie was having an educational holiday in London after his little breakdown at school. Next year he would be a senior at Colorado State (his parents had enrolled him in a grade school program for gifted students, making him younger than his class), and this summer he was considering slashing his wrists rather than returning home.

For now, Leslie tied on a semitransparent latex gaff to hide his male bulge. His cock tucked securely away, he pulled on a pair of black silk French-cut knickers and checked the result in his wardrobe mirror. Credible. Perhaps he'd get the operation someday.

The estrogen seemed to be taking some effect meanwhile. Leslie hoped to have real breasts in time. He squeezed his growing breasts hopefully. Maybe soon, with a padded platform bra. For today he struggled into a soft black bra, fastening the hooks in front and then sliding the cups to the front, fitting Spenco Soft Touch Breast Forms into the cups as he shifted them over his own small breasts. He inspected himself in the mirror. The bounce of the breast forms felt real; the darkened areola and preformed nipple protruded from the soft nylon to good effect. Someday silicone implants. Damn the risk.

Leslie Lancaster was slight of build—another failing for which his father had never forgiven him. The 38-C padded bra fit him well, and he could sometimes slither into a size 8 dress. He had been secretly crossdressing since puberty, for three years now with his sister's help, and he was not a virgin except with a woman. After his breakdown, Lydia had urged him to make the transformation here in London, away from Mom and Dad and Colorado. Long pendant earrings framed his face and made the short pageboy look sexy.

Preliminaries completed, Leslie tugged on a pair of opaque black tights and a very brief black miniskirt. Then a loose black silk blouse that allowed his silicone breast forms to bounce with his gait, and a black cotton jacket with minimal shoulder padding. His shoulders were small, and he looked very sophisticated in an off-the-shoulder party dress. His legs were good, and the jacket and micro-miniskirt made his slim hips less obvious. Black stiletto pumps finished the ensemble, and Leslie had already learned to walk on five-inch heels on London pavement. He examined his face in the mirror, decided a hat wasn't required, and picked up his handbag. No trace of Colorado.

And he was a she.

▼▼▼

Leslie usually turned her tricks in Soho when the tourists were about. Arabs paid well. When money was tight, it was Nightingale Lane and Ramsden Road and Oldridge Road and hanging around The Grove. No Arabs in limos. Quickies in side streets. Maybe a beating. Best to work Soho. Or Kensington. Quiet park bench and a knob job. Chase down the come with a half lager at The Catherine Wheel. Ten quid extra without the condom. Sometimes she got extra when the John groped her cock. Sometimes a bloody lip. She carried mint-flavored Mates, not-lubricated, reservoir tip. Kept her breath clean and fresh.

Now then. Leslie Lancaster was sitting inside The Munchkin on St. Giles High Street off Charing Cross. The pub had earlier been named The München and had just been renamed The Conservatory, but would always be known as The Munchkin. Leslie had three friends she often met there before strolling over to Soho or wherever.

There was Samantha Starr, a lovely transsexual just beginning to show her age, which was probably twenty-five but old enough to advise Leslie on her chosen path: she was Leslie's best friend and everything Leslie wanted to become. There was Jo Crowther, a slim dyke who had her suspicions about Leslie, but who was too caught up in her abstract paintings to bother pressing further. And there was Philip Anthony, a graying poet, extensively published, peripherally distributed, eternally inebriated, who was clueless about Leslie or he would have been interested. Leslie had met the latter two through Samantha, and she had met Samantha whilst crouched over the toilet with an unsecured door one evening at the Ladies' in the Munchkin. Yes, women are far messier: never sit down on the seat. Samantha had become her mentor and guide, and sometimes Samantha arranged special sessions for better money than the streets.

Samantha said "You're looking very trendy this afternoon. Very much the London office girl." Samantha had on a long blond wig, but was otherwise dressed almost identically to Leslie—thus the joke.

"Yes," said Leslie. "I fear it's catching this season." Her low American accent translated well as a woman's voice to British ears, accustomed as they were to overseas mauling of their language.

"It suits you well," Jo commented, lighting her cigarette. She waved the smoke away, remembering that it made Leslie cough. Jo was Irish and had lovely auburn hair, shorter than Leslie's. They were of a size, but Jo was wearing a black leather jacket and artfully torn jeans.

"Thank you." Leslie had never made it with another woman, although Samantha had shown her what to do. She sensed mutual interest and made her eyes wide and innocent as she finished her half lager.

Philip stood up and pointed at their glasses. "Same again, ladies?" He and Jo were drinking pints of bitter, Leslie and Samantha half lagers. Philip saw himself as an aging cavalier poet, surrounded by a court of adoring young ladies, and as such he was good always for more than his share of rounds. He was fond of doffing his tweed hat and bowing over their hands, and he was harmless.

Leslie scanned the rest of the patrons. Early in the evening, and mostly the science fiction crowd who hung out here. No money there, although several of the guys had tried to pick her up. Leslie kept it on a business level, although there was the wicked thrill of it. Turn a few tricks every other night or so. Found in the street: over and above her parental allowance. Paid for the flat and a growing wardrobe. On the street she gave only head. No undressing. Unzip his fly, and face in his lap. Quick and easy and out of there. Twenty-five quid for five minutes, ten extra without the condom, swallowed or sprayed over her face. She much preferred a condom. No aftertaste, no sticky mess to ruin her make-up. And no choking. With practice she could now deep-throat an entire cock and hold it there as he ejaculated, feeling the warm spasms of come pulsing into the condom against the back of her throat. She enjoyed the sensation, and the sudden detumescence that meant job over and money in hand. No taxes withheld.

"Here you are, ladies." Philip was back, sloshing glasses. He resumed his chair and lifted his pint. "A toast to the summer solstice, the longest day of the year."

"Is that today?" Leslie could not believe that she had been here in London nearly three months. Two months more, then back to Colorado. She couldn't do it.

"Bad time to be a vampire," Jo said, concerned at Leslie's sudden dismay. "Or to be a Druid sacrifice."

"Oh, the Druids never sacrificed anyone," Philip jumped in, blissfully uninformed as usual. "You know, I'm thinking of joining Wicca. When I was a bit younger, I used to participate in Morris dancing."

"And got hit over the head by a stick." Jo was on a roll, and she got Leslie to giggle.

Leslie got beer up her nose in the process and made for the Ladies'. Samantha followed her in and watched as she fixed her face.

"Look. Do you have any real plans for tonight?" Samantha knew well she hadn't.

Leslie blew her nose. "What did you have in mind?"

"I have an address. Private session." Samantha had dubious connections and had taken Leslie under wing.

"Have you been putting those cards into phone boxes again? The ones that read 'Ultimate Mistress For Lovers Of The Bizarre. Dial 229-something' and that sort? Because the last time you talked me into participating in one of those sessions, I was made to wear a gym slip and to take ten strokes of the cane from a nasty old man—among other things."

"And your share for the evening was fifty knicker."

"I had serious welts for days."

"At five quid a welt. Besides, it was safe sex." Samantha's sex change had been expensive, and her heroin habit wasn't cheap. The weirdos paid well, and she considered their money hers for the taking. Leslie ought to feel more grateful for the work.

"This isn't going to involve water sports, is it?" Leslie drew the line at getting pissed on. Once a geezer had fastened her head in some sort of portable toilet while Samantha squatted over her face. The Brits were a kinky lot, she thought, but then, who was she to talk. She just wanted their money, quick and easy.

"There may be a little B&D, perhaps some spanking. Look, they've seen you with me and asked about you. I told them you were a submissive teenage model who only posed and nothing more. Well, I hinted that you might give a little head for the right knicker. And anyway, I'll be there with you. Safe as houses, and we split two hundred quid plus tips."

"Two hundred quid! That's more than just spanking!"

"Well, there will be several participants." Samantha put her arm around Leslie. "Come on, love. They want the both of us, but I can always phone up another friend."

A woman entered the loo then, so Leslie adjusted her lip gloss while she thought about it. Probably mean a bright red bum in the morning, but a hundred quid plus whatever extra the geezers paid was better than trolling for Arabs in Soho. And Samantha did know the ropes. Literally.

And there was the strapless black leather minidress she'd been dying for in Kensington Market. With the right underwired push-up bra, she'd look smashing in it.

Back at their table, Philip was entertaining Jo with much lurid misinformation about primitive fertility rites performed at the changes of seasons. Jo was very happy to leave Leslie and Samantha to Philip while she bought a round. Philip was a dear old poofter, and at least he hadn't begun to recite his poetry. Yet.

Later, as they were leaving The Munchkin, Jo caught Leslie by the arm. She said in a low voice "Will you listen to me? Just mind yourself following about Samantha so much. She's wild, and she's well clueless."

Jealousy? Leslie wondered. She left the pub with the trace of a blush. She had also had a bit more lager than she'd intended. Philip had recited three of his latest poems, and drink was required.

▼▼▼

It was a warm night as they stood out on the pavement for a taxi. Taxis used St. Giles High Street as a shortcut, so even this close to nine they had no difficulty. The sky was still bright, owing to the summer solstice, with shadows now dissolving into deeper shadow.

Leslie studied her face in her compact mirror, feeling anxious. "Do they know about me?"

Samantha shared some of her Valiums. She was in a giggly mood. "I just said that you were an American teenage runaway out for a spanking good time!"

That was the funniest line either of them had ever heard, and they hugged one another in a fit of snorting laughter. The driver wondered if they were likely to get sick in his cab. Probably sisters having a reunion, he decided, although the younger one had picked up a slight American accent while abroad.

They got off in Battersea at a pub called the Northcote, as Samantha wanted another half lager and both needed a slash. Also they were early, and the driver couldn't find Auckland Road owing to the car dealership that had obliterated the street sign at this end of Battersea Rise. After, they clopped quickly down the pavement like giddy schoolgirls, clutching their handbags to their middles, laughing away as they talked, paying no mind to their surroundings. Leslie envied the bounce of Samantha's implanted breasts. She'd have hers done at the same clinic.

"Shouldn't we have dressed better for this?" Leslie asked. She had had three of Samantha's Valiums together with the lagers, and she was no longer on Planet Earth.

"I don't think our clothing will long be a factor," said Samantha, starting another run of giggles.

Leslie felt wonderful. Colorado was only a bad dream.

Then Auckland Road began to oppress her. It was a tiny side-street of row houses, brown bricks showing urban decay. Some houses showed diffident potted plants upon the stoop, others appeared abandoned. Leslie could smell curries cooking somewhere. Reggae music thumped in the gathering darkness. The pub at the end of the street looked cheerless and silent.

"Here! They've said two hundred pounds? Look where we are."

Samantha took her arm. "Obviously they've let a flat, love. Hardly discreet to plan their gatherings where their neighbors are all watching, is it?"

They rang a bell near the end of the street. Leslie was reassured when a young man in pinstripes welcomed them inside. The houses on either side were dark and appeared vacant; this house had an empty feel to it, and Leslie told herself that it was one of those places sublet by the hour or night for special needs. Once Samantha had taken her to a sinister flat in Clapham where Leslie had been dressed into a latex maid's costume and required to give head to a similarly clad Japanese gentleman, while Samantha pranced about in a leather corset and whipped them both with a riding crop. Afterward the John had given both of them head.

Whips and costumes left with the management. Most hotels did not offer this service.

Leslie sighed as she entered. Just do the trick, take their money, go home. Beats working the burger-doodles in Colorado.

Outside, it was finally dark.

Upstairs, there must have been a dozen people scattered about the large sitting room and kitchen: men and women, mostly well dressed with a few leather-clad punkers. A skinhead in knicker boots handed Leslie and Samantha cups of some hot mulled punch from a bowl in the kitchen.

"God, it's an orgy!" Leslie whispered to Samantha, smiling graciously as she sipped her punch. "Why do they need us? Looks like we're to put on a show for them."

The punch was well laced with rum and probably much more. It hit Leslie between the eyes after the earlier imbibements. She swayed and found herself hanging onto a professorial gentleman, who listened to her every word. Samantha was quickly counting fifty pound notes and shoving them into her handbag. She nodded to Leslie and patted her bag, then headed for the loo.

Someone gave Leslie another cup of punch. The walls were decorated with primitive masks and paintings that reminded Leslie of ancient cave drawings. There was a ballet barre standing in the center of the room, sturdily fastened to the floor. A spanking stand, Leslie guessed. The whips and leather gear were likely in another room.

"Just over here," said the professorial gentleman, leading her to the ballet barre. "Have you quite finished with your punch?"

"I think I've had a glass too many." Leslie sensed more at work than the alcohol and Valium, and she began to feel panic.

"Just lean against this barre," advised the kindly gentleman.

Leslie placed her hands upon the barre, trying to keep on her feet. Two women were tying her ankles to the uprights of the barre, while the skinhead bound her wrists together to the horizontal bar. One of the women fitted her with a collar and chain, pulling her head down so that she was bent over the barre, legs widespread, ass exposed, and totally helpless. The other woman expertly strapped a rubber ball-gag tightly into her mouth, then thoughtfully rearranged Leslie's hair and earrings over the strap.

She sensed this had all been done here before. Often.

Here's where I earn my hundred quid, thought Leslie, wondering why the Brits had this thing about spanking. The school system probably. She looked about for Samantha. People were removing their clothes now. Well, she couldn't give head with this gag in place. Samantha would look after her if things got rough.

"Shall I strip her now?" asked the skinhead.

"Leave that for Him to enjoy," said the professor.

Leslie blinked, trying to stay alert. She tottered in her stiletto heels and would have fallen, but her bonds held her in a fixed position, and she could only slump forward. She felt someone pull up her miniskirt, then hands groped her ass. Someone poured some sort of warm liquid over her tights. Was that blood? It smelled like a goat pen. Sick.

She hoped they wouldn't use canes; that one session had been enough. She chewed on her rubber gag, looking about for Samantha. Everyone was quite naked now, except for Leslie. They were circling about her now. She turned her head. She couldn't see Samantha anywhere. This wasn't Colorado.

Leslie managed to count. There were thirteen of them in the room. Naked men and women. Someone was drawing a star in a circle about her as she clung to the barre. She supposed the words at the points of the star were Latin, just as she supposed their chanting was Latin—or something else unintelligible. Leslie hadn't a word of Latin, and she knew absolutely nothing about either witchcraft or Satanism; but she had seen horror films, and she couldn't see Samantha. Maybe she was off getting into some dominatrix gear.

They were copulating now as they circled her—women bent over and men riding their backsides like herd animals mating, shuffling all around her, chanting.

It wasn't just a weird orgy with a lot of kinky perverts at all. Through the veil of drugs, Leslie knew real fear.

A moment later, the horned man appeared with the pentacle behind her, and then Leslie *knew real fear.*

She strained helplessly at her bonds, trying to tell herself it was the drugs, that it was only a man with very much body hair and some fake antlers tied to his head. This was like watching *Rosemary's Baby.* Surely the enormous erect phallus was fake— at least a foot in length and dart-headed like an animal's. Leslie caught a glimpse of his eyes and knew none of it was fake. She lowered her face and moaned into her gag. Maybe *this* was the bad dream.

He snuffled the animal menstrual blood and urine that had been poured over her buttocks. Flat-taloned hands then ripped apart her black tights, shredded her silk knickers, exposing her ass to the chanting coven and its master. Her gaff still concealed her shrinking cock and balls from their sight, and Leslie felt a strange sense of relief that they still hadn't guessed.

The enormous head of the penis rubbed impatiently against her, seeking an opening, skidding across the crack of her ass. Leslie had only been sodomized on occasion—usually by Saman-tha's double-ended dildo—and she hadn't liked it at all. But needs must when the devil drives.

The room was dimly lit. As the taloned hands pulled her hips closer, Leslie wriggled her ass to meet the questing penis head, felt it lodge in her asshole, and pushed back against it quickly.

She screamed as the pointed head popped suddenly past her overmatched sphincter muscles. She kept screaming as the twelve-inch cock brutally penetrated her rectum, glanced off her prostate and pushed deep inside her colon. She kept on screaming as the horned man began to thrust vigorously in and out of her ass, grasping her hips and grunting with each stroke.

But, of course, that was the reason for the ball-gag.

Only the ropes and the horned man's hands held Leslie from falling. She had bitten deeply into the hard rubber gag, her sobs and gasps replacing her useless screams. She began to echo the horned man's grunts with each thrust, angling her hips as best she could to accommodate his assault. The huge animal phallus was stuffing her, ripping in and out of her insides, as she jolted helplessly in her bonds.

The others were circling them, switching partners, copulating like rutting animals to match the movements of their deity and his virgin bride. Leslie knew she could never pull free from the horned man's grip on her—not until his seed had been spent within her. Despite the terror and the pain, Leslie was joining into their sexual frenzy. She knew Johns. She knew she was giving this one a terrific fuck. She rocked her hips into his loins, wanting every massive inch of him inside her body.

When the horned man came, Leslie screamed anew against her gag—screaming now in passion rather than pain, although the pain was intense. Molten iron seemed to be gushing into her rectum, filling her insides with a rush of inexpressible energy. She thought of an endless cocaine enema, shaking her total being. In that same surge, she felt her own orgasm shudder through her, as her penis jetted spurts into her latex gaff.

As the horned man slowly withdrew from her bleeding ass, Leslie collapsed against her bonds. She was barely conscious when she felt a taloned hand explore her wet gaff, then rip it away. She thought she heard an outraged snarl—like a chainsaw hitting barbed wire in a dead oak.

She was totally unconscious just as the *real* screaming began.

▼▼▼

Dawn came early with the summer solstice, and dawn found Samantha sprawled upon the bathroom floor. That last hit of smack had been over the top after all the rest. She collected her works, amazed to find it all there, and went to look for Leslie.

Leslie was where Samantha had last seen her, slumped over the barre. From the look of it, things had become a bit too wild during the night. Samantha untied her, wincing at the blood and semen that had dried on Leslie's torn tights and thighs. She pulled her skirt down to cover her and helped Leslie to a couch; then went into the kitchen for tea. She settled on a bottle of brandy and shared some with Leslie.

"Rough night?" She inquired sympathetically, as the brandy brought Leslie around. They must have all done her ass. Tough on the kid, but it was just a job. Actually they'd only wanted Leslie for the night, but Samantha had insisted on coming along to chaperone and to collect.

"You bitch," said Leslie. She wanted to strangle her but was too sore.

Jo was right: Samantha was clueless. "Look. I told you there'd be a little B&D involved. And now we have our two hundred knicker."

"Half of which you got just to set me up."

"That's still one hundred pounds to your gain. And you're no virgin—though I swore you was. And I meant to help. Really!"

Samantha looked about, unrepentant, still well knackered. "Where did they all go? Look! They've left their clothing all about!"

"I'm certain they're all warm enough without it," said Leslie.

Glancing down into her blouse, she felt her enlarged nipples pressing against her breast forms, pushing them uncomfortably against her tight bra. Her silk blouse, unscathed through it all, was about to burst open. Leslie tugged out the forms, and her breasts filled the bra cups completely.

Her black miniskirt covered her thighs and torn undergarments.

Soon Leslie would have to look.

MOTHER AND CHILD
REUNION
▼▼▼

TIM SULLIVAN

BILLY knew that he shouldn't have stayed for the second feature. It was called *Dark Sabbat*, and he told himself as the creepy opening titles unrolled that he would just watch for a few minutes. He could get away with that, but if he came home after dark, he was going to be in trouble.

But the sight of a beautiful woman locked in an iron maiden, blood gushing out from beneath its suggestively carved lid, transfixed him—as did the witch's rising from her grave; the bloody murders of several minor characters; and the final burning at-the-stake scene which seemed to rid the earth of the evil but sexy witch once and for all. Watching her writhe, her smooth skin shiny with sweat, Billy felt something new and yet oddly familiar. His penis grew until it wedged his shorts uncomfortably into his backside.

As the final credits rolled and the lights came up, Billy didn't get out of his seat right away. Not just because of his erection, but also because he had enjoyed the film so much that he didn't want it to end.

Soon the deliciously weird images gave way to dark thoughts

of what was going to happen when he got home. He got up and made his way through the deserted lobby of the decrepit movie palace. Only an old man stood at the door, wearing a maroon uniform with gold epauletes on his sloping shoulders.

It was dark between the streetlamps, and the wind was blowing pretty hard. Billy pulled up his collar against the cold and started walking. The sidewalk smelled of stale piss. He caught sight of the clock on city hall: seven-thirty. God, was he gonna get it.

He tried to keep thinking about the movie, but his dread increased as he got closer to home. He turned the corner of his street, walking very slowly up the hill. He wasn't thinking of the movie at all by the time he opened the front door and stepped softly inside.

The odor of cooking meat filled the front hallway. His parents must have been in the dining room, having dinner. Or maybe the food was warming in the oven while they waited for him. They were gonna kill him.

Maybe if he sneaked upstairs real quietly, got into bed, and pretended to sleep . . . maybe he could come down in the morning and pretend he'd been in his bedroom the whole time. He could say he'd been reading; that's why they didn't hear him. And he'd dozed off before dinner. . . . They'd never realized he was in the house, ha ha, and it had all been a big misunderstanding.

Of course, they'd never believe it. He'd have to face them sooner or later. Might as well get it over with.

Still wearing his jacket, he went into the dining room. He was surprised to see the table set, but Mom and Dad not there. They must be in the kitchen. Sighing, he passed through the swinging doors.

Dinner was in the oven, all right—smelled like beef cooking— but the kitchen was empty, too. Where was everybody?

Even more than he did before, he wanted to go up to his room and hide out until morning. He had a feeling that something awful was about to happen, and the best thing to do was just keep away from it, just sleep through it.

He passed through the silent house and returned to the staircase. He clutched the newel post, looking up. It seemed a long way to the top. He swallowed air and started for the second floor.

Each step groaned underfoot. About halfway to the top, he heard another groan. It was coming from his parents' bedroom.

"Oh, God!"

It was Mom!

He froze.

"Oh, Jesus! God!"

Someone was hurting her! There was somebody else in there, grunting, wheezing like an animal. Dad?

Looking around wildly, he tried to think. Somebody was doing something to his parents in their bedroom, maybe holding them at gunpoint. Threatening them. Torturing them.

His mom cried out. "Jesus! God! Oh, God!"

Whatever was happening, Billy had to put a stop to it. But what could he do? He was just a kid.

He looked around, desperately trying to think of something. His eyes were level with the second floor, and at the end of the hallway he saw the gun cabinet. He had to go past his parents' room to get to the rifles. If he should make any noise, he might get killed!

It took another scream from his mother to make him take the next step. The creak of the step scared him to death, but he heard more grunting and screaming that seemed to cover the sound of his footsteps. He was sweating so much his shirt was clinging to him under his coat.

Five more steps and he was on the landing. His parents' bedroom was just ahead to the right. He had to *really* be quiet now.

The bedroom door was ajar. As Billy moved toward it with agonizing slowness, he heard his father's animal grunting more clearly. He didn't want to think that his dad could make noises like that, but there was no mistaking his voice.

"Oh! Oh! Oh! Ooooohhh!" Mom shrieked.

That made him hurry up. He crept past the door and made his stealthy way to the cabinet. His hands were slippery as he tried to open it. It wouldn't budge.

He strained to free it, smearing sweat on the wood and glass, but he couldn't. It was locked. So where the hell was the key?

"Oh, no . . ." he muttered. He remembered where he'd seen the key when he'd gone hunting with Dad. It was on Dad's key chain, the one with the plastic family crest.

A horrible, sputtering, wheezing cry came from the bedroom. It was Dad, and it sounded like he was dying.

Gritting his teeth so hard he thought his jaw would crack, Billy balanced himself on his left leg and raised his right foot. He kicked hard, and watched in amazement as glass cascaded down in front of him. He leaped back to avoid being cut.

The glass under his feet crunched and tinkled as he reached into the cabinet and touched the stock of Dad's twelve-gauge. The ammunition was stored in boxes in a drawer under the rifles. He fumbled with it frantically.

"What the hell do you think you're doing?"

Billy whipped around. He was greeted with the incredible sight of his parents, neither of them wearing a stitch of clothing, standing in the hallway.

"I . . ." Billy didn't know what to say. Where was the kidnapper? What was going on? He had never seen his parents naked before. Actually, Mom wasn't *completely* naked. She was pulling a robe over her soft, pale shoulders. But he could see her breasts, and down below, a dark triangle of—

"Answer me!" his father demanded. He took a threatening step forward, and Billy watched in astonishment as his dad's penis swung from side to side, wetly striking his hairy thighs.

"I thought somebody was hurting Mom . . ." Billy heard his voice trail off.

Dad stopped. Mom was standing behind him, putting on her robe to cover her nakedness. "Hurting Mom? Hurting her? Don't you know what man and wife do when they're alone, at your age? Did I raise a half-wit?"

Billy didn't say anything. When Dad got like this, there was no way to talk to him.

"Answer me, goddammit!"

Dad lunged, swinging his arm in a blind rage. Billy ducked, slipping under Dad's armpit, his face passing near the hairy crotch. He caught a whiff of some strong odor he'd never smelled before, though it was oddly familiar.

"*Jesus Christ!*" Dad screamed. Billy couldn't see him, but he heard a sickening crunch of glass and the heavy sound of Dad falling to the floor.

Billy tried to run. Mom blocked his path, though, stretching her arms out to enclose him. He looked up into her icy blue eyes, and knew that he couldn't escape from her.

"You're hurt," she said, a statement rather than a question.

Billy started to say that no, he was all right, but she wasn't talking to him. She looked past him at Dad.

Billy couldn't resist looking over his shoulder. He saw Dad picking himself up off the floor. Dad's big hands were red, and as he stood, he smeared blood across his chest, clutching his heart as if he were about to die.

"You'd better go into the bathroom and clean up," Mom said. "I'll be in to help in a moment."

Muttering, Dad walked past them with a hangdog expression on his face, and holding his dripping hands against his chest, went through the bedroom door.

Mom still had her arms around Billy, and he felt her warmth against his sweating body. He smelled the same odor he'd noticed on Dad, almost as if they were two parts of the same salty creature. It didn't smell like either one of them, but somehow like both.

"Billy," his mother said in much the same tone she had used to tell Dad to go clean up his cuts, "go downstairs and get cleansers, a bucket and sponges from under the kitchen sink."

"Okay, Mom." He backed away from her and started downstairs. His face was level with her lips for just a moment, and as she turned to go into the bedroom, her robe parted. He saw what looked like blood on her thighs.

But that was impossible. The blood hadn't even spattered on

Billy, and he was *between* her and Dad. And Dad hadn't touched her on his way into the bathroom. So how could she have blood on her like that . . . especially down there?

She was gone, and he couldn't be sure of what he'd seen, but it sure looked like blood. What *had* they been doing in there when he disturbed them by breaking the glass? As he headed to the kitchen, he remembered what Dad had said about man and wife, and realized that he had never thought of his parents making love before.

He got the cleansers, bucket, rags, and sponges, filled the bucket with hot water, and toted it back upstairs. It sloshed onto the carpet as he set it down. Billy got down onto his knees, sprayed some cleanser on the carpet and dipped a sponge into the bucket. He wiped the blood up as best he could by the bedroom door, and worked his way back toward the gun cabinet. The cleanser frothed as he listlessly rubbed it in circles, turning the yellow carpet to orange.

"Ow!" He felt the glass shard pierce his fingertip, popping through the skin like a knife point through paper. Holding up his shaking hand, he looked at the crystalline bit protruding from his index finger. A gleaming maroon bubble swelled around the penetration point, grew until gravity could no longer hold it, quivered, and dropped onto the carpet.

He watched it fall straight into a tacky puddle of Dad's blood. Staring at the spot, he couldn't be sure exactly which was his blood and which was Dad's. He pulled out the sliver and absently wrapped a rag around his sore finger.

He heard Mom and Dad talking, but he couldn't tell what they were saying behind the closed bedroom door. Just the sound of their voices was enough to get him moving again.

Still, he worked around the area where his blood had fallen. He was reluctant to wipe it away for some reason. He couldn't explain why, but it had something to do with his relationship with Mom and Dad.

The red stain spread on the rag around his finger as he

worked. The cut stung, but he would wash the cleanser out of it later. It was best to finish this job, so Mom wouldn't be so mad at him.

Not that she would do anything to him. No, it was always Dad who punished him. But he knew that Dad was only carrying out Mom's wishes. He'd heard Grandma say it once—Mom was strong-willed. That was why she got her way. It was a good thing, though, most of the time; things wouldn't go so good if Dad was running things, which Dad himself admitted.

He heard his mom calling: "Finish that up, Billy, and get ready for dinner."

He scrubbed harder.

▼▼▼

The shepherd's pie was pretty dried out by the time they had dinner. The way things were going, he didn't feel very hungry anyway.

"Pass the peas," Dad grunted, reminding Billy of the noises that had come from the bedroom earlier.

Billy did as he was asked, picking up the bowl of peas and passing it to Dad. His index finger pressed against the warm ceramic and made him wince. He almost dropped the bowl, and it slammed down pretty hard on the table. Dad didn't seem to notice, though. He just spooned some peas onto his plate and kept eating grimly.

"Billy," Mom said, "where were you?"

Billy stopped chewing. "Huh?"

"Don't talk with your mouth full," said Dad, chewing.

Billy swallowed the mass of potatoes and stringy beef.

"Well?" Mom demanded. Her eyes were as silver-blue as the sky before a storm. "Why did you get home from school so late, Billy? Where were you?"

"I . . ."

Mom leaned forward expectantly. Dad kept chewing while she said, "Yes, tell me."

". . . went to the movies."

"The movies. And what did you see?"

"Two shows."

"The titles, please."

"Well, one was *The Chuckling Brain from Outer Space.*"

Dad's shoulders shook a little, but his mouth was so full it was hard to tell if he was smiling.

Mom never took her eyes away from Billy's eyes. It was as if there were an invisible thread connecting her left eye with his right, her right eye with his left. "And the other film's title, Billy?"

Here, he was on shakier ground, and he knew it. Maybe he should make up something. No, because all Mom had to do was look in the paper, and she'd see what the double feature was. He had to tell her the truth.

Dad swallowed his food with an audible gulp. "Answer your mother," he said.

He looked at Dad with pleading in his eyes, but the Old Man's frown told him he wasn't gonna get out of this. He cleared his throat. "*Dark Sabbat.*"

Mom just kept looking at him, completely still. Dad didn't actually say anything, but he kind of rumbled, like he had gas or something. The cooling oven pinged softly.

Finally, looking confused, Dad spoke: "Some kind of devil worship thing?"

"Just a horror story, Dad."

Dad was thinking about that, but Mom leaned forward. "You know you're not supposed to see those kinds of movies, don't you, William?"

William. This was getting ominous. He said in a low voice, looking down at his plate: "Yes, ma'am."

She smiled at him, which was the worst thing that she could have done. "And yet you did go to this movie, coming in very late, so that dinner's spoiled, breaking the glass in the gun cabinet, and causing your father to have an accident. You did all this, just to see this movie, didn't you?"

"I didn't mean for any of that to happen, Mom."

"You didn't mean it?"

"No, really—I'm sorry."

It was so quiet that the only thing Billy heard was the squeaking of his chair. His leg was shaking so hard under the table that he thought it would come off at the hip.

Mom took a sip of water. Then she set her glass down, and said, "That's not good enough, William."

William. When she called him that, he was as good as dead. His punishment was gonna go on and on and on.

"Is it?" she said.

"No, I guess not." Maybe his punishment had already started. . . . Maybe it had been going on for a while now.

"You guess not. What should we do about that, your father and I?"

His voice seemed tiny and far away. "I don't know, Mom. It's not up to me."

She smiled. "No, it isn't. But if it were up to you, William, what would you do?"

She was really messing with his brain now. She knew that he would let himself off easy if it was up to him. But if he said what he really thought, she'd probably make it a lot worse for him. On the other hand, he didn't want to give her any ideas. Maybe he could find a nice compromise.

"I guess I'd send myself to my room without dinner."

"But you've already had dinner."

It was true. Gross as the shepherd's pie had been—and he could feel a lump of it congealing in his guts—it *was* dinner. He couldn't deny that. "Without dessert? Grounded for a week?"

At last Mom looked away from him, just for a moment. She glanced at Dad, smiling with condescension. "Did you hear that, Will?" she asked without a trace of mockery. "Did you hear the severe punishments that our son has recommended for himself?"

"Yeah." Dad wasn't smiling, though.

"Don't you think those punishments are a bit mild for what you've done, William." She turned her blue, blue eyes on him again, and he felt so helpless, so lost, looking into them.

"Maybe a good licking," Dad said.

"But your hand's hurt, dear," Mom said.

"That's true."

"So any physical punishment will have to wait."

"Yeah."

"Meanwhile, William, you will go to your room. And you'll stay there until we tell you to come down. And you'll think about what you've done."

He gulped. This was *all?* He couldn't believe it. They were just gonna send him to his room for a while? There had to be more to it than that. Mom was just gonna sit around planning some awful torture for him while he sweat it out upstairs. Pretty sadistic.

What they didn't know was that he had some secret stuff hidden in his room. If they ever found out, he was a dead duck.

▼▼▼

Billy waited until he heard the TV come on downstairs before he went to the closet. The hanging clothes caressed his hands and face as he knelt and pried loose the board at the back of the dark enclosure.

Carefully setting the board to one side, he reached in and pulled out his secret treasure trove—a box of books and magazines that his parents would have forbidden him to look at, if they'd ever seen them. He made sure they didn't. He'd discovered the loose board in the back of the closet by accident a few months ago. There was a space behind there, so he'd ended up hiding his books in there instead of under the bed, where Mom could have easily found them.

He pulled a book out that he'd been reading for a while, *The True History of Witches*. Leaving the others in the closet in case he was disturbed, he lay down, covering the book and his flashlight with the blankets, and started leafing through the book, trying to remember where he'd left off.

It was the chapter on the Salem Witch Trials, he remembered. He opened to a picture of Tituba, the Haitian servant who told four teenage girls about voodoo in the kitchen of a Puritan judge. They'd become possessed, and this was depicted in the illustration as a cloud of smoke coming out of the fireplace behind Tituba, demon faces visible in the vapor. The girls were cringing at the evil sight, and the judge was coming through the door, looking astonished in his buckled hat and black, seventeenth-century clothing.

The result of the witch trials was public hanging for several people, and one person was tortured to death. It seemed that the only thing to do with a witch was kill her. Otherwise, she kept spreading her evil around. Just like in the movie, where she had to be burned at the stake. Naked.

He read on about how witches frequently had men under their power. The men, physically strong though they might be, were helpless in the presence of the witch's supernatural strength. The witches had knowledge other people were ignorant of.

It reminded him of Mom and Dad. Mom always seemed to know things that other people didn't know. And she had an undeniable power over Dad . . . and over Billy, too, when you came right down to it. She even got her own way with Grandma and Grandpa, Dad's parents. Mom didn't have any family, of course, except for the people on Dad's side and Billy.

Mom couldn't be a witch, could she? Not really? It was true that Billy always got along better with Dad when Mom wasn't around. And things happened to Dad when Mom was there, as if to keep him in his place or something. Dad wasn't ordinarily clumsy enough to fall down into that glass, not when Mom wasn't there, at least. He'd taught Billy how to play baseball, and taken him fishing and hunting. Mom always stayed home, having parties with women friends of hers.

Maybe these other women were witches, too. Maybe they got together when the men were away, and planned their spells. Maybe they had black masses, sacrificed animals . . . even babies . . . to Satan.

But that was crazy. Wasn't it? How could a bunch of women living here in this town be witches? That Salem stuff was a long time ago.

Still, the book said witchcraft went on even in the present day. Some experts believed it was more common than ever. If that was true, then it wouldn't be all that surprising if Mom and her friends were witches, would it?

Billy shut the book, snapped off the flashlight, and placed both under the bed, since he was too sleepy to get up and stash them in the hiding place in the closet. He knew he should put them away, but he didn't. He was just too tired. After all that had happened, he welcomed sleep.

He had bad dreams. He was in a cave, and he wasn't alone. Things were brushing against him. Bugs. Rats. Spiders and bats, only not like any he'd ever seen before. Bigger and badder, nasty things that got on you and made your heart stop. Hairy and creepy things that sucked your blood and got on parts of your body and wouldn't get off, no matter what you did. Slime dripped on him, smelly, wet, gloppy stuff that smelled like . . . like Mom and Dad. . . .

He awoke abruptly, on his elbows, sweating and out of breath. He knew it had been a dream, but it didn't matter. He was still afraid. Still filled with dread.

As he caught his breath, he began to realize why. The fact was, he was still worried about his coming punishment. If Dad had walloped him, it would be all over. But Mom was being much harder on him than Dad ever could be. He could almost hear her asking him what he would do to punish himself.

She was torturing him right now, even though she was downstairs. That must have been why he was having nightmares. He lay back down, feeling the dampness of the sheets against his skin. He felt slimy and uncomfortable. Miserable. And it was all Mom's doing.

"Witch." The word came out unbidden. It just seemed natural to say it when he was thinking of his mother. He didn't have any proof, really, but that didn't mean it wasn't true. She wouldn't advertise the fact that she was a witch, after all.

The door opened, casting a long rectangle of light across the floor. He watched the shadow; it didn't move for the longest time.

From the shape, he saw that it was Mom. He pretended to sleep.
Would she come into his room? He hoped not. There was a time
when he would have felt otherwise, would have been glad to have
her come in and softly stroke his head.

"Billy," she said. Her voice was soft, but firm. She knew he
was awake. Why not? She knew everything, didn't she? Everything except the book hidden under the bed. He began to sweat
again.

"Billy, I know you can hear me."

"Yes, Mom." He tried to sound as if he were half-asleep,
even though he could not have been more awake than he was
now—fearing what would happen, fearing her.

She entered the room and sat on the edge of the bed. She
reached over him and placed one hand on the bed, forming a
triangle with him as the base. He was afraid she'd see the book
and flashlight hidden under the bed. She said, "Billy, have you
been thinking about what you did?"

"Yes, Mom."

"You know it was wrong, don't you?"

"Yes, Mom."

"And you won't do it again, will you?"

"No." He wasn't telling the truth, not completely. He would
have risked getting in trouble anytime, if he could watch two
swell pictures again.

"Tell me something," Mom said. It wasn't a command. Billy
waited.

"Sure."

"Do you believe in the Devil?"

"Yes." Sunday School didn't have it quite right, as far as Billy
could see, but there was some evil power in the universe, he was
sure of that much.

"And do you believe that the Devil has servants here on
Earth?"

"Sure."

"Do you think you know who they are?"

He thought about her question for quite a while. Was she

trying to trick him in some way? Find out if he suspected any-thing? Knew anything? "Sometimes I do," he said carefully.

"Sometimes . . . I wonder if you know anyone in league with Satan?"

Jeez. "Mom, I'm just a kid. How could I know anybody like that at my age?"

"Wickedness knows no limitation on age. In fact, it knows no limitations at all."

She pulled the covers up around him and touched his cheek with the back of her hand. "Why, you're very warm, Billy," she said.

"It's hot in here, Mom."

"No it isn't. It's a comfortable temperature, Billy. I think you're sick."

Maybe she'd put a spell on him, he thought, to make him run a temperature. Maybe she'd given him a disease to punish him. And now she was here in his room to torment him. Witches could do things like that, couldn't they?

"I'm okay, Mom."

She pressed her palm against his forehead. "No, you're not. You've got a fever."

She was right. He was still sweating a lot, and his head hurt. His cut finger was throbbing, and felt as big around as a knock-wurst. He really was sick . . . but had she caused it?

"I'll be right back," Mom said. She got up and left the bedroom.

Remembering the book, Billy reached down to pick it up, along with the flashlight. He got out of bed, and found that his legs were wobbly. In fact, he felt really lousy. The book and flashlight seemed to weigh a hundred pounds, and the closet seemed far away. He was wheezing and tired by the time he opened the door. Crawling inside, he groped around for the loose board in the dark.

"Where are you?"

Oh, no!

"What are you doing out of bed?" It was Mom. She was back already. He stood up straight, in a panic, and a robe covered his head like a loose turban. That gave him an idea. He removed the robe from its hanger and came out of the closet, making a show of putting on the robe.

"I was cold, Mom."

He couldn't see her eyes, the way she was backlit from the doorway. The lights in his bedroom were still turned off, and he could see little besides Mom's silhouette. She held something in her hand, but he couldn't tell what it was.

"I would have fetched your robe for you, dear," she said. "But I thought you were hot, not cold. That's why I got this damp washcloth."

"I, uh, got a chill, Mom," he gasped. He got back into bed, muscles aching from the effort.

Mom pulled the covers up over his chest. She pressed her hand over his forehead, cooed, and laid the washcloth where her hand had been a moment before. It felt good, cool and comforting. He closed his eyes and enjoyed the refreshing sensation. His trip into the closet had really tired him out. He lay still while Mom slowly swabbed his forehead.

"This is what you get for being disobedient, Billy," she said. "It's made you sick."

She was practically admitting it. She was punishing him with some kind of spell, making him sick. He felt his heart beat faster. This *was* black magic, wasn't it?

"You know you take movies too seriously," Mom said. "You fantasize too much. That's why Dad and I like to know what you're seeing, what books you're reading, and that's why we don't let you collect comics. Besides, you know we like to take you to the movies ourselves."

Yeah, sure, but there was only so many times he could see *Pinocchio* with them. He wanted to see things they—she, really—didn't want him to see. Know things she didn't want him to know.

"Now you've made yourself sick," she clucked. "Seeing those awful movies."

But the movie was about witches, and if she really was a witch, as he suspected, it was no wonder she didn't want him to see it. Maybe he'd learn something she didn't want him to know, just from seeing a movie about witches. He'd learned more from the book, but the movie had stirred him in the way the book never could. There was something about seeing the witch's face, ten feet high on the screen, eyes staring icily. Not to mention her soft breasts. Seeing her victims being stricken with horrible afflictions. Seeing her glee as she tormented them with her supernatural ways.

"Don't you have anything to say, Billy?" Mom asked.

He shook his head.

Mom's eyes narrowed. "You're not even going to say you're sorry?"

He wasn't sorry, of course. But she would never accept that. He had to apologize. For some reason, the words wouldn't come. All he could think of was his punishments in the past—punishments that went on and on, for days or weeks or months. He was never forgiven for anything he did wrong, for making mistakes. So why should he be sorry? He didn't say anything, just shut his eyes and pretended to be unconscious.

"Maybe you're not sorry," Mom said. "Maybe you're happy that you made your father and me worry until we were sick, while you were out having fun."

Worry until they were sick? They weren't even up when he got home, for crying out loud. What had they been doing in the bedroom, anyway? You heard stories at school, but not about your own parents. Had she fuzzed his mind, so that he couldn't think about such things? Well, there were more pressing matters at hand. She was just messing with him now. This whole punishment thing was phony. He was like a guinea pig for her spells, a lab specimen or a rat in a maze that she was watching for those cold eyes.

Was she really his mother? He didn't have blue eyes, and he didn't feel close to her at all. She was a witch, and she had no love for him in her heart. If she had a heart.

She removed the damp washcloth from his head and stood up. "Try to get some sleep now, Billy."

She backed away from the bed and went out of the room, closing the door behind herself. Billy was left alone in the dark, certain now that she was a witch, and that he was under her power, just like Dad.

What could he do about it? He was just a kid. And he was sick anyway. If Dad couldn't resist her, strong as he was, how could Billy, especially while he had a fever? He shuddered, as much from fear as from illness.

Grandma, Dad's mother, had always said that strength wasn't in muscle, but in brain power. Grandma always said that Billy was smart, that he was the one in the family who would amount to something. If she was right, maybe he could outsmart Mom, figure out some way to save himself.

But how?

He heard Dad and Mom talking downstairs, through the vent that came up from the kitchen. It was hard to hear what they were saying, but he could make out a few words: ". . . overactive imagination . . . monsters . . . silly things . . . no sense of responsibility . . . crazy ideas . . ."

This was all Mom; Dad just grunted every once in a while, agreeing with her. He always did, at least to her face. Sometimes he said things when Billy and he were together, and Mom wasn't around. But when he was with her, he just said whatever she wanted him to say, like he was a zombie or something.

Maybe that was it. Maybe she had him so far under her power that he wasn't even fully conscious when she was around. He could only be himself when he was away from her.

Should Billy try to wake Dad up, make him aware of what he was doing? If he understood how things looked to somebody else, maybe it would help him get free of Mom's power. Billy doubted it, though. Dad was probably too far gone by now.

If that was true, then Billy was alone. Maybe he was just a kid, but he was the only one who could stand up against this evil.

". . . weird kid . . . don't know where he gets these ideas . . . almost think he hates us. . . ."

She was right about that. His jaw clenched as he thought about the terror he'd been going through because of her. What kind of mother was she, to treat a kid like this? Maybe she wasn't really his mother at all.

". . . send him to military school . . . learn to obey . . . make him realize what the world's like . . . selfish kid . . . no concept of reality. . . ."

No concept of reality! He tossed the covers aside and dragged himself painfully out of bed. She'd like people to think that, wouldn't she? That he was nuts. Then nobody would take him seriously when he said she was a witch.

His robe was soggy, and he ached all over, especially his head. But he wasn't going to let that slow him down. He had to show some guts here. He had to do something. He didn't know what it would be, but by the time he was through, Mom would know she wasn't fooling him anymore.

He put on his slippers and went to the door. He opened it softly, and looked out. Shadows angled crazily in the hallway. Something looked funny, out of whack. Oh, yeah, it was the glass in the gun cabinet. Even at night it cast a reflection . . . or it used to cast one, before he broke the glass. Now it just looked like a jagged black hole in the dim light.

Light from downstairs made a faintly glowing rectangle of the staircase. Billy stepped into the hallway and waited a minute, hearing only his own ragged breathing.

He crept along, thankful of the carpet that kept his footsteps from sounding. Pausing at the head of the stairs, he glanced at the gun cabinet once again. Could he do it? Could he actually take a rifle down and use it . . . ?

As if in a dream, he found himself moving toward the gun cabinet. He hardly knew he was moving now. All the pain in his body was gone, and it was almost pleasant, the way he was drifting toward the end of the hallway. Now he had a goal, a mission. That was something that he found pleasing, satisfying, something that really gave him hope and strength for the first time in his life that he could remember. His mother had kept him in his place, along with his dad, from the beginning. She'd kept him from understanding things clearly.

He was at the gun cabinet. He almost thought he would see the bats and spiders creeping around, but he didn't. No, this dream wasn't creepy. This dream was *cool*. He made his selection. The ammunition drawer opened, he took out a box of shells. He efficiently broke open the twelve-gauge and put in two shells— just as Dad had showed him—closed it up, and clicked off the safety.

Not only didn't he hear the steps creaking, he couldn't even feel his feet *touching* the steps. He ran his hand along the railing, all the way down to the newel post. The painted wood felt like the purest silk. He was floating past the front door, through the hall, into the living room, cradling the shotgun in his arms as if it were a newborn infant.

The TV was on. He heard an audience laughing, and the host of a talk show ragging on somebody. The room was awash with a blue glow, matching Mom's eyes. She and Dad sat on the sofa. A bottle of Diet Coke and some chips in a bowl were on the coffee table in front of them. They were staring at the TV.

They didn't see him.

He had them right in his sights. Not that he needed to sight a shotgun. All he had to do was point in their general direction, and . . .

Dad looked up. The TV's glare revealed his angry face, but the anger drooped into a gape as he saw the shotgun, now leveled at the sofa. At Mom. At him.

He said something, but either he spoke too softly or the TV was too loud. Or maybe it was Billy's fever that prevented the sound from carrying across the living room.

"Get out of the way, Dad," Billy said, his voice sounding surprisingly strong.

Dad's mouth kept working, but no words came out.

Mom looked up at him. She didn't seem surprised.

Billy knew what to do; he'd seen this kind of thing enough times on TV. He waved the shotgun, indicating that Dad should move. "Go on, Dad, get away from her. I don't want to hurt you. Move."

Dad's features were distorted with powerful emotions. He opened his mouth wide to shout. But Billy couldn't hear him. Dad looked really scared, but he didn't move.

"I'll shoot you if I have to," Billy said. "I'm not fooling."

"Yes you are."

It was Mom, coming through to him loud and clear. He didn't understand how he could hear Mom and not hear Dad, but that was the way it was. He squinted to see her face through the flicker cast by the TV. Her mouth didn't move, but she calmly said: "You'll put that gun down now."

How was this possible? Magic. Black magic. Just like in the movie. Just like the preachers on the religious cable channels said. Evil has great power. She was using it against him now. Entering his mind. She'd been doing it all his life, but never so openly. This was an urgent situation, so she was going further than she'd ever gone before. Showing her hand.

"Get out of my head," Billy said.

Dad's brow furrowed. He looked from Billy to Mom and back to Billy again.

"Yes, you're out of your head," Mom thought at him. Adding as an afterthought: "William."

William. She was in his head, calling him *that* name. She was trying to drive him insane. He felt heat rise through his body as if an oven flared in his guts.

"That's not what I said. You're in my head, and you're trying to control me. You're evil."

"I'm evil? Who was bad today? Was it me? Or you?"

"You're bad all the time. You're in league with the Devil, and I know it."

A smile formed slowly on her face, showing her canines. "The Devil?"

Dad looked at her again. He was lost.

"That's right. You're a witch, and your power over Dad and me is over."

"Oh, you're protecting your father from me, are you? That's very noble. William."

"Don't call me that!" He thrust the barrels of the shotgun forward menacingly. "Don't ever call me that again!"

"It's your name," she said simply.

"I don't care. Don't call me that."

She smiled at him. "You don't give orders. You're a child. You're my child. Though I'm not very proud of that right now, William."

He couldn't stand it. She wasn't even afraid of him when he was pointing a gun at her. "Don't you know that I've got the power now!" he screamed. "All I have to do is move my finger a little bit and you'll be blasted into two pieces! You want me to do that?"

She kept smiling. A stain spread across the lap of Dad's robe. He'd pissed himself.

Billy was disgusted, enraged at his father. The Old Man was a wimp. And Mom was a witch.

"When did you sell your soul to Satan?" Billy asked.

She laughed—a long, harsh staccato sound that withered Billy's brain. He felt like he was in a wind tunnel filled with the searing engines of her contempt. He trembled, trying to find a way to kill her, but he couldn't do anything. She'd taken over his brain, just as she'd taken over Dad's, and turned him into a sniveling, gutless coward. Her laughter disarmed him.

He lowered the shotgun, knowing that terrible things were about to happen, but not caring. He was dead already. She couldn't do anything to him that was worse than what had just happened. He didn't care what she did to him, or what she made Dad do to him.

He felt tears roll down his cheeks, and dropped the gun on the floor. It thudded dully on the carpet. He saw Dad jump, scared that the gun would go off. Billy smiled, amused at the Old Man's cowardice.

"God damn you!" his father's voice finally crashed through the silence. His face was purple with rage in the colored light of the cathode ray tube. "You gonna be sorry you ever picked up that gun!"

Dad came lunging across the floor at him, the sash of the bathrobe swinging, reminding Billy of his penis earlier, when he'd come out of the bedroom in pop-eyed rage. Billy couldn't help it; he threw back his head and laughed.

"*You fool!*" Billy cried between gasps of furious laughter. "You stupid fool!"

Dad stopped cold in the middle of the living room floor. His lower lip quivered in confusion. He'd threatened to clobber Billy many times and never got a response like this. He didn't know what to do, so he just stood there, reeking of piss, looking idiotic.

"Will," Mom said to Dad, "sit down."

"Yeah, *siddown, Will,*" Billy said. He felt power spreading through him as if it were being pumped from his heart, through his bloodstream, to every part of his body. He'd never felt like this before. This was all right, really all right.

"Don't you want me to . . ." Dad was almost whimpering in this little, tiny voice.

"I want you to go clean yourself up," Mom commanded him.

Dad stood there for a few seconds, looking like Dan Quayle being asked a hard question, and then he turned and marched off to the bathroom for the second time today. The bandages on his hands flashed in the TV light.

"And I want you to come here and sit next to me, Billy." Mom patted the sofa cushion to her right.

Billy hesitated. He was afraid of her again. He'd had his chance to fight back, to get rid of her, but it was gone forever. She was in charge now. He might as well face it. Sighing in resignation, he moved toward the sofa.

For a moment, he stood looking down at her. She smiled at him, once again showing her canines. She looked like a wild animal.

"Come on, Bill," she said. "Sit down."

Bill. She only called him that when she was pleased with him. But that was impossible. He had just threatened to kill her.

How could she act like this now, like he'd just won the spelling bee at school? Confused and fascinated by her attitude, he sat down next to her.

"You know, Bill," she said, reaching out to brush a lock of hair out of his eyes, "you don't take after your father. You're much more like me."

"Huh?"

"You take after me, darling." She looked at him with her freezing eyes, transfixing him.

"What do you mean?"

"Call it what you want. But you've got my genes. Recessive though they are, you've got them."

"What are you talking about, Mom?"

"Heredity, Billy. Don't you know what that is?"

"It's what's passed down from generation to generation, isn't it?"

"Yes, and there are a few people who carry this unusual gene that makes them special. Do you see what I'm driving at?"

"Witches."

"That's right. It's as good a word as any to describe us, but don't use it out in public. Some people get very worked up about us. They don't really understand what we're all about, you see."

That comment begged the question. "What *are* you all about, Mom?"

"Not just me. *You*, too, Billy. You're one of us."

"No, not me . . ."

"Yes, you! You're a witch. You've got the latent ability to read minds, exercise power, resist the evil spells of others. You're a *witch*, Billy. A witch."

"But a witch is evil."

"No, just powerful. How do you think we got this house, our cars? Everything we own? Do you really think your father could do it alone? He can barely tie his own shoes without my help. He just doesn't have the brains."

He wanted to argue with her about this, but when he thought about it, what she was saying wasn't so much different than what he'd been thinking about the two of them.

"Didn't they teach you about genetics in school?"

"You mean like Gregor Mendel and that stuff from biology class?"

"Yeah, that's it, Bill."

"But that was just like, like spots on guinea pigs and stuff like that."

"On the outside. But humans are more complex. Do you remember how they said an inherited trait might skip several generations and then pop up again somewhere down the line?"

"Yeah."

"That happens a lot to witches. They seem to die out in certain areas, and then they come back when people least expect it."

"But what about the evil stuff? Why do people believe in that stuff?"

"People always have to have someone to hate and fear, unfortunately."

God, this was weird. His mother was sitting here telling him she was some kind of mutant. What was worse, he was beginning to believe it. Of course, he had accused her of being a witch himself, but more of a supernatural type. It was actually kind of a relief to think that she was more of a scientific witch than a black magic one. He hadn't learned all that much bad stuff about science in Sunday School, though the minister had frowned on the theory of evolution, which was what Mom was talking about here. So it was probably all right, even if people mistakenly thought it was witchcraft.

How did Billy know she was telling the truth, though? He wanted to, but there was a possibility she was making the whole thing up to save her own skin. No . . . she had won before she told him about it. It was the truth, and he had to face it—he was a witch, too.

"You might think I've been hard on you in recent months," she said, reading his mind. "But it was so I could test your potential abilities. And I must say you've passed with flying colors."

"But what have I done? I can't read minds."

"You *will* be telepathic. You knew I was a witch, didn't you?"

"I read about witches in a book. It made me think about you."

"No, you sought out the book because you already knew somewhere deep down that I'm a witch. You wanted to know more, that's all. You weren't conscious of it, but that's what actually happened."

"Honest?"

"Honest.

He thought about all this for a long time. And then something occurred to him. "Mom, you know what?"

"What, Bill?"

"This is gonna be some Hallowe'en."

She laughed. He laughed, too. They were together again, for the first time in Billy couldn't remember how long. It was great.

"Now I've got to teach you about sex," Mom said.

"Huh?"

"You know. What your father and I were doing when you got home. I didn't want you to think about it before I was sure, but now it's time you learn all about it."

She was looking deeply into his eyes, and suddenly his mind flooded with understanding. Those rumors he'd heard, the things that go on between men and women—as Dad had put it—all came flooding into his memory as Mom telepathically filled his mind with knowledge. He became wildly excited by the images she sent to him. She put her hand on his, and it was warm. Hot. She leaned forward and kissed him.

"Let's go upstairs," she said.

Billy didn't know what to say, so he didn't say anything. He just got up and went with her. He felt his heart jerking in his chest, and his guts seemed to be in his throat, but he felt reassurance emanating from Mom's mind. They were in the hallway, turning to go upstairs.

"Just a goddamn minute!"

Dad was standing in the doorway, pointing the shotgun at them.

"What do you think you're doing, Will?" Mom asked.

"What do I think *I'm* doing?" Dad demanded. "What the hell do *you* think *you're* doing, Barbara?"

"I'm initiating Billy. We've got to preserve the gene."

"Preserve the gene! You're talking about seducing your son, for God's sake."

"It has to be done, Will," Mom said, as if explaining something to a very young child. "You should be proud to be a part of this."

"I'm not part of it!"

"Oh, yes you are. We couldn't have had Billy without your genes. You're a carrier."

Dad didn't want to hear that. He pointed the gun at Mom. "You can talk all you want, but if you try and take the boy upstairs . . ." He cocked both barrels using his bandaged thumb, wincing a little with the effort.

Mom smiled. "You can't do that, Will. You could never do that. And you know it."

"Don't be so sure." But he didn't sound all that convincing.

"All right, then." She held out her arms, and her robe fell open, exposing her pale breasts.

Dad looked queasy, seeing the flesh that he had caressed so many times. He glanced down at the shotgun, imagining what the buckshot would do to her soft parts.

"Will, be reasonable."

"Reasonable?" He looked as if he were about to cry. "Is any of this reasonable? I feel like I've gone out of my mind, like I'm stark raving mad. Crazy as a bedbug."

"No, you're not crazy. I've kept you placated, but this situation has forced you to see things as they are for the first time. I don't need you anymore, Will."

Pain glazed Dad's eyes, but after a moment it hardened into anger. Hatred. Billy watched it happen, as if he were observing a flower opening. Dad made a sound like an animal. Not the grunting sound he'd made earlier, but an anguished lowing sound, like a bull being slaughtered. Dad even shook his head like an enraged bull and snorted in rage. He would have been frightening, except that Mom's mind was already beginning to control him.

Billy could feel it, sort of a disturbance that passed through him—a by-product of what Mom was doing. Kind of like when you rub your feet on the carpet and the hairs on the back of your neck stand on end.

Dad looked confused, scared. He'd never realized how much power Mom had over him before; she'd always been very subtle about it.

But no more. Now she was turning on her witching juice full throttle. Dad was twitching like he was sitting on a live wire. He was finding it harder and harder to point the shotgun at Mom. It was bobbing all around. Billy knew that all Dad had to do was squeeze the trigger and he'd be blown all over the hallway, but he wasn't all that scared. He could see that Mom wouldn't let him do it.

"Unnh . . . ," was the closest Dad could come to saying something.

Billy expected Mom to make the Old Man drop the shotgun, but she didn't. Dad slowly moved his arms around, shaking like a leaf the whole time, until both barrels were pointed straight at his jaw.

Dad's face was shiny with sweat. The trigger was slick, and drops flew from Dad's clenched, trembling fingers. He made an absolutely pitiful sound.

"I told you, you're not needed around here anymore," Mom said.

The roar of the shotgun blast was amazingly loud inside the house. Dad's head was gone in a flash, separated into a zillion wet, red specks that just appeared everywhere, even on the second-floor banister. Dad's body was slammed back against the wall. His bandaged hands clutched the smoking shotgun for a moment, as if nothing had happened. Then they relaxed and the gun slipped to the floor with a thump. Dad's headless body sagged and slumped with a slithering sound, until it was sitting on the floor with the feet apart. One slipper was off and one was on. The feet quivered a little and then were still.

"Wow!" Billy shouted. This was incredible. He didn't even mind the way the hallway now smelled like exploded firecrackers and raw meat. "You made him do it!"

"Yeah. And now we've got to clean it up."

Clean it up? "God, Mom, I'll puke."

"I don't mean like you cleaned up your father's blood earlier. I mean just get rid of this place."

"Get rid of it?"

"Burn it down," she said.

For a second or two, Billy didn't get it. He'd always thought the house was important to her. But then he realized how much fun it would be to torch it. "Just burn it down, huh?"

"Sure, our homeowners' insurance will cover it."

"But I thought we were going to . . ."

"Plenty of time for that later."

"What about Dad?"

"He killed himself after setting fire to the house. Business has been bad lately, and he's been filled with despair. We did all we could to help him, but he was beyond our reach. Killed himself while we were out. Tragic."

"Cool. But will the police believe it?"

She smiled with her icy blue eyes. "They'll believe anything I tell them."

"Yeah, I guess they will. Well, too bad about Dad." He'd kind of liked Dad, sometimes. As he stepped over the headless body, he remembered the times they'd gone fishing and hunting. Dad had blown a squirrel to bits once, just to see what his thirty-odd-six could do. Kind of ironic the way he'd ended up, when you thought about it.

Billy got some matches from the kitchen and set fire to the curtains. They went right up, and the wooden beams, floorboards, and rafters burned well, too. He kept on lighting things until he started to choke from inhaling smoke.

Hopping over Dad's body, he joined Mom in the front hallway

again. She took him by the arm and guided him toward the door. Before opening the door, she looked back with satisfaction at the flames raging in the living room. Her powers helped make it burn faster. Billy smelled something like when Mom left the pork roast in the oven too long, and wondered if it was Dad.

Mom opened the door and they went out. The cool night air felt good, and Billy's fever seemed to have miraculously vanished. Mom had fixed him up with her mind.

None of the neighbors were on the street or in their driveways. The bright flickering of TV sets could be seen through their windows. Sooner or later one of them would notice the hotter orange flickering coming from Billy's house and call the fire department. You couldn't really notice it from outside yet.

"Well, where do you want to go while the fire burns?" Mom asked, unlocking the car door. "Can you think of a place?"

Billy frowned, feeling Mom inside his head, knowing that she really wanted to please him. "I do know a place we can go," he said.

"Where?" She got into the car and reached over to unlock his side.

He opened the door and slid inside. "To the movies."

"Oh, are they open this late?"

"I know a theater that's open all night."

She turned on the ignition. A fiery glow came from behind the venetian blinds as she backed onto their street. "What's playing?"

"A double feature. *The Chuckling Brain from Outer Space*, and. . . ."

"This sounds familiar. What's the title of the other movie?"

"*Dark Sabbat.*"

"Scary. What's it about?"

"About witches being burned at the stake."

She put the car into drive and started cruising slowly toward the theater. "Those Hollywood writers never do get it right, do they?"

Billy laughed. Then he and his Mom went to the movies, and lived happily ever after.

SNATCHER
▼▼▼
DEAN R. KOONTZ

BILLY Neeks had a flexible philosophy regarding property rights. He believed in the proletarian ideal of shared wealth—as long as the wealth belonged to someone else. If it was *his* property, Billy was ready to defend it to the death. It was a good, workable philosophy for a thief, which Billy was.

Billy Neeks's occupation was echoed by his grooming: he looked slippery. His thick black hair was slicked back with enough scented oil to fill a crankcase. His coarse skin was perpetually pinguid, as if he suffered continuously from malaria. He moved cat-quick on well-lubricated joints, and his hands had the buttery grace of a magician's hands. His eyes looked like twin pools of Texas crude, wet and black and deep—and utterly untouched by human warmth or feeling. If the route to Hell were an inclined ramp requiring some hideous grease to facilitate descent, Billy Neeks would be the Devil's choice to pass eternity in the application of that noxious, oleaginous substance.

In action, Billy could bump into an unsuspecting woman, separate her from her purse, and be ten yards away and moving fast by the time she realized she had been victimized. Single-strap purses, double-strap purses, clutch purses, purses carried over the shoulder, purses carried in the hand—all meant easy money to

Billy Neeks. Whether his target was cautious or careless was of no consequence. Virtually no precautions could foil him.

That Wednesday in April, pretending to be drunk, he jostled a well-dressed elderly woman on Broad Street, just past Bartram's Department store. As she recoiled in disgust from that oily contact, Billy slipped her purse off her shoulder, down her arm, and into the plastic shopping bag he carried. He had reeled away from her and had taken six or eight steps in an exaggerated stagger before she realized that the collision had not been as purposeless as it had seemed. Even as the victim shrieked "police," Billy had begun to run, and by the time she added, "help, police, help," Billy was nearly out of earshot.

He raced through a series of alleyways, dodged around garbage cans and dumpsters, leaped across the splayed legs of a sleeping wino. He sprinted across a parking lot, fled into another alley.

Blocks from Bartram's, Billy slowed to a walk, breathing only slightly harder than usual, grinning. When he stepped out onto 46th Street, he saw a young mother carrying a baby and a shopping bag *and* a purse, and she looked so defenseless that Billy could not resist the opportunity, so he flicked open his switchblade and, in a wink, cut the straps on her bag, a stylish blue leather number. Then he dashed off again, across the street, where drivers braked sharply and blew their horns at him, into another network of alleys, all familiar to him, and as he ran he giggled. His giggle was neither shrill nor engaging but more like the sound of ointment squirting from a tube.

When he slid on spilled garbage—orange peels, rotting lettuce, mounds of molding and soggy bread—he was not tripped up or even slowed down. The disgusting spill seemed to facilitate his flight, and he came out of the slide moving faster than he had gone into it.

He slowed to a normal pace when he reached Prospect Boulevard. The switchblade was in his pocket again. Both stolen purses were concealed in the plastic shopping bag. He projected what he thought was an air of nonchalance, and although his calculated expression of innocence was actually a dismal failure, it was the best he could do.

He walked to his car, which he had parked at a meter along Prospect. The Pontiac, unwashed for at least two years, left oil drippings wherever it went, just as a wolf in the wilds marked its territory with dribbles of urine. Billy put the stolen purses in the trunk of the car and drove away from that part of the city, toward other prowling grounds in other neighborhoods.

Of the several reasons for his success as a purse snatcher, mobility was perhaps most important. Many snatchers were kids looking for a few fast bucks, young hoods without wheels, but Billy Neeks was twenty-five, no kid, and possessed of reliable transportation. He usually robbed two or three women in one neighborhood and then quickly moved on to another territory, where no one was looking for him and where more business waited to be done.

To him, this was not small-time thievery committed either by impulse or out of desperation. Instead, Billy saw it as a business and he was a businessman, and like other businessmen he planned his work carefully, weighed the risks and benefits of any endeavor, and acted only as a result of careful responsible analysis.

Other snatchers—amateurs and punks, every one of them— paused on the street or in an alleyway, hastily searching purses for valuables, risking arrest by their inadvisable delays, at the very least creating a host of additional witnesses to their crimes. Billy, on the other hand, stashed the purses in the trunk of his car to be retrieved later for more leisurely inspection in the privacy of his home.

He prided himself on his methodicalness and caution.

That cloudy and humid Wednesday in late April, he crossed and re-crossed the city, briefly visiting three widely separated dis- tricts and snatching six purses in addition to those he had taken from the elderly woman outside Bartram's and from the young mother on 46th Street. The last of the eight also came from an old woman, and at first he thought it was going to be an easy hit, and then he thought it was going to get messy, and finally it just turned out weird.

When Billy spotted her, she was coming out of a butcher's shop on Westend Avenue, clutching a package of meat to her breast. She was *old*. Her brittle white hair stirred in the spring breeze, and Billy had the curious notion that he could hear those dry hairs rustling against one another. A crumpled-parchment face, slumped shoulders, pale withered hands, and shuffling step combined to convey the impression not only of extreme age but of frailty and vulnerability, which was what drew Billy Neeks as if he were an iron filing and she a magnet. Her purse was big, almost a satchel, and the weight of it—in addition to the package of meat—seemed to bother her, for she was struggling the straps farther up on her shoulder and wincing in pain, as if suffering from a flare-up of arthritis.

Though it was spring, she was dressed in black: black shoes, black stockings, black skirt, dark gray blouse, even a heavy black cardigan sweater unsuited to the mild day.

Billy looked up and down the street, saw no one else nearby, and quickly made his move. He did his drunk trick, staggering, jostling the old biddy. But as he pulled the purse down her arm, she dropped the package of meat, seized the bag with both hands, and for a moment they were locked in an unexpectedly fierce struggle. Ancient as she was, she possessed surprising strength. He tugged at the purse, wrenched and twisted it, desperately attempted to rock her backward off her feet, but she stood her ground and held on with the tenacity of a deeply rooted tree resisting a storm wind.

He said, "Give it up, you old bitch, or I'll bust your face."

And then a strange thing happened:

She seemed to *change* before Billy's eyes. In a blink she no longer appeared frail but steely, no longer weak but darkly energized. Her bony and arthritic hands suddenly locked like the dangerous talons of a powerful bird of prey. That singular face—pale yet jaundiced, nearly fleshless, all wrinkles and sharp pointy lines—was still ancient, but it no longer seemed quite *human* to Billy Neeks. And her eyes. My God, her eyes. At first glance, Billy saw only the watery, myopic gaze of a doddering crone, but abruptly they were eyes of tremendous power, eyes of fire and ice simultaneously boiling his blood and freezing his heart, eyes that saw into him and through him, not the eyes of a helpless old woman but those of a murderous beast that had the desire and ability to devour him alive.

He gasped in fear, and he almost let go of the purse, almost ran, but in another blink she was transformed into a defenseless old woman again, and abruptly she capitulated. Like pop-beads, the swollen knuckles of her twisted hands seemed to come apart, and her finger joints went slack. She lost her grip, releasing the purse with a small cry of despair.

Emitting a menacing snarl that served not only to frighten the old woman but to chase away Billy's own irrational terror, she shoved her backward, into a curbside trash container, and bolted past her, the satchel-size purse under his arm. He glanced back after several steps, half expecting to see that she had fully assumed the form of a great dark bird of prey, flying at him, eyes aflame, teeth bared, talon-hands spread and hooked to tear him to bits. But she was clutching at the trash container to keep her balance, as age-broken and helpless as she had been when he had first seen her.

The only odd thing: she was looking after him with a smile. No mistaking it. A wide, stained-tooth smile. Almost a lunatic grin.

Senile old fool, Billy thought. Had to be senile if she found anything funny about having her purse snatched.

He could not imagine why he had ever been afraid of her.

He ran, dodging from one alleyway to another, down side streets, across a sun-splashed parking lot, and along a shadowy service passage between two tenements, onto a street far removed from the scene of his latest theft. At a stroll, he returned to his parked car and put the old woman's black purse and one other in the trunk with the six taken elsewhere in the city. At last, a hard day's work behind him, he drove home, looking forward to counting his take, having a few beers, and watching some TV.

Once, stopped at a red traffic light, Billy thought he heard something moving in the car's trunk. There were a few hollow thumps and a brief but curious scraping noise. However, when he cocked his head and listened closer he heard nothing more, and he decided that the noise had only been the pile of stolen purses shifting under their own weight.

▼▼▼

Billy Neeks lived in a ramshackle four-room bungalow between a vacant lot and a transmission shop, two blocks from the river. The place had belonged to his mother and had been clean and in good repair when she had lived there. Two years ago, Billy had convinced her to transfer ownership to him "for tax reasons," then had shipped her off to a nursing home to be cared for at the expense of the state. He supposed she was still there—he didn't know for sure because he never visited.

That evening in April, Billy arranged the eight purses side by side in two rows on the kitchen table and stared at them for a while in sweet anticipation of the treasure hunt to come. He popped the tab on a Budweiser. He tore open a bag of Doritos. He pulled up a chair, sat down, and sighed contentedly.

Finally, he opened the purse he had taken off the woman outside Bartram's, and began to calculate his "earnings." She had looked well-to-do, and the contents of her wallet did not disappoint Billy Neeks: $309 in folding money, plus another $4.10 in change. She also carried a stack of credit cards, which Billy would fence through Jake Barcelli, the pawnshop owner who would also give him a few bucks for the other worthwhile items he found in the purses. In the first bag, those fenceable items included a gold-plated Tiffany pen, matching gold-plated Tiffany compact and lipstick tube, and a fine though not extraordinarily expensive opal ring.

The young mother's purse contained only $11.42 and nothing else of value, which Billy had expected, but that meager profit did not diminish the thrill he got from going through the contents of the bag. He looked upon snatching as a business, yes, and thought of himself as a businessman, but he also took considerable

pleasure simply from perusing and *touching* his victims' belong-
ings. The violation of a woman's personal property was a violation
of her, too, and when his quick hands explored the young mother's purse, it was almost as if he were exploring her body. Sometimes, Billy took unfenceable items—cheap compacts, inexpensive
tubes of lipstick, eyeglasses—and put them on the floor and
stomped them, because crushing them beneath his heel was somehow almost like crushing the woman herself. Easy money made
his work worthwhile, but he was equally motivated by the tremendous sense of power he got from the job; it stimulated him, it
really did, stimulated and satisfied.

By the time he had gone slowly through seven of the eight
purses, savoring their contents, it was 7:15 in the evening, and
he was euphoric. He breathed fast and, occasionally, shuddered
ecstatically. His oily hair looked oilier than usual, for it was damp
with sweat and hung in clumps and tangles. Fine beads of perspi-
ration glimmered on his face. During his exploration of the
purses, he had knocked the open bag of Doritos off the kitchen
table but had not noticed. He had opened a second beer, but he
never tasted it; now it stood forgotten. His world had shrunk to
the dimensions of a woman's purse.

He had saved the crazy old woman's bag for last because he
had a hunch that it was going to provide the greatest treasure of
the day.

The old hag's purse was big, almost a satchel, made of supple
black leather, with long straps, and with a single main compartment that closed with a zipper. He pulled it in front of him and
stared at it for a moment, letting his anticipation build.

He remembered how the crone had resisted him, holding fast
to the bag until he thought he might have to flick open his
switchblade and cut her. He had cut a few women before, not
many but enough to know he *liked* cutting them.

That was the problem. Billy was smart enough to realize that,
like knifeplay so much, he must deny himself the pleasure of
cutting people, resorting to violence only when absolutely necessary, for if he used the knife too often, he would be unable to

stop using it, would be compelled to use it, and then he would be lost. The police expended no energy in the search for mere purse snatchers, but they would be a lot more aggressive and relentless in pursuit of a slasher.

Still, he had not cut anyone for several months, and by such admirable self-control, he had earned the right to have some fun. He would have taken great pleasure in separating the old woman's withered meat from her bones. And now he wondered why he had not ripped her up the moment she had given him trouble.

He had virtually forgotten how she had briefly terrified him, how she had looked less human than avian, how her hands had seemed to metamorphose into wicked talons, and how her eyes had blazed. Deeply confirmed in his macho self-image, he had no capacity for any memory that had the potential for humiliation.

With a growing certainty that he was about to find a surprising treasure, to put his hands on the purse and lightly squeezed. It was crammed full, straining at the seams, and Billy told himself that the forms he felt through the leather were wads of money, banded stacks of hundred-dollar bills, and his heart began to thump with excitement.

He pulled open the zipper, looked in, and frowned.

It was dark inside the purse.

Billy peered closer.

Impossibly dark.

Squinting, he could see nothing in there at all, not a wallet or a compact or a comb or a packet of Kleenex, not even the lining of the purse itself, only a flawless and very deep darkness, as if he were peering into a well. *Deep* was the word, all right, for he had a sense that he was staring down into unplumbable and mysterious depths, as if the bottom of the purse were not just a few inches away but thousands of feet down—even farther— countless miles below him. Suddenly he realized that the glow from the overhead kitchen fluorescents fell into the open purse but illuminated nothing; the bag seemed to swallow every ray of light and digest it.

Billy Neeks's warm sweat of quasi-erotic pleasure abruptly

turned icy-cold, and his skin dimpled with gooseflesh. He knew he should pull the zipper shut, cautiously carry the purse blocks away from his own house, and dispose of it in someone else's trash bin. But he saw his right hand slipping toward the gaping maw of the bag. When he tried to pull it back, he could not, as if it were a stranger's hand over which he had no control. His fingers disappeared into the darkness, and the rest of the hand followed. He shook his head—no, no, no—but still he could not stop himself, he was *compelled* to reach into the bag, and now his hand was in to the wrist, and he felt nothing in there, nothing but a terrible cold that made his teeth chatter, and still he reached in, down, until his arm was shoved all the way in to the elbow, and he should have felt the bottom of the purse long before that, but there was just vast emptiness in there, so he reached down farther, until he was in almost to his shoulder, feeling around with splayed fingers, searching in that impossible void for something, anything.

That was when something found *him.*

Down deep in the bag, something brushed his hand.

Billy jerked in surprise.

Something bit him.

Billy screamed and finally found the will to resist the siren call of the darkness within the purse. He tore his hand out, leaped to his feet, knocking over his chair. He stared in terror at the bloody punctures on the meaty portion of his palm. Tooth marks. Five small holes, neat and round, welling blood.

He stood for a moment, numb with shock, then let out a wail and grabbed for the zipper on the bag to close it. Even as Billy's blood-slick fingers touched the pull-tab, the creature came out of the bag, up from a lightless place, and Billy snatched his hand back in terror.

It was a small beast, only about a foot tall, not too big to crawl out through the open mouth of the purse. It was gnarly and dark, like a man in form—two arms, two legs—but not like a man in any other way at all. If its tissues had not once been inanimate lumps of stinking sewage, then they had been some sludge of mysterious though equally noxious origins. Its muscles and sinews appeared to be formed from human waste, all tangled up with human hair and decaying human entrails and desiccated human veins. Its feet were twice as large as they should have been and terminated in razor-edged black claws that put as much fear into Billy Neeks as his own switchblade had put into others. A hooked and pointed spur curved up from the back of each heel. The arms were proportionately as long as those of an ape, with six or maybe seven fingers—Billy could not be sure how many because the thing kept working its hands ceaselessly as it crawled out of the purse and stood up on the table—and each finger ended in an ebony claw.

As the creature rose to its feet and emitted a fierce hiss, Billy stumbled backward until he came up against the refrigerator. Over the sink was a window, locked and covered with filthy curtains. The door to the dining room was on the other side of the kitchen table. To get to the door that opened onto the back porch, he would have to go past the table. He was effectively trapped.

The thing's head was asymmetrical, lumpy, pocked, as if crudely modeled by a sculptor with an imperfect sense of human form, modeled in sewage and scraps of rotten tissue as was its body. A pair of eyes were set high on that portion of the face that would have been the forehead, with a second pair below them. Two more eyes, making six in all, were located at the sides of the skull, where ears should have been, and all of these organs of vision were entirely white, without iris or pupil, so you might have thought the beast was blinded by cataracts, though it was not. It could see; most definitely, it could see, for it was looking straight at Billy.

The thing reeked—a stench reminiscent of rotten eggs.

Trembling violently, making strangled sounds of fear, Billy reached to one side with his bitten right hand, pulled open a drawer in the cabinet next to the refrigerator. Never taking his eyes off the thing that had come out of the purse, he fumbled for the knives he knew were there, found them, and extracted the butcher's knife.

On the table, the six-eyed denizen of a nightmare opened its ragged mouth, revealing rows of pointed yellow teeth. It hissed again and, to Billy's astonishment, it spoke in a thin, whispery voice that managed to be simultaneously soft yet shrill yet gravelly: *"Billy? Billy Neeks?"*

"Oh, my God," Billy said.

"Is that you, Billy?" the beast inquired.

I'm dreaming this, Billy thought.

"No dream," the beast whispered.

It's from Hell (Billy thought), a demon straight up from Hell.

"Give the man a big cigar."

Twisting its deformed mouth into what might have been a grin, the demon kicked the open can of beer off the table and let out a hideous dry sound halfway between a snarl and a giggle.

Suddenly lunging forward and swinging the big butcher knife as if it were a mighty samurai sword, Billy took a whack at the creature, intending to lop off its head or chop it in half. The blade connected with its disgusting flesh, sank less than an inch into its darkly glistening torso, above its knobby hips, but would not go any deeper, certainly not all the way through. Billy felt as if he had taken a hack at a slab of steel, for the aborted power of the blow coursed back through the handle of the knife and shivered painfully through his hands and arms like the vibrations that would have rebounded upon him if he had grabbed a crowbar and, with all his strength, slammed it into a solid iron post.

In that same instant, one of the creature's hands moved flash-quick, slashed Billy, revealing two of his knuckle bones.

With a cry of surprise and pain, Billy let go of the weapon. He staggered back against the refrigerator, holding his gouged hand.

The creature on the table stood unfazed, the knife embedded in its side, neither bleeding nor exhibiting any signs of pain. With its small black gnarled hands, the beast gripped the handle and pulled the sharp instrument from its own flesh. Turning all six scintillant, milky eyes on Billy, it raised the knife, which was nearly as big as the beast itself, and snapped it in two, throwing the blade in one direction and the handle in another.

"*Come to get you, Billy,*" it said.

Billy ran.

He had to go around the table, past the creature, too close, but he did not care, did not hesitate, because his only alternative was to stand at the refrigerator and be torn to bits. Dashing out of the kitchen into the bungalow's little dining room, he heard a thump behind him as the demon leaped off the table. Worse: he heard the *clack-tick-clack* of its chitinous feet and horny claws as it scrambled across the linoleum, hurrying after him.

As a purse snatcher, Billy had to keep in shape and had to be able to run deer-fast. Now, his conditioning was the only advantage he had.

Was it possible to outrun the devil?

He bounded out of the dining room, jumped across a footstool in the living room, and fled toward the front door. His bungalow was somewhat isolated, between an empty lot and a transmission repair shop that was closed at this hour of the evening. However, there were a couple of small houses across the street and, at the corner, a 7-Eleven Market that was usually busy and he figured he would be safe if he could join up with other people, even strangers. He sensed that the demon would not want to be seen by anyone else.

Expecting the beast to leap on him and sink its teeth into his neck at any moment, Billy tore open the front door and almost plunged out of the house—then stopped abruptly when he saw what lay outside. Nothing. No front walk. No lawn, no trees. No street. No other houses across the way, no 7-Eleven on the corner. Nothing, nothing. No light whatsoever. The night beyond the house was unnaturally dark, as utterly lightless as the bottom of a mine shaft—or as the inside of the old woman's purse from which the beast had clambered. Although it should have been a warm late-April evening, the velvet-black night was icy, bone-numbingly cold, just as the inside of the big black leather purse had been.

Billy stood on the threshold, swaying, breathless, with his heart trying to jackhammer its way out of his chest, and he was seized by the mad idea that his entire bungalow was now *inside* the crazy old woman's purse. Which made no sense. The bottom-less purse was back there in the kitchen, on the table. The purse could not be inside the house at the same time that the house was inside the purse. Could it?

He felt dizzy, confused, nauseous.

He had always known everything worth knowing. Or thought he did. Now he knew better.

He did not dare venture out of the bungalow, into the unre-mitting blackness. He sensed no haven within that coaly gloom. And he knew instinctively that, if he took one step into the frigid darkness, he would not be able to turn back. One step, and he would fall into the same terrible void that he had felt within the hag's purse: down, down, forever down.

The stench of rotten eggs grew overwhelming.

The beast was behind him.

Whimpering wordlessly, Billy Neeks turned from the horri-fying emptiness beyond his house, looked back into the living room where the demon was waiting for him, and cried out when he saw that it had grown bigger than it had been a moment ago. Much bigger. Three feet tall instead of one. Broader in the shoul-ders. More muscular arms. Thicker legs. Bigger hands and longer claws. The repulsive creature was not as close as he had expected, not on top of him, but standing in the middle of the living room, watching him, grinning, taunting him merely by choosing not to end the confrontation quickly.

The disparity between the warm air in the house and the freezing air outside seemed to cause a draft that sucked at the door, pulling it shut behind Billy. It closed with a bang.

Hissing, the demon took a step forward. When it moved, Billy could hear its gnarly skeleton and oozing flesh work one against the other like the parts of a grease-clogged machine in ill repair.

He backed away from it, heading around the room toward the short hall that led to the bedroom.

The repugnant apparition followed, casting a hellish shadow that seemed somehow even more grotesque than it should have been, as if the shadow were thrown not by the monster's malformed body but by its more hideously malformed soul. Perhaps aware that its shadow was wrong, perhaps unwilling to consider the meaning of its shadow, the beast purposefully knocked over a floorlamp as it stalked Billy, and in the influx of shadows, it proceeded more confidently and more eagerly, as if shadows eased its way.

At the entrance to the hallway, Billy stopped edging sideways, bolted flat-out for his bedroom, reached it, and slammed the door behind him. He twisted the latch with no illusions of having found sanctuary. The creature would smash through that flimsy barrier with no difficulty, Billy only hoped to reach the nightstand drawer, where he kept a Smith & Wesson .357 Magnum, and indeed he got it with plenty of time to spare.

The gun seemed considerably smaller than he remembered it. Too small. He told himself it seemed inadequate only because the enemy was so formidable. He told himself the weapon would prove plenty big enough when he pulled the trigger. But it still seemed small. Virtually a toy.

With the loaded .357 held in both hands and aimed at the door, he wondered if he should fire through the barrier or wait until the beast burst inside.

The demon resolved the issue by *exploding* through the locked door in a shower of wooden shards, splinters, and mangled hinges.

It was bigger still, more than six feet tall, bigger than Billy, a gigantic and loathsome creature that, more than ever, appeared to be constructed of feces, wads of mucus, tendons of tangled hair, fungus, and the putrescent bits and pieces of several cadavers. Redolent of rotten eggs, with its multiplicitous white eyes now as radiant as incandescent bulbs, it lurched inexorably toward Billy, not even hesitating when he pulled the trigger of the .357 and pumped six rounds into it.

What had that old crone been, for God's sake? No ordinary senior citizen paying a visit to her butcher's shop. No way. What kind of woman carried such a strange purse and kept such a thing as this at her command? A witch? A witch? Of course, a witch.

At last, backed into a corner, with the creature looming over him, the empty gun still clutched in his left hand, the scratches and the bites burning in his right hand, Billy really *knew* for the first time in his life what it meant to be a defenseless victim. When the hulking, unnamable entity put its massive, saber-clawed hands upon him—one on his shoulder, the other on his chest—Billy peed in his pants and was at once reduced to the pitiable condition of a weak, helpless child.

He was sure the demon was going to tear him apart, crack his spine, decapitate him, and suck the marrow out of his bones, but instead it lowered its malformed face to his throat and put its gummy lips against his throbbing carotid artery. For one wild moment, Billy thought it was kissing him. Then he felt his cold tongue lick his throat from collarbone to jaw line, up and down, again and again, an obscene sensation the purpose of which he did not understand. Abruptly he was stung, a short sharp prick that was followed by sudden and complete paralysis.

The creature lifted its head and studied his face. Its breath stank worse than the sulfurous odor exuded by its repellent flesh. Unable to close his eyes, in the grip of a paralysis so complete that he could not even blink, Billy stared into the demon's maw and saw its moon-white, prickled tongue writhing like a fat worm.

The beast stepped back. Unsupported, Billy dropped limply to the floor. Though he strained, he could not move a single finger.

Grabbing a handful of Billy's well-oiled hair, the beast began to drag him out of the bedroom. He could not resist. He could not even protest, for his voice was as frozen as the rest of him.

He could see nothing but what moved past his fixed gaze, for he could neither turn his head nor roll his eyes. He had glimpses of furniture past which he was dragged, and of course he could see the walls and the ceiling above, over which eerie shadows cavorted. When inadvertently rolled onto his stomach, he felt no pain in his cruelly twisted hair, and thereafter he could see only the floor in front of his face and the demon's clawed black feet as it trod heavily toward the kitchen, where the chase had begun.

Billy's vision blurred, cleared, blurred again, and for a moment he thought his failing sight was related to his paralysis. But then he understood that copious but unfelt tears were pouring from his eyes and, doubtless scalding, were streaming down his face. In all his mean and hateful life, he had no memory of having wept before.

He knew what was going to happen to him.

In his racing, fear-swollen heart, he *knew*.

The stinking, oozing beast dragged him rudely through the dining room, banging him against the table and chairs. It took him into the kitchen, pulling him through spilled beer, over a carpet of scattered Doritos. The thing plucked the old woman's black purse from the table and stood it on the floor, within Billy's view. The unzipped mouth of the bag yawned wide.

The demon was noticeably smaller now, at least in its legs and torso and head, although the arm—with which it held fast to Billy—remained enormous and powerful. With horror and amazement, but not with much surprise, Billy watched the creature crawl into the purse, shrinking as it went. Then it pulled him in after it.

He did not feel himself shrinking, but he must have grown smaller in order to fit through the mouth of the purse. Still paralyzed and still being held by his hair, Billy looked back under his own arm and saw the kitchen light beyond the mouth of the purse, saw his own hips balanced on the edge of the bag above him, tried to resist, saw his thighs coming in, then his knees, the bag was swallowing him, oh God, he could do nothing about it, the bag was swallowing him, and now only his feet were still outside, and he tried to dig his toes in, tried to resist, but could not.

Billy Neeks had never believed in the existence of the soul, but now he knew beyond doubt that he possessed one—and that it had just been claimed.

His feet were in the purse now. All of him was inside the purse.

Still looking back under his arm as he was dragged down by his hair, Billy stared desperately at the oval of light above and behind him. It was growing smaller, smaller, not because the zipper was being closed up there, but because the hateful beast was dragging him a long way down into the bag, which made the open end appear to dwindle the same way the mouth of a turnpike tunnel dwindled in the rear-view mirror as you drove toward the other end.

The other end.

Billy could not bear to think about what might be waiting for him at the other end, at the bottom of the purse and beyond it.

He wished that he could go mad. Madness would be a welcome escape from the horror and fear that filled him. Madness would provide sweet relief. But evidently part of his fate was that he should remain totally sane and *acutely* aware.

The light above had shrunk to the size of a small, pale, oblate moon riding high in a night sky.

It was like being born, Billy realized—except that, this time, he was being born out of light and into darkness, instead of the other way around.

The albescent moonform above shrank to the size of a small and distant star. The star winked out.

In the perfect blackness, many strange voices hissed a welcome to Billy Neeks.

▼▼▼

That night in late-April, the bungalow was filled with distant, echoey screams of terror from so far away that, though carrying through every room of the small house, they did not reach the quiet street beyond the walls and did not draw any attention from nearby residents. The screams continued for a few hours, faded gradually, and were replaced by licking-gnawing-chewing sounds of satisfied consumption.

Then silence.

Silence held dominion for many hours, until the middle of the following afternoon, when the stillness was broken by the sound of an opening door and footsteps.

"Ah," the old woman said happily as she stepped through the kitchen door and saw her purse standing open on the floor. With arthritic slowness, she bent, picked up the bag, and stared into it for a moment.

Then, smiling, she pulled the zipper shut.

BIOGRAPHIES

▼▼▼

JANET ASIMOV is the author of *The Second Experiment, The Last Immortal, The Package in Hyperspace, Mind Transfer,* and *The Mysterious Cure and Other Stories of Pshrinks Anonymous.* She is co-author (with the late Isaac Asimov) of *How to Enjoy Writing* and the "Norby" series.

JOHN BETANCOURT began his editing career at the age of 19, working as an assistant on *Amazing Stories* magazine. He left five years later to start his own horror magazine, *Weird Tales,* with George Scithers and Darrell Schweitzer. Since then he has moved on to book editing for Byron Preiss Visual Publications, Inc. He is also a popular short story writer and novelist whose books include *Rememory, Johnny Zed,* and *The Blind Archer.* His next novel is a children's fantasy scheduled to appear from Atheneum in 1994, written in collaboration with Kevin J. Anderson.

JONATHAN BOND currently lives in Eugene, Oregon, where he works as editor for *Pulphouse* magazine.

RAY BRADBURY, one of the greatest writers of fantasy and horror fiction in the world today, has published about 500 short stories, novels, plays and poems since his first story appeared in *Weird Tales* when he was 20 years old.

Among his many famous works are *Fahrenheit 451*, *The Illustrated Man*, and *The Martian Chronicles*. He has also written the screenplays for *It Came from Outer Space*, *Something Wicked This Way Comes*, and *Moby Dick*. Mr. Bradbury was Idea Consultant for the United States Pavilion at the 1964 World's Fair, has written the basic scenario for the interior of Spaceship Earth at EPCOT, Disney World, and is doing consultant work on city engineering and rapid transit. When one of the Apollo Astronaut teams landed on the moon, they named Dandelion Crater there to honor Mr. Bradbury's novel, *Dandelion Wine*.

ADAM-TROY CASTRO lives in New York state, where in between occasional forays into cartooning and stand-up comedy he contributes short stories to magazines including *Dragon*, *Science Fiction Age*, and *Pulphouse*, and anthologies including *Journeys into the Twilight Zone*, *Book of the Dead III*, *Beneath the Tarmac*, and *Grails*. His nonfiction has appeared in *Spy*, *Premiere*, *Amazing Heroes*, and the *Quayle Quarterly*.

LYNN CROSSON has been writing for 22 years, having completed her first novel at the tender age of 12. This is her first published work of fiction. She has led a nomadic existence, but currently resides on Long Island with her nomadic cat and two somewhat nomadic friends. While she will admit to a flirtatious nature, close inspection of her basement will reveal nothing out of the ordinary.

PHILIP JOSÉ FARMER has written 73 novels and short-story collections, including biographies of Tarzan and Doc Savage. He is credited with breaking the tabu on the mature use of sex in science-fiction with his short novel *The Lovers* in 1952. He has garnered three Hugos and a Playboy award. His most popular series are the *Riverworld* and *World of Tiers* books. His works have appeared in nineteen languages, though, he regrets, not in Albanian. One of his ancestors was a Massachusetts witch who barely escaped hanging. Some of his other ancestors were not so lucky. He has been married to the same woman for 52 years, and has two children, five grandchildren, and one great-grandchild. At the age of 75, he is embarking on his first mystery novel and plans to write several mainstream and historical novels. He wishes Homo sapiens good luck in the future but knows too much history to believe that our species will get it.

NINA KIRIKI HOFFMAN has been pursuing a writing career for ten years and has sold more than 80 short stories, three short story collections, a novel (*The Thread that Binds the Bones*), one novella (*Unmasking*), and one collaborative young adult novel (*Child of an Ancient City*). So far.

Trained at the Philadelphia College of Art and the Royal College of Art in London, England, LARS HOKANSON is an award-winning artist who specializes in woodcut illustrations. Among others, his clients include *The New York Times, Random House, Viking/Penguin, Rolling Stone, Time, The London Observer*, Stephen King, Isaac Bashevis Singer, and the Sultan of Oman. His art has been exhibited in the permanent collections of a number of major museums, including the Museum of Modern Art in New York, the Philadelphia Museum of Art and the Tate Gallery and National Portrait Gallery, both in London.

NANCY HOLDER has sold three horror novels to Dell/Abyss, two in collaboration with Melanie Tem. *Making Love*, the first Tem/-Holder novel, was published in August of 1993. Her solo effort, *Dead in the Water*, will be released in early 1994. She has also sold three dozen short stories and articles to anthologies and magazines such as the *Women of Darkness, Borderlands, Shadows*, and other series; and to *Die, Elvis, Die!, Still Dead, Obsessions, Pulphouse, Narrow Houses, The Mammoth Book of Vampire Stories, Phobias*, and others.

In addition, she has written 13 romances and two mainstream

novels. Her romances have placed on the Waldenbooks Romance Bestseller List seven times, and received awards from *Romantic Times*. Her books have been translated into more than 15 languages. She is Director of Mythology for FTL Games and contributing editor to *The Gila Queen's Guide to Markets*. She is also a member of The Board of Trustees of the Horror Writers of America.

In 1992 she received the Bram Stoker Award from the Horror Writers of America for Superior Achievement in the short story category, for "Lady Madonna."

She is coordinator of the pet grief support area on AmericaOn-Line. She lives in San Diego with her husband, Wayne, and their Border collies, Mr. Ron and Maggie, where she is writing another horror novel and more short stories.

JOHN KAIINE is completing his first novel, *Fossil Circus*, a psychological contemporary gothic-horror tale of Madness and the Mad.

He lives in England with his wife (the writer Tanith Lee) and one black and white cat.

STUART M. KAMINSKY is the author of 27 published mystery novels and numerous short stories. His novels, which have been translated into ten languages, include the Inspector Porfiry Petrovich Rostnikov novels, one of which, *A Cold Red Sunrise*, won the 1989 Edgar Allan Poe Award of the Mystery Writers of America for Best Novel and the 1990 Prix Du Roman D'Aventure for the best mystery novel published in France. His 1984 entry in the Rostnikov series, *Black Knight in Red Square*, was an Edgar nominee as best original paperback. Kaminsky also writes the popular Toby Peters mysteries. His nonseries novels include *Exercise in Terror* and *When the Dark Man Calls*, which was filmed in France as *Frequence Meurtre* starring Catherine Deneuve.

Kaminsky wrote the dialogue for the Sergio Leone film *Once Upon a Time in America*, and wrote the story and co-scripted *Enemy Territory*. In addition he scripted *A Woman in the Wind* with Colleen Dewhurst for the Arts and Entertainment Network's

Short Stories series. His other screenwriting work includes *Ain't Got No Tears Left* for MGM, *Growing Up Rich* for GUR Productions, and *Get Serious* for Lambert Productions.

Kaminsky's nonfiction books include: *Don Siegel: Director*; *Clint Eastwood*; *John Huston: Maker of Magic*; *Coop: The Life and Legend of Gary Cooper*; *American Film Genres*; *Basic Filmmaking* (with Dana Hodgden); *Writing for Television* (with Mark Walker); and *Ingmar Bergman: Essays in Criticism* (edited with Joseph Hill).

Kaminsky, who is Professor and director of the Florida State University Conservatory of Motion Picture, Television and Recording Arts, formerly chaired the Radio/Television/Film Department at Northwestern University in Evanston, Illinois, and headed Northwestern's Program in Creative Writing for the Media.

MARVIN KAYE is one of those rare writers equally adept in many different genres. His pioneering books on games and magic (*The Handbook of Magic*, *A Toy Is Born*) are seminal in their field; his mystery novels (*Bullets for Macbeth*, *The Grand Ole Opry Murders*) are perennial favorites; his horror novels (A *Cold Blue Light* [with Parke Godwin], *Ghosts of Night and Morning*) are bestsellers. His latest novel, *Fantastique*, is already being hailed as a modern masterpiece. Kaye currently resides in New York, where he writes, edits, and manages a theatrical group, The Open Book.

When he was a senior in college, DEAN KOONTZ won an *Atlantic Monthly* fiction competition and has been writing ever since. His books are published in 31 languages; worldwide sales total more than 100 million copies, and that figure currently increases at the rate of more than ten million copies a year. His most recent five novels have risen to number one on the *New York Times's* bestseller list.

Dean Koontz was born and raised in Pennsylvania. He graduated from Shippensburg State Teacher's College (now Shippensburg University), and his first job after graduation was in the Appalachian Poverty Program, where he was expected to counsel and tutor underprivileged kids on a one-to-one basis. His first day at work, he discovered that the previous occupier of his position had been beaten up by the very kids he'd been trying to help and had landed in the hospital for several weeks. The following year was filled with tension, and Koontz was more highly motivated than ever to build a career as a writer. He wrote nights and weekends, which he continued to do after leaving the poverty program and going to work as an English teacher in a suburban school district outside of Harrisburg. After a year and a half in that position, his wife Gerda made him an offer he couldn't refuse: "I'll support you for five years," she said, "and if you can't make it as a writer in that time, you'll never make it." By the end of those five years Gerda had quit her job to run the business end of her husband's writing career. Dean and Gerda Koontz live in southern California, which they have called home since 1976.

British by birth, and a scientist by training, **ANDREW LANE** has been gainfully employed for the past eight years by Her Majesty's Government. His second life as a professional writer started in 1985, when he began writing articles and reviews for many UK genre magazines. He has also co-written *Lucifer Rising*—an original novel based upon the long-running British television science fiction series *Doctor Who*, and is currently working on a solo *Doctor Who* novel entitled *All-Consuming Fire*. "Crawling from the Wreckage" is his first "serious" short story to be published.

Born in 1947, **TANITH LEE'S** first fantasy novel *The Birthgrave* was published by DAW Books in 1975. She has now published more than 50 books and around 130 short stories.

Currently, she is working on Scarabae Blood Opera—novels so far, *Dark Dance, Personal Darkness*—a series about an ancient and perhaps immortal family with vampiric leanings, set in the modern world and the limitless past. She is also working on a series of Victorian gothic horror novels (so far: *Heartbeast, Elephantasm*) and on a sequel to her young-adult novel for Atheneum, *Black Unicorn.*

She is married to the writer John Kaiine.

THOMAS J. LINDELL lives in Seattle with his wife, two cats and a brand new freezer that he is currently filling with homemade ravioli. When he isn't writing, he is the computer administrator for the Western Washington March of Dimes.

BYRON PREISS is the editor of the books *The Planets, The Universe, The Microverse,* and *The Dinosaurs: A New Look at a Lost Era,* which was featured in *Life* magazine. He has collaborated with Arthur C. Clarke, Isaac Asimov, and Ray Bradbury, and edited the Grammy Award winning *The Words of Gandhi.* His monograph on *The Art of Leo & Diane Dillon* was a Hugo Award nominee. He holds a B.A. from the University of Pennsylvania and an M.A. from Stanford University. He currently resides in New York City.

KATHRYN PTACEK was raised in Albuquerque, New Mexico. She received her B.A. in Journalism, with a minor in history, from the University of New Mexico, Albuquerque, where she was graduated with distinction. After the sale of her first novel, an historical romance, in July 1979, she became a full-time novelist.

She has written 18 novels—fantasy, historical romances, a Regency, and horror, among the latest being *In Silence Sealed* and *Ghost Dance.* Her suspense novel, *The Hunted,* was published by Walker Books in January 1993. She has also edited three anthologies: the critically acclaimed *Women of Darkness* and its companion *Women of Darkness II,* and *Women of the West.* Her short stories have appeared in a number of anthologies, including *Freak Show, Doom City* and *Phobias.* A member of Horror Writers of America and Sisters in Crime, she writes an anthology review column for *Cemetery Dance,* and edits and publishes a monthly market newsletter for writers and artists, *The Gila Queen's Guide to Markets*.

She is married to novelist Charles Grant, and has two cats, Lucyfur and Huckleberry Fang; they all live in New Jersey. She collects gila monster stuff and unusual teapots and cat whiskers, although no one ever believes that.

DARRELL SCHWEITZER is the author of three novels, *The White Isle, The Shattered Goddess*, and forthcoming *The Mask of the Sorcerer*, plus about 150 published stories, and hundreds of essays, columns, reviews, interviews, and poems. He has written or edited a number of nonfiction books, including *Discovering H.P. Lovecraft, Pathways to Elfland: The Writings of Lord Dunsany*, and *Discovering Modern Horror Fiction* (two volumes, with a third forthcoming). He is currently editor of *Weird Tales* magazine (for which he won a World Fantasy Award), a regular contributor to anthologies, a Pennsylvania resident, and in, as he vaguely puts it, his "suspiciously late thirties." His novella, "To Become a Sorcerer" was a finalist for the 1992 World Fantasy Award.

T. DIANE SLATTON is a wife, mother, and former sergeant in the U.S. Army. So far in her new writing career, she's garnered Honorable Mention in both the Writer's Digest Short Story Competition (1991), and Article Competition (1992). In 1991 she also won a grant from the Illinois Arts Council.

Her first published story, "Seventh Son of A Seventh Son," appeared in the anthology, *Abortion Stories: Fiction On Fire*. Her most recent sale is to *Pulphouse* Magazine.

S.P. SOMTOW was born in Bangkok, Thailand and grew up in Europe. He was educated at Eton College and at Cambridge, where he obtained his B.A. and M.A., receiving honors in English and Music. Although he has received international acclaim as an avant-garde composer, he is most known for his best-selling horror novels, including *Valentine, Moon Dance*, and *Vampire*

Junction. His work has been nominated for numerous awards and been translated into many languages. In 1981, he won the John W. Campbell Award for Best New Writer. His young adult novel *Forgetting Places* was honored by the "Books for Young Adults" program as an Outstanding Book of the Year. Currently he alternates between working on books and motion pictures; his films include *The Laughing Dead* and *Burial of the Rats*, which he scripted for Roger Corman.

E R STEWART was born on Charles Dickens's 146th birthday in Altoona, Pennsylvania. He began writing in earnest eight years later, and submitting eight years after that. He's married and has three children. His credits include fiction, nonfiction, criticism, poetry, maps, cartoons, and photography in such publications as *Marion Zimmer Bradley's Fantasy Magazine, Asimov's Science Fiction Magazine, SF Review, Aboriginal Science Fiction, Military Lifestyle, Family, Macon, Thrust/Quantum, The Mountaineer-Herald, Cricket for Children,* and *Ladybug for Young Children.* He is a contributor of novellas, maps, and world building to Baen Books' *War World* anthology series, and has placed other stories with J.E. Pournelle & Associates for upcoming anthologies.

TIM SULLIVAN has published more than 30 science fiction, horror, fantasy, and mainstream stories in such publications as *Isaac Asimov's Science Fiction Magazine, Pulphouse, Amazing Stories,* and any number of anthologies. His short fiction includes "Zeke," a finalist for the Nebula Award, and "The Comedian," which appeared in the last Donald Wollheim's annual best SF anthology. Mr. Sullivan has also published nine books: seven novels (the most recent of which are *The Martian Viking* and *Lords of Creation*) and two anthologies, *Tropical Chills* and *Cold Shocks.* In recent years, he has turned to screenwriting, having sold an original script entitled *Without a Thought* to Aspect Pictures, as well as receiving screen credit for Rubicon Films' thriller, *Fatal Ambition.* He's acted in a few films too, such as *The Laughing Dead* and *Angel of Passion,* and is currently trying his hand at producing as well as writing the screenplay for an adaptation of Stanley G. Weinbaum's *A Martian Odyssey*.

PACO IGNACIO TAIBO II has been the recipient of numerous awards in Mexico, Latin America, and Spain, most recently including the Planeta/Mortiz Prize. Taibo's novels, which include *An Easy Thing, Calling All Heroes, The Shadow of the Shadow*, and *Some Clouds*, have all been published in the United States. Taibo is one of the founders of the International Association of Crime Writers, and currently serves as president of the organization. He lives in Mexico City.

Among **STEVE RASNIC TEM'S** recent and forthcoming story publications are: *In Dreams, The Mammoth Book of Vampires, Psycho Paths 2, Stalkers 3, Tomorrow Magazine, Swashbuckling Editor Stories, Pulphouse* Magazine and a chapbook from Necronomicon Press: *Decoded Mirrors: Three Tales After Lovecraft*.

LOIS TILTON lives in the Chicago suburbs, where she no longer teaches philosophy. She has published two novels about vampires: *Vampire Winter* and *Darkness on the Ice*. Since 1987 over 30 pieces of her short fiction have appeared in magazines and anthologies that feature science fiction, fantasy, and horror.

MARY A. TURZILLO has recent sales to *Asimov's Science Fiction, Xanadu, The Magazine of Fantasy and Science Fiction, Modern Gold Miners and Treasure Hunters, Tomorrow*, and *Universe*. While teaching at Kent State University, she founded the Cajun Sushi Hamsters from Hell. She lives in Warren, Ohio, with a teenage son, two gifted cats, and several dying houseplants.

KARL EDWARD WAGNER was born on December 12, 1945 in Knoxville, Tennessee. In 1967 he moved to Chapel Hill, North Carolina, where he graduated from medical school and practiced psychiatry. Following publication of several novels, he left his practice, and has been a full-time writer since 1975.

Wagner has written or edited more than 45 books in the fantasy and horror genres, including the Kane series of heroic fantasy and two volumes of his short fiction, *In a Lonely Place* and *Why Not You and I?* He has also edited DAW Books' *The Year's Best Horror Stories* for the past 15 years.

Wagner has twice won the World Fantasy Award and has won the British Fantasy Award four times. The latter possibly reflects his fondness for hanging out in London pubs. "A Walk on the Wild Side" is one of a number of his London stories, based upon observations over a pint glass.

JANE YOLEN, author of more than 130 books for children and adults, has been called "America's Hans Christian Andersen" for her many original fairy tales. Winner of the World Fantasy Award, the Kerlan Award, the Regina Medal, the Mythopoeic Society Award, and many other honors, she is a past president of the Science Fiction and Fantasy Writers of America and has been on the board of directors of the Society of Children's Book Writers since its inception. She is editor-in-chief of Jane Yolen Books, an imprint of Harcourt Brace, specializing in children's books and young adult novels of fantasy and science fiction. Mother of three grown children, she and her husband, Dr. David Stemple, spend their time between their home in Hatfield, Massachusetts, and St. Andrews, Scotland.